HARTSBURG, USA

By the same author

Political Animal

HARTSBURG, USA

A NOVEL

DAVID MIZNER

BLOOMSBURY

Published by Bloomsbury USA, New York
Distributed to the trade by Holtzbrinck Publishers

All papers used by Bloomsbury USA are natural, recyclable products made from
wood grown in well-managed forests. The manufacturing processes conform to the
environmental regulations of the country of origin.

LIBRARY OF CONGRESS CATALOGING-IN-PUBLICATION DATA

Mizner, David.
Hartsburg, USA : a novel / David Mizner.—1st U.S. ed.
p. cm.
ISBN-13: 978-1-59691-326-4
ISBN-10: 1-59691-326-6
1. School elections—Fiction. 2. Ohio—Fiction. 3. Political campaigns—Fiction.
4. Political fiction. I. Title

PS3613.I96H37 2007
813'.6—dc22
2006032977

First U.S. Edition 2007

1 3 5 7 9 10 8 6 4 2

Typeset by Westchester Book Group
Printed in the United States of America by Quebecor World Fairfield

For my friends from Waterville:
Kip, Todd, Kev, Rob,
Nish, Joe, and Gurney.

Reality, it burns
The way we're living is worse

—Jay Farrar

PART ONE

PROLOGUE

IN 1991, ADDRESSING the languid, chewing crowd gathered to celebrate Hartsburg's 175th anniversary, Mayor Bob Sundstrom said, seemingly apropos of nothing, "Might as well cut my balls off and put a bell round my neck." People looked up from, or down at, their stuffed chicken breasts. What just happened? Was this some saying along the lines of "Well, tickle my toes and call me Louie"? Until now the speech had been suitably boring, no less so because he'd been speaking as if he were the town: "Hartsburg" had become "I," as in "I was born in 1817" and "My steel was used to make tanks that helped defeat the Nazis." So he was talking about cutting the town's balls off?

In the back of the room, a man who'd just been put out of work by the closing of the town's last steel mill, said "Amen."

Most people didn't understand that the mayor had been commenting on Hartsburg's status as a political bellwether, and most of those who did still didn't see what testicles had to do with it. Even the farmers in the audience, who got the joke—male sheep, wethers, were often castrated—couldn't summon a laugh for poor old Bob. It wasn't his fault that the town was dying—what's a mayor next to the exigencies of "free"trade?—but people tended to read civic significance into the age spots and booze veins on his forehead. Two years later to the day, Bob jumped off the bridge that linked Hartsburg's halves and ended up in a coma—a failure-to-fail failure whose metaphorical meaning was so obvious people barely bothered to comment on it. Bob had completed his transformation from human being into symbol. Few people had really known Bob, and no one went to visit him as he lay, half-dead, in the remotest corner of the nursing home. Out of sight, almost out of mind. But now, in the game show–bright ballroom of the Holiday Inn, he was in sight, on mind, and

3

sweating terribly. "As I go," he said, still speaking as Hartsburg, "so goes the nation." People clapped. They clapped because they wanted to help Bob get through this and because most residents—at least most residents who went to events like this—were proud of the town's reputation as a trendsetter.

It was probably more accurate to say that Hartsburg followed, rather than set, trends; in any case, the town had, as of '91, voted for every presidential winner of the twentieth century. In the sixties, journalists began to flock to the town to gauge the national mood. There were other bellwether towns, but perhaps none better suited to play that role on TV. The river and the factory provided a picturesque backdrop, a vision of America that people liked. Situated in south central Ohio, near Kentucky, it was Midwestern but also vaguely Southern. It was not rich and not poor. It had some, but not too much, racial diversity. With around twenty thousand residents, Hartsburg was neither a small town nor a city. It was a little of this and a little of that and not too much of anything.

The journalists who came to town in the sixties, seventies, and eighties wanted to talk to "ordinary Americans." Undecided voters were especially precious. Hartsburgers were amused to see who ended up speaking for the town and therefore the nation. Before both the '84 and '88 elections, Gladys Peters appeared on national telecasts. It was no mystery how she'd attracted their attention: outside the gas station that she owned she posted signs that revealed the kind of "character" the media loved. Also, as a hater of all politicians, she came across as undecided. In the run-up to the '88 election, for example, her sign said, "Stick your Dukakis in my Bush."

For the journalists who walked into the service station, Gladys lived up, or down, to their idea of an ordinary American. With her dry, yellowed skin, she was so real she looked fake, like a wax sculpture. Her smile, if that's what it was, looked like grilled corn on the cob. The journalists quickly learned, to their delight, that the divorced mother of three was a fan of NASCAR, *Wheel of Fortune*, and country music, and that she went to church, and that she still had faith, albeit diminished, that the lives of her children would be at least as good as hers. What they didn't discover was that she hadn't produced a cohesive bowel movement in years, and that she used a battery-powered nose-hair trimmer to masturbate while watching *Cool Hand Luke*, and that she had more doubts about the existence of God than she let on. An ordinary American? Absolutely.

In '92 and '96 the bellwether wandered off, voting for two losers, George Bush and Bob Dole. While Bill Clinton slowed the rightward thrust of the country—or at least softened it—it raged on in Hartsburg. In '92 Jonathan Wedgwood, a preacher from Colorado, established a ministry. Drawing people away from mainstream churches and finding converts among farm families and laid-off steelworker families, Wedgwood's outfit was like a nonstop Baptist revival. It occupied a campus below the river on the southern edge of town, a factory of dogmatism whose salespeople went door-to-door, agitated for political change, and formed satellite churches. While liberals tended to exaggerate the power of the religious right, there was no question that this town was vastly different from the one that had voted for Lyndon Johnson.

No longer a bellwether or even a toss-up, solidly "red" before the term existed, just another factory town without a factory, Hartsburg had lost its sporadic spotlight. Not a single national journalist went there for years. Then, in '03, a school board race got dirty—dirty enough to briefly capture the attention, if not the imagination, of the nation.

CHAPTER 1

ON A CLOUDY FRIDAY evening in September of '03, Wallace Cormier drove up The Drive. Some pleasant feeling lingered from a forgotten thought, which he tried to remember so that he might maintain the feeling. It occurred to him that he could feel good without the benefit of a thought. Then he looked to his left.

He couldn't believe what he saw, although what he saw was nothing if not believable: the movie theater, *his* movie theater—which had shut down three weeks before—was now a church. Trying to read the sign where movies were once listed, he sensed that his eyes had been off the road for too long.

He was calm as he skidded toward the stopped truck.

The seat belt caught him, tightening as his lips grazed the top of the steering wheel—a passionless kiss. His body thudded into the seat, his head snapped back, his chin hit his chest, bounce, bounce, bounce . . . bounce . . . then he was still, except for his heart. His heart didn't understand that he was safe. So he'd been afraid, then, not calm. Burnt rubber. Bad breath. He put on his glasses, which had been thrown onto the dashboard, and looked at the sign: "Want something sweet for the soul? We're not Dairy Queen, but we've got great Sundays!" Cormier punched his palm, almost hard enough to hurt.

Cinema Center—CeeCee, as he secretly called it—was where, as a teenager alone in the eighth row, he had consumed Coppola and Ashby and Lumet, and where, having returned to Ohio after six years in Hollywood, he had watched the movies that he reviewed in the *Hartsburg Informer*. Even after he had gotten his own column, he had continued to review movies. When a movie showed promise, he would throw his notepad on the floor and remove the camping light from his head. For

Cormier, movies weren't a means of escape: sitting in the theater he didn't forget that he was living in the town he used to dream of leaving or that his nineteen screenplays were buried unsold and unloved in a U-Haul box. On the contrary, a good movie—especially one that evoked what one of his reviews called "the pain of being human"—woke him up to his life.

He shifted into neutral and yanked the emergency brake. This was the longest light on the more reputable of Hartsburg's commercial strips, both of which, unlike Main Street, sometimes filled with traffic. Here on The Drive (Stuckney Drive, officially), which stretched from the river up through the western part of town to the highway, Wal-Mart and the other superstores seemed to cast their glow on surrounding businesses. Cars gleamed in showrooms. Gliding from the Outback Steakhouse to Barnes and Noble, your vehicle driving itself, you felt safe and efficient. You had to be a full-blown crank or commie (and Cormier was only a touch of both) not to take comfort in all the comfort.

But now The Drive, all of Hartsburg, had no movie theater. Cormier had considered using his column to try to save CeeCee, but what could he say? Not many people were going to miss an old dusty, sticky multiplex. The original four theaters had become eight; during quiet moments in your movie you heard the one playing next door.

"What are you going to do?" said Clyde, the old, pockmarked ticket taker, on the last night of CeeCee's existence. Clyde couldn't stop doing DeNiro, like DeNiro himself. "Enjoy duh show," he added. The show was *Lost in Translation*. Feeling pressure to enjoy an intense last night with CeeCee, Cormier had trouble watching the movie, as opposed to watching himself watch it. He wondered if the movie was pretentious. It was definitely slow. But he claimed to like slow movies. The Japanese people were props. In his pad he'd written: "Pretentious? Slow! Racist? Something is wrong with me." Eventually he relaxed, and the movie won him over. When Bill Murray left the girl at the end, Cormier felt saddened yet heartened by the universality of struggle, and vowed to live better, love harder.

Where there had once been salvation there was now superstition.

* * *

Beverly Baer was standing with her husband in the black-floored show-room of his GM dealership, watching their twins pretend to drag race. When she heard the screech, she thought the car that held Kyle or Karl had started. She gasped, bent her knees, looked at Peter, and knew every-thing was okay. The screech had come from The Drive.

"A Saab," Peter said, scornful of both the car and its owner.

She was grateful for his calm; he would have stayed calm even if one of the cars in the showroom had by some miracle gone on. Peter was her wall. She leaned on him to brace herself against dangers real and imag-ined.

She took a breath, not as deep as she'd intended, and nodded as though someone had asked her a question. "You all right?" Peter asked.

"Yes," she said. "I'm good."

She looked past the site of the near accident to Faith Evangelical, which a breakaway faction of the Baers' church had formed—the second such spin-off. While the intimacy of a smaller church appealed to her, the idea of someone other than Reverend Wedgwood delivering the message did not. Faith Evangelical's attendance had already grown, but it was un-clear how many of the newest members had come from Hilltop, the Baers' church. It wasn't supposed to matter: they were all brothers and sisters in Christ.

"Let's go home," Peter said.

"Not yet."

Len, Peter's employee, dropped an imaginary flag. The boys, sitting up on their knees, pretended to steer and made *brmm brmm* noises.

Beverly was glad not to be moving. She was a busy woman. Her busy-ness defined her no less than her loud laugh or lush chestnut hair. Busy Bevy, her friends called her, with mocking affection. (Jealousy, Bevy knew, was in there too.) Her friends were busy as well, but most of them had three or four children, not five, and their husbands were more apt to help out around the house. Also, her friends were more efficient. "Slow down," her mother-in-law, Kay, often said to her, "and you'll get more done."

Bevy had learned to cook, clean, prioritize, multitask, and even sew but still felt like a fraud when it came to housework. Her house looked fine, but God (and Kay) knew she never cleaned in the crack by the stove and always forgot to buy things and couldn't get her towels fresh smelling.

Still, with effort, ingenuity, and a few fallback rules (when you're not sure what to do, vacuum), she'd kept the household chugging along all these years—or she had until last May, when she'd launched her campaign for school board.

She had trouble thinking about anything but the campaign. (Truth was, she didn't *want* to think about anything else.) With her mind on issues and itineraries, even simple chores became chores. She'd be drafting a speech in her head only to discover she'd put SpaghettiOs in the dog's bowl. Yesterday she'd been unable to go grocery shopping because she'd lost her wallet. She'd found it this morning in the refrigerator, in the bin that should have been full of veggies.

"Let's go," Peter said. "I've been on my feet all day."

"And I haven't?"

"I didn't say that."

"Let them race one more time, so they can each win two."

"So nobody wins, or everybody? That's one heck of a lesson." He let out a gruntlike laugh, and his face twitched. Sarcasm didn't suit him.

Bevy, by contrast, had no trouble being sarcastic: "Yeah, let them win a few fake races, next thing you know they're liberals."

Peter put his finger over his mouth to shush her. There were some things you just didn't joke about. "It's time to head home," he said. "I'm hungry."

"Me too," Bevy said.

The truck in front of him, jacked up several inches above tractorlike tires, was taller than some houses. This fucking town. Cormier had been born in Hartsburg and he loved it. He loved it the way he loved himself: with reservations. His living here—again, still—felt like a defeat. It was de rigueur among his dinner party companions to disparage the town. (These friends, as well as his wife, were New Yorkers.) He sometimes participated in the bashing; his anger toward the town was a component of his love. Other times he defended Hartsburg with the prickly passion of a patriot.

Even the town's apologists—some of whom, by no coincidence, held positions of power—acknowledged that Hartsburg had a problem: it had been hemorrhaging jobs and residents since the steel factory had closed in '91. (A smaller one had shut down in '78.) But the town's sophisticates, expert at finding flaws, had a broader range of complaints. What racial diversity there was (and there was more than you'd expect) created tension. The notable "cultural" events were the Christmas pageant, the Octoberfest Festival, and high school musicals. The restaurants were tragic. Worst of all, in their view, was the rise of fundamentalist Protestantism.

The fundamentalists—perhaps 20 percent of the town's population— had erected a garish crèche in the town square at Christmastime and hung a door-sized framed copy of the Ten Commandments in the lobby of the courthouse. Also, they'd gone after sex education, stores that sold "pornographic" materials, and, most recently, evolution. Eighty years after the Monkey Trials, the school board was debating whether science teachers should teach religion. Cormier hadn't attended any school board meetings but could be confident that no Darrows or Bryans were holding forth. ("Big bang, big schmang" was the quote that had stuck in his mind.) Proponents of creationism had given it a facelift and a new name, intelligent design. If and when they got control of the board, it would be taught in addition to evolution. Balance, they called it.

Cormier had responded to the rise of the religious right with an equanimity that, he knew, didn't befit the resident liberal columnist. The changes at the high school might have worried him if his daughter, a junior there, had questioned evolution or crammed prayer club into her schedule, but Carly seemed safely secular, and would be unlikely to find religion unless she learned that it looked good on a college application.

He'd written only one column on the religious right, and even that piece, inspired by objections to a teacher's screening of *Schindler's List*, was little more than a tweak. But then his pieces these days were tweaks at best. More often, they were stories about a half-blind barber or a persevering widow or a handy handicapped fellow. Pluck was what he praised. In the midnineties he'd exposed Hartsburg's history of racism and called into question the town's famous hospitality; now he profiled youthful seniors and precocious children. His column had gone soft. When he'd started writing human-interest stories, he'd reasoned that they were an effective means of conveying ideas. Readers, he told himself, would swallow political arguments if they were mixed with life-affirming narrative. Sure, the town was hurting, but did you know that Dot Ferguson made ends meet by harvesting and delivering eggs? Truth be told, Cormier had figured out that he didn't enjoy making people feel bad about the town. Not that he was really thinking about other people. At this stage of his life he wanted adulation. Actually, he'd always wanted adulation; these days he wanted adulation and *ease*. When he walked down Main Street, he wanted waves, not glares. Better yet, he wanted to be left alone.

Perhaps he was reluctant (okay, afraid) to take on Wedgwood and his adherents; the *Schindler's List* column had prompted a month of crank calls. But he was of two minds about the religious right. He was of two minds about most things political. (The war in Iraq, which he hated, was an exception.) He questioned the whole notion of a culture war. Wasn't it a diversion from the war waged by people with lots of money against everyone else? And given all the stuff that children could get into, was conservative Christianity that bad? Abstinence, for example: where Carly was concerned, he was all for it. On balance he'd found the crusaders more amusing than maddening.

No longer. Glancing again at the sign—"great Sundays!"—he vowed to write a series of columns blasting the religious right. He'd been brave before, a long time ago, and would be again. Just not tonight. Tonight he would bowl.

The car behind him beeped, and when Cormier stuck his head out the window to look past the truck, he saw that the light was green. Still the truck didn't move. Cormier was tempted to beep his own horn. If the vehicle in front of him had been, say, a Subaru Outback, he certainly would have beeped. He might have even honked. So he should honk now; it would be cowardly and condescending not to.

Just as he decided to beep, not honk, the truck sped away. He put his car in gear, stepped on the gas, and stalled. The emergency brake.

Burnt rubber. Bevy loved this smell. She pulled it into her lungs as she turned onto The Drive. The twins looked back from Peter's SUV and waved. To try to stop them from competing for her attention, she steered with her thighs and waved both hands, but after they'd pulled up at the light, Kyle slapped Karl's hand, then his face, and Karl let out a scream that Bevy thought she could hear.

Peter wasn't one to raise his voice—she liked that about him—but he didn't have much choice at the moment. "Come on," Bevy said. "Do something." They had different ways of dealing with the twins. Although Peter agreed that Kyle needed to learn to control himself, he was more concerned that Karl learn how to defend himself. "The world's a tough place," Peter said, echoing his mother, and Bevy couldn't have agreed more, but when you're four years old you shouldn't have to worry about "the world." Or about your brother beating on you while your daddy just sits there.

Finally, Peter reached back and grabbed Kyle, quieting him. Bevy's shoulders dropped and she blew out so hard she was surprised the windshield didn't steam up.

When they started moving again, Karl waved at her, his sad little face all lips and lines. She smiled but didn't wave for fear that Kyle would see. What'd it matter whether she waved or not? It mattered. Waves, touches, smiles, looks, words, silences: they added up. Bevy wasn't one to believe you could mess up a child with a bad minute or even a bad month—children tended to survive the blunders of their parents—but you had to be good more often than not, and the price of being bad seemed higher with twins.

Just when she'd gotten good at being a mother, the twins had come along. Karl and Kyle got the lion's share of her time, and much of what remained went to Brent, whose need for attention was the strongest, or the loudest. Somewhere along the line, Ronnie, their oldest, had wandered off the path—how far was hard to say. Sometimes he seemed like a typical ornery teenager; other times she felt that he would be the heartbreak of her life. Loretta, the middle child and only girl, seemed content to lay low, but Bevy wanted to find more time for her now that she was working her way into adolescence.

They lived near The Drive, on a smooth circular road carved out of forest in the seventies. Their olive-colored house was low-slung and larger than it looked. The front yard, cut down the middle by a slate stone path, was bigger than the backyard. They owned an acre of land, which included a chunk of the woods out back.

She parked her SUV in the garage alongside Peter's and, in anticipation of her campaign meeting tonight, decided to take a minute. In the rearview she looked less tired than she felt. "If I lose," she said, practicing her new stump speech, "then we all lose. You see, liberals want to use the public schools to demean what we stand for. I know it's hard to believe. It can't be, right? It's too bad to be true—"

The garage got dark as the doors fell behind her.

Walking through the entryway between the garage and the kitchen, she heard JB bark, Kyle laugh, and Peter speak in a harsh tone. Her stomach tingled with a dull pain, like a funny bone, letting her know she'd messed up.

JB, their rottweiler, had pulled the taco pie down from the stove, where it'd been cooling. The pan was facedown. JB, trying to get it turned over, had pushed it all the way across the kitchen, leaving a trail of pie on the white linoleum. JB was taking his time eating, as if such bounty came along every day. Peter, Ronnie, and the twins were watching the show but only three of them were enjoying it.

"Good Google, Bevy," Peter said. "How many times are you going to leave him inside with our dinner?"

"It's only the second time," Bevy said.

"In a month," Peter said.

"Ouch," Ronnie said.

With the cheese and taco sauce binding the meat and veggies, the pie was a paste, like Spackle. "I'm sorry," she said, meaning it. If she accomplished nothing else, Bevy needed to get dinner on the table. Peter had said from the start that the campaign would get in the way of family life, and it was like she was out to prove him right.

"I figured JB might as well finish," Peter said. "It's no good to us."

"I don't know about that," Ronnie said, dropping to his knees. He put his head down near JB's and starting chowing.

Bevy put a hand on a shoulder of each twin to make sure they didn't mimic their brother. "Don't be doing that, Ronnie," she said, but couldn't help smiling.

"Get up," Peter said. "That's disgusting." Ronnie stood up like he had a bad back. He moved slowly and talked quietly. Some people mistook him for mellow, but anyone halfway perceptive could sense the pistons firing beneath the surface.

As JB went along he not only ate the chunks, he also took the time to lick up the sauce and the grease. The poor thing didn't realize his beef-dream might not last.

"He's cleaning up for me," Bevy said.

"Oh, yeah," Peter said. "Dog saliva, that's real sanitary."

"I was only kidding," Bevy said.

"On second thought," Peter said, grabbing JB's collar, "he shouldn't be rewarded." After putting up a brief struggle, JB allowed himself to get dragged away, although he looked back and licked his black lips. From across the kitchen JB appealed to Bevy with a moan. "He doesn't even have the decency to feel guilty," Peter said. "The beast."

"Should I call Domino's?" Bevy said.

"No," Peter said, putting a point on it as if to say, You shouldn't be rewarded either. Or maybe money was on his mind. "I was really looking forward to taco pie."

"I could make tacos," Bevy said.

"But not pie?" Peter said.

"There's not time," Bevy said. "I have to get to my meeting."

"Right," Peter said. "Your *meeting*." Peter took JB into the family room, where a glass door slid open to the backyard.

Ronnie stuck around while Bevy peeled an onion, which would wreak havoc on her makeup. She looked at him and he put on a smile. Ronnie was striking—he had longish chestnut hair, the color of Bevy's, and his green eyes seemed to give a view of the fire inside—but he never talked about the girls who must have been interested.

"Yes?" Bevy asked.

"Morgan got me a ticket for a show tonight."

"That a first name?"

"Last. He's Hilltop."

Time was when you could be sure that a Hilltop family were good people, but the church had gotten so large you could no longer be sure. Some people, it seemed, came over from the lenient churches without making any other changes in their lives.

"He the one who dropped you off yesterday, the one with the sixty-nine Mustang?"

"That's him. Can I go or not?"

"You *know* you need to tell me more."

"It's Kanye West, a Christian singer. He's dope."

"Dope, hunh? Well, how can I say no to someone who's dope?"

"I'll be home by midnight."

"I doubt your father will let you go, but if he does, it's fine by me."

"Cool," he said, and the tremor in his voice, all false hope, made her regret saying he could go. Ronnie was about to go ask his father, then decided to do it later, after Peter had gotten some food in him. Ronnie's head could have been made of glass for how easily she saw what was going on in there. The boy wasn't a total mystery.

"Dinner's in fifteen," she said as he walked away with a limp that looked like a reason to call the doctor but was probably a style.

Peter came in and shook his head in annoyance, as if JB had done this to spite him. Peter was unflappable in a crisis—his siblings still marveled at the strength he'd shown after their daddy's death—but inconveniences rattled him. The only thing that could make him yell was his computer, and he took traffic jams personally. If a bomb fell on Hartsburg, he would stay calm and take charge, but the other night, when the cable went out, he'd kept punching the catcher's mitt he wore when he watched Reds' games. He'd had it in him, however, to pray till he cooled down. She'd never known anyone else who was so much man and so much boy all at the same time.

"Are you going to clean this up?" he said.

"No. I figure we'll get used to it. Learn to live with it, you know?"

Peter raised his hands, as if to acknowledge that he had come into her kitchen, so to speak. He walked over to her, put his hand on her shoulder, and kissed her temple. She kissed him on the mouth, but he kept his teeth clenched. Peter had to be in the right mood to French kiss. Or freedom kiss, as the kids were calling it these days.

"Now get out of here," Bevy said, looking at the knot that had been tight on his neck for twelve hours. She patted his chest. "Go relax."

The hamburger she'd planned on using smelled rank. Knowing that good cooks improvised, she took a box of Steak-umms out of the freezer and dropped them in the pan one by one as she peeled off the plastic, then sliced them up while they cooked. Like a Japanese chef, maybe. But they fried down to not much, so she dumped in two cans of tuna and mixed it all up with taco seasoning and a half cup of Ragu.

While the meat simmered, she checked the message on the machine. It was from Marybeth Sheldon, wanting to know if there was still a meeting tonight now that Bevy's opponent had dropped out. This was why Bevy had wanted to go through with the meeting, to guard against cockiness. The libs, as Rush called them, might come up with another candidate, and part of Bevy, the fighter in her, hoped they did.

When she got off the phone with Marybeth, Bevy found the twins playing in the pie. Kyle was rubbing Karl's hair with it, and Karl seemed to be enjoying the abuse. Kyle started rubbing the food all over himself, like it was soap in the shower. Bevy might as well have been wearing leg irons. She just watched.

Loretta, her hair clumped and wet from swim practice, walked in the front door, as did Brent, who passed her on the way to the kitchen. "JB got our dinner again?" he said.

"No," Bevy said, tempted to lie down in the paste herself. "Don't you know modern art when you see it? I got a grant from the NEA."

"Any *A*?" Brent said.

"She's joking, bonehead," Loretta said. "Our mother can actually be pretty witty sometimes. Too bad it's wasted on you."

"I don't see you laughing," Brent said.

"You don't laugh at wit," Loretta said.

"*You* never laugh at anything," Brent said.

"I call this work Tex-mess," Bevy said, and for a nauseating moment she actually saw meaning in the pie. It was the scattered, sorry young woman she'd been in Texas. But it was the smell of the mess, more than the sight of it, that recalled her dark years. Mexican food, margaritas, and futility. False hope.

She'd gone years without thinking about her old self—that time in her life had seemed as lost to her as early childhood—but in recent months it'd been returning in flickers and flashes, afterimages like from a dream, or a drunken night.

Kyle stuffed a chunk of tomato in Karl's ear while Karl licked the goop from his palm. "You're letting them play in it?" Brent said. With five children, you had to put up with a lot of disorder. She pretended to be unfazed by it, especially when Peter called attention to it, but she felt great relief every night when the kitchen was clean, the children were in bed, and the doors were locked.

"No snacking," Bevy said as Loretta opened the fridge.

"There was pizza at prayer club," Brent said, "but I didn't have any." His smile was asking for a smile, but Bevy didn't oblige. With Ronnie being Ronnie, it was left to Brent to be the good son and he was getting too good at it.

"What's for dinner?" Loretta said.

"Fish and steak tacos," Bevy said.

"Wow," Loretta said. "Haute cuisine."

"I don't *want* oat cuisine," Brent said. He was fifteen but seemed younger than Loretta, who was six months shy of fourteen. Girls developed earlier than boys, of course, but Loretta had always been old for her age; she'd started speaking in sentences at two and a half. Bevy's mother-in-law, Kay, had been concerned that Loretta wouldn't be able to fulfill her potential in the public schools. Having homeschooled Peter and her three other children, Kay had put pressure on Bevy to do the same for Loretta, but Bevy didn't want to set her apart; the girl had trouble enough making friends. What Bevy hadn't told Kay was that she lacked the school smarts to feel confident teaching her.

Bevy grabbed the twins by their collars. "You two, stop." She looked at Loretta, then Brent, fixing them with a low-grade glare. "You two, leave."

She pulled off Kyle's shirt and lifted him up to the counter near the sink. She ran the water warm and, using the spray nozzle, washed the pie from his armpits.

"What were you thinking?" Bevy asked.

"You shouldn't waste food," said Kyle with a knowing smile.

"You were rubbing it on you like it was going to get you clean," Bevy said.

"What makes clean clean?" Karl asked. He was still playing with the pie, using his foot to paint the floor. He was the thinker of the two.

"What do you mean?" Bevy asked. "How do you know something's clean?"

"Yes."

"Well, you can tell just by looking and smelling. Right now you boys are *not* clean."

"Are you clean, Mom?" Karl asked.

Kyle started to fall into the sink headfirst and she caught him, her back seizing up, and she whimpered out a laugh.

Her life was hard, yes, but there were different kinds of hard. This hard was easy compared to the hard in Texas, before she'd met Peter. They'd only known each other for a month when he flew in to visit her and, in a truck stop near her hometown outside Midland, brought her to the Lord. Her conversion began in the truck stop but didn't really end until two years later when she'd given birth to Ronnie. She was home. Motherhood was real, like God Himself. It didn't fade like fun or lose its luster like a good idea. To this day she could look at any one of her children and burst into tears. It was love she felt but also amazement: she'd gotten lucky, been saved, and only God knew why.

"Karl!" she yelled as he reached up for the handle of the frying pan. He froze and looked at her but didn't lower his hand.

She ran and scooped him up and hugged him, not caring about getting messy. She kissed his cheek and kept kissing it until it was free of taco pie, which tasted spicy and good, and which she now couldn't wait to clean up from the floor.

"Never touch something that's on the stove," she said. "Even if Mama messes up and leaves the handle sticking out like that, you can never, ever touch it."

CHAPTER 2

O N THE LAST FRIDAY of every month Cormier bowled with friends from childhood, the two who'd stayed. Before heading into the alley, he checked himself in the rearview. His vanity was nothing new, but now that he was wearing his hair longer, it was placing greater demands on his time. He adjusted a curl cluster as if turning a page, then raked the whole grayish tangle back off his forehead. This latest look of his, Ruffled Intellectual, worked, he felt, because it made use of his thick hair and was not undermined by his thin frame or slight effeminacy. It also legitimized his aloofness: the Intellectual wasn't talking because the Intellectual was *thinking*.

Stu and Jimmy were sitting there, hunched behind bottles of Busch. Stu used his middle finger to blow him a kiss, and Jimmy smiled. The three of them had been friends since fifth grade, brought together by a snowball fight on the playground that had bloodied Debbie Wheeler's nose and landed them in the principal's office. As teenagers they had been part of a larger group, ten guys who, to an unusual degree, had transcended the social and economic divisions that had cut through the school like hallways. The group included jocks and preps, stoners and straight arrows, working-class kids and wealthy kids, plus a smart, shy, skinny, middle-class boy who was never left behind by his more-popular brethren. Cormier's parents had tried to pass along their idealism, but if he had hope for humankind, his friends deserved some of the credit.

Cormier exchanged one of his brown bucks for bowling shoes and took a stool at the little round table. "About time," Stu said, his bottom lip bulged with Skoal. The tobacco juice in his cup, rimmed with tiny bubbles, looked like espresso.

"I got caught at work," Cormier said.

"What's this one about?" Stu said.

"Margie Stone turned a hundred."

"Poor bitch," Stu said.

A few lanes down, teenagers were bowling badly. Big hair, tattoos, concert T-shirts: not Carly's crowd. Tonight his daughter was watching movies at Lisa Zimmerman's house, where, Carly hoped, Dave Chin would acknowledge his fondness for her, to which he had admitted to Cammy Slater in the library. How that might happen—in the midst of an alcohol-free gathering with parents upstairs—was beyond Cormier's comprehension. Having kept his personal life as a teenager hidden from his parents, Cormier was amazed by how much he knew about Carly's; understanding it, though, was another matter.

"A hundred years old," Jimmy said. "Can you imagine?"

"Nope," Stu said. "If by some miracle I hit eighty, I'll blow my brains out."

"Jesus," Jimmy said.

For guys who had grown up in the same two-family house, then worked together in the factory, Stu and Jimmy couldn't have been much more different. You got the sense that they were different not despite all their time spent together but because of it; like a comedy duo, they'd forged their identities in opposition to each other.

"And if I don't have the strength to do it," Stu said, "one of you is going to do it for me. Probably you, Jimmy. I wouldn't trust Hollywood with a firearm. He'd half-kill me, then he'd have second thoughts and try to shove my brain back into my head."

"*Then* I'd have a story," Cormier said. The minty-ashtray smell of the tobacco competed with the lemony Lysol that'd been sprayed in their shoes. Bowling's bonding power was due in part to the dandyish tricolored shoes. Every time they came here, Cormier pictured the three of them breaking into a song and tap-dance routine.

"I've got a story for you, Wally," Jimmy said. "Went on a call down on Riverfront. Bad fire, but we kept it in the kitchen. The girl who called it in has got Down's."

"Not another heroic retard story," Stu said.

"It's not," Jimmy said. "It's, like, a . . ."

"Human story?" Cormier said.

"Yeah," Jimmy said.

"You want a story?" Stu said. "I'll give you a story. There's this rugged, good-looking guy"—pretending to primp, he ran his fingertips over his thick eyebrows and thinning hair—"who works at Wal-Mart. One day last week he catches a woman shoplifting clothes, and she offers to pleasure him orally in the changing room so long as he doesn't turn her in. Guy can't help noticing she's got beautiful lips, so he takes her up on the offer, and the be-low job is so exquisite he lets her walk out with the clothing."

"No way," Jimmy said with a smile. "You're full of it."

Stu made his eyebrows bounce. His forehead—traversed with crevices that set off lobes of weathered skin—looked like an antique basketball. "What's the matter, Wallywood?" Stu said in response to Cormier's blank face. Normally he was his best audience; some people didn't enjoy the Stu show at all.

Cormier reminded himself that opening up to these guys was always the right move. "I just saw what they did to Cinema Center," he said.

"Oh yeah," Jimmy said. "You loved that place."

"What were you hoping for?" Stu said. "A hippie commune?"

"I don't know. Nothing, a store. Home Depot maybe? But a *church*?"

"Fucking Bible thumpers," Stu said. "When someone says he's more righteous than you, hide the cows and the kids. Most thumpers are pedofags."

"No they're not," Jimmy said. "They're good people."

"Some are, some aren't," Cormier said.

"The voice of reason has spoken," Stu said. With his tongue he pushed out his wad and it plopped into his spit. "Let's toss the rock."

The wager was five bucks a game. It had seemed like a lot of money in high school and it seemed like a lot of money now. Cormier had trouble holding his own even when he wasn't battling a mild case of whiplash. Jimmy, a lefty, had perfect form; he slid into his shot and ended with his hand above his head, keeping it there as his ball curved toward the center and the pins exploded. Meanwhile Stu picked up every spare that wasn't a split. Part of this tradition was the ridicule heaped on Cormier as he rolled his soft straight balls. *Nice one, Molly. Don't hurt your typing finger. Pussy.*

Sadly, Cormier was better at bowling than at any other sport (and yes, it was a sport). On most bowling nights, this one included, he got into a groove. The first tender touches of his drunkenness massaged away his self-doubt, and he bowled with his body not his brain, the ball seeming light, the lane short. Fun was what it was. Cormier won the third game with a 188, marking on every frame but one. During his fourth or fifth beer, the wheels came off the Wallywagon, but he didn't care; he had won one game, cutting his losses and upholding his manhood.

Only Jimmy had the strength to keep powering balls through the dead spots in the lanes, which hadn't been rebuilt since the alley opened in '69. Cormier had celebrated his twelfth birthday here. While he and the other boys did their best to wield the balls, Cormier's father had sat there reading. The bookish son of Cleveland public school teachers, James had never bowled. Cormier urged him to try it, not knowing that an old wrist fracture would force him to bowl with both hands—the infamous diaper wiper. There were snickers from some of the boys, but Stu and Jimmy knew not to laugh.

Now, thirty-two years later, Jimmy readied his attempt for a turkey. His ball caught the wrong side of the center pin, but all the pins went down, and he pumped his fist. "You see that?" he said.

"Your gay little fist-pump?" Stu said. "Yeah, I saw it."

"Seriously, boys," Jimmy said, "when was the last time I ended up paying?"

They considered his question, and it became clear, at least to Cormier, that the answer was never. "Fuck you," Stu said, and they all laughed.

Stu's laughter turned into a groan and he rubbed his eyeballs with his palms. His hands were always in motion: rubbing, scratching, picking, flicking.

"What?" Cormier said.

"I just remembered about my life."

"Yeah," Cormier said.

"I shouldn't go to work tomorrow," Stu said. "It's just of matter of time before I punch someone in the Adam's apple."

"I suggest you don't," Cormier said.

Stu was a performer but not a phony; his rage was pure. He had a righteous resentment that Cormier could only guess at. Did Cormier romanticize Stu? Cormier's wife thought that he did—"your own little Joe Six-pack"—and Cormier had to admit that he liked the *idea* of Stu. Early in college Cormier had presumed to believe that he had outgrown his friends from home, especially the ones who'd stayed in Hartsburg. Before long, though, he'd found himself impressing his college friends with mostly true tales about his hard-core, working-class buddy. Stu visited him once at NYU and his anarchic spirit, as well as his shit-kickers, meshed with the punk sensibility that Cormier and his friends were doing their pitiful best to embody.

Cormier's fondness for Stu, in any case, was genuine and deep. Stu was honest to a fault (if that was possible) and he kept Cormier honest (if that was possible).

Afterward in the parking lot, they stood near Jimmy's truck and each smoked one of Stu's cigarettes, their attention drawn to the bar at the Holiday Inn across the street. Done-up women got out of an SUV. Even at a distance, especially at a distance, they triggered in Cormier those fantasies that would never die or be fulfilled. Women walking into a bar on a Friday night. A game for younger men, although Stu, long divorced, might be heading there later. An eighteen-wheeler stopped at the light, blocking their view.

"So I've been going to Hilltop," Jimmy said.

"Hilltop?" Stu said.

"Wedgwood's church," Cormier said, trying to show no reaction.

"Jill's been going there since last year, with her sister and the boys. I just started. This last month she's been too tired to go, so I've taken the boys. That's why when you talked about them being fags—"

"I was just—" Stu said.

"I know," Jimmy said. "But you're not going to 'just' anymore. Jill loves it there. It's given her peace, so it's got to be a good thing."

Cormier nodded so heartily that he felt the pain in his neck; light-headed from the Marlboro Red, he tried to believe in his nod, wishing the world were simpler than he knew it to be. Jill had advanced breast cancer. "How is she?" Cormier said.

"Hanging in there." Jimmy might have said more if Stu weren't there. They were best friends, Stu and Jimmy, absolute brothers, but Jimmy tended not to reveal vulnerability in front of Stu. That was Cormier's role, the softy to whom Jimmy showed softness, although the two of them hadn't talked much in recent weeks.

Jimmy flicked away his butt, getting so much distance that Cormier wanted to cheer. Jimmy Lynn was once a name on everyone's tongue, the three-sport star headed for the big time, which around here meant the Big Ten.

Quick good-byes were said and then Cormier was driving home with the exaggerated caution of a medium-drunk driver. His beer bloat had diminished, leaving behind an empty, juicy stomach, a bag full of fart. He'd skipped dinner but felt more ill than hungry. Water was what he needed, water and a be-low job; of this there was no chance, not in his condition and not with the sexless streak that was now a potential Topic for Discussion. His lower back pain had commenced, ahead of schedule. He was looking forward to a Saturday of sloth. Contentment, they said, was a curse, but "they" had never camped out in Cormier's leather recliner surrounded by snacks.

He didn't look at the church as he drove by.

The left-turn arrow went green on cue, pleasing him until he thought about it. An efficient ride home: yippee. But that was life, wasn't it? His life, anyway. Nothing to be sniffed at, perhaps, these tidy pleasures, these flashes of accomplishment. A felt-tipped pen, a nice heavy one. Sweet and sort-of-healthy fig bars kept spongy in a ziplock bag. You twisted the ice tray and heard the *crack* and watched the cubes jump.

The Saab shook its way through a pothole, and Cormier wondered if it was his liver or kidneys that hurt, not his back. Maybe he just had to piss.

He kept making turns but was moving essentially south toward the river. People saw the town as a hamburger, the river as the meat, but the image, with its oversized bun, had never pleased Cormier, who tended toward realism. The north side, Cormier's side, had more people and Main Street; the south had the abandoned steel factory and Hilltop.

The streets were empty, the houses dark. He could have made it home unnoticed on a camel, on a parade float. He drove by the Zimmermans' house, where Carly was perhaps consummating her crush. No reason to think about *that*.

The blocks in his neighborhood were squarish, as were the houses. He drove by his mother's house, the house he'd grown up in. He was still amazed to be living here, in Hartsburg, yet he'd lived away for only a decade, including his years at NYU. More than three quarters of his life had been lived here, so maybe it was amazing he'd ever lived elsewhere. Maybe he was meant to live here. Except that no one was *meant* to do anything. He didn't believe in fate, and hated that catchall prayer of the self-deluded: "Everything happens for a reason."

He had *chosen* to live in Hartsburg and not all of his reasons were fear-based ones. Too often his life seemed like a dream, like dust, and his living here was an attempt to create a sense of permanence. His roots here felt almost real.

Turning off the car, he saw the light upstairs, where Robin was reading and waiting for her drunken husband and sober daughter, and he felt grateful for that, for home, and ashamed for not feeling grateful more often. Jimmy was walking into the hospital that his house had become. Bodies were getting blown apart in Iraq.

Fragments of his last script, a sci-fi romantic comedy, flashed in his mind, each one an embarrassment, an insult, a moral indictment. The pain they brought seemed physical but quickly faded, like the ache of a stubbed toe. Good lines never came back and he might have doubted their existence except that he knew he could write. Tomorrow a few thousand people would read strong sentences about the pluck of an old woman whose cruelty toward her caretakers he'd had no choice but to portray as charm.

No choice, sure.

A faraway dog barked, and trees rustled: sounds that seemed closer to silence than noise. He closed his eyes. To Cormier no other quiet was as quiet as Hartsburg's.

In his pants pocket, amid lint, was a warm piece of Dentyne, and he chewed on it as he might have at sixteen, before walking into a house four blocks away where a different woman would have been waiting, unable to sleep until she knew her boy was safe.

CHAPTER 3

BEVY HAD DECLARED that she wanted to run for school board at the dinner table. It was Memorial Day, and rain had pushed their barbecue inside. All eyes went to Peter, whose balled-up lips were working in a circle. With the twins now in preschool, Bevy's load had lightened—she'd even found the time to start counseling drug addicts at Hilltop—and everyone in the family was happy that there was more of Bevy to go around. Now here she was, talking about running for the school board?

Peter's mother, Kay, was there, and she looked at the ceiling as if to appeal for help. Peter had barbecue sauce on his nose. Although his eating habits seemed as meticulous as all his other habits, somehow food often found its way onto his face, and ribs were a challenge even for the neatest of eaters, like Kay. "Why?" he asked.

"Isn't it obvious?" Bevy said.

Kay cleared her throat and touched her nose. She was being subtle so as not to make Peter look silly, but it was a little late to worry about that: the man had sauce on his nose. Peter wiped off his nose and looked across the table at Bevy. Used napkins, stained black-red, were piled high around a big bowl of bones. Sauce streaked the coleslaw. The children weren't usually interested in what passed between their parents, but now all of them except Ronnie were keyed in. "I know why *someone* needs to run for school board," Peter said. "But why does it have to be you?"

"Why not me? I think I'd like it. But this isn't for kicks and grins. I've been thinking about this and praying on it and I truly believe that God wants me to run."

Ronnie pushed away from the table, and the chair, missing the rubber tips that Bevy had forgotten to buy, scraped bumpily on the floor, vibrating the table. Kay cringed and Karl, aping his beloved grandma, did too.

"Sit down," Peter said. "We're having a discussion." It took Ronnie half a minute and two sighs to sit down, the table vibrating again as he pulled his chair tight.

"It'd keep me pretty busy for the next five months," Bevy said. "After that, it'll be just one night a month."

"If you win," Kay said.

"Oh, I plan on winning," Bevy said, and Loretta smiled.

"Never know with all the libs in town," Peter said, making a fist around his knife. "It sure would be nice to beat them."

At this point Bevy knew she had him, and an hour later, after some cajolery in his study during which she hinted that she would do "the thing he likes best," he granted his permission. Bevy let out a holler that made Peter cover his ears.

When she walked out, Brent gave her a high-five, but Kay kept to herself. She was scrubbing underneath a burner. To hear Kay talk of her household, well, the kids' clothes never had a wrinkle and all the meals were served on time. Peter shared this view of his childhood, so there were three possibilities: he was afraid to contradict her or time had reshaped the reality or Kay was the Super Mother she claimed to be.

"I know you don't think much of public schools," Bevy said, "but that's where our children are; that's where most children are."

Kay set down the sponge and used her thumbnail. It'd been years since Bevy's own mother had done much mothering—Deidre had a new husband and a new family—and Bevy had long hoped that Kay would be, if not a mother figure, then at least a friend. But Bevy felt little warmth from Kay and lots of judgment. Peter claimed, however, that Kay thought highly of her daughter-in-law. The woman was confusing: hard to read, hard to know. Her reserve made Bevy miss Texas, where people were more likely to spill their emotions all over the floor. Still, Bevy had respect for Kay and wanted to hear her opinions on things—especially things having to do with Bevy herself.

Confrontation, Bevy decided, was the wrong approach. This occasion called for her Southern-belle voice, which had softened up everyone from crusty old cowboys to cops to the woman in the supermarket last week who had grabbed the last box of Blueberry Morning. "Talk to me, Mama," Bevy said, going for it. Kay's gray hair was pulled back so tight her eyes edged upward, Chinese-like. The eyelift gave her a look of disapproval, which she was probably going for. "I respect your opinion. I want to know what you think."

"All right then. I believe running for school board—politics—is something Christians, especially Christian women, ought not be doing."

Big modern churches, the stock market, televangelism, and, as it turned out, politics were all on Kay's list of no-no's. Yet Bevy used to talk politics with Kay. Maybe Kay's worldview was narrowing as she got closer to heaven. Or maybe she'd taken this position just because it was different from Bevy's. Kay would claim to be above spite, but Bevy felt that she still blamed her, ten years later, for their move to Hilltop.

"Who do you want running for office?" Bevy said. "Atheists and Muslims?"

"All I know is when Christians get involved in politics, it's not long before they start doing un-Christian things. It dirties up your faith."

This exchange came back to Bevy four months later as she drove to her meeting at Hilltop. Her faith hadn't been dirtied up. Yes, the give-and-take had gotten nasty there for a bit, but where in the Bible did it say "Thou Shalt Not Make Clear that the Man You're Running Against Is a Radical Old Kook"? And who said Christians couldn't be tough? As a matter of fact, the very problem with the country was that they hadn't been tough enough these past forty years. The campaign had reminded Bevy how tough she could be. When there was something to win, watch out for Beverly Carmen Baer, sister to two older brothers and daughter to Lieutenant Colonel Lamar H. Northcutt Jr. She had won riding contests on horses and bulls. She had become head cheerleader, only to quit the squad two weeks later. She had won drag races against men with better cars.

There was nothing un-Christian about winning—and nothing better to win than political campaigns. Kay lived in a fantasyland. Her white clapboard country church was straight out of the 1920s: men in suits, women in dresses. They took pride in their own purity; meanwhile the world went to hell around them.

Bevy liked the area around Hilltop; it was less congested. And less congested was how her mind felt. Kyle's aggression, Karl's whimpiness, Ronnie's anger, Loretta's loneliness, Brent's need to please, Peter's annoyance about the campaign, Kay's opposition to the campaign, the rank meat she should have tossed, the clogged drain upstairs—all of it blew out the window. For the first time in years, she was spending large chunks of time in her own head, and it was an exciting place to be.

Hilltop consisted of a main church, a chapel, a school, an administrative office building, and an event center, all linked by dark cement walkways that cut through well-kept lawns. The school housed the preschool, Sunday school classes, Bible study groups, counseling sessions, and Bevy Baer for School Board meetings. Fifty people had attended her meetings, although never more than twenty at once, and a mere eleven had pounded the pavement on her behalf. She wasn't sure what to make of this. People had lives as full as hers, but the congregation, drawing people from five towns, was four thousand strong. This much was clear: that crusading army of Christians—often seen marching across TV screens to the sound of ominous music—was nowhere in sight.

After parking, she stayed in the car, closed her eyes, and prayed out loud for guidance, choosing one her favorites, from Psalm 19: "May the words of my mouth and the meditations of my heart be acceptable in Your sight."

Tonight only nine people were there, and she knew why when they clapped: everyone thought she'd won. "Ladies and gents," said Ted Culp, standing up from his spot in the semicircle, "the newest member of the school board!" The twerp had wanted to run himself and was the likely source of the rumors. Although people knew Bevy had been saved not a moment too soon, her past was hazy even to Peter—even to herself, at this point—and Culp, she'd heard, had added color to the picture in hopes of undermining her, as if Marlin Dreifort (her opponent until a few days ago) would comb through her dirt. What'd Culp think Dreifort was going to do, hire a private investigator?

The informal primary had come to an end when Reverend Wedgwood had seen Bevy in a Bible study and raved about her to the whole group. (It was no coincidence that Bevy had picked that moment to hold forth.) Though not in the room, Culp had gotten the message. Then, trying to atone, he had become a fan.

"Thank you," she said. "That's very kind. But this is exactly why I wanted to see you all tonight. You see, this race is far from over."

"But Dreifort dropped out," said Rhonda Shoate. A single woman with a facial hair problem, she was Bevy's most loyal volunteer. In fact, Rhonda seemed to revere her. Bevy liked the idea of having a groupie—she would have liked a horde—but was unsettled by the intensity of Rhonda's attention. Something wasn't right with Rhonda.

"They've got till Tuesday to find someone else," Bevy said. "And you know they're going to. Liberals are like weeds: they keep coming back." The crowd appreciated this, Rhonda leading the smiling nods. "So I wanted to get together to implore y'all not to relax, and to recruit a few folks—five, I hope—to do door-to-door work tomorrow."

Bevy made a point of handing the clipboard to Pauline Bumpers, who was new to Hilltop. Bevy wanted to show Pauline and everyone else that Pauline's deformity didn't discomfort her, even though it did. Pauline had stubs for arms. Disabled people made Bevy feel dour and ungrateful. The effect on Bevy of disabled people was like that of overly cheery people (Marybeth Sheldon, also in attendance, fell into this category). Why couldn't Bevy just love all people, whatever their level of cheer or length of arm?

"I need a pen," Pauline said, and Bevy dug through her pocketbook, not surprised she'd forgotten something.

"Does anyone have a pen?" Bevy said.

"I've got one."

The voice sent a quiver through the room. It was the smooth, husky voice that for some reason made Bevy think of a cabin in the mountains, the crackle of a fire.

Reverend Wedgwood, his bulk filling up the doorway, pulled a pen from the pocket of his suit jacket. "I'd like it back." He smiled. "I do love my Sharpie."

"Sharpies are excellent pens!" Marybeth said.

"I like Uni-balls!" Rhonda shouted, and Bevy tightened with embarrassment, like a teacher presenting her class to the principal.

"Thank you, Reverend," Bevy said.

"Please pay me no heed," he said, like that was possible. An aspiring public figure herself, Bevy studied the way the Reverend took over the room as he walked across it. Bevy could be confident, but *that* confident?

He sat down next to Marybeth, who let out a titter and patted her headdress of hair. Women who acted like schoolgirls in front of him embarrassed Bevy.

Pauline's arms were so short her hands seemed to jut from her ribs. She didn't seem self-conscious as she held the clipboard against her chest and signed it. The woman had grace. Bevy had heard a rumor that Pauline was a liberal on economic issues. If so, she was a special kind of liberal, the loveliest of the species—so lovely that, like a ladybug, she seemed to be something else altogether.

Bevy said, "I want to stress to y'all the importance of what we're doing. This is the only contested race this year, and conservatives already have two seats. One is held by a Hilltop brother and another is held by a man called Paul Lapin, who's a Jew but strong on moral values, so if we win this seat, we could go a long ways toward making the public schools a safe place for our values, and our children."

"Amen," the Reverend said, and Bevy felt his eyes on her, his power joining with hers. She had on a postman-blue dress that was all business yet all woman and, underneath, a super-support bra that restored to her what nursing had taken away.

"But if I lose, then we all lose. Liberals want to use the public schools to demean what we stand for. I know it's hard to believe. It simply can't be, right? It's too bad to be true. Remember when a student at the junior high was told she couldn't write a report about Jesus, and we all thought, well, that's got to be a mistake. But it's no mistake, friends. The effort to push liberal, atheistic values onto our children is intentional and infuriating, and when we win this race, it's going to be *over*."

People clapped, as did the Reverend. There were only ten people here—at the VFW she'd spoken to two hundred—but the feeling was the same. In another life she'd fantasized about being a country rock star. This was a performance, all right, although she was just saying what she believed, sharing her fears and hopes. Her hopes had been hard-won. Hilltop made her feel less alone, but she could still feel like a dazed tourist, searching for someone who spoke her language. The Supreme Court had legalized abortion and banned school prayer. You could get money from the government to urinate on an image of Christ but you couldn't praise Christ if you worked for the government. Those who thought marriage was a sacred bond were intolerant; those who thought

31

it was a prison were enlightened. Black was white, down was up, queer was normal.

Faced with such madness, Christians could be forgiven for despairing. (In weak moments Bevy wondered if Kay, tucked inside her bubble, had the right idea.) But with the help of Reverend Wedgwood, Bevy had come to see that the state of the nation wasn't madness, or if it was, it was *explainable* madness: Christians, complacent and naïve, had been outmaneuvered, not outnumbered.

But the majority would be silent no longer. Their exile was coming to an end: "What in God's name are we waiting for? How loud a wake-up do we need? Just last week a child wrote a note saying he wanted to blow up the school like Osama bin Laden. Is that loud enough? Maybe not. Maybe we want to wait until there are condom machines in the bathrooms. Or until the Pledge of Allegiance is banned. Or until some troubled student, schooled in secularism, straps a bomb to his chest. I suggest to you, brothers and sisters, that we cannot wait a second longer. We've already waited far, far too long."

Pauline looked like a seal when she clapped. Bevy's brain did that sometimes, thought cruel thoughts.

When the clipboard came back to Bevy, seven people had signed up to work tomorrow. It took an effort not to hug Reverend Wedgwood when he approached her afterward. Rhonda, lingering by the door, stared at Bevy like she was an Apostle. "Rhonda," the Reverend said, "would you be a dear and give us a moment?" Rhonda cast a longing glance at Bevy before waddling out.

Being alone with the Reverend was unprecedented and possibly inappropriate; feeling a need to do something with her hands, she shoved the clipboard into her bag, the camel-colored leather stretching out to accommodate the board. She had to pee. The Reverend had a dimpled chin, and his dark hair, gray at the temples, was brushed straight back, creating a bouffant effect. His hands were as large as her daddy's but soft-looking. Indeed, Bevy regarded him as a father figure even though they were the same age. "Your message was spot-on," he said. "It was strong but secular, and I urge you to make sure that everyone involved with our campaign is on the same page. My point being, we don't want people canvassing and preaching the Gospel at the same time."

"Of course not. The separation of church and state, right?" She spiced her words with the perfect lilt, and the Reverend leaned back his head, his chin dimple opening up as he chuckled. Bevy had more fire in her than all the other Hilltop ladies, including his wife, Minnie, a dowdy dud unworthy of the Reverend.

He put his hand on Bevy's shoulder and walked her toward the door. Bevy tightened the muscles in her calves to support her knees but could do nothing about the pee dribbling into her underpants. "There is a time for proselytizing and a time for politicking," he said. "We don't need everyone in Hartsburg to be Christian, at least not yet; we just need them to vote Christian."

Bevy wasn't even through the door when Peter called to her from the living room. She found him in his chair, his feet flat on the floor, his head pulled back, looking like a man during takeoff who hates to fly. "Ronnie ran off," he said. "He didn't tell me where he was going, didn't tell me anything."

Her backward plunge into the couch wasn't quite voluntary. "He had a ticket to a concert. I can't remember the singer's name. Kentay or something."

"I don't like the sounds of that."

Peter went upstairs, and she knew he was fetching Brent, who would tell them about this singer. Bevy pushed herself up and leaned on the arm of the couch, her legs bent and stacked on their sides. Having taken off her underpants, she felt naked.

"Okay," Peter said, retaking his seat. Brent, always eager to help, stood between them. "Ronnie snuck off to a concert. You have any idea which one?"

"It's something like Kentay or Kenay?" Bevy said.

"Kanye West," Loretta said. The house was carpeted everywhere but the kitchen and the upstairs bathrooms, and Loretta, with her light step, could walk into rooms unnoticed. "He's very acclaimed. It's hip-hop."

"I don't like the sounds of that," Peter said.

"Ronnie said he's Christian," Bevy said.

"He asked you if he could go?" Peter said.

"That's right," Bevy said.

33

"And you said no?"

"No. Not exactly."

Peter rubbed his chin. She couldn't see his scruff but she heard it, hard on his fingers like sand on a sheet. Once the children had left, he said, "Not exactly?"

"I said he could go if you said yes."

"So you wanted to play good cop to my bad."

"No. I don't know. I just get tired of saying no to him."

"Maybe if we said no to him a little more often, he wouldn't be so screwed up."

"He's not screwed up."

"What would you call it? Is he just a little lost? Is he *finding* himself?"

"Not everyone goes in a straight line. God knows I didn't."

"Honestly, Beverly, that doesn't give me much comfort."

And there it was. He'd never stated it so bluntly, his belief that Ronnie's wildness was her legacy to him, passed along through genes or shoddy mothering or both. And Bevy didn't disagree. She'd learned to be a mother with Ronnie. She now knew it was a mistake to watch your children too closely, to react to their every move. And even before he had started to act out, she'd seen herself in him. Riding home one evening after hitting two home runs in a Little League game, he'd seemed sad. Strawberry ice cream dripped down his cone onto his dirty hand. "Aren't you happy?" she asked him. "I guess?" he said. She could see it in his eyes, all that want. He was her child, no question.

"I turned out just fine," she said.

"But you've told me a thousand times how lucky you got. Do you want to leave it to chance? Do you want to just let Ronnie go and hope for the best?"

"That's not what I'm saying."

Brent came leaping down the stairs and jumped to a stop in front of Peter. "I downloaded a song by this Connie guy," he said, and breathed hard through his smile.

"What I'd tell you about downloading music?" Peter said.

"I know, I know—"

"Right, I understand. You were helping us out." Peter stood up and put his arm around Brent and they walked up to his room.

Bevy took this opportunity to retrieve the panties from her purse, which she'd left in the entryway off the kitchen. She held them at arm's length as she went down to the basement. The laundry room—a box of a room tucked between the guest bedroom and the furnace—was where she went to be alone, and she liked it best when the old dryer was rumbling, giving off warmth. She dropped her underpants in the washer, but it seemed she could still smell them, so she gathered up the clothes that were strewn about.

As the machine filled, she cupped her hands under the cold water and held them to her face.

When she went back up, Peter was standing in the kitchen, eating ice cream. Brent was doing nothing but watching him. "It's all f-word this, n-word that," Peter said, his lips creamy in the corners with Ben & Jerry's. The family did their best not to give money to those hairy freaks, but the Chunky Monkey flavor made a true boycott difficult. "If that's a Christian singer," Peter said, "I'm Hillary Clinton."

"Want to hear it, Mom?" Brent said.

"No, that's all right."

"Go on upstairs, son," Peter said. "And thank you. You did good."

Bevy waited for Brent to walk away. "Where I come from, that's called tattling. I'm not sure we should be encouraging it."

"What should we be encouraging, Beverly? Should we be encouraging them to stay out to all hours of the night listening to Kunte Kente sing f-this, n-that?" His voice was calm, but his eating was furious, all loud scrapes and quick bites. "You know, I was thinking. If you weren't at that meeting . . ."

"So it's my fault?"

"I didn't say that."

"I think you did."

She managed not to hear what he said as she walked out. Going up the stairs she let tiredness run through her. It was like lifting up a dike.

But she was awake when Peter got in bed. And she was awake a minute later when he started to snore. And she was awake two hours later when the clock said midnight. She got up and walked to the window: no Ronnie.

Peter, lying on his back, looked smug. She couldn't remember a single night that she was asleep when he wasn't, and how could he sleep now?

Downstairs, through the window of the front door, the street was still. In winter, skidding cars posed a threat to mailboxes, so Peter had put an extra post on theirs, and at the moment it looked to Bevy like the body of a farm animal, a headless animal. The streetlight, which Bevy could hear humming, allowed her a view of Kelly Beale-Wallis's flowerpots across the street. A good neighborhood all in all, but the year before, the police had broken up a dispute at the house just four doors down, and at a house on the other side, around the loop, teenagers were always coming and going, a party raging while the parents, if they were there, pretended not to notice. She was pretty sure that Ronnie didn't drink or drug, but she didn't like this Morgan character, Hilltop or no. For one thing, there was that car of his. Bevy knew about Mustangs.

CHAPTER 4

CORMIER AND ROBIN liked their house: it was one aspect of their life about which they had no reservations. Sure, they wished the house were farther from the street—there was no front yard to speak of—and farther from other houses, but these were quibbles. The previous owners had knocked down walls, so the downstairs had the feel of a loft; it was all air and light. Meanwhile the rooms upstairs—three bedrooms and Robin's study—retained their turn-of-the-century coziness. They'd added new windows and antique chestnut floors. The house seemed a perfect blend of the old and the new.

Cormier had been living in the house for a month when he began to sense that he had known it in a former life. And he had: Stu informed him that the house had been the site of an infamous party thrown by Danny Pastorelli. Cormier was living in the house where he had long ago vomited, dared to dance, and sucked face with a drunken senior. A coincidence, yes, but a hundred other houses in town held similar memories.

Their decision to live in Hartsburg had been a practical one. Two days after Cormier had come back home to help take care of his father, Robin called from Los Angeles to tell him that she was pregnant. This was '87. His father was upstairs getting killed by cancer and his mother was at the stove frying chicken cutlet. Cormier walked the phone as far out of the kitchen as the cord would allow. He implored himself to *say the right things*, and he did, during that conversation and the several that followed. Decisions were not their strength, but they made one. She'd had an abortion as a teenager and another was out of the question, they'd been together for six years, she loved the idea of owning a house, fuck LA, Dad might stay alive for months, Love you, Love you too, so.

It happened quickly—within four months they were moved and

married—and it made sense; what didn't, perhaps, was their decision to stay. They had reasons: the house, the comforts that a low cost of living allowed them, the continuity (for Cormier), the garden (for Robin), and, above all else, their daughter, who was thriving; there was always a friend or teacher or team Carly didn't want to leave. But these reasons felt like rationalizations; both Robin and Cormier had trouble accepting that *this* was their life. In their life, after all, they weren't going to live in the Midwest, weren't going to have to travel sixty miles to see a decent play, weren't going to be one of those couples who stopped striving. So they waited for their life to begin, fearful that it wouldn't come, resentful of the other person for not making it happen.

They talked about their disappointments, talked and talked. If Cormier had ever been a typical Midwestern male in his lack of expressive capacity, he was no longer, not after twenty-two years of brain-dancing with Robin Birnbaum. But they couldn't seem to get out from under the sense of incompleteness and failure. The therapist they'd tried had urged them to distinguish their own problems from those they shared, as if that were possible. "Marriage," Stu liked to say, "is a pool you both piss in."

"You stink" were the first words Cormier heard on Saturday morning. He turned onto his back to spare her the breath that he'd been blowing on her.

He had an erection, and it felt wonderful against the silk sheet. A strange thing, hangover horniness. The Internet could have told him the physiological reason for it, but he hated doing research. Good thing he wasn't a journalist.

"Every time you go out with Stu," Robin said, "you drink too much."

"You just notice that?"

"I feel compelled to mention it once every five years."

Robin understood Stu. Or she at least understood Cormier's connection to him. She tolerated Stu because she had to; like Cormier's farting or lack of handiness around the house, Stu was an aggravating and occasionally amusing part of her husband.

Robin, now sitting up, took her legal pad off the nightstand. She had short dark hair, slate blue eyes, fair skin, and a chin that seemed to nudge her thick lips up toward her flat nose—a kind of beauty that only men of intelligence and refinement understood. He loved to have sex with her. When he was inside Robin, feeling her feel him, he felt like a man.

Cormier pulled the sheet tight around his erection. Their problem of late wasn't sexual per se. It probably wasn't even a problem, just an inevitable stretch of laziness, where sex seemed like a task, a task with an unspectacular payoff, like a hike up a small mountain.

"Stop snoring," she said.

"I'm not asleep."

"Then why are you snoring?"

She'd had a bad night, apparently: maybe she'd had her buried-alive dream. The people dumping dirt on her coffin varied, ranging from Robin's mother to Ariel Sharon. (If Cormier had ever appeared in the dream as a shoveler, she'd been considerate enough not to tell him.) He wanted to protect her from her mind's tumult, but what could he do? Be kind. "You okay?" he said.

"Unclear. I've got to ask you something."

He turned toward her, keeping his head on the pillow. He tried to figure out what he'd done wrong, and the effort tightened the vise on his temples. He imagined his eyes popping out and blood shooting out onto her white T-shirt.

She said, "Who's CeeCee?"

"CeeCee?"

"You kept saying 'CeeCee' in your sleep."

He laughed the laugh of the innocent. "She's, uh, the bartender at the bowling alley. I'm in love with her. We're in love with each other."

"You wish."

"CeeCee is my name for Cinema Center."

"You're serious."

"Afraid so. I think that was my last secret. Now you know everything."

She smiled, stroked his hair. "Baby, did you dream about CeeCee?"

"I drove by her last night. My sweetheart is now a church."

"This fucking town."

Coming from Robin, criticism of Hartsburg seemed like criticism of him, and he normally would have put up a defense. This morning, though, wanting sex, he let her remark pass. But her eyes were back on the pad.

Robin sent stories to journals and had a binder full of rejection letters to prove it. It was brutal, this fiction business, no easier on the ego or the digestion than Hollywood. The trajectory of Cormier's screenwriting had been similar to that of his journalism, from earnest and hard to obsequious and soft. His early scripts were weighty and, he now knew, pedantic. As the rejections mounted along with his debt, he'd blunted the edges on his work, writing films that were more John Hughes than John Sayles. He'd never made a penny off his screenwriting—he'd waited tables—but had sold out nonetheless.

He admired Robin for still putting her ego out there to be stabbed, even if he was tired of editors at, say, the *Okiehunga Quarterly* influencing his family life. The arrival of the mail, marked by the squeak of the rusty mailbox lid, was cause for concern.

There was a knock on their door, and then Carly was surging in and crawling into their bed. She smelled like tonic water. "How are you, sweetie?" Robin said.

"Oh my God," Carly said, rolling onto her back and resting her head on Robin's crossed calves. "I've got a total migraine or something."

"Did you take aspirin?" Robin said, massaging Carly's temples.

"I couldn't find any. What am I going to do? I've got a calc test on Monday."

"You'll feel better," Cormier said.

"Well, isn't this heartwarming?" Robin said, using a word that she could only use ironically. "The whole's family here." She was referring to the arrival of Peeve, their gray tabby cat, who walked on top of Carly to get to Robin's hand, which he butted with his head. "All right, all right," Robin said, using one hand to rub Peeve and the other to rub Carly. No rubs for Cormier. Peeve looked at him but didn't gloat. He was too high-minded for that. Peeve had a serious disposition, even for a cat. He seemed to think you silly for finding him cute. Peeve was the son of one of Cormier's mother's cats. Cormier had chosen the name for the purpose of being able to say, "There's my pet, Peeve"—a rare pleasure because Peeve spent almost all his time outside.

"Did you have a good time last night?" Cormier said.

"*That*," Carly said, "went very well. Dave totally asked me to hang out."

"Does that mean you're going on a date?" Cormier dared to ask.

"Dad, come on. It is what it is. The Zimmermans have this wine cellar, and Lisa's mom let us drink a couple bottles."

Robin looked at Cormier. "You had wine?" Robin said.

"Two glasses."

"That headache, dear girl, is a hangover," Cormier said.

"It's awful," Carly said. "I'm never drinking again. I mean, how do you *do* anything when you feel like this?"

Cormier placed a pillow over his face. He'd long ago accepted that he would never feel like an adult, but he could still be surprised by how far he hadn't come.

"Lisa's mother let you drink?" Robin said. Lisa Zimmerman was Carly's best friend and chief rival. According to the latest class rankings, Carly was third and Lisa was fourth. The smartest non-geeks, Carly had said. The competition between the girls was obviously unhealthy, but Cormier got caught up it. This morning he found himself wondering if Lisa had only pretended to drink wine to keep herself fresh.

"You'll feel better," Robin said. "Go get in bed, and I'll bring you some Advil."

Peeve left with the women and Cormier spread his arms and legs so that Robin would have to touch him when she came back. Left unoccupied, Cormier's brain did what it often did when left unoccupied: it worried about Carly. They had made an effort not to project their disappointments onto her, and it was possible to conclude that they had succeeded. After all, she was supersocial, diligent, and driven. On the other hand, she was supersocial, diligent, and driven. There was something going on when two people who viewed themselves as underachievers raised an overachiever.

"Move your arm," Robin said.

He got up, although not quite upright—back pain—and with his wife ensconced in an imaginary world, he stumbled into the real one, if this world of his could be considered real. He was inclined to spend the day reclined.

By the time he got downstairs after a seven-part pee, Robin was at the table, dribbling soy milk over Optimum Zen. The tones of NPR caressed the kitchen.

"No oatmeal?" he said.

41

"I want to get back to my story," she said as if she'd ever left it.

Her break from routine brought him to the brink of tears. He was fragile this morning—his muscles felt like ice melting inside his hot skin—and he had an urge to talk to Robin, maybe even cry to her, but unloading now would have been selfish, with Robin caught up in her work, and he doubted he would get the attention or affection he craved. Neither he nor Robin was a caretaker by nature. One of their jokes was that they needed an adult in the relationship, someone to hold them and tell them that everything was going to be okay.

"You'll clean the gutters today?" Robin said.

"Yeah," he said, dizzied by the thought of being on the roof.

"And make dinner?"

"Can I take it one meal at a time, please?" He considered his own break from routine. His body was asking for naughtiness, for pork and yolk and cheese, a treat that recalled his pre-sensitive-stomach, pre-pseudo-vegetarian days, a slippery sandwich that would grease his dry, depleted system like motor oil.

He stood in the middle of their new sky-blue-tiled kitchen, trying to make up his mind, as though the fate of men and nations rode on the decision.

Footsteps on the front porch. "Oh, Jesus," Robin said.

"Exactly."

"Let's pretend we're not here."

Sometimes he didn't do the easy thing. Sometimes (once) he didn't cross the street to avoid hypercritical readers of his column. Sometimes he didn't screen phone calls. Sometimes, apparently, he didn't hide from proselytizers on his porch. He slid in his socks toward the door, swinging his arms like a speed skater.

What greeted him was staggering. Teeth and perfume and "Good morning" sung by a tall, square-shouldered woman and two little blond boys. Squinting in the light, Cormier looked at one boy, then the other, trying to find a way into this confounding scene.

"Yes," the woman said, and barked out a violent laugh. "They're twins."

"I'm Karl!"

"I'm Kyle!"

"We didn't mean to disturb you," she said.

Then why did you? he wanted to say. Cantankerousness fell under the Ruffled Intellectual rubric, but he seldom dared to go for it. With a fake yawn plus stretch—hand on head, elbow out—he brought relative order to his hair.

If they were proselytizers, their pitch was sneaky. Her name was Beverly Baer, call her Bevy, they lived up on Laurel Terrace, she and he were both Ward Three-bees . . . She had a Southern accent, the real deal, not the Ohioan accent people mistook for Southern. Cormier watched this woman's dark lips move. She was technically attractive, with a symmetrical face and gleaming brown eyes, but her stiff pink dress and stiff auburn hair sapped her of sexuality. Almost. Was she winking at him?

"You look familiar," she said.

Cormier often got half-recognized because of the drawing that accompanied his column. "I've lived here a long time, was born here."

"That's wonderful," she said, oddly. She put her hand on her sternum, next to a silver brooch that could have stopped a bullet. "My children are growing up here in this great town of Hartsburg, which is why I'm running."

He nodded for no reason. "What?" She handed him a flyer. She was running for school board, on a platform of parental control, which was code. He got the picture.

"We know what's best for our children," Bevy said. "Teachers need to teach."

This woman was responsible, indirectly, for violating CeeCee. Yet he admired her. She was out here trying to change the world while he contemplated the pro and cons of a pork-centered breakfast. "Who are you running against?" he asked.

"He dropped out due to health problems."

"So you're running unopposed?"

"You could say that."

"Well, what *else* could you say?"

"Pardon me?"

"Forget it."

"Okay, I will," she said, and laughed that laugh again. It was as if she were having an asthmatic attack and loving it. When her wide-eyed wheezes finally subsided, she reached down to remove Karl's or Kyle's pinky from his nose, then patted his head; the beatific tableau restored, the three of them looked at him.

"You're running unopposed yet you're out here on a Saturday morning?"

"Can't take anything for granted."

"It must be too late for someone else to get in."

"Why, are you thinking of running?"

He didn't say no. He'd had too much coffee—there was an egg-timer ticking in his sternum—except that he hadn't had any coffee. Too little, then. "Now that you mention it," he said, theatrically stroking his chin, and the two of them got a big laugh over that, ha ha ho ho, just two Ward Three-bees having a good time on a Saturday morning. Across the street Mr. John was clanking around under the hood of his Pontiac.

"Tuesday is the deadline for filing," she said.

"Did you know that Cinema Center is a church now?"

"I did," she said, letting her smiley front fall. Bevy Baer wasn't an idiot, not by any means. "Supply and demand," she said.

Cormier crossed his arms and tried to get large in the doorway. "The Lord works in mysterious ways." Here inside his hangover he was discovering some verve and pop.

"He sure does, Mr . . ."

"Cormier. Wallace Cormier."

This was the name on his column, and it seemed to register in Bevy Baer's glassy eyes. "Are you married, Mr. Cormier?"

Taking this as a shot at his masculinity, he said, "Yes" in his best baritone, using his morning voice to his advantage.

"Well, I'd appreciate your wife's support as well."

Trying to take the offensive, he pointed at the piece of armor disguised as a brooch and realized that he was also pointing at a sizable and possibly excellent breast. "That's really nice," he said, sounding like Lou Rawls with a sore throat.

"Thank you. My husband, Peter, gave it to me."

"Hope you didn't mind me *broaching* that subject."

They leaned forward into their laughs, ha ha ho ho. A final moment of fake joviality before the battle commenced. As he stepped back, he knew there was a chance he'd do it—run for office—and by the time he'd said,

44

"Good luck," and shut the door, he was sure he would, and only after he'd made up his mind was the excellence of the idea revealed to him, the excellence so layered and deep that he was simultaneously ecstatic and mournful for the years he had spent not running for school board. It was a perfect idea.

He walked back into the kitchen and pushed Bevy's flyer across the table. "I'm going to run against her. This is it: this is what I've been looking for."

Robin looked at him as if he'd said he'd joined the merchant marine. When her upper lip was raised and curled, it looked like an exotic mushroom. "Why?"

"It's a good idea."

"I'm not saying it's not. I just want to *talk* to you about it, okay? Why are you so sure this is what you want to do?"

"Well, for one thing, they turned Cinema Center into a church."

"She's one of the flock?"

"I'd say so."

"Then you wouldn't win."

"Thanks. Thanks for your support."

"It's just the truth."

"This ward is pretty moderate."

"What do you know from wards?"

She always went Jewish on him when she was angling for an advantage. "I know this neighborhood," he said.

"*Do* you?"

"What the fuck is that supposed to mean?"

She pushed her chair back and stood up, hands raised. "If you think yelling is going to help your case . . ."

Cormier hadn't been this angry in a long time, not since she'd told him that his memoir about his Hollywood years was no good. "I don't see why I have to even make a case. Why can't I just tell you that this is what I want, and you say okay?"

"Because you're part of a family, you big bonehead." She shook her head and managed a laugh. The soggy flakes in her bowl reminded him of the leaves in the gutter. "Let me ask you a question," she said. "How's Jill doing?"

"What is *this*?"

"You always come back from bowling a little unbalanced, and I figure it must have something to do with Jimmy. I mean, one of your best friends' wives is dying."

"You always do this. Whenever you don't want me to do something, you suggest that my motives are weird or dark."

"I'm not talking about your motives; I'm talking about your state of mind."

"I feel good, Robin, better than I have in a long time."

"Are you feeling the way you felt a few years ago when you were going to write—what was it again?"

"*Rodentia.*"

"What?"

"The horror movie, where all the rodents in the world—"

"No, no, no. It was a book. You were going to quit your job to write it."

"Oh. Yeah. The book about rock songs in movies."

"Right."

"What's your point?"

"That you're impulsive."

"But I didn't quit my job and I didn't write the book."

"Because you soured on the idea."

"No, I didn't. I still think it's a great idea."

"Then why'd you give it up?"

"Because you didn't want me to do it."

"It's my fault you gave it up?"

"No. I'm lazy."

"You're lazy yet you're going to run for office?"

"You can call me impulsive or you can call me lazy. You can't call me both."

"Why not? Impulsiveness is a form of laziness."

He'd long suspected that she was smarter than he was. He paused to think. "I want to do something socially useful."

"So this is altruism?"

"Partly. This town's in trouble."

"But it's been in trouble for years, and all of sudden because of a movie theater—"

"That's what woke me up, okay? I mean, whatever it takes. Like they say, 'Revolution begins when the complacent are denied their dinner.'"

"I've never heard that."

"You've heard every saying?"

"But if you want to take on the kooks, you already have a forum. You don't have to write about"—she pointed at the paper—"old ladies."

"Oh, great. We're doing cheap shots now."

"It was a good piece, actually."

"Don't patronize me."

"You could be writing more substantive stories."

"I know I could be, and I know you know I could be. How do I know you know I could be? Because I've told you about a thousand times I could be. But now I'm telling you something else. I'm telling you that I really, really want to run for school board."

"It's one thing to want it, but . . ."

"You don't think I'd be a good candidate."

"Do you?"

"Yes, actually, I do. I think I might surprise you."

She smiled at the notion that he could still surprise her. It was not a nasty smile. "There's someone else to consider," she said.

"What's she care either way?"

"She's part of this family, and it's something that will affect her."

"I need her permission?"

"You need her opinion."

"And if she signs off?"

Robin blew out, fluttering her lips, and rubbed her forehead. She'd been tired, it seemed, for a long time. They all had. He wanted them not to be tired. First, though, he wanted to run for school board. He looked at his wife and let her look at him. Seventeen years before, in their kitchen in Santa Monica, after he'd told her that he was going to give up screenwriting and move back to Hartsburg indefinitely, she had looked into his eyes and known she had to support his decision. Back then they'd had a way of lifting each other up. He believed, he had to believe, that they still could.

"Okay," she said.

He hugged her, kissed her, and swept her into a dancelike move. Yes, you could call this dancing. NPR was playing a Latin number and they did a mambo or a tango or a rumba, a mumbo-jumbo-cowabunga across the kitchen. He turned his back to her and tried to shake his ass like a woman in a rap video but Robin, cackling, hugged him from behind. "Stop it," she said. "Please, stop, I can't take it."

They went back to dancing together, cha cha cha. They could go deep, the two of them, they could talk about pain and parents and what did it all mean, but it was this silly side of theirs, often dormant, that made him feel most at home.

He spun her into the fridge, and stuff fell to the floor, photos and magnets and receipts and Carly's perfect report card. "Leave it for now," he said, but Robin was already on her knees, sorting through the mess.

CHAPTER 5

I T'D TAKEN BEVY several years to feel comfortable in Hartsburg. She'd missed Texas, the openness of both the land and the people. The people in Hartsburg were nice, but nice was different than friendly. It might have had something to do with her accent; even in people's smiles Bevy picked up a *you're-not-from-around-here-are-you?* But eventually people let down their guard and she let down hers. Hartsburg had become her home, and she loved it. The people were decent, hardworking, and patriotic. They weren't flashy or loud. Unlike Texans they didn't need to show you how tough they were. They had a quiet dignity. They kept to themselves but were there when you needed them. On the evening of 9-11, everyone had gathered at the town square, thousands of people, white, black, and brown, Protestant, Catholic, and Jewish. Standing in the crowd, warmed by all the candles and bodies, she had felt that this worst day had turned into the best.

Bevy liked downtown Hartsburg. It reminded her of a past she'd never known, a less coarse time. After canvassing on Saturday morning, she walked down Main and imagined that the sidewalks teemed with people and shopkeepers waved and men tipped their hats and it was safe and sunny. Which it was now, in real life, safe and sunny. But empty.

For the second time this morning, she went to Kohl's Coffee to meet with her volunteers. Bevy had gotten a coffee the first time and decided to get another one now. She had stayed up till three-thirty, which was when Ronnie had gotten back, and Peter had poked her awake at five-thirty, wanting to make sure Ronnie was home. Then they'd stayed up to figure out what punishment he deserved.

Aside from the espresso drinks, which Bevy's budget denied her, the coffee at Kohl's was help-yourself. While her volunteers waited for her at a corner table, Bevy pumped herself a small one and took it to the counter, where Jenny Kohl gave her a smile. Jenny was a large woman, with smooth skin and a shapely figure. She glowed. A natural beauty, although she could have used some makeup around the eyes.

"Another round, barmaid," Bevy said. "One of those days."

"All my days are one of those days," Jenny said.

Bevy felt free to laugh because she knew Jenny was just being self-deprecating. Jenny seemed comfortable in her life. Bevy guessed that her faith was strong. Not that strong faith guaranteed a life of ease: when Bevy had accepted Jesus into her heart, life had not stopped being hard; it had stopped being bad.

"You have a great laugh," Jenny said.

"Thank you, darling. You have a great smile."

As if to prove her correct, Jenny showed Bevy her straight teeth.

When Bevy turned around, Kyle had Karl pinned, his knee on his back. Karl wasn't even putting up a fight; he just lay there with his cheek on the floor.

"Get off him, Kyle," Bevy said, and in case he planned on disobeying her, she took his arm and escorted him to the table next to the volunteers.

Karl was still on the ground, the poor thing. "Get over here," she said.

Only four of the seven who'd signed up had showed up: Marybeth, Ted, Pauline, and, of course, Rhonda. But the five of them had covered most of the ward. How successful they'd been was another question; this wasn't the best group of pitch-people. Marybeth was more bubbly than a cheerleader on the last day of school. Rhonda had facial hair and a mental problem. Pauline had almost no arms. Ted's lip was lined with a caterpillar mustache that only a better-looking man could have pulled off.

"Wow!" Marybeth said, pointing her long silver fingernail at Bevy's cup. "You're a real caf-fiend!" This was typical Marybeth. It wasn't quite criticism, but what else could it be? The twins, at the next table, were pretending to read the newspaper.

"How'd we do, folks?" Bevy said as they gave back her lists, which she hoped were marked up the way she'd instructed.

"I did well, I must say," Marybeth said. "I got people fired up!"

"I didn't," Pauline said. "People weren't friendly at all." With her no-nonsense manner, she was the opposite of Marybeth. Pauline had on jeans and a jean vest, a denim suit, which didn't do justice to her pretty face. Brown eyes sat peaceably above rosy cheeks. She had an oval face, which looked even squatter because of her braids.

"At first," Pauline said, "I thought the problem was, you know"—she clapped—"my flippers, but I think people just didn't want to be bothered."

"Did you smile?" Marybeth said.

"I think so," Pauline said. She displayed a smile, and it was not a good smile; she kept her teeth together.

"Why, you have the smile of an angel!" Marybeth said.

"I can smile when I talk," Rhonda said with a smile.

"People thought I was there to preach," Pauline said.

"So what if you were?" Ted said. Bevy, working on her own smile, gave Ted one, and he closed one eye like he was looking through a telescope.

"Well, this is all new to me," Pauline said, "going door-to-door. It's hard."

Pauline's gentle bluntness impressed Bevy. First, she had referred to her disability without making anyone uncomfortable. Then she had told an under-told truth about witnessing, whether for Christ or for Bevy Baer: it was daunting to enter someone else's space. "It's not easy, I know," Bevy said. "The rejection, people's moods. The judgment. You have to keep re-minding yourself that you're doing something good."

Bevy recalled her odd conversation with Wallace Cormier. There'd been subtexts. She wondered if he might run, and if she wanted him to.

"It's so sad," Rhonda said.

"What is?" Pauline said.

"All these people, all around you. You look at them and you know they're going to Hell, and it's so sad—it makes me so sad. I don't want people to burn in Hell."

"I know, hon," Bevy said, rubbing Rhonda's arm. Bevy didn't disagree with the sentiment but people like Rhonda, with their glazed eyes and gloominess, gave Christians a bad name. In the interest of PR, and just plain decency, Christians needed to talk about Heaven, not Hell. Bevy re-alized now that she didn't want Rhonda out there speaking for her. "I need someone to coordinate my direct mail," she said, "and I was thinking that you, Rhonda, with your work ethic, would be the perfect person for the job."

With a quick turn of her head, Rhonda looked at Bevy, and Bevy feared that Rhonda saw through her ploy. "Really?" Rhonda said, smiling while she spoke. "I would love to direct your direct mail, Bevy Baer."

Bevy checked her clipboard to see if she had anything more to say; what she found was a prayer list, topped by Jill Lynn. "Before we go, can we say a prayer for Jill Lynn." She reached across the table to take Marybeth's hand, which was heavy with rings, then took hold of Rhonda's hand, which was heavy with fat. It tweaked Bevy's heart to see Pauline lean forward so that Rhonda could reach her hand. "We ask you, God Almighty, to bring comfort and healing to our ailing sister. May you stop the spread of cancer in her body. Please, God, return her body to good health. Praise *God*, amen, and . . . amen."

Rhonda didn't cling to Bevy after the meeting or follow her out. She was relieved but also let down, as if Rhonda were an annoying boy who'd stopped liking her. Bevy caught up with Pauline and asked if she wanted a ride.

"No, thanks. I live just down there." She pointed to the area between Main and the river, an old area that had been modest when Bevy moved here, and was now shabby, the poorest part of town except for maybe the projects on the other side of the river. Pauline's husband, Ricky, was a former steelworker who managed a Laundromat down on Lincoln. Bevy wondered if she'd declined a ride because she didn't want Bevy to see her house.

"I hope this morning doesn't put you off the campaign," Bevy said.

"It won't. I'm good at not caring what people think."

This was plainly true, like everything else Pauline said, and now Bevy knew Pauline wasn't embarrassed by her house. "So what brought you to Hilltop?" Bevy asked.

"It was gradual." Her short arms, the way they moved, gave the impression that she was walking fast; in fact they were strolling. Bevy glanced at her car as they passed and saw a can of whipped cream that'd escaped from a shopping bag. "I was brought up Catholic. It started to seem kind of tired. And empty: people just going through the motions." She crossed herself as best she could. "Forgive me, Father."

Bevy was taken aback, unless this was joke. Even if it was a joke. Pauline looked at Bevy and winked. The girl had a mischievous streak. "But if I had to point to one thing that led me to Hilltop, it was my son going to Iraq. I needed to renew my faith."

Bevy had heard about Zach, one of three Hilltop children in Iraq. "How's he doing over there?" Bevy asked.

"Okay, as far as I know. But I don't know much."

Peter and Bevy had talked about the military for Ronnie. Having grown up in a military family, Bevy liked the idea in theory, liked it less the more she thought about it. She and Peter hadn't brought up the idea with Ronnie, knowing he'd reject it because they'd brought it up. Bevy was either hoping or not hoping he'd come to it on his own.

They stopped on the corner of Deeb Street, which was where Pauline, Ricky, and their daughter, Lucy, lived. A little farther down Main Street, on the top floor of a beat-up old house, Jill Lynn lay ill. "Can I ask you a question?" Bevy said.

"You just did."

"Yes."

"And you didn't ask if you could ask it."

"Oh. Well . . ." Bevy's mind had gotten all twisted around. Pigeon poop, white as white paint, dropped and splattered on a windshield of a parked car.

"Bevy," Pauline said. "I'm kidding."

"Oh." Bevy had a strong humor radar, but Pauline's, it seemed, flew too low.

"People are too careful with me." She flapped her arms against her ribs.

"That's not why—I mean, people are just careful."

"I know, and I don't like it. Life's too short. Ask away."

"Is it true you're a liberal?"

Pauline smiled her real smile, which allowed her teeth to part. "News gets around."

"If you're looking for a church that doesn't gossip, you best look elsewhere."

"I'll tell you what I told Marybeth. I could see myself voting for a pro-life Democrat. You see, my guiding principle is that each life—whether it's two seconds' old or black and poor or stub-armed and middle-aged—is precious, and as far as I can tell, that's more in line with the liberal take on economic issues, taxes and spending and all that."

Bevy was tempted to get into it, to point out, for example, that the welfare state hardly valued life, but she decided to give Pauline the last word, for now.

Driving home, Bevy thought about the only disabled person she'd ever been close to. Maurice was a friend of her father's, a fellow Vietnam vet who'd had an arm amputated at the shoulder. A black man with a gentle, sleepy manner, he'd been like an uncle to her, and after her father had died, Maurice would come to the driving range where she worked. She'd stand there talking to him and trying not to seem hungover or anxious while he hit balls—an impressive feat for a man with one arm. She could tell that he was there to check up on her. One time, holding back tears, she almost confided in Maurice—she wanted to ask for his help—but pride, and its opposite, kept her silent.

There she was, Bevy's old self, rearing her ugly soul, wanting for some reason to be seen. That girl had always been desperate for attention. Bevy didn't want to look at her, not because she was afraid to—at this point her old self could do her no harm—but because she didn't want to give her the satisfaction.

It was no coincidence that Ronnie waited until Bevy got home before coming down from the bedroom that he shared with Brent. Bevy and Peter always made sure to present a united front, but her presence softened the proceedings.

If it'd been left to Bevy, tired as she was, she might have let Ronnie slide, but discipline wasn't discipline if it wasn't consistent. And Peter wasn't Peter if he wasn't consistent. There'd been times when Bevy thought she didn't like his sameness, but she needed it. She knew she needed it because on those rare occasions when he deviated—when, say, he got loopy on wine or went to bed without washing up—the world seemed like a creepy, distorted place, with horns and fangs.

"Can I make you something for lunch?" Bevy asked. "Or breakfast."

"We've got business to take care of," Peter said from the head of the table.

"He's got to eat," Bevy said.

"Fried eggs?" Ronnie said.

"I didn't get eggs this morning," Peter said.

"You want eggs, Peter?" Bevy said.

"I thought you were making ham salad," Peter said.

"You want eggs, I'll make eggs."

"I'll take both," Ronnie said.

"Before you take anything," Peter said, "you're going to listen to what your mother and I have to say." Ronnie sat down across from Peter, in Bevy's seat. She went to stand behind Peter and put her hands on his shoulders. Ronnie was wearing a ribbed tank top T-shirt, which reminded her of men she'd known back in Texas. His biceps were ridged with veins. "It's hard to know where to begin," Peter said. "You go to a concert without asking, knowing that your mother and I would disapprove of this . . . singer. Then, to add insult to injury, you get home at three in the morning."

"I messed up, all right?" Ronnie said, blending those last words so that they sounded like, "I eat." Hip-hop talk, Bevy supposed. "But that doesn't mean I did something, like, sinful, you know what I'm saying?"

"What do you call dishonesty?" Peter said.

"That's not what I'm talking about."

"The music," Bevy said, wishing now that she'd listened to it.

"The music?" Peter said. "Oh, I heard the music."

"You didn't understand it," Ronnie said.

"Is it hard to understand n-word, f-word?" Peter said. "Does that have some sort of deep meaning? And that's beside the point. Even if you'd gone to see Billy Graham himself, you blew your curfew, so your mother and I have decided to ground you for a month. That means no nights out except Hilltop functions, and no TV."

"Oh, frick," Ronnie said.

"Don't frick me, boy," Peter said, pointing at him. "Do not be fricking me."

"What about lunch?" Bevy said as Ronnie stood up to leave.

"I'll eat when The Peter's done," he said, and walked out.

Peter tilted back his head and looked up at her. He pressed his lips together, giving his chin dimples that made it look, upside-down, like a furrowed brow. "He thinks I want him to be miserable," he said. "I want him to be happy."

"You should let him know that."

"How?"

"With your mouth. This thing right here." She leaned down to kiss him and found the feeling of his nose on her chin oddly erotic.

She smiled down at him, but he was looking serious again. "Did you try Liquid Plumber on the drain upstairs?"

"Twice. I need to call a plumber."

"No, no. I'll take care of it."

Peter was pretty good at fixing things but not as good as he thought he was, not as good as Kay thought a man should be. A few years earlier the pieces of the VCR he'd taken apart had ended up in the trash. But he couldn't hurt a drain.

Loretta, researching a paper about the civil rights movement, was watching a video. Or was supposed to be. Bevy, her instincts at work, sped into the family room before Loretta could find the remote. "You have got to be kidding me," Bevy said. On-screen a black guy jumped into a hot tub, where two naked women waited. MTV had been kind enough to blur his genitals. "Is that Martin Luther King?" Bevy said.

"This is a documentary about American youth," Loretta said. Sometimes Bevy had trouble knowing if she was joking.

"I don't live in a cave. This is *The Real World*, so-called. It's about as real as Marybeth Sheldon's blond hair."

"Mom," she said, giving the word an extra syllable. "That's so catty."

Bevy looked at her daughter, sitting on the couch with her arms wrapped around her shins. An old soul trapped in a pubescent body. Bevy had named her Loretta thinking it would become Lori, but the formal name had stuck and rightly so.

The African American man on TV made reference to the sizable size of his penis. Racist stereotypes, no less. The three people in the tub were talking about the possibility of a threesome, like they weren't already in one. The cultural air was toxic. Bevy was concerned about her sons, but you didn't have to be a feminist to believe the world could be extra confusing and cruel for girls, especially when sex came into play.

Thanks to the better board members, the schools in Hartsburg now taught abstinence, which, the curricula said, could be achieved through self-respect—self-esteem, they called it. (Of course, you couldn't teach girls to "esteem" themselves without also teaching them that God loved them, but Bevy could settle for a program that didn't do active harm.) No one, however, knew how to defend against pop culture. Bevy read *People* magazine, which told her all about the money-worshipping moguls and the self-hating female stars who preached false liberation and the young male writers, fresh out of the Ivy League, with their stubble and their sneakers, who'd learned about sex in frat houses. Bevy believed in the First Amendment but wanted these people punished.

"Turn it off," Bevy said.

"*You* were watching it," Loretta said, picking up the remote.

"I was waiting for the part about Rosa Parks."

"Very funny," Loretta said without the slightest smile.

Time alone with her daughter was rare, so Bevy sat down next to her and put her feet up on the coffee table. One of the twins opened the sliding door, letting the dog in, and JB, a real ladies' man, rested his chin on the couch between them. Bevy and Loretta took turns petting him. "So how was swim practice yesterday?" Bevy asked.

"Not so good. Nikki wasn't there, and I don't care for the others girls on the team."

"How come?"

"What they talk about just doesn't interest me."

"What do they talk about?"

"Boys."

"Boys don't interest you?"

"Not the boys they talk about. They're totally immature. To be honest with you, I'm looking forward to the boys in high school."

"You best not tell Daddy that, not unless you want to give him a heart attack."

"I relate better to older boys." Bevy tried to hide her smile, but Loretta caught sight of it. "You see, Mother? That's why I don't tell you things, because you get all goofy."

"I'm not goofy."

"You're so goofy."

"All right, I am," Bevy said, only hinting at what she was thinking, that she wished her daughter could get goofy every now and again. "I hope you understand that *The Real World*—that's not the way life really is, or should be."

"Who do you think I am? Brent? Of course it's fake, like all the reality shows. They just try to shock you. I find them amusing."

This was what Bevy wanted to hear, but Loretta, smart as she was, knew what Bevy wanted to hear. "Amuse yourself in other ways. And be nicer about Brent."

From the kitchen came a clanging sound, the sound of glass getting tapped by a piece of silverware. "There are hungry people in here," Peter said, which meant that Brent was now waiting on lunch as well.

"One minute," Bevy yelled. A deep, back-cracking yawn squeezed tears into Bevy's eyes. "You hungry, Lo?"

"I'll make my own lunch."

CHAPTER 6

CORMIER WAS SO INDECISIVE that he was good at making decisions. Too anxious to weigh pros and cons, to sit with doubt, he made quick choices that struck him as self-evidently excellent. What felt to him like certainty was in fact the opposite. He'd decided, for example, to abandon his movie-writing "career" and move back to Hartsburg in about a minute. The decision had turned out to be a good one—probably—but he'd given it almost no thought. Good instincts? In any case, it was unwise to think too deeply about the potential downsides of a decision (unless you were, say, invading and occupying a divided, oil-rich country). Had he fixated on all that could go wrong in life, or in a school board race, he never would have been able to get out of bed.

Now, during the inaugural moments of his political career, he sensed that Robin was right—he was being impulsive—but this, for better or worse, was how Wallace Cormier went about changing his life. Wanting to dance some more, he tried to pull Robin into the living room, but she insisted on sticking everything back on the fridge. He put on the Ramones—thinking of Carly, he kept the volume lower than the Ramones demanded—and went into the dining room so that the record wouldn't skip.

His favorite way of dancing was to jump as high as he could. He was naked under his robe and his balls began to hurt from flopping around, but he jumped all the way through "Do You Wanna Dance?" "Yes!" he kept answering. "Yes!"

He still hadn't eaten by the time Carly came downstairs, and he convinced her to come to Riverside Café, which wasn't near the river at all; it was on Lincoln Ave., at the end of a mini-mall. Riverside was where Cormier had gone the morning after senior prom. His date, Leanne

DAVID MIZNER

Grubach, was a sophomore with purple acne, a pigeon-toed gait, and a habit of saying "fuck, yeah." Everything he looked at that morning, from her prom-dress-created cleavage to the yolk spreading out on her plate, reminded him of all the sex he hadn't had.

Carly hadn't been to Riverside since she was a young child, and Cormier was excited to reintroduce it to her. Riverside, like Kohl's Coffee, was an island of authenticity, yet Carly and her friends ate at Applebee's and got coffee at the Starbucks in Barnes & Noble. If only she would give these better places a chance, she would love them; this was his belief, a belief he called into question as soon as they walked into Riverside. "The air's like margarine," she said. "Do you know what this is going to do to my skin?"

He'd not fallen in love with his daughter the moment he'd first seen her. She'd captured his heart in the subsequent weeks as her generic human sweetness became a personality that knew him and needed him. He wasn't sure if the depth of his love made it sadder or less sad that she had grown into a teenager he didn't much like. If she weren't his daughter and if she were more in touch with her Jewishness and if he weren't opposed to using ethnic slurs, Cormier would have called her a Jap.

Robin, who had been more of an outsider than Cormier in high school, was pleased to have a daughter who fit into the mainstream. They were buddies, Carly and Robin. Vicariously experiencing a conventional, nonsuicidal adolescence, Robin loved to chat with Carly about boys and makeup and clothes. "There's nothing honorable about being unhappy," Robin said in Carly's defense. This from the woman who refused to take an antidepressant for fear that it would alter her "essential self."

After all these years Cormier still didn't know the waitress's name. He couldn't trust her nametag, which said "Cher." The freckled fat on Cher's upper arms hooded her elbows. "Gross," Carly said, probably referring to the "Horny Trucker" (steak, eggs, and pancakes, all covered with sausage gravy). Or to the shiny pink abscess doming out of the orange scruff of the man at the next table. He wore dark sunglasses and a yellow mesh-backed baseball cap that said "Shovelhead." An actual horny trucker.

Carly eyed her cup of cloudy water with a lip-curled look she'd learned from her mother. "Feeling better?" Cormier asked.

"Not really."

"Take the day off."

"I can't."

"Yes, you can."

"You have no idea how much work I have." She blew out in such a way that remarked on the airlessness of the place, then pulled her curly brown hair into a ponytail. Carly was attractive, maybe beautiful—he had no way of knowing. She'd gotten Robin's blue eyes and Cormier's delicate nose and mouth. "What if I'm still sick tomorrow?"

"You won't be. That's not the way it works."

"You can't be hungover for two days?" Shovelhead grinned at this. Cormier imagined the abscess filling up as the miles ticked off on his odometer.

"Not from two glasses of wine," he said. "You'll feel perfect tomorrow."

"I want to feel perfect now."

"Know the best thing for a hangover? Alcohol."

"Yuck. There's no way I could get it down."

"You'd be surprised," he said, thinking of his own wants.

"Do you think they'd serve me?"

After Carly had ordered pancakes and Cormier had ordered the three-egg special, he said, "And a couple Bloody Marys."

"You old enough?" Cher said without looking up from her pad.

"Yes," Carly said, sitting with a straight back and her hands clasped on the table. He wanted to hug her. "I'm twenty-two."

"What the hell," Cher said. "I wouldn't mind if this place got shut down."

Carly clapped. "How fun," she said, and Cormier had to look away. He focused on Shovelhead's abscess to stop from tearing up. Her excitement reminded him of when she was young—younger. When she was four and five and six, everything had fascinated her, including her father. He'd sing a nonsensical song and she'd laugh with joy. He'd tell her about crickets or Dumpsters and she'd sit rapt. He missed her wide-eyed appetite even more than he missed her chunky legs. These days she knew everything, pretended to. A classic teenage stance, perhaps, but jadedness seemed to hit kids earlier and harder than it once had. It was as if ignorance and in-nocence were now shameful.

"I need to tell you something," he said.

DAVID MIZNER

"Uh oh," she said, seriously.

"I'm hoping to run for school board, and I want to make sure—well, I want to know how you feel about it."

"Are you going to have be, like, *in* the school?"

"No. Not when you're there."

"Fine, then. Is there actually a chance you might win?"

"That's not what this is about," he said, realizing that he was doing this for Carly, in part. Sleepwalking through his days in recent months, he'd been in no position to lament her lack of passion. "But yeah," he said. "I've got a shot."

The Bloodies were almost as tall as the celery stalks that came as garnish. Cormier had forgotten about this reason to love Riverside. "Yum," Carly said after taking a long pull on the straw. "Are you sure there's alcohol in here?"

"Yeah. Be careful."

But she took another pull and the color seemed to go straight from her glass to her face. "Oh my God," she said. "I feel better already." Was it possible she was drunk? Why else would she be pretending the celery were a cigar?

"Maybe save the rest till after you eat?" He went to grab her glass, but she snatched it away and took a drink, then puffed on the celery.

"You know what?" she said. "It's almost like I'm drunk again."

"Stu calls it the shampoo effect."

"That's brilliant. It's a total metaphor." She smiled, and he smiled because she was smiling and because the vodka was sandpapering his hangover. This was a longtime habit of his, drinking away his hangover, feeling either good or guilty about it depending on the state of his life. Today, having become a Candidate, he felt good.

"I love being drunk," Carly said. "Why can't I be drunk, like, all the time?" Her elation seemed to turn all at once to sadness. The food came, and Cormier was tempted to feed her. "Can I ask you a question?" she said.

"Of course."

"It's a little bit—I don't know how to ask it."

"Just ask." He was eager to tell her something she didn't pretend to know. "There should be nothing you can't ask me."

62

"No, that's okay. I'll ask Mom."

"Ask *me*. Please."

"It's about sex."

"That's okay."

"I saw *The Man Show* the other night?"

He chewed his limp, buttery toast and smiled as if he were glad to be having this discussion. This was karmic retribution for getting his daughter drunk. The one episode of *The Man Show* he'd seen had featured a mock game show in which contestants tried to identify people by their ass cheeks, their actual ass cheeks. Cormier had tried to imagine what the mullahs in the Middle East would make of it.

"It's a trashy show, Carl," he said.

"I'm well aware of that, Father. You know what? Forget it."

"No, no. I want to know what you saw."

"It was about butts?"

"Butts."

"Yeah," she said. "Holes."

"Holes."

"Right. Buttholes."

"Yup, got it. What about them?"

"Forget it."

"Okay."

For the first time in his life he was happy to hear Carly's cell phone. She squinted at the phone and said, "It's Dave!"

Cormier pointed at her untouched food as she answered the phone. "Hey you . . . Guess what? . . . I'm drunk . . . I'm totally drunk . . . Yup . . . Like, some diner down on Lincoln . . . I know . . . Yup . . . My dad . . . Totally."

Carly looked at him and smiled. "Yeah. He's pretty cool."

It shamed Cormier how much those words gratified him. He was critical of Robin for allowing her teenage demons to influence her parenting—she was too accepting, he thought, of Carly's conventionality—but in his weaker moments with Carly, he was back in high school, the shy guy hoping to win the popular girl's approval.

Her phone voice was drawing glances, and Cormier felt justified saying, "Please hang up or go outside."

"Fine," she said, standing up.

Cormier had been virtuous enough not to order bacon but the eggs and potatoes had been cooked in bacon grease, so this was another of his fake vegetarian meals. He wiped his plate clean with his final piece of toast, which he'd saved for this purpose.

Two cups of coffee later, Carly still hadn't returned. He would have brought the pancakes home but she'd put syrup on them. Uneaten food saddened him. Shamed him. He put a plate on top of the pancakes, concealing evidence of the crime.

Waiting for change at the counter, he saw an old woman at a table of old women smiling at him. Before he could look away she waved him over.

The woman took his hand and sandwiched it with her hands, which were soft, like an old baseball glove. "I have to tell you," she said. "You made me cry this morning."

"Sorry about that."

"No, no. It's good to cry every now and then."

"It sure is," Cormier said, and he was about to demonstrate.

"This is Wallace Cormier, everyone. You've seen his column, haven't you?"

"I read it all the time," a woman said. This one was wearing a baseball cap. Old women did not look good in baseball caps. "How do you come up with your ideas?"

"Well, you know," he said, trying to remember his answer to this question. "I keep my eyes open and my ears to the ground. And if that fails, I just make stuff up."

Their laughter gave him a chance to escape. He waved and smiled his way out the door. Carly was nowhere near. He found her at the other end of the mall, standing in the warmth coming from a Laundromat.

She winced when she saw him and put the phone against her chest. "Sorry. I've been talking a long time, haven't I? Sorry."

"It's okay. It's fine."

"What happened to my pancakes?"

"I threw them out."

"I'm sorry. I'll pay for them."

"Don't worry about it. Please."

"Would if be all right if I just talked for one more minute?"

"Sure. Take your time." It was hard to be hard on a daughter who was hard on herself, although perhaps she was hard on herself because they weren't hard on her. This morning he'd responded to her getting drunk by getting her drunk.

The butthole on her mind, he realized, probably belonged to Dave Chin. It was a flaw in the human arrangement that fathers had to endure their daughters' sexual development. Carly faced dangers greater than men, even greater than men educated by *The Man Show*, but at the moment he couldn't remember what they were.

She was coming of age in a country that was as confused as ever about sex, obsessed yet prudish. Obsessed because it was prudish. Like a fifty-dollar hooker, the country subsisted on sex yet loathed its own cheapened sexuality. A phony frankness coexisted with a phony righteousness. Americans laughed knowingly at sitcom cunnilingus jokes, then feigned shock when hunger for cock or pussy led people astray. Meanwhile conventional opinion refused to acknowledge that the two most divisive issues, the ones that held the political system hostage—abortion and homosexuality—were about sex. Sex, sex, sex. It was everywhere yet Americans couldn't see it. They made too much of it, and too little, and Cormier was probably no exception.

He found himself standing in front of a T-shirt shop that catered to Hilltop, which was less than a mile away. The shirts in the window said "Not All Religions Are Created Equal" and "My God Can Kick Your God's Butt" and "Satan Sucks."

Cormier stood there longing to do something to take back his town. Then he remembered that he already was. He walked back into the restaurant. The woman in the baseball cap looked at him, then at his table to see what he'd forgotten. She was delighted to realize that he had returned to speak to them. In a voice loud enough for Cher and Shovelhead to hear, he told them about his campaign, making it real.

CHAPTER 7

Monday was cold. When Peter called home during lunch, she asked if she could put the heat on. "You can take the girl out of Texas," he said, and sighed. "Do what you think is right." He had a way of turning everything into a matter of right and wrong, and Bevy did the moral math despite herself: comfort equaled working better, and working better was greater than the financial cost. Whatever. Her tootsies were chilled.

The heat hadn't been on since May. The heaters, which lined the bottoms of the walls, clicked and gave off a roasted-wet smell, and then a clanking came from the basement. They'd had almost no work done on the house in their twenty years here, and Bevy feared that everything would go at once: the pipes, the wiring, the furnace. Last week, when a lightbulb had blown out, Bevy had braced for an explosion. Peter agreed that preemptive repairs were called for, but the money wasn't there.

Bevy didn't hate housework. She saw it as the price she paid for her blessed life, and a small price it was. Until the campaign had invaded her thoughts, she'd been able, more often than not, to get into a groove, a trancelike state that shrunk the world to the task at hand. She liked the quick results—lemony kitchen, vacuumed rug, shiny bathtub—and she loved being with her family in a house she'd made nice.

Midafternoon on Monday, she walked away from a sink full of water and dishes when the garbage disposal didn't go on. The sink was where Bevy started—she worked outward from there—and now she felt thrown off, backed up.

She popped her head into the family room—the twins and Patrick Sheldon, Marybeth's kid, were playing with trucks—then went down to the laundry room. Feeling efficient as she moved clothes into the dryer in one clump, she recalled last night's message, wondering if the Reverend's insights about religious freedom could become part of her stump speech. On her way back upstairs she noticed that the furnace's clanking had given way to a clicking. Or ticking.

It was time to get dinner going, baked lemon chicken, but she didn't want to deal with the sink just yet, so after another check of the boys— "not so hard, Kyle"—she scooted upstairs to her bedroom, passing through thumping music. Ronnie had gone straight to his room without even saying hello. It was good he wasn't out gallivanting, but holing up in his room didn't seem so healthy either.

Listening to Rush while she made the bed, she heard him say "licentious libs." She wasn't sure what that word meant, but she liked it. Safe to assume it didn't mean lovely. She practiced saying it as she sprayed Formula 409 on the mirror in the bathroom off their bedroom. "Licentious libs," she said. "Licentious libs."

With a paper towel she wiped off the spots of spit that Peter had flicked onto the mirror with floss and got a surprise glimpse of her stern housework face. It was rare to get a candid look at yourself. She changed her face with a smile. "I'm Bevy Baer and I'm going to wipe the town clean of licentious libs."

The soap scum on the sink specked with Peter's whiskers could wait another day, she decided, but the tub still hadn't emptied from her shower, so she reached into the frigid water and pulled a clump of her hair from the drain. A half-measure: there was junk in there she couldn't clear away herself. One of these days she was going to get a plumber over here with that special tool. The snake, it was called.

She immediately regretted flushing; like an idiot she'd tossed the paper towel into the toilet and now watched it fill up. "Stop," she said. "Please." She promised God that she would do better housekeeping if the water stopped. She grabbed Peter's cup, thinking she might catch some of the water, but it stopped just in time, the hair-cake floating on top.

Trying to stay a step ahead of her tiredness, she walked into the hallway, her sights set on the kitchen, but couldn't resist knocking on Ronnie's door. He turned down the music, and she took that as an invitation, which she wasn't supposed to need.

"Open doors during the day," she said.

"No other families have that rule."

"I don't know about that. And we're not other families."

"No," he said. "We're not." Lying on his back without a shirt, he looked lean. He had Bevy's pale, yellow-tinted skin, which made everything stand out: his moles, his nipples, his patch of chest hair. The room was stuffy, and it smelled of sweat, not BO, just maleness. The walls were bare. For a moment the room brought back rooms and trailers she should never have entered. You wake up parched and you slide out from under his arm. You take a twenty from his wallet and call a cab from a pay phone, your skimpy outfit stupid in the morning chill, and you hope Colleen's home to turn the night into a funny story, and when the Mexican cabbie eyes the morning whore in the rearview, the thought fills you up with its fever-hot truth: *I hate myself*.

"It's boiling in here," Ronnie said. "I take it you checked with The Peter before you turned the heat on."

"What are you doing, Ronnie?"

"Nothing."

"You been doing nothing this whole time?"

"I'm listening to music."

"You call this music?" she said, although on a closer listen she found a melody inside the noise. "This is a buzz saw."

"Do me a favor, Mom?"

"What?"

"Leave."

The music got loud again as she went downstairs. She passed through the kitchen—that was next on her list—and into the family room, where Patrick, that meek boy, was sitting in a corner while the twins crashed their trucks head-on. "Enough with the trucks, boys. Time to play Legos. Show Patrick those nice skyscrapers."

Caffeine. Her delivery vessel of choice was that sweet cherry nectar, Dr Pepper. She kept both diet and regular on hand and the choice depended on which she deserved. She opened a can of diet and stared at the sink. Maybe she could drain it without getting the disposal working. She could prepare the chicken without draining the sink, for sure.

It was getting dark out. A cat or something darted across the back lawn. Probably running from JB, who needed to be fed.

A scream came from the family room. That little wuss. She felt sympathy when she saw Patrick's face. Karl was crying too. There was blood on the carpet, dripping from Patrick's finger. She located the culprit, a jagged truck fender.

"I told you, boys," she said. "No more trucks."

Patrick screamed again. She picked up the truck, then Patrick, bending at the knees to try to spare her back, which ached till she was upright, and she walked into the kitchen, tossed the truck, put a tissue around Patrick's finger, and wrapped his hand around the tissue. Karl had followed, and she kissed his forehead. "I need you to be my big strong boy and stay here with Patrick."

But there were no Band-Aids in the bathroom downstairs, and the box in each bathroom upstairs was empty, so after marching into Ronnie's room and making him turn down the music, she picked up the phone in the bedroom, skipping over the normal deliberation, the cost-benefit analysis of leaning on Kay. "It's me," Bevy said. "Listen, little Patrick Sheldon cut his finger, and I seem to—"

"I keep a first-aid kit in the bureau of the guest room."

The most maddening thing was not that Kay kept a first-aid kit in Bevy's house; it was that Bevy had forgotten about her own first-aid kit. An unnecessary favor-request of Kay was a horrible thing. "Thank you, dear," Bevy said.

Patrick stopped crying just before the doorbell rang, then ran into his mama's arms. When Bevy told her what had happened, Marybeth got wide-mouthed with horror, then bent down and kissed her son about fifteen times. These days even Christians were behaving like children were made of saltine crackers.

"What if it's infected?" Marybeth said, holding his finger up to the light.

"It's not."

"They need to be watched closely, don't they?"

"I was."

"Okay."

"I mean, not every minute. I had to clean."

"Oh, Busy Bevy. What are we going to do with you?" Marybeth's smile glowed inside her fake tan. She starved herself but her big bones didn't allow her the thinness she craved. Her face looked like a bank robber's in a stocking. "When I clean the house," Marybeth said, "I make sure my children are nearby."

"I should have dragged all three boys into the bathroom?"

"Forget about it, okay? It's fine. But for future reference, there are rooms next to the bathrooms, right?" She laughed. "Or do your bathrooms float in midair?"

Marybeth stood up and Patrick hugged her leg. Bevy felt bad. She should have shown sympathy at the start—anticipating Marybeth's reaction, she'd been matter-of-fact—and now she'd have trouble showing sympathy with Marybeth smiling at her like they were having a fun time, as if she hadn't just called Bevy a bad mother.

"I'm sorry Patrick got cut," Bevy said.

Marybeth reached out and squeezed Bevy's wrist like she was taking her pulse. She couldn't wrap her fingers around it because of her nails. "Please don't worry about it," she said. "Patrick is a tough little boy. He'll be okay."

Bevy made herself kneel down and kiss Patrick good-bye. Can't take it out on the children, can't make them pay for their parents.

"See you on Wednesday!" Marybeth yodeled on her way out. "I hope you got rid of that truck."

Bevy passed through the kitchen—it'd become a monster in her mind—and put the twins in front of a video, then went downstairs. The clothes weren't quite dry. Bevy decided to wait there till they were.

"You all right, Mom?" Ronnie had put on a tank top T-shirt and the beige cowboy hat that Bevy had gotten in Texas. She'd been back only once, to visit her mother, who'd moved to Houston years earlier, right after she and Bevy's father had separated. To her credit, Deirdre had gotten herself a new life, complete with a new man and stepchildren. Unfortunately, that new life didn't include much time for her old family.

It was unusual for Ronnie to pick up on her mood; that was more Loretta's style. "Just one of those days," Bevy said, checking the clothes: still damp.

"The kitchen sink's backed up."

"Is that what you came down to tell me?"

"No."

"Do you need something?"

"No." But he stayed in the doorway, his bare feet hugging the rise. She would do her best not to talk about his toenails. It was no wonder half his socks had holes.

"Ronnie?"

"Mom, I'm, like . . . I'm suffocating."

"Go somewhere. You're free to roam in the afternoon."

"I'm not talking about that. I'm sick of you and Dad riding me. You're all over me. I feel like, like a bug under a microscope."

What an awful image. She worried about all the emotion pent up in Ronnie. There was no doubt that Ronnie's belief in God was strong, but both Peter and Bevy felt that he hadn't sufficiently submitted. He was still trying to be the master of his life.

"I'm almost eighteen," he said.

"Uh oh," Bevy said. "Look out."

"You see? You don't take me seriously."

"I promise you there is no one I take more seriously. But your father and I do worry about you, I can't deny that."

"I'm doing fine."

"I don't believe that you are."

He pointed at her. "That right there. I hate that. You think I'm a bad Christian."

"I most certainly do not."

"My faith is strong. It's not easy being a Christian."

"No, it's not."

"And I'm out there, being a Christian."

"And that makes me very proud to hear."

"I mean"—he made a scary wince-face and lifted up his elbows, his arms winging out—"I'm representin' yo."

"Okay." She didn't like this black style of his, not because it was black, but because it was a front. Sometimes even Bevy had trouble seeing the boy who was hiding in there, but she knew he was more interesting and passionate than Mr. Cool Hip-hop man.

"But I'm not, like, down with the whole program," Ronnie said.

"What do you mean?"

"I see things different."

"Like what? Give me an example." She dropped the pile of clothes onto the table and began to fold. What she wanted to do, though, was to curl up with the warm clothing and go to sleep. Beware of the talks with your children you wish for. "Well?"

"Music. It's messed up that rock and hip-hop aren't cool."

"And you have lots of company. I mean, there are Christian rock bands all over the place. Some things you can't compromise on. Music's not one of them."

"So I can listen to what I want?"

"What were you doing all afternoon?"

"You weren't happy about it."

"Jeez, Ronnie. You want to do what you want to do, and you want me to be happy about it too? I'm okay with it. Let's not create a problem where there isn't one."

He smiled and did a little dance, his shoulders seesawing.

"Now dancing's another matter," she said. She threw a pair of his boxers at him, and he let them land on his hat. "Especially when you move like that."

"You kidding? I've got mad moves."

"You like to dance, hunh?"

"In my bedroom I do."

"Not at dances?"

"Nobody fast-dances at dances except girls and drunk clowns."

"That's a shame."

"And you've seen the Hilltop dances. They're murder."

"Is that all you got a problem with? Music?" She could hope.

He shook off the boxers and scratched the whiskers on his cheek, which were too soft to call scruff. "Your speech the other night?"

"At the Rotary Club?"

"You talked about Bronson Tavares, remember? And you made him out to be some kind of major menace to society. But I know the kid. He's not dangerous."

"You couldn't possibly know that. He threatened to blow up the school."

"He's a little messed up."

"A little messed up? He wants to go, quote, 'bin Laden' on the school."

"Okay, maybe he's dangerous, maybe he's not. But here's my point. Just listen, all right? I'm sitting there, listening to you talk, and it comes to me that the Christian thing to do is to help this kid, know what I'm saying? I mean, we're supposed to help the weak, right? You want weak? This kid is weak, yo."

"I'm not suggesting that this child should not be helped. But as long as he's a danger, he should not be going to school with y'all. This is a tough issue, one you don't fully understand. Professionals and parents and, yes, even school board candidates who happen to be your mama have a better grasp of the complexities involved. Yo."

He lifted up his hat and pushed back his hair and stared at the floor. She'd beaten him down with her verbal barrage. She didn't like her defensive tone, but she was peeved he'd criticized her speech, and she had a right to be.

He went upstairs a few minutes ahead of her and when she walked into the kitchen, he was at the sink, holding a bent fork. There was a gargle as the last of the water drained.

"My hero," she said, and kissed his cheek. "I hope you know that your father and I aren't strict with you for the sake of being ogres. We know what it takes to be at peace in this world, and the next one. That's all we want for you."

"I know," he said, and handed her the fork.

"Ronnie," she said as he walked away. "Please cut your toenails before you kill a small animal."

Her head had cleared along with the sink. The recipe called for lemon rind mixed in with the bread crumbs, which seemed weird, so she made the chicken plain. While the oven preheated, she straightened up the family room, then nestled for a minute with the boys on the couch. Once the chicken was cooking, she went up to the bathroom with a sponge, paper towels, and a garbage bag. She splashed warm water all over the sink, then squirted Soft Scrub on the soap scum and let it penetrate while she wiped up the hair in the shower and let the shower run and squirted Soft Scrub in the shower and took a plunger to the toilet. Once the water in the toilet had gone down, she scrubbed the sink and the shower, singing "I'm scrubbing" to the tune of "I'm Walkin'," then wiped them shiny. The plunger had pushed water onto the floor, so she wiped it up first with paper towels, then with a normal towel, which she took down to the laundry room along with the sheets she'd stripped off Loretta's bed, tossing out the bag of paper towels as she passed through the kitchen. The towel and the sheets went in the washer, and back in the kitchen she greeted Brent and got started on the fried cheese-broccoli and instant mash.

The faster she moved, the more energy she had. A paradox of being Bevy was that despite her fear of darkness and disorder, despite her awareness of all the evil in the world, she felt capable of accomplishing extraordinary things. There was greatness in her, she was sure of it. She cleaned as she cooked—Kay had nothing on her!—and it was in a gleaming lemony kitchen that the Baers sat down to eat.

Peter walked in just as Bevy set down the platter of chicken. "My, my," Peter said. "Doesn't this look nice."

She kissed her husband, then sat down across from him, and they all held hands. "Ronnie, dear," she said. "Why don't you say the prayer."

CHAPTER 8

H E CALLED THE MANAGING EDITOR to tell her about his candidacy. Concerned about "equal space implications," Jeanette said he would have to "steer way clear" of politics in his column. She was younger than Cormier, an up-and-comer in the chain that owned the *Informer*. "Conservatives are pissed at us," she said. This was a mantra among the editors, who worried that the paper was as liberal as they were, which wasn't very. "Objective" stories were ones that wouldn't inspire angry e-mails and phone calls from right-wingers. With seventy-five signatures to gather in three days and who knew how much political ground to make up in a month, he asked to take his vacation now. Not possible, Jeanette said, but she suggested he take an unpaid leave of absence. He didn't ask why he could take a leave but not a vacation; he was happy just to be free.

It turned out that even people leaning toward Bevy Baer wanted a contest; he had enough signatures by Monday afternoon. He had forgotten and possibly lost his checkbook, so he handed the woman at City Hall his MasterCard—an act that struck him as appropriately American, entering an election on credit.

The restaurants in Hartsburg were a source of frustration for the town's sophisticates, like Robin Birnbaum, who abstained from nostalgia except in regard to the culinary wonderland of her Upper West Side youth. When they ate out, they went to fast-food places, which were cheaper and no less sad than the places trying to be good. Monday evening they celebrated his candidacy at Pizza Hut. A festive occasion it wasn't. All through dinner Carly text-messaged friends, and Robin ate only a salad. She regarded any pizza west of the Hudson with an apprehension that bordered on anger, but Cormier suspected her of making a point about their income-less month. They'd be okay, though, financially. Robin's inheritance from her grandfather had paid for their house and would put Carly through college. Robin also did freelance copyediting, which supplemented Cormier's $51,500 salary. They lived well and saved nothing. The idea of planning for retirement depressed them. Why not just buy adjoining plots at the cemetery?

When Robin and Carly went to the bathroom after dinner, he wondered, with fleeting interest, why their habit of peeing together irritated him, then went outside looking forward to a few minutes of communion with Jackson Browne, music to which his women objected. He'd forgotten that they'd taken Robin's Honda, not his Saab, and it was locked. He burped hotly and decided that this would be his last taste, ever, of Pizza Hut pizza. It was like a tomato and cheese doughnut.

Pizza Hut was on the crest of The Drive's largest hill. He walked past the bright blue Dumpster and found himself on a dirt path, which ran parallel to the lot's curb before bending down the hill. It was probably an offshoot of Tripp's Trail, so named by Stu in honor of William Tripp, a freaky guy with a cleft palate who walked on it from school back to his house in the country. Other paths snaked out of the forest and fed like tributaries into Tripp's Trail, which itself snaked into the forest out near the highway. Or used to: the Wal-Mart parking lot had probably closed it off.

Cormier walked the length of the lot, then went partway down the hill, far enough to shut off his northern view. He looked south toward the Mobil Mart and the GM dealer and CeeCee's corpse. Faith Evangelical, shut down for the night, could barely be seen.

He walked back toward Tripp's Trail, staying on the grass some ten feet below the concrete, and discovered a discarded mini-refrigerator, which he used as a platform. Standing on the wobbly refrigerator, imagining that he were about to give a speech to a crowd packed into Mobil Mart's parking lot, he felt instantly nauseous. To stop from falling, he bent his knees and held out his arms like a tightrope-walker.

It dawned on him that fear—of public speaking, of humiliating himself—was what he was feeling, and that fear was what he needed to be feeling.

A grinding anxiety had been Cormier's companion during his last years in Los Angeles. The excitement of the writing life had surrendered to fear—of failing, of not being talented enough, of going broke. It wasn't selflessness that had inspired him to come back to care for his father; he'd been looking for an honorable way out of Hollywood, not that he'd ever really made it in.

His anxiety hadn't abated the moment he moved to Hartsburg. In the weeks leading up to his marriage, he'd suffered from hot-face, which had occasionally erupted into sweating attacks—he'd had to change his undershirt moments before the ceremony—and as a new father, he'd had trouble sleeping for reasons more complicated than the crying in the next room. Writing a column had also been a challenge at first, a challenge intensified by his determination to write provocative pieces.

Over the last few years, however, Cormier had half-consciously created a pillowy life. Robin, pummeled by rejection, suffered enough for them both. He worked thirty-hour weeks and took half-hour showers and arranged his day around lunch. He was known to watch three *Law and Orders* in a day. He'd even started checking reviews written by famous critics to make sure that his own opinions weren't eccentric. (They weren't.) In his most contented moments he believed that he'd figured out how to live—why suffer?—but there was sporadic dissent from within. Some fundamental part of him, call it his soul, ached with hunger when he saw a great movie or read about the war in Iraq or contemplated Carly's future. The soul was a selfish, ravenous beast. It demanded to be fed regardless of the pain it caused its host. Perhaps it was the pain itself that nourished the soul. You gave it pain and it gave you peace.

Yes, the time had come to feel terrible again.

"Where the fuck is he?" His wife's sexy, raspy voice.

He turned toward them—he wanted them to see him—but the refrigerator came off the ground, so he jumped backward and fell onto his stomach, then clutched the grass with both hands, as if he might keep falling.

On Tuesday he got up early (for him), ate Grape-Nuts, did ten push-ups and ten squat thrusts, took a long shower, shaved, and flossed for the first time in years. Now that he was a Candidate, he had a tangible reason to look and feel good, to *be* good. The pain in his gums and the taste of blood and the pink pulpy water that spiraled down the drain struck him as poignant, harbingers of the battle that lay ahead.

He was in his recliner trying to figure out how to figure out what to do when Robin emerged from her study and came downstairs. She looked at him. To her eyes, he realized, this campaign of his could look like a vacation. He shoved his things into his briefcase, kissed her cool cheek, and scooted out the door.

The weather was hard to read, the sky white but bright. Before getting into his Saab, he nodded at Mr. John, his across-the-street neighbor who was about to take a chain saw to a tree stump. Usually he was content to ignore Mr. John, but every neighbor was now a potential vote. Mr. John, a former Navy Seal, had signed his petition but without much apparent enthusiasm. The bumper sticker on his Pontiac said, "I love my country, but the government scares the hell out of me." A libertarian, then, which might or might not make him receptive to Cormier's message, once he had a message.

He drove downtown, excited by the prospect of a noontime latte. A half-mile strip of three- and four-story brick buildings, Main Street had been in decline for years but refused to succumb. It hovered between life and death (not unlike Mayor Bob Sundstrom, suspended in a coma since jumping off the bridge in '93). Businesses still sprouted up, places trying to meet needs unmet by the superstores: a French restaurant, a tattoo parlor, a chair-cover boutique. You couldn't get pants or milk on Main Street, but if you were in the market for a doily or repulsive coq au vin, this was the place for you.

For some reason, it was hard to find parking on Main. The joke was that the parked cars were props in a plan to make the town look alive. Cormier found a spot a full two blocks away from the coffee shop. The inconvenience outraged him; what was the point of living in Hartsburg if it wasn't easy? But as he power-walked toward his latte, he realized that the exercise would do the Candidate good. He wanted to picture himself as a movie hero but couldn't think of a movie in which the politician didn't lose his soul.

There had once been a movie theater on Main. Cormier had a vivid memory of seeing *Spartacus* there with his parents. Some people must have been opposed to the building of Cinema Center—it'd been first-generation sprawl—yet Cormier had loved it, and if a new theater came to town, people would make it their own. Still, in his opinion, newer wasn't better; even better wasn't better. The country, he felt, was in decline, and in denial about its decline. He didn't want to be a fogy—it was a short fall from crankiness to conservatism—but he'd seen his town and country grow more anti-intellectual, more divided, more repressive, louder, courser, crasser, grosser, faster, fatter, worse.

Sitting at the one table in front of Kohl's Coffee, eating tall sandwiches, were two guys in business suits. Cormier knew one of them: Denny Lake. Two years younger than Cormier, Lake had once been a ladies' man—or girls' man, since it was during high school. Senior year, when Cormier was supposedly dating Leanne Grubach, she'd given Denny a blow job. Denny was heavy now but still handsome, with sharp blue eyes and his orange hair cut short. He seemed pleased to be playing the part of a loud-talking, power-lunching businessman. When Denny gave Cormier a lazy nod, he wanted to yell. This is Hartsburg! You're a businessman in a town with no business!

Jenny Kohl greeted Cormier with a beneficent smile. Her parents used to run a brewery, and Jenny had the bearing and boobs of a German barmaid. She could have hoisted Cormier over her head and pinned him to the floor. And he wished she would. "The usual?" she said.

"Better make it a double."

"That kind of morning?"

"That kind of week."

"I hear you. Work or family?"

"Said 'double' for a reason." Decent banter, he felt. "Running for office," he said, and she flinched. Had he yelled? Bad breath? "School board," he said, looking away.

"Good for you. When's that?"

"The election?"

"Oh. Election Day." She knocked on the side of her head. "Been up since five."

"You and me both."

He took the thick-brimmed mug to his spot in the corner. On his table was the *Informer*, which for the first Tuesday in months didn't contain his column. He tossed the paper onto another table to make room

79

for his laptop and the packet he'd received upon filing, which included a map of his ward, financial disclosure forms, and ethical guidelines. He sat down, sipped foam, and seriously considered making a list.

The person to whom he needed to turn was obvious. Cormier had learned that the seat he hoped to win was held by his old favorite high school teacher, Marlin Dreifort. Heart problems had forced him from the race. Cormier was shy when it came to calling people—another limitation that made strange his choice of career—but in his new capacity he didn't have the luxury of being himself. He dug around in his briefcase until he found the pleasing, dense lump of phone.

Dreifort answered on the first ring. "Glad you called," he said in a loud whisper.

"Good."

"But you can't call me."

"Okay?"

"Are you free this afternoon?"

"Let me check." Cormier took a sip. "Yes."

"Benches by the river at four." With that he hung up.

Cormier felt a sense of accomplishment. Not only had he set up a meeting, he had set up a mysterious meeting with cinematic overtones. He allowed himself a moment of longing for his job: not the writing, the watching. He liked to go alone, in the middle of the day; but sometimes he went with Robin and Carly. He couldn't help but be influenced by their reactions. Sitting between them, he had trouble knowing how he felt.

The next person he needed to call was as self-evident as the first. A friend from college, Zev Dreskin, was a political consultant in DC. A former fat person and fellow film geek, he had been Hardy to Cormier's Laurel at the Kubrick Society's Halloween Bash. His transformation into handsome political sage had astounded Cormier. Zev was humble about it, but Cormier had trouble dealing with his success and his slickness, and was only half-pleased when he took his call. Cormier felt embarrassed telling him about his meager campaign, but Zev seemed excited. Politics was politics, apparently.

"How are you positioning yourself?" Zev asked.

"Well, I'm a liberal."

"No, you're not."

"Yes I am, and I'm not ashamed to say it."

"You should be ashamed to even think it. You're a common-sense pro-gressive with solid Midwestern values."

"Jesus."

"Wally, I don't think you understand the political dynamics of Ohio."

"I've lived here all my life."

"I ran a *race* there. You've got to think very seriously about the image you're projecting. If you still have bushy hair, cut it. And don't run as Wallace."

"That's how most people know me."

"True: your name ID is a strong point. But Wally is warmer, more down-to-earth. You're in politics now, man. Everything you do—what are you doing right now?"

"Right now?"

"This second."

"I'm just sitting here drinking a latte."

"Are you kidding?"

"No?"

"You can't drink lattes."

"But I love lattes."

"Have a cappuccino."

"What's the difference?"

"I don't know, but cappuccinos are tougher; they're Italian. Lattes are French."

"No, café au laits are French."

"Just lay off the lattes, okay? And cappuccinos for that matter. Here's a rule for you: Don't touch anything that's frothy. Drink Sanka."

"No one drinks Sanka anymore. Do they?"

"Whatever, 'good to the last drop.' Maxwell House. Folgers. Drink Folgers, wear flannel, eat beef. You may think this shit is stupid, but you ignore it at your—oh Christ."

"What?"

"Does Robin hyphenate?"

"I beg your pardon."

"Did she take your name?"

"No. She's Robin Birnbaum."

"Oy. And that car you drive! You need help. I'm coming out there."

"No, you're not."

"I've got a slow cycle. End of the month, I'm coming out."

There were reasons to want Zev to stay away—his debaucherous tendencies, the flirtatious Jew-boy rapport he had with Robin, Cormier's instinct that he needed to follow his own instincts—but these all cowered in the face of Cormier's towering wish to be taken care of. "Okay," he said. "What do I do in the meantime?"

"Are there debates?"

"I'm not sure."

"Got to be. Forums, at least."

"For-*a*."

"Like that, right there. You can't talk like that."

"That was a joke."

"Oh . . . Jokes are good, but they've got to be good. I mean, what was that, Latin humor? Are you going for the dead-language demo?"

"I'm not going for any demo. I'm talking to my friend."

"Fair enough, but I suggest you start being who you're going to be. What else? Know the issues, meet people, print up literature. Have a kick-off event as soon as possible. Get press there. Make news, preferably good news. If you remember nothing else, Wally, remember this: You love your family and you love America."

"I do, actually. Except when I don't."

"None of that, man. I'm serious. No liberal, soul-searching, there-are-no-absolutes, Hamlet crap, okay? You love the *shit* out of America and you love the *shit* out of your family. I'll call you soon and we'll figure out what to do about God."

Zev hung up before Cormier could thank him.

He wrote an announcement of his kickoff party, to be held tomorrow night, chez Birnbaum-Cormier. He remembered to clear it with Robin. She screened calls and the minute spent waiting through the rings was dead time, lost life, like the moments before an elevator door closed. Pissed off by the wait, he had taken to singing into the machine, always choosing a song by a classic rock artist of earnest bent. Although she genuinely preferred edgier fare, he suspected that her animus for these songs had to do with her feelings about certain of Cormier's own qualities, in particular his sentimentality. Could she really hate James Taylor? They had turned their mild mutual hostility into a little game. Ah, marriage. Today he went with "Beautiful Loser" by Bob Seger.

"That's the worst one yet," she said. "But apropos."

"Mind if I throw a kickoff party at our house tomorrow night?"

"As long as I don't have to do anything."

"I love you," he said, the feeling hitting him out of nowhere as it had to, a moment of clarity that could put the lie to a month of murk.

She grunted her surprise. "I love you too."

He gathered up his things and returned his mug to the counter, where Jenny had another smile for him, plus a double clap and three inches of cleavage.

"Seger," she said. "I love Seger."

He waved good-bye and wondered if Jenny Kohl would be attracted to his message, once he had a message. Jacked up on his last latte for a long time, and on his love for at least one woman, Cormier walked toward his car. Chickie Shea, smoking in front of the Cigar Store, waved to him, and he waved back without breaking stride. This was a new Cormier. The Intellectual—somber, ruminative, weighed down by the burden of having to face hard truths—had never hurried and had often stopped to study mundane objects, a broken bottle, say, which, judging by his bunched-up brow, held a metaphorical meaning hidden to less-evolved minds. The Candidate, by contrast, was pragmatic, optimistic, and efficient. Instead of thinking about problems, the Candidate fixed them.

The Candidate was fast. The Candidate was happy.

CHAPTER 9

BEVY WAS TRYING to create space in the Lynns' freezer when the hospice nurse walked in. "I have to run out to buy a few things," the nurse said. She was mousy and dressed like a pilgrim. "I should tell you, Jill's been having a rough go of it."

The casserole Bevy had brought was her own invention. Under the breadcrumb crust, which she had spiced with Parmesan and brown sugar, were egg noodles, Velveeta and ricotta cheese, chunks of honey ham, onion, green pepper, and a splash of good barbecue sauce. If you wanted fine food, Bevy wasn't the girl for you, but if you craved something hearty and creamy, food that would cozy up to you from the inside, Bevy could bake it up with the best of them. There was no room in the freezer, so she searched for a spot in the fridge. Bevy put her casserole on top of Marybeth's lasagna, with its arrogant green noodles, and walked down the hall.

The words of the nurse hadn't sunk in, and Bevy's breath caught in her throat. "Hey, darling," she managed to say. Jill lifted her chin in what might have been a smile. Her wig was crooked. Bevy tried to straighten it out when she kissed her cheek, but her head was on the pillow and what did it matter anyway?

She sat down and took Jill's hand, which was like tissue paper. "How you doing?" Bevy said, and Jill, confused, looked down at the hand Bevy was holding, giving an answer of sorts. She'd been dying for weeks; still, it was a shock. Now she was *dying*. It would be up to Bevy to do the talking. "I brought you a casserole."

Jill looked away. This room, Bevy realized, was the last she would know of this world. It was like a fancy old hotel room, with high ceilings, swirly moldings, and even a little chandelier. You would say the place had character, if only to avoid calling it a dump. There was the hum of traffic, which you could just about ignore except when a big truck or bad muffler went by. You could smell exhaust, but you could also smell the river, and its sweetish, earthy odor was fitting if not pleasant, very Hartsburg.

"There's a lot going on with the casserole. It's creamy, cheesy, spicy, salty, sweet, but you're not really interested in food, are you?"

Jill looked at her dead-on for the first time. The veins in her forehead looked like tree roots, and every part of her was shrinking except her eyes. With her skin receding, her nostrils looked huge, the nose of a skeleton. Bevy decided that it did matter that her wig was crooked. "I'm just going to lift your head up, that's it, good. There, that's better."

She slid her chair closer and rubbed Jill's upper arm, which felt like a chicken bone through her nightgown. Bevy thought about her father, who'd died from a heart attack when she was twenty. Bevy tried to nail down a specific memory of Lamar—how his hand felt on her back as he pushed her into her first bike ride, how he stood at the sink as he shaved with his straight-edge—but what she got was this: she's wasted at his funeral and can't stop giggling during "God Bless America" and at the reception afterward her stepmother calls her a piece of trash and kicks her out.

Bevy again wondered why her old self had been visiting her. Her volunteer work seemed like the obvious explanation, but she'd counseled drug addicts for months without thinking of her past. The memories, hazy at first and now vivid, had surfaced right after she'd kicked off her campaign, but she couldn't see a connection. Maybe the explanation was simple: when you spend time inside your head, you see everything in there, including stuff that's not pretty or pertinent.

Bevy wedged her arms behind Jill's warm, wet back and rocked her side to side. Either the wig or her head smelled like cheese corn; that nurse needed to do a better job. Bevy dared to squeeze her tighter and was pretty sure she could feel Jill's arms on her back. It was a miracle that Jill had found her way to Hilltop. Her sister had been a member for years but Jill had shown up only a year before. They weren't close, Bevy and Jill; yet for whatever reason, Bevy was the first person at Hilltop she'd told. In the parking lot, after a Bible study, Bevy was about to get in her car when she saw Jill standing there, all five-foot nothing of her. It was snowing; big wet flakes clung to Jill's hair and wool coat. "I'm dying," she said. Bevy asked

Jill if she'd been saved, she needed to make sure, and Jill nodded; then the two of them cried and hugged. "You made it," Bevy said, resting her cheek on top of her wet head. "You're home."

Yes, Jill was at peace, but that didn't mean she would go peacefully. Her eyes were moist and bulging. It seemed that her living self, fleeing from the cancer as if from a fire, had crowded into her eyes, hoping to be rescued.

"What is it you want to say?" Bevy said, back in her seat. "What are your eyes telling me? That you're worried for your children? Yes, of course you are. I want you to know that all of us, everyone at Hilltop, will help Jimmy take care of your children. Our love for them won't match yours, of course, but love it'll be. What else, sweetie pie? Heaven? That's a tough one. I don't really know what it's going to be like. Being in the presence of our Lord, that's not something I can really put words to . . . Oh, darling. I know. I know. You don't want to leave. You're not scared to, you just don't want to. Yeah, this here might not be Heaven, but it's pretty darn beautiful, isn't it? . . . Enough with the heavy talk? Fine by me. My casserole? Where'd I get the recipe? It's my own creation, actually. Okay, okay, I admit it; I'm proud of it. No need to poke fun. I'll leave a note for Jimmy on how to heat it up. He can handle that, right? I'm not sure Peter could. Peter, Peter, Peter. He's having a real hard time with me running for school board. He went so far as to blame me when Ronnie snuck off—"

Jill squeezed her eyes shut as if faced with a bright light, then opened them wide and looked at Bevy. "I like chicken," she said.

"Me too, baby." She kissed her hand. "Me too. I made chicken the other night, lemon chicken without lemon, and I asked Peter how it was, and he said, 'dry.' Don't you think he could have just said, 'good'? Is that so hard?"

Jill shook her head and Bevy felt that she was finding fault, pointing out that Bevy claimed to cherish Peter's honesty. "That's true," Bevy said. "But part of being a good spouse is knowing when to fudge the truth." Bevy laughed and Jill seemed to smile. Here she was, confiding in and laughing with someone who maybe had no clue what was happening. If Bevy had distance on the scene, if, say, she was listening in on the other end of that baby monitor, she might conclude that the woman talking and laughing was crazy or lonely. She was neither. She couldn't deny, though, that she could have used a close friend or two. She had lots of friends, almost all Hilltop, but they tended to gather in groups, and the conversation didn't allow for much soul baring. She wanted a friend like Colleen, closeness like that. Colleen had gotten a running commentary on Bevy's up and downs, and Bevy likewise had wanted to know all of Colleen's secrets. In the years after high school, those bad times, they'd been inseparable.

Bevy didn't like to think about Colleen because she didn't like to think about who she'd been back then, but the memory that came to her now was a good one: she and Colleen have made the remarkable decision to stay in for the evening. Out on the deck they eat a real meal and watch the sky close up around the orange sunset, then go inside and curl up on the couch and chat like schoolgirls—which, practically, they are. Colleen rubs and scratches Bevy's head as they talk about every little thing.

Jill pouted and said, "I don't think I'm going outside tomorrow."

The sad cuteness of that remark made Bevy want to hug her again, but she decided to leave her be. It seemed selfish to go on blabbing about her little concerns. Not so little, really. She was talking about her marriage. It was life, and maybe when you were near death, you wanted to hear about life. If she could hear at all. Bevy started rubbing her arm again, because there was no way she wouldn't want that, human touch.

"So Peter wanted to wake Ronnie up just to give him a talking to, and I convinced him not to, and we stayed up and talked about Ronnie's future. Then I had to go out and campaign on two hours' sleep, then go home to make lunch, then campaign some more, then go home to make dinner. I'm not complaining. Or maybe I am; it's a lot. Peter thinks my campaign is getting in the way of our family life. But you know something? There's part of me that sees it the other way around. Is that awful of me?"

Jill was looking at her, paying attention or at least listening to her voice like it was music, a twangy tune. "So, yeah, things have certainly been better between Peter and I. We're not communicating, and it's also been a little lackluster in the, you know, bedroom department. The good news is, Peter has agreed to see a counselor. The man is still capable of surprising me, and that's got to count for something. He won't do it at Hilltop, not with all the chatter-bugs buzzing around, so we're going to have someone come to the house. Don't you just love the modern church—marriage counselors making house calls."

Jill closed her eyes and scratched her forehead, like she was trying to remember something. "Oh, sweetheart," Bevy said.

Bevy heard the front door open and adrenaline flushed away her fatigue as she got ready for a discussion with the nurse. Bevy liked confrontation. And she liked being right. But she could tell by the creak of the old floors that it was someone heavier than the nurse. She propped up Jill's head and made sure the wig was straight.

Jimmy swept into the room, a large man taking large steps, and bent down to kiss Jill's forehead. Only then did he notice Bevy. Till now she'd seen Jimmy only from across the church. He was cute. "My wife been talking your ear off?"

"I'm afraid it was the other way around."

"That's good." He took Jill's hand and Bevy just about lost it, seeing her tiny hand in his big mitt. She had a thing about hands. "She hears everything."

Thinking about what she'd revealed—bedroom problems!—Bevy worried that Jill had understood, then hoped she had. It was important, she felt, to sometimes show yourself to people as if to God, with no fronts.

"It's snowing?" Jill said, staring up at her husband.

"Nah, honey. Won't be snowing for another month or two." Jill grunted and tried to lift her head off the pillow. "What do you want?" Jimmy said. "You want a kiss?" He kissed her on the lips, but she shook her head in what looked like disgust and slapped the bed with both hands, then quickly calmed down.

Bevy hoped Jill would soon be released; maybe that was wrong to want, life being sacred, but why suffer when paradise was waiting? Maybe she wasn't suffering. Maybe medication had numbed her pain, and maybe she was too out of it to see the pain in the eyes of her sweet, sweet husband. Too many maybes for Bevy's taste.

Jimmy had nice wavy blond hair but a bad haircut, probably self-given; his hair stuck out on one side like the branch of a Christmas tree. Bevy wanted to take care of him, wanted to hug him and feed him and put him to bed.

"You're Bevy," he said.

"Yes. I brought a casserole."

"Jill really likes you. She talks about you, don't you, sweetie?"

Jill looked up at Jimmy and said, "Nanna?"

"No, that's Bevy. She's your friend. And she's running against Wally."

"What?" Bevy said.

"Oh," Jimmy said. "You wouldn't know, would you? My friend Wally, he's planning on running for school board."

"Are you talking about Wallace Cormier?"

"That's him. Known him forever."

This was a lot to absorb. For one thing, she now had a race on her hands. For another, her opponent was a friend of Jimmy's; the man whose columns she'd read last night online would have had nothing to do with these people. "I met him. In fact, it might have been me who put the idea in his head about running."

She was excited and it felt wrong to feel this way here, so she kissed Jill's caved-in cheek, smiled at Jimmy, and walked out. Jimmy followed her down the long hallway and into the kitchen. He looked like he wanted to speak but said nothing.

"I left a casserole in the fridge for you," she said. "It should cook for forty minutes at three-fifty. I think you'll like it."

He put his hands in the front pockets of his jeans—tried to; with the thickness of his hands and the stiffness of his new jeans it took some doing. Weird the way emotions worked: she didn't cry when she was with Jill, but now, watching her husband try to stuff his hands in his Wranglers, she was tearing up.

"Thought it'd be better having her home," he said. "Not so sure anymore, with the boys seeing her like this."

"I think that's better than them not seeing her at all."

"I hope so."

"She's a great girl. I've loved knowing her."

"She got pregnant. That's why I married her."

"I didn't know that."

"It was the best thing that's ever happened to me, best thing I've ever done, being her husband. Loving her. I've done it well. It gives me some peace, knowing that."

"It should."

"People feel bad for me. They did even before, because I used to be a star athlete, a million years ago. Tarnished glory, all that. Boo hoo. If you ask me, this town should get better at forgetting. If you've got to feel bad for someone, feel bad for Jill, okay?"

"Okay." Bevy watched him walk back down the hall, his hands still in his pockets.

Stepping out of the house, Bevy wanted to feel every bit of what her life was at that moment—she was a healthy woman walking tall and breathing autumn air in the middle of the greatest country that God had ever created—but her mind kept falling forward to the fight against this Wallace Communist character.

CHAPTER 10

ON THE DRIVE old people were out in full force, sitting low in their gargantuan sedans. Cormier slalomed past them, loving his Saab. The conversation with Zev had excited him—it seemed to validate his endeavor—but he wasn't about to change what he drove or how he looked. He had to admit, however, that his hair could prejudice people against his message, once he had a message. He was due, in any case, for a trim.

At Staples he ran off two hundred flyers and bought a staple gun, something he'd always wanted to own. Back in his ward he posted flyers on telephone poles next to announcements of yard sales and lost cats. Leaving his car running, he sprung out and pumped four staples into the soft wood. It was a satisfying task, borderline manly, and once he'd taken off his cotton sweater, he imagined that he was a working-class pol, a champion of the people, a staple-gunning slayer of the immorally rich.

Halfway down Deeb Street, which ran between Main and Riverfront, someone said, "What's going on?" A man he recognized stood smoking on a second-floor porch. It was Ron Something-ski, who'd played a role in the remodeling of their kitchen. Cormier could barely see his eyes beneath the curved brim of his baseball cap.

"I'm running for school board," Cormier said.

Something-ski nodded and sighed as if to say, Aren't we all. Cormier couldn't think of anything more to say. He had grown up with guys like Something-ski—Stu's and Jimmy's old house was right behind this one—but he had donned a stiff new role: Candidate talking to Ordinary Guy. He conversed daily with Jenny Kohl, however, and she wasn't exactly Susan Sontag. "How's business?" he asked plausibly.

"How's it look?"

"Right." What a scene: this guy on his sagging porch smoking a butt in the dead heart of a Tuesday. His lawn was dirt. The windows on the house next door were cardboard. This had been a vibrant, lower-middle-class neighborhood when Cormier was young; now it was speeding through working-class on its way to poor.

Something-ski's greasy hair, squeezed by his cap, stuck out sideways by his ears. People in Hartsburg made Cormier sad. That wasn't reason not to like living here; on the contrary, it made him feel connected. Like the winter wind, the sadness of the town blew through him and caused him to shiver and ache. He added to it, was part of it; like the sadness of Robin or Jimmy, the sadness of Hartsburg was indistinguishable from his own. He was saddened by people in Hartsburg who were sad, like Something-ski, and by people who were happy, like the high school seniors he'd seen at Olive Garden on prom night, digging into vats of gloppiness and taking full advantage of the all-you-can-eat breadsticks. They cheered as dishes arrived. People tried, tried so fucking hard, and who was Cormier to say they weren't succeeding? Something-ski wasn't succeeding. Cormier knew nothing of his kind of sadness—it was presumptuous to think he did; it was presumptuous to think Something-ski had a "kind" of sadness—yet he shared with Something-ski a memory of better days in this town, which, like youth, had slipped away before people had thought to appreciate them. No, people had appreciated them, people other than Cormier, who'd been too young and too arrogant to recognize the magnificence of a majority-middle-class town. The eighties had been better than the nineties, the seventies better than the eighties, the sixties better than the seventies. Prosperity had peaked in the midsixties. Some people in town were suffering back then—Cormier heard about them every night at the dinner table—but there was hope that they could be helped and money available to try, and more people than not, more people than ever, were doing well enough, and the result, Cormier now knew, was a communal feeling of peace. American Dream? Don't laugh. American Dream? Damn right. The town was a dream that had once come true.

He walked up the steps and mounted the banister; then, pressing one hand to the eaves, he reached up and handed Something-ski a flyer—a formidable maneuver for someone who used to walk around fences while his friends scaled them.

He braved a jump and went down the steps in a stumbling run that sent him across the sidewalk and into the street, where the hood of his Saab caught him. He pushed himself up and turned around sporting a straight face, as if he'd nailed the dismount. Something-ski seemed to be staring at him. "Hope to see you at the party," Cormier said. "And even if you can't make it, please keep me in mind on Election Day."

"Will do. Keep me in mind when you need work done."

"Will do," Cormier said, trading favors for votes like a pro.

Jimmy lived on the top two floors of a four-story house at the end of Main Street, where it met Shawnee Avenue, which a quarter mile to the south became the bridge. He and Jill lived there with their two sons and their daughter, Shannon, who, at twenty-five, was struggling to put together an adult life. It was nicer inside than its exhaust-dirtied siding suggested, but the location was awful, one of the few traffic-loud places in town. If the mill hadn't shut down, Jimmy might have been able to give Jill a quiet place to die.

It pained Cormier to think of what had become of Jimmy's life. In high school he'd had beauty, grace, strength. Cormier had been witness to thousands of mundane yet astounding athletic feats, a day-to-day decathlon. Hoisting a keg over his head or sprinting to brace a lady slipping on the ice or catching everything thrown his way, Jimmy made life itself look like a game of toss. Girls loved him and guys were disarmed by his kindness and lack of guile. In Hartsburg High's 1977 yearbook, he was "Best Athlete" and "Nicest Guy," a remarkable twofer.

Now, a quarter century later, he carried the heavy aura of a tarnished golden boy. It was a measure of his humility, and obliviousness, that he had no awareness of the role he played in the town's story of itself. Except for comatose Bob Sundstrom, Jimmy probably best embodied Hartsburg's misfortune. He didn't complain about his life—not once, as far as Cormier knew—but his sadness wasn't merely the projection of others.

Looking back, Cormier could see that his sadness had always been there. At parties he'd been no more comfortable than Cormier, and the two of them usually ended up together on the edge of the action. Cormier directed questions at the soft spots in Jimmy's psyche, and he opened up, sealing their unlikely bond, a bond that granted Cormier a status he wouldn't have otherwise achieved. There were rumors about the two of them, rumors likely started by girls whose advances Jimmy had spurned. They were only a little gay, though, and when Jimmy was with a girl, Cormier wanted to be him, not her.

The summer before senior year, working a construction job, Jimmy broke his leg when a scaffolding collapsed, losing his chance at an athletic scholarship and therefore college. Jimmy seldom fucked around, but when he did, once, with a quiet girl named Jill Piper, he became a father and a husband. Her cancer was discovered in '91, three months after their youngest was born and six months before the factory shut down.

As he put up a flyer on a pole near Jimmy's house, Cormier scolded himself for not going up to visit Jill. His last visit, a month earlier, had been awkward. He'd had trouble talking to her even before she'd lost her hair and twenty pounds. Now there was the issue of her presumed support for Bevy Baer, who, Cormier had learned, also attended Hilltop.

He was up against the town's most powerful institution. Who was on his side? His old teacher Dreifort, probably. Stu, definitely. Robin, maybe.

There was someone else whose support he could count on, a political player no less. While collecting signatures he had avoided two houses, Bevy Baer's and Annie Cormier's. He hadn't been prepared to give his mother the news. A longtime advocate for the poor, she would be thrilled—and inclined to take control. For the sake of his marital and emotional health, Cormier needed to resist the temptation to put the campaign in her hands. She was already very involved in his life. Too involved, Robin believed, an opinion she'd expressed only three days before, after Cormier had made the mistake of relaying Annie's thoughts about Carly. Cormier responded by making a comment about Robin's father, who managed to exert a strong influence on their lives from a thousand miles away, and then they played a round of that always-edifying game: Your-Relationship-with-Your-Parent-Is-More-Messed-Up-Than-Mine.

After posting flyers on almost every block, he stopped by his mother's house. He knocked and walked in; Annie refused to lock her door against the crime that had come to town when the jobs had left. The crime consisted mainly of meth-fueled robberies, but once or twice a year, in one of the sketchy parts of town, there was an incident of blood-gushing violence, each one further confirmation that Hartsburg wasn't the town they used to know.

Annie's excitement struck him like a gust of wind; gone was the calm that made this house a refuge from the storms in his own home. "Congratulations! You've got large shoes to fill. Dreifort was quite good, that coot. Of course, first you need to win . . ."

On the floor a brown bag of yarn bundles had tipped over, making a nice bed for Leon, one of her cats. The coffee table was covered with journals and newsletters, one of which was *Utopia Today*. A mug rested on the unabridged dictionary that sat on the couch. His father had been the force behind the order in the house. Annie, it had turned out, was something of a slob—a funny quality for someone with her aristocratic air. She was from a Waspy Maryland family, Episcopalians, old money long spent. Her bun of white-yellow hair looked like an onion.

She stopped talking once she had tuned into his mood. "What's the matter, my boy?"

"Just tired. Been up since five."

"Are you hungry?"

"Starving." This made her smile. Suspicious of Robin's low-fat food, she loved feeding her son. The array of dispossessed souls she'd dedicated her life to helping didn't include animals, who were always getting roasted and fried in her kitchen. She wasn't much interested in causes not directly related to economic justice. What kind of platform would the old radical recommend for him? Curricula on class-consciousness? A student government with actual power? Disbandment of the school board?

"You're truly not eating meat?" she said after Cormier had twice asked her not to put ham on the grilled cheese sandwich that was browning in a pool of butter.

"Trying not to."

She shook her head and smiled, as if to say, Kids these days. This touch of the traditional brought back bittersweet memories. His parents used to mystify Cormier's friends. When they weren't holding forth about justice, Annie and James were engaging his friends in discussions about How to

Live a Meaningful Life. Cormier made sure his friends stayed for dinner. Mom's pork roast and potatoes seemed to redeem the family.

As for Cormier himself, he used to view his parents' eccentricity with both admiration and anger. Vietnam was the big issue, and even at the height of the war's unpopularity it wasn't unpopular in Hartsburg. Annie and James brought him to protests, and when he looked into the faces of cops and counterprotesters, he intuited that his parents were doing something brave. His parents stood apart even from the other antiwar activists; having come of age in the fifties, they didn't like the new generation's drugs or free sex or trendy talk about self-actualization. Annie and James were a minority of two, and that was just fine with them. Perfect, probably.

But Cormier's desire to be popular, or at least normal, clashed with his desire to please his parents. In seventh grade he followed his father's suggestion that he protest the war by refusing to stand for the Pledge of Allegiance. His protest caused a minor stir, bringing him scorn and snickers and occasional praise. Now, years later, whenever he lamented his ambivalence about dissent, he thought back to the precocious breasts of Trish Metzger, who, speaking to him for the first and last time, said that when her brother got back from Vietnam, he was going to cut off Cormier's toothpick dick.

"I've been making calls," Annie said. "People are excited about your campaign, but we need to get out there and hit the streets. What *is* the matter, Wallace?"

Unprepared to tell her that he didn't want her to take over, he tried to think of what else might be bothering him. "I'm worried I'm not up to this."

"Oh, I think you are. I know you are. It's a marvelous thing you're doing. People are positively aching to hear an enlightened voice."

Annie was an incorrigible optimist. A progressive revival was always in the offing, never mind that corporate-sponsored conservatism had all but triumphed, or that her brand of politics had become an anachronism, or that her own daughter had devolved from a nuclear freeze activist into a Bush-loving "Security Mom." Annie surveyed the barren political landscape and saw only flowerings of hope. It was a kind of faith, a fervent belief in people, an almost unreasonable commitment to reason. Progress, Cormier guessed, was almost always brought about by those who shared

Annie's faith. Maybe, for at least the next thirty days, he could believe.

She grimaced and put her hand against her lower back, fighting a pain that probably would have put Cormier in bed. She wasn't a silent sufferer—she'd talked at length about her torment after James's death—but compared to Cormier, she was a stoic. He might have been reluctant to unload on her, except that she invited him to. Although she worried about him, she seldom judged him, even when his problems were the sort her worldview wanted her to mock—like a dispute with Robin over what size TV to buy. Unlike James, Annie didn't put politics before people. Cormier's older sister, Marcie, the conservative, got no less warmth than Cormier. (She did, however, get more e-mails.)

Annie brought him the sandwich along with a jar of bread-and-butter pickles, then sat down across from him. The table was a hunk of oak that he loved. The four of them had sat down here every evening. Annie and James had been intent on creating a shelter for their children, free from the intensity of not only the outside world but also of their own adult lives. Peace had prevailed, and this, Cormier believed, was why he had few concrete memories of his childhood. People tended to recall trauma, and trauma had been uncommon in 18 Bartlett Street.

"Is Carly going to work on the campaign?" Annie asked.

"I'm not sure she has the time."

"Well, she should find it." In Annie Cormier's world, there were creatures even worse than conservatives: conformists and careerists. She feared that Carly was going to become both. Her concern about Carly, which resembled Cormier's own, infuriated Robin, who did her best to pretend Annie didn't exist—no easy task. James and Annie had liked Robin from the start—their approval had been essential—but Cormier had since accepted that the two women in his life would never be close.

"This could stir some genuine passion in her," Annie said.

"Her father's school board campaign?"

"Perhaps not. It's not exactly a sexy cause, is it? But it is important, make no mistake. Your father would be proud."

"Yeah?" He said this casually, as if he had only a passing interest. His father had been disappointed when Cormier had stopped writing political films. Before coming home one Thanksgiving, Cormier had edited his latest screenplay into something he dared to show his father. *Hat Trick*, his raunchy yet curiously life-affirming film about a love triangle on a women's college hockey team, became *The Edge of the Ice*, a tale about the challenge of self-liberation in a consumerist society.

Cormier knew his father had loved him, but only in the way an office worker knows the weather when he looks out the window: knowing without feeling. For all his father's rhetoric about the importance of communication, of airing grievances when they arose, the two of them had ended up with, or had always had, a conventional relationship, a cliché, with Cormier needing more than James could give. Aided by Robin, a master at assessing the psychic damage done by parents (especially other people's), Cormier had come a long way toward forgiving his father—and, by extension, himself. He could be fairly certain that the goal of this campaign was not to win Daddy's approval.

"Oh yes," Annie said. "James, more than anyone else, stressed the importance of local elections. That was part of the plan."

Annie and James had met in Chicago, Catholic Workers both. They soured on the movement's religious underpinnings, so in the early fifties they and dozens of their comrades moved to towns throughout the Midwest, hoping to sow the seeds of a radical revolution. Annie and James picked Hartsburg out of a hat. James taught seventh-grade science, was a welfare caseworker, and wrote copy for Kohl's Brewery just long enough to encourage workers there to unionize. In the midsixties, with War on Poverty funds, he and Annie formed the Community Center, a catch-all nonprofit that helped people in need. Annie, now ostensibly retired, still went in almost every day.

"Money," she said. "That's what public office is about, and school board is no exception. Really, Wallace, I wish you'd tell me what's bothering you."

"I'm glad that you're excited about my campaign, and I want you to be involved—"

"But you don't want me taking charge."

"Believe me, Mom, there's part of me that would love to lean on you, but I can't. I need to do this by myself. You can understand that, right?"

"I can, yes, but I don't appreciate the implication that I'm overbearing."

"This has nothing do with you."

"Now you're accusing me of egomania?"

"Come on, Mom."

"That was a joke, Wallace."

"Oh. Good one."

"I hope that you will at least take advantage of my contacts."

"Of course," Cormier said, now fearing that she wouldn't do enough. Mama's Boy runs for office. "Don't get me wrong, I want your help. I need your help."

"Well, you have it."

"Good."

"How's the sandwich?"

"Great," he said, and it was. Underneath the tomato and white cheddar was a thick layer of her homemade mayonnaise.

"I must say, I'm surprised Robin signed off on this plan of yours."

"How do you know she signed off?"

She stared at him with pursed lips, her skin tightening on her cheekbones. When her radiance failed her, she could look severe.

"She's more supportive than you think," he said.

"No, no, no. That's not what I mean. It's that Robin is, well, she's a cynic."

"This again?"

"I'm not making a judgment."

"Yeah, you love cynics."

"I adore Robin, you know that. But she has a rather bleak outlook."

"She doesn't have a bleak outlook. She writes fiction, for fuck's sake—"

Annie turned her head away and closed her eyes, as if he'd showed her a hideous wound. She disliked crude language—an eccentric distaste, he felt, for someone who'd marched with steelworkers and antiwar veterans.

"Robin believes in art; how not-cynical is that? She's actually a romantic. She just doesn't feel hopeful about the state of the world, but can you blame her?"

"I have an idea, then. Let's all sit around and mope."

"Who's moping?" Cormier smiled. "I'm running for school board."

He handed out the rest of his flyers, leaving them between doors when people didn't answer, then drove down to the *Informer* offices. The benches that Dreifort had suggested as a meeting spot were nearby, and Cormier sat down feeling optimistic even as dark clouds blew in from the west and colored the sky with the certitude of a paint roller.

He looked at the abandoned factory across the river, a mass of steel and stone, its main chimney giving the town the finger. A couple of miles beyond the factory sat Hilltop, where people were plotting his demise. So much for his optimism: he now felt like a teased boy, too small for this world. He used to sit on these benches and envision not only his release from Hartsburg but also his triumphant return, as a director or writer or musician using his pull to bring jobs to his hometown. Now here he was, filling up with dread at the thought of running for one of five little school board seats. Fear was what made the undertaking worthwhile, the risk, but such wisdom was small comfort when you had a desperate urge to pee, crap, cry, and run away.

What was he afraid of? Losing. No, looking stupid. Shaming himself in front of friends and family and, even worse, acquaintances and strangers—people who'd doubted him or disliked him or never bothered to have an opinion. But even if he did okay, he might not be able to find an audience for his message, once he had a message. Fifteen or twenty years ago he'd have had a better chance; back then the town was evenly divided, a bellwether, a magnet for national media. The night before Cormier's senior year began, his father turned on the news, and there was Don Nedney, Stu's father, in front of the factory, supposedly speaking for the common man. Of course, the reporter had no way of knowing that Dirty Donny would tie one on, then go home and slap his family around. Or that a month later he would leave for work and never come home. Or that a year later he would be found naked and dead from a sleeping-pill suicide in a hotel room in Ashton. "The fucknut ran away," Stu had said, "but only made it a few miles."

Cormier heard a honk behind him. The car that had pulled up in the breakdown lane, an Audi, was not one that Dreifort would drive. Bill Samuels, Cormier's best friend from work, was in the driver's seat, waving him over.

"New car?" Cormier said.

"It's Tina's."

"You two are back together?"

"It seems that way."

Bill had a fear of commitment that Cormier did his best to understand. Marriage had scared Cormier, the fact of it, but he'd readily committed to Robin. He'd known early on that she was substantial—she had a brain that he could fall into forever—and it'd been a relief to know where sex was going to come from. If he'd had a worry, it'd had to do with her depression, but at some point marrying her had become a pleasant inevitability.

Bill said, "We had a pool going on your campaign till Jeanette shut it down."

"She's right, for once. I mean, people were going to win money if I lost?"

"Not everyone. Some people bet on you."

"Really?"

"They got great odds."

"Who you'd bet on?"

Bill smiled and said nothing. Blue-eyed, conventionally handsome, he'd have looked like an L.L. Bean model except that he was balding. He was outdoorsy, a biker and a hiker. Cormier made fun of him for all the money he spent on gear.

"Are you guys going to give me a fair shake?" Cormier said.

"Why wouldn't we?"

"Because you bend over backward to be fair to conservatives."

"That's drivel."

"It's drivel I first heard from you."

"I doubt it."

"I'm pretty sure."

"Well, things look different when you have to make decisions."

"You mean when you have power?"

They'd started at the *Informer* around the same time. Cormier had been taken with Bill's dry humor and his disdain for the editors. Then, last year, he'd become an editor. They'd joked about his promotion hurting their friendship, then allowed it to happen, a little. On the first day of his editorship, he'd sent out an e-mail saying he wished to be called William, not Bill, to which Cormier had sent out an e-mail saying he wished to be called Bill, not Wally. Bill had only pretended to take Cormier's e-mail in stride.

"Just remember," Cormier said, "there's not two sides to every story."

"No. There's seven."

There was a loud beeping. Cormier was surprised to see that it was coming from a small black pickup, which backed up over the curb and onto the walkway.

"There's my meeting," Cormier said.

"Looks very professional."

Remembering to be who he wanted to be, Cormier smiled.

"Good luck, Wally."

Dreifort stopped his truck next to a bench, then edged forward, as if that would make his parking spot legal. He put the pickup in park but kept it running in order to listen to the classical music, which was a nice accompaniment to the rain that had begun to fall. He closed his eyes, his hands chopping the air, conductor-style. In the dirt on the door someone, probably Dreifort himself, had written, "Love Me Tender."

Dreifort had taught a class called Humanities, which could have been called A Cultural History of the World in No Particular Order. He told incomprehensible jokes, had a weakness for alliteration, and overenunciated every word. Some of what he said might have been bullshit, but his passion, rare among the tired, check-marking mimeographers of Hartsburg High, was a lifeline for dreamers, depressives, and druggies.

"Sorry I'm late," he said, "but not so sorry that I didn't opt to enjoy the rest of that piece. That's a lotta sonata. It reminds me of a Chinese-food feast." A hefty man, he walked with a limp offset by a cane. What hair he had hung to his shoulders, and his white facial hair was more than scruff but less than beard. His hunter's orange sweatpants were pulled up over his belly. He squinted at Cormier as if his glasses obscured his sight.

"Mr. Dreifort," Cormier said, shaking his hand.

"Call me Marlin. Or Dreifort. Or diphthong. No time for pleasantries, in any case, or pleasantness." He lowered his posterior onto the bench, a time-consuming act that called for back-up beeping of its own. "My beloved believes me to be at the pet store. I'm not supposed to be taking part in this campaign *in any capacity*. Emphasis added."

"Are you all right?"

"Define your terms. I had a triple bypass last spring and was doing well until Bevy sought to portray me as an old fool. The turbulence of political battle sent my BP into the DZ, and my doctor ordered me to cease and desist so that I wouldn't cease to exist." He squinted at the sky, his nostril lifting to reveal a tuft of hair. "Shall we take cover?"

"I'm fine," Cormier said, stifling a shiver in a senseless attempt to seem tough.

Dreifort rocked himself until he had the leverage, with the help of his cane, to stand up. "To Truck Family Robinson we go. Better yet, let's duck into St. Catherine's."

"Can you do that, just go into a church?"

"That's the only thing you can do to it. In any case, Cathy's is my church."

"I didn't know you were religious."

"I don't know that I am. I like the peace of the place, and Father Muller is one perspicacious padre."

"I went to St. Catherine's when I was kid. My dad wanted me to get a taste of religion. It was long before Muller's time."

"Onward," Dreifort said, pointing at the church with his cane. "Muller challenges me to challenge my beliefs about what in the name of God or lack thereof we're all doing on this spinning sphere of water and dirt."

The church was modest but for the row of stained glass windows, which were getting peppered by the storm. The pews looked newly polished. Father Muller was crouched on the dais, working on what appeared to be a problem with the lectern. Dreifort gave him his trademark, arm-flapping wave, meant to evoke Nixon getting on the helicopter. Muller answered with an easy smile and the peace sign.

They took a seat in back and Dreifort, water dripping off the tip of his nose, tried to talk quietly. "Let me tell you why I wanted to rendez-vous avec vous: I'm hoping you'll allow me to serve as your informal adviser."

"Yes, of course. Please."

"Congratulations. You just made a good decision. Today I want to impart to you a single message, to wit: Get ready. Get ready, boy, 'cause they're coming for you. They want this. A Baer victory would mean a morbid majority."

"Yeah, I know."

"You don't know it enough." He leaned toward Cormier, his hands stacked on the curved head of his cane. His odor, stirred up by the rain, recalled for Cormier his bachelor stink, damp towels picked up off the floor. In the wood grain on the pew in front of them Cormier saw countryside: rolling hills and clouds. "I like you, Cormier. I've liked you ever since you pointed out, absolutely astutely, that Robert Mitchum was getting short shrift in my class. But I recall that you're something of a romantic—"

"That was a long time ago."

He growled. "This ain't your grandma's school board, Cormier. This ain't Frank Capra, much less Frank Zappa. I can just imagine the sparkling speeches you're already drafting betwixt your ears, phrases singing straight to people's better angels. Well, Godspeed, good sir, but you better be ready to get down in the muck, because we're playing tackle football here, not touch. I've never metaphor I didn't like, so let me add that you need to hit back and hit first or this'll be a TKO sooner than you can say 'here comes the story of "Hurricane" Peter McNeeley.' Last time I had to make it known that the home life of my opponent didn't comport with the compost he pushed in public."

"And how'd that feel?"

"Fine, said the survivor of the plane crash. 'Tis to say, Compared to what? I decided I'd spend to win, and I don't mean cash, sweet cheeks. Politics ain't for the faint of heart or prim of posture. If you haven't heard me yet, hear me now: a surgeon ought not complain about blood. You'll need a strong stomach."

"My stomach is stronger than you think," Cormier said, watching himself play a role. He had no intention of playing dirty, but he had long wanted his life to be a movie—if this was sickness, then most people were sick—and here he was, living the church scene from *The Untouchables*. But the screenwriter in him wanted him to tone it down.

"Doctors save lives," he said.

"Precisely," Dreifort said.

Cormier was tempted to mock his old teacher's grandiosity; instead he found himself thinking about Dreifort's class, the importance of which he had never appreciated until this moment. It was the one place he'd gone as a teenager (other than the movies) where the world had consistently opened up. "Thanks, Dreifort," Cormier said.

CHAPTER 11

IN THE MIDDLE of the session, feeling double-teamed, Bevy regretted not suggesting to Peter that Reverend Wedgwood act as their counselor. Unlike young Chip here, the Reverend wouldn't have been intimidated by Peter; plus the Reverend had an interest in seeing that Bevy's campaign continue. On the other hand, Scripture was Scripture and probably not even the Reverend could have found a loophole.

It was too weird. Here she was, revealing her marital problems to the youngest of Hilltop's associate pastors, a man closer in age to Loretta than to Bevy, while across the street Kelly Beale-Wallis unloaded groceries and children from her minivan. "Just to be clear," Bevy said, "if Peter wants me to drop out of the race, I have to?"

Chip scratched his peach of a cheek; aside from the razor burn on his neck, which could have grated Parmesan, he was soft as a newborn. His strawberry-blond hair was scruff-short on the sides but long enough on top to make a part. She pictured him in his bathroom pushing a wet comb through his hair while his wife sneaked a love note into his bag lunch. He was a newlywed: what'd he know about marriage?

Chip locked eyes on Bevy. Clearly, he was working out of some playbook. He'd placed his chair midway between Peter and Bevy and every time he spoke or was spoken to, he made eye contact and looked like he was about to weep. Chip overdid his look of concern to the point where Bevy wanted to say, Oh, come *on*. If what Chip was going for was compassion, a lack of judgment, the result seemed like the opposite.

"Yes," he said. "If that is Peter's final decision, you have to respect that."

"Then I don't know that there's much to talk about," Bevy said.

Chip looked at her with his moist eyes. This delay might have been by design, a way of making sure not to say the wrong thing, but she felt like she was trapped in a dubbed movie. "For one thing," he said, "we can talk about whether that is what he wants."

This was their third trip round this discussion. Peter was suck-biting a bologna and cheese sandwich. A Bee-and-Chee was what he and Kay called it. The two of them had all sorts of adorable nicknames for the food he had eaten since childhood. His Sunday breakfast of two fried eggs and two scrambled eggs was the Mega-Egga, and Bevy had once heard Peter ask Kay to make him something called a Musty. "A Crusty-Musty?" Kay had needed to know. Peter shook his head. "Just a Musty."

Two squares of paper towel hung from Peter's collar, a bib, and he was eating off the tray on wheels he'd assembled this weekend. The project had gone better than his plumbing: yesterday evening he'd spent an hour upstairs with his toolbox, but the water had gone down just as slowly today. She was sick of cleaning the shower.

Peter said, "I'm behind her campaign, but I want her to have more time for our family. As far as I'm concerned, the family comes first."

"And it does," Bevy said. "I'm working maybe twenty hours a week on the campaign and the other hundred whatever, I'm at home."

"It's not just a matter of hours," Peter said. "It's a matter of focus."

"It's only for another month," she said. "Not even."

There was a silence while whatever happened in Chip's brain happened. JB came into the room and went straight to Bevy. She gripped the skin on his neck with both hands and kissed his cold nose and let him lick her lips and tongue. He was a good dog. Peter had gotten him and named him after his favorite ballplayer, Johnny Bench, but JB had taken more to Bevy—an unspoken source of sadness for Peter.

Chip said, "Could you work less on the campaign, perhaps fifteen hours?"

"I don't think so. I mean, there's no point in doing this if I don't try to win, right?"

"Could the time come from somewhere else?" Chip said.

"Counseling," Peter said.

"I have to go there right after this," Bevy said.

"This can be your last time until after the campaign," Peter said.

"It's only two hours a week," Bevy said, dreading having to break the news to Wilma, whom she had come to know and love and fear for.

"It's two hours that the family needs," Peter said.

"All right," Bevy said.

Peter said, "And could you do less campaigning on Saturday?"

"That's when people are home."

"That's when *we're* home."

Now it was Bevy who waited to speak. She didn't want to give any more advantages to Cormier, who already had Sundays to himself. Peter always talked about the need to take back the country, yet here he was, making it harder for Bevy to do her part. It seemed to Bevy that every Christian in town should have been helping her free up time. Brothers and sisters, do my laundry while I kick Wallace Communist's butt.

"All right," she said. "Fine."

Chip wrote something in his notebook. "I am very impressed with the way the two of you talked it through. It seems to be a very reasonable compromise."

The phone rang and Bevy, unsure if they were finished, stayed seated, but the ringing was so loud there was no use in talking, and if whoever it was left a message, they'd have to listen to that too. When Bevy heard the voice—just the tone, not the words, which she couldn't make out—she stood up. She sometimes imagined that her body was a machine, an old appliance that took a while to turn over, but it was firing away now in an instant. Grinding, spinning, shaking. The caller was Colleen, her old best friend from Texas.

"Who was that?" Peter said.

"I'm not sure." Bevy sat down, her hand pressed on her tingly abdomen.

Chip said, "Is there any other matter which you would like to discuss?"

"Our love life," Bevy heard herself say.

"Good gravy, Bevy," Peter said.

Chip didn't know what to do: his eyes went back and forth between Bevy and Peter and settled on Bevy. "Are you referring to sex?" he said.

"Yes," she said. "Carnal pleasure."

"Oh," Chip said.

"We're done here," Peter said. He pushed on his tray, and it rolled across the room and stopped just short of Chip, who'd raised both hands and one foot in self-defense.

Most Christians didn't like to talk about sex; this was a stereotype that happened to be true. A respect for its sacredness kept Christians quiet; that and discomfort, a sense that sex was dirty. Which it wasn't, unless it was. It was confusing, Bevy had to admit. She herself wasn't comfortable talking about sex compared to some believers, like her mother and stepfather, who, much to Bevy's mortification, raved about all the heaven-shaking that went on in their bedroom. Bevy's mother had sent her a book about sex written by Beverly Lahaye, the head of Concerned Women for America, and Tim Lahaye, coauthor of the Left Behind series. The book had answered some, but far from all, of Bevy's questions about what was acceptable.

Despite his discomfort, Peter, a virgin till marriage, had been happy when they'd started having sex. In fact he'd been as grateful as a rescued hostage. Bevy should have done a better job of bringing him along. Their sex was pretty good—Peter could be a ten-minute tiger—but they didn't have enough of it, and the whole bit should have been more relaxed. He didn't initiate it or want Bevy to, so she had to make the move without appearing to—a game she didn't always feel like playing after a long day. This seemed like a solvable problem. Not one, however, that she would share with Chip, who, having just lost his virginity, probably thought all sex was just as peachy as peach pudding.

Bevy was suddenly anxious to hear Colleen's husky, cigarette-cooked voice. "Just kidding," Bevy said. "I wanted to get a rise out of you, Pastor Chip."

He didn't smile. "Well, sex is indeed an area that I deal with; it is, after all . . ."

Peter, Bevy, and even JB, it seemed, waited for him to finish his thought: tell us, dear Chip, what, in your uninformed opinion, is sex?

"The physical expression of love."

"Thank you, Reverend," Bevy said. "This was very helpful."

They all stood up and Peter pulled off his bib and handed it to Bevy. With Chip watching, Peter had no choice but to kiss her cheek good-bye.

She watched Peter walk Chip to his car. Chip pointed at his old Ford and Peter knelt down to show him something. Peter stood up, his arm curled as if hugging a beach ball, and pushed one palm crossways into the other; the punch line, it seemed, involved an accident. When Chip was done laughing, Peter gave him his card.

Bevy pivoted away from the window and leaned back against the wall. "A good marriage is hard; a bad marriage is easy." This was wisdom from Reverend Wedgwood, and she used it on an as-needed basis, like a tranquilizer. Her parents had divorced when she was sixteen, so even before she had become a Christian, she knew she would marry for life. Marriage had been easy at first, so easy she thought it would stay easy. Then reality happened. They had settled into a normal, good marriage. It took effort to build a normal, good marriage. That was the tightness in her chest: that was the effort.

When she heard the garage door open, she walked into the kitchen and listened to the message: "Hey, girl, guess who? I know: weird, right? It's been way too long. My number's 432-776-8443. Give me a call, all right? I want to talk to you about something. Actually I want to talk to you about *everything*."

Bevy erased the message, wishing she had a number that was harder to remember. Some bridges were better left burned.

Bevy liked working with addicts, although the work could be frustrating. Some clients skipped sessions, and some were interested only in the meal provided after counseling. "You can eat all you want," went the saying in the cafeteria as freeloaders loaded up, "but you're never going to get full." Reverend Wedgwood understood that addicts were caught in a web of problems, so Hilltop provided parenting and literacy classes, meals, child care, and a job-placement program. Of course, government provided these same services but made matters worse. Trying to help someone without speaking to his soul was like bailing water out of a sinking ship. Hilltop tried to fix the holes.

Bevy's success story was Wilma Chapwell, a pregnant heroin addict who hadn't shot up in six months. For the last three months she'd been Bevy's only client, and Wilma had missed only two sessions. Now it was Bevy who'd be absent.

Wilma was one of the many African Americans who participated in Hilltop's programs; no one saw them in that way, however: they were God's children like everyone else. Wilma was incredibly shy; it had taken her at least a dozen sessions to open up. Bevy had come to discover that she was sharp, though undereducated, and funny; the two of them had shared more laughs than cries.

On a muggy Tuesday in June, maybe the hottest day of the year, Wilma had been saved. In all her years of witnessing, this had been one of Bevy's most joyful moments. The school's air-conditioning was busted, so they were outside, under a tree. Wilma's thin blouse was sticking to her belly and her breasts. Her skin, which had been mustard-colored, was getting its gleam back. Bevy remarked on how good she looked, but Wilma shook her head. "I look okay on the outside," she said, "but on the inside I don't feel good. I'm nervous all the time. I want what I see in you, that calm kind of feeling."

Only once, early on, had Bevy talked to Wilma about salvation; she had wanted her to arrive at this point on her own. Bevy said, "That calm feeling? That's the presence of God." Bevy opened her Bible to the book of Romans, as Peter had done for her in that truck stop some twenty years before. Reading from Paul's letters, Bevy said, "God says, 'I will save you and you will have eternal life; all you have to do is accept it.' You see, God *wants* to save you. He wants you to be what the Bible calls 'born again.' The question is, do *you* want to be born again?" Wilma nodded, tears rolling with sweat down her cheeks.

Wilma was in the classroom when Bevy walked in, seated on the couch in the preschool reading area. "Don't get up, darling," Bevy said, bending down to hug her. "I know what it's like trying to stand up when you're shaped like that."

She was wearing a normal white button-down, not maternity wear, and where it met her black slacks, a triangle of belly was showing. "I feel like a hot water balloon."

"Inflated?"

"Right? Like someone opened up one of them life rafts inside me. I mean, check me out, Bevy. My baby's getting *big*."

"Well, it's a good thing you don't have to push the baby out of your body."

Wilma made a clicking noise and pointed at her. "I got good news. Jerren is going to come to the parent class with me."

Jerren was the child's father. He wasn't dangerous, Bevy hoped, but he was negligent, a slacker and slider-by who seemed never to get off the couch. The baby needed a father, however, and Wilma was thinking about moving in with him.

"He always says he'll go," Bevy said.

"I know, I know, but this time he means it truly."

"You've got to get him to come to church."

"But he works at the warehouse on Sunday."

"Then bring him here on Sunday evening. And if that doesn't happen, bring him Wednesday night. And if that doesn't happen, get him to come to a prayer breakfast or a Bible study. See what I'm saying? He's got the time if he's got the will, and getting him right with God, that's the most important thing you can do, okay?"

"Okay." She folded her hands on her belly as if on a desk, like a student trying to look well behaved. "But him coming to class, it's a step."

"Yes, it is . . . I need to tell you something, Wilma." Bevy, avoiding Wilma's eyes, looked at a child's drawing of a sun with a face, rays bending downward to make what looked like a mane. The sun, she realized, was a lion. "You know, I'm running for school board, and well, between that and my family, I have hardly a free second, so for the next few weeks, I'm not going to be able to make it to our meetings."

"But I only got a month till my baby's born," Wilma said.

"I'll probably see you before then. If not, right after."

"But I've been doing so good."

"And you're going to keep doing good."

"I need you."

"No, you don't. You've got God's love and guidance. That's all you will ever need."

"Come on. Let's get real. I mean, if that's all I need, why'd I be coming here in the first place? I had a system, a routine, know what I'm saying? I come here, I go to church, I go to AA. It was working for me, Bevy."

She looked at Wilma; fear was what she saw. If she thought these sessions were keeping her whole, then they were. Every morning when Bevy was trying to stay clean, she had walked to a diner, counting her steps the whole way, and treated herself to a raspberry-cheese danish and coffee. Sitting at the speckled counter on the stool with the ripped red vinyl, its hole sealed by air-browned masking tape, she listened to the cook sing in Spanish over the sound of sizzling eggs and thought about Peter waking up in Ohio, the life that waited for her at the end of her long walk. She left a two-dollar tip and resealed the tape, which was warm on her fingertips. Charmain, the diner's kindly-despite-herself matriarch, rung her up, and if her six-inch nails made key-pushing difficult, she didn't let on. Bevy stood there until her bill was on the little pole. She liked it when the pole went through the circle that looped the $2.15, but it was okay if it didn't. You wove a net out of what you had and eventually the net felt as real as Jesus.

"You really got to do this board thing?" Wilma asked.

"Oh, I have no choice. You'll be okay. You have no idea how strong you are. But you need to keep coming here; other counselors would love to meet with you. I know you won't need to call me, but just in case, here's my cell phone number."

She wrote her number on a business card of Peter's, but Wilma, her mouth hanging open, didn't take it. Bevy took her hands and kneeled. With their hands stacked on Wilma's belly, Bevy said, "I ask you, God Almighty, to give Wilma the strength to continue to resist temptation. And next month, after Wilma has given birth to a healthy, happy baby, and after I've won a landslide victory, we will, Jesus, with your guidance, continue our work together. Praise *God*. Amen."

With the session ending early, Bevy had a free fifteen minutes before she had to fetch the twins from nursery school. She should have gone to buy American flag stamps for the mailing that Rhonda was organizing. Instead, she took a walk around the campus, which was bustling. Normally Bevy liked the activity, but today, haunted by Wilma's stunned face, she wanted to steer clear of people.

As she walked up the hill toward the main church, Lincoln Avenue, with its billboards, came into view. She walked behind the church, hoping to see countryside, but the forest, she discovered, shut off the view. Surprised by all the butts strewn along the back of the church, she wondered who had sneaked smokes. When she was in high school, she'd told herself that skipping class to smoke cigarettes was harmless fun, and she'd probably believed herself; when you're on a gradual decline, you don't notice it. Looking back now through time's telescope, Bevy could see that October of her junior year was when it had begun. One day your parents are together and you're an A student. The next month your parents are separated and you're sneaking smokes. The next year you're drinking tequila and letting men do unspeakable things to you.

The decline got steeper. Her father died when she was twenty; two weeks later she had her "accident." She'd been out of the hospital for probably a month when Colleen introduced her to cocaine. "It'll give you a little lift," she said, after convincing Bevy to join her at a party. So much, and so little, happened between that night and the morning years later when she woke up on the floor of the Dallas airport. She didn't have her wallet or any memory of how she'd ended up there. She was trying to figure out how to get back to her life, such as it was, when a man with pressed white pants offered her a handkerchief. She couldn't see his face—the rising sun was shining in her eyes—but she could feel his strength. It wasn't the swaggering strength of the men who normally appealed to her. It was quieter. This stranger emanated solidity like a well-made piece of furniture. In his presence her mind slowed.

What'd Colleen want to talk about? Bevy would never know.

Walking back down the hill, Bevy heard Reverend Wedgwood call her name. She pretended not to hear him because she probably looked like a smudge, what with her crying jag after Wilma had walked out, which had also given her a breath issue. But she feared that the Reverend would see through her, so when he called her name again, she spun on her heels and gave him what could have been a smile of surprise. He waved her over with one finger, and she had no choice but to go to him.

He was standing with a big-headed bald man in front of the event center, and when the Reverend turned to him, she took out her pocket mirror and a tissue, wiped below her eyes, searched for gum, found a gum wrapper, sucked on it, disposed of it. She did all this without breaking stride, and by the time she'd reached them, she was back to being Bevy.

"How fortuitous," the Reverend said, "you walking by at this very minute. I'd like to introduce you to an old friend of mine. Bevy Baer, this is Arch Cook."

Arch Cook kept his hands in the pockets of his beige raincoat and nodded in a twitchy way, like he was trying to shake snow out of his hair. He wasn't bald, after all: his hair was the color of his skin.

"Back in Colorado," the Reverend said, "I took an interest in a state senate candidate whose campaign Arch was running. He's one of the foremost operatives—"

"Strategist," Arch said.

"Whatever," the Reverend said.

"No," Arch Cook said. "Not whatever." Bevy had never heard anyone be short with the Reverend. "Language matters."

"Okay then." The Reverend cleared his throat. "Strategist it is. Arch will be in Ohio for the next week, and I thought you might avail yourself of his expertise."

"That would be wonderful," Bevy said, and meant it. Arch Cook seemed odd—he still hadn't looked at her—but the Reverend's word was enough for her. "I need all the help I can get, especially now that I have an opponent again."

"Liberals," the Reverend said, stressing each syllable. A breeze lifted his yellow silk tie; he grabbed it and tucked it inside his buttoned suit jacket.

"Wallace Cormier is this one's name," Bevy said.

"Oh, I'm familiar with Monsieur Cormier," the Reverend said, putting a funny French twist on it. Bevy laughed and Mr. Cook's head bobbed. "A few years back his anti-Christian propaganda prompted me to have a chat with the editors of that rag."

"He's a tried and true liberal," Bevy said.

"Well, he's certainly true"—the Reverend smiled—"but I don't believe that little Wallace has ever been tried."

"We can destroy him," Arch Cook said, and took a sideways step toward Bevy, his eyes fixed on the pavement.

"Destroy him?" Bevy said.

Arch Cook looked over his shoulder. He squinted when he spoke and breathed through his mouth, as if his glasses had shut off his nasal passages. He was a bit of a social retard, it seemed, but he had a way of commanding your attention. "We'll pick him apart like an overcooked chicken."

"Let's do it," the Reverend said.

"By all means," Bevy said.

"You're an attractive candidate," Arch Cook said with his eyes closed.

"Indeed you are," the Reverend said.

"Thank you," Bevy said, and now it took no effort to smile.

"I need your phone number," Arch Cook said.

Taken aback by his brusqueness, Bevy had to collect herself before thinking to give him the card that Wilma had refused to take. He held the card up to his glasses, handed it back to her, and poked his cell phone with a plastic toothpick.

"The boy's come a ways since Colorado," the Reverend said.

"So have you, Rev," Mr. Cook said.

"But we're getting started."

"Yup."

"It's one heart, one soul at a time," the Reverend said.

"Or one country," Arch Cook said.

"Yes," the Reverend said, and laughed. "Let's start with America, and you, Mrs. Bevy Baer, are going to play your part."

Bevy's tendency when she got excited (an impulse left over from her youth) was to sing ZZ Top songs and dance. It wasn't proper music for a Christian woman—the beat was too strong—and at any rate, as she made her way across the Hilltop campus, dancing wasn't an option, so she jogged to her car and, as soon as the door was shut, let out a scream so long and loud she was out of breath by the end of it.

CHAPTER 12

Not until his house was crowded did it occur to him to be nervous, but once the idea had struck him, it became irresistible. Some fifty people—friends, Annie's activist allies, faces he recognized from canvassing—had shown up to support Wally (don't call him Wallace) Cormier. Carly, whose presence had been requested, wasn't among them. Nor was Something-ski. When Stu had walked in carrying two cases of Busch bottles, Cormier had regretted not telling Something-ski that there'd be beer.

Annie, on the couch with Stu, waved Cormier over, and he left his post at the front door. As he made his way through the people clustered around the snacks, he started to run his hand through his bush of hair only to discover that it wasn't there. Yesterday, afflicted by barber-seat myopia, he'd kept asking Dawn to take a little more off. His hair was no longer distinctive; it was . . . normal! But it was longer than his mother's; Annie had recently chopped off her waist-length hair.

She said, "Stuart and I were just reminiscing about the time James and I found him passed out on the couch. James had to literally slap him to wake him up."

"I'm a deep sleeper," Stu said.

"Oh yes," she said. "Deeply drunk. Speaking of which, it's rather unusual to serve alcohol at an event such as this."

"This is an unusual kind of campaign," Stu said.

"Right," Cormier said. "Unconventional."

"Indeed," Annie said. She winced as she pushed herself up, then kissed the cheek of a tall black woman with cornrows and black-framed glasses. "This is Star Mourning," Annie said, "the best teacher at Hartsburg High. And the best grant writer in the world."

"Come on, A," Star said. "Are you trying to make me blush?"

"I don't think that's possible," Annie said.

"I'm blushing right now," Star said. "You just can't tell."

The strength of Star's handshake made Cormier feel inadequate. "Congratulations," she said. "You've got no choice but to kick butt."

"And this," Annie said, "is Stuart Nedney, one of Wallace's oldest friends and one of the town's chief perpetrators of mayhem."

"Good—" Stu swallowed a burp.

"Stuart, you might be able to help us. One of the things we're hoping to do is to finally make use of the abandoned factory. It's such a dispiriting eyesore. You know that space as well as anyone. Any ideas about what it might be good for?"

"Burning," Stu said.

There was a silence that Cormier, in his tense state, couldn't bear, so he retreated to the kitchen, where Robin was chatting with their friends Paul and Zora Clymer. It felt good to be around Robin; although her head and heart were often racing, she tended to give off a mellow vibe. "Good turnout, huh?" Robin said. "This is great." Cormier thought she could have infused her disingenuous words with some disingenuous emotion. She'd taken refuge in the kitchen after one malodorous, trembly gent had stepped up onto an ottoman to spout conspiracy theories about 9-11.

"How you doing?" Robin asked, rubbing his upper arm.

"Nervous," he said.

Both Clymers cast concerned eyes at him: not what he needed. He wanted them to say he seemed fine, not to look at him as if he had told them that he had schizophrenia.

"What are you nervous about?" Zora said.

"My speech."

"You're articulate," Zora said. "You'll do well." Although this was what he thought he'd wanted, reassurance, it infuriated him. She wasn't taking his nervousness seriously.

"And it's not like you have to say anything earth-shattering," Paul said.

The Clymers were well traveled and knowledgeable—they both taught at a private high school—but Cormier couldn't quite give himself over to them. A few weeks before, at an Italian restaurant outside Columbus, Paul had sent back a pasta dish because it wasn't al dente, then chuckled when the waitress said, "Al what?" The Clymers derived satisfaction from living in a place to which they felt superior. Cormier himself wasn't immune to the pleasures of alienation, which he indulged at dinner parties. Like exiles in some backward land, they gathered to revel in each other's intelligence and to disparage the culture, or lack thereof, in which they found themselves. But someone would go too far, and Cormier would end up defending his place of birth. The consensus among his dinner companions was that Cormier believed that only he was entitled to criticize Hartsburg. But there was a line, a line separating frustration with a place from disdain for the people who lived there. He knew there was a line because he sometimes crossed it.

"Earth-shattering is what I'm going for," Cormier said. "I would very much like to shatter the earth." There was a chance he was in deep trouble.

Robin tried to tousle Cormier's hair and frowned when she couldn't. If he had just asked Dawn to stop before the final round of snipping, then he would have had enough hair right now. Here his rational mind gained back some ground, pointing out that the link between his anxiety and hair length was elusive at best.

Cormier was pretending to mingle when Carly walked in with an Asian boy who could only be Dave Chin. Cormier watched him saunter over to the snack table. He hadn't known that letterman jackets still existed.

Carly had on a peach sweater and khakis. In her freshman year Carly had gone through an exposed-navel stage. It was a relief that adolescent fashion had taken a turn away from nakedness. With Dave's back to her, she dared to kiss Cormier's cheek. "Sorry I'm late," she said. "Got stuck in yearbook." She checked the contents of her book bag and couldn't find something, something important judging by the way she was picking through the books and files and papers. "Oh God," she said.

"What is it?" Cormier said. "What's wrong?"

"Shit shit shit." Her face was clenched, and Cormier looked at the vertical line between her eyebrows, which she would mold into a permanent feature.

"What?" he said. "Tell me what's wrong."

He understood, with more clarity than ever, that her anxiety was his, that he'd given it to her. He knew how it felt and didn't want her to feel it.

What were you supposed to do? Accept the pain of your child? Watch TV and eat cereal and live your life, ho hum, while your child suffered?

"Phew." She tilted her head back, closed her eyes. "I found it."

"Good," Cormier said, wanting to escape with Carly to the mountains.

"We've got tons of studying to do," she said as Dave returned, munching smoked almonds that Cormier could smell.

"We, meaning you and your friend you've yet to introduce?"

"It's a pleasure to meet you, sir," Dave said. He brushed salt off his hands with three quick claps and gave Cormier a slap-and-shake. "Dave Chin. This is a great home you have here. And you have a great daughter as well."

"Thanks," Cormier said, deciding to make the easy joke. "We like the house."

"Damn," Dave said, his hand over his mouth. "That's cold."

Dave Chin was a little too comfortable, a little too confident, for a teenager meeting the father of the girl he liked. The phone rang; both Cormier and Carly started to make a move toward the kitchen, but Robin picked it up.

"So," Cormier said, "You two are in the same classes?"

"Yup," Dave said. "Not that I'm in the same league as her."

"Oh, please," Carly said. "He gets great grades."

"Good enough to get me where I want to go."

"And where is that?" Cormier said.

"Out of Hartsburg."

"Tell me about it," Carly said.

"Actually," Dave said, "I'm thinking about Georgetown. I like the idea of being in Washington—you know, politics and all. I think I'd like to make a difference."

"That's great," Cormier said, and when he looked over his shoulder, he was saved by Robin, who told him that Zev was on the phone.

Up in the study, he found Annie and Dreifort powwowing: the proverbial back room. Dreifort was wearing a sombrero and women's sunglasses. "I'm going incognito lest word should get back to my beloved."

"Yeah, I hardly recognized you," Cormier said. "I've got Zev on the phone."

"His political-consultant friend in DC," Annie explained.

"Ooh-la-la," Dreifort said. "A professional operative."

"Very much so," Annie said.

"Shhh," Cormier said, putting on the speakerphone. "Hey, man. I'm here with my mother and Marlin Dreifort, who currently holds the seat."

"Greetings from the heartland!" Dreifort bellowed.

"Hello, Zev," Annie said.

"Hey, folks," he said. "My instinct on a night like this is to keep it simple and upbeat. We just want to stoke some enthusiasm, get some phone numbers."

"I'd agree with that," Annie said, "but it can't be entirely content-free."

"I concur," Dreifort said, speaking to the phone.

"What are we looking at for demographics?" Zev said.

"There's some money in the ward," Dreifort said. "Old money, since that's the only kind here in Hartsburg—and there are middle-class people, and on the other side of Main live the less-lucky classes. Many of the middle class have been here for years, which means they predate the revival and likely lean left or at least libertarian. But there are also newer homes in which reside Bevy and a lot of her lot, and some of the poorer folks have found comfort in Christ."

"Yup," Zev said, as if none of this were new to him. "And it's white?"

"Mostly," Dreifort said. "Many Latinos aren't legal and live on the outskirts of town whereas most of the blacks live in the projects on the south side."

"What are the issues?" Zev said.

"There are a batch of biggies," Dreifort said. "A new issue is an old issue, by which I mean student safety. A note was found in which a student expressed a desire to, quote, 'go bin Laden' on the school. In response, Bevy has proposed tougher get-tough measures. She'd turn the school into a fortress, and this must be opposed."

"Here, here," Annie said.

"However," Dreifort said, "after Columbine and Nine-Eleven, parents want to feel secure that their children are secure. My experience in the military as well as my image as a cranky old crank with a fondness for firearms accrued to my advantage. I predict that B. Baer will portray my heir apparent as soft on student crime."

"No doubt," Zev said. "She'll question his manhood."

"My *man*hood? She's a woman. I mean, I'm more of a man than she is, right?"

"Yes, dear," Annie said. "But you have the sensitivity of a woman."

"Mom," Cormier said.

"What?" Annie said. "It's a compliment."

"Either way," Zev said, "let's don't put that on a pamphlet. What else, Marlin?"

"There is—pardon me, partner—the sticky issue of homosexuality, how it's presented to students. Also the minor matter of how it is that we humans are being. Bevy wants teachers to teach intelligent design, which is a creative name for creationism."

"Sounds about right," Zev said, his interest waning. Cormier pictured him with his shiny shoes on his desk, tossing a ball in the air. "I assume Wally's going to take the ungodly positions on these issues, which is fine, I guess, except that on his candidate profile, in the space marked 'religion,' it's going to say, 'none.'"

"How about 'none of your business'?" Annie said.

"Wally, didn't you go to church when you were young?" Zev said.

"Oh, please," Annie said. "James took him and his sister to church as a form of education. Imagine, letting children think for themselves."

"I spotted you in church just the other day," Dreifort said. He was looking at Cormier, possibly winking behind his glasses, which were round, retro, and humongous: portholes. "As did Father Muller."

"Tell me more," Zev said.

Annie groaned and Cormier spoke before she could. "There's no way to say I'm religious. The most you could say is that I believe in God."

"You *do?*" Annie said.

"Maybe," Cormier said, learning of his possible non-atheism along with everyone else. "Sometimes I think I do."

"Well, if you're willing to talk about God," Zev said. "We should be fine."

Dreifort raised his arm, like a student in class. "Politicians have been lying about their faith ever since they invented God."

"I dig your style, Marlin," Zev said. "You're helping Wal prepare for the debate?"

"Affirmative."

"All the issues we've spoken about are theirs," Annie said. "I suggest we talk about the things we want to talk about, such as, oh, I don't know, education?"

"We will," Zev said. "But if we don't handle these hot buttons, people will never even hear our message."

Cormier, staring in the direction of Zev's disembodied voice, could feel his mother make a face. He now had a brain trust, complete with conflicting advisers, quite a luxury for a school board candidate, yet he was less than thrilled. Classic Cormier: desperate to be taken care of, angry when taken care of.

Downstairs there was still no sign of Lars Molofsen, the reporter, or Jimmy. On the other side of the picture window, Stu was smoking, and it was a comforting picture, a sign of normalcy, so Cormier walked out. The street was lined with cars on both sides.

"No Jimmy," Cormier said. "I've got to say, it pisses me off a little."

"Yeah, it's not like his wife's got cancer."

"I know he's got a lot on his plate, but I can't help thinking he's not here because they've been going to Hilltop."

"If she was healthy, he'd be here even if you were running on the al Qaeda ticket, which, for all I know, you are."

"I guess you're right."

"Congratulations," Stu said, having turned around to look in the picture window. "You've got some Negroes on board."

"Nice."

"Star Mourning. That's why blacks are good at sports: they're named to be stars. Lennox Lewis. Sterling Sharpe. Stuart Nedney: What am I going to do with that? Work at Wal-Mart, that's what." He patted his pants before finding his cigarettes in the pocket of his quilted flannel. "Senorita," he sang, in reference to the chunky, pretty Guatemalan who had maintained her inside position at the snack table throughout the evening.

Cormier longed to be in the Johns' house, where the missus was drying dishes and the mister was watching *Wheel of Fortune*. But their son Brian was in Iraq, so the tranquility went only so deep. Mrs. John had lived in that same house while Mr. John was in Vietnam. And now she was waiting again. They both were. Mr. John would have switched places with Brian, he'd told Robin. Fighting was easier than waiting, he'd said.

"My baby likes her cheese," Stu said.

"She works with my mother."

"Oh yeah? Think Annie would put in a word for me?"

Cormier tried to think of a way to be tactful, an arduous task with anxiety gumming up the wheels in his brain.

"Just kidding, fucknut," Stu said. "*I* wouldn't put in a word for me."

"Come on, Stu. You'd be great for some women."

"Just not the cheese-eating Latin goddess."

"She's, like, twenty-five."

Cormier expected him to say, That's right in my wheelhouse, but Stu grabbed his face, fingers splayed, as if trying to pull off his leathery coat of skin. His hair, given its lack, was as messy as it could be. "I hear this Bevy woman is hot," he said.

"Maybe. In a hairspray kind of way."

"Yummy."

"Her husband owns Baer Motors."

"Yeah. He's a fucking weenie."

"I want to beat them, man. I want to win so I can do good stuff and all that, but I really, really want to beat them, you know? And it starts tonight."

"You giving a speech?"

"Yeah. I can't wait to get it over with."

"You should do what I do when I've got to give a pep talk at work."

"*You* give pep talks?"

"Yessir, and people eat it up. Annie was just getting on me about organizing the workers, but most of those fucknuts like it, probably 'cause their lives are so miserable otherwise. When I've got to speechify, I remind myself that everyone there is going to be dead in a hundred years. Or probably fifty with all the fat fucks in Wal-Mart."

"Fat fucks in Wal-Mart," said someone from the sidewalk: Bill. "And beer. Now this is my kind of political event."

"That was off the record," Cormier said.

"Don't worry," Bill said, bouncing up the steps. He seemed to love the feel of being in his body. "I come as a civilian."

"This is Stu," Cormier said. "I think you guys have met."

"William Samuels," Bill said, and Cormier, moved that he'd shown up, decided to forgive him the pretension.

"We met a few years ago at Wok and Roll," Stu said. Stu had an astounding memory; only recently had alcohol begun to poke holes in it. "We talked about video poker and fly-fishing. You work at the *Informer*, right?"

"Yup," Bill said, stepping away from Stu's smoke. "I'm part of the problem."

"Aren't we all," Stu said.

Then there was silence. Cormier had long wanted friends from the different parts of his life to hang out together—he imagined it to be liberating—but at the moment he was too tense to foster a discussion. It was all he could do just to hear what was said.

"Is Lars here yet?" Bill said.

"No," Cormier said. "I can't get this over with until he is."

"The fucking press," Bill said, trying too hard to be self-deprecating.

"If you ask me," Stu said, "people fixate too much on the media. Don't get me wrong, I hate the press, but if you want to take control of the country—"

"And I do," Cormier said.

"You don't go after the press," Stu said.

"I agree," Bill said. "People exaggerate our importance."

"I wouldn't say that," Stu said. "But if you get political and economic power, the press will get in line."

"Sure," Bill said. "It's as simple as that. We don't tell people the truth because George Bush and Sam Walton don't want us to."

"Exactly," Stu said. "But go easy on my boss. Let that stingy bastard rot in peace."

Cormier couldn't read Bill's smile. The door opened: Annie, with Star Mourning behind her. "Reporter or no," Annie said, "we need to get started."

The sensations he picked up were elusive yet intense, like in a dream: bright light, faceless faces, dense heat. He could have sworn that his old teacher, small-headed under a sombrero, was in front of his fireplace, gesticulating like an aerobics instructor. This world was distorted yet familiar, déjà vu passing by then settling like a TV picture dropping into place. He's standing in a classroom, students laughing at him as he turns to mush. He wanted to run away but felt a hand on his forearm, his mother's.

Dreifort took off his hat, rubbed his dome, said "hair apparent." Then the Candidate was speaking, words coming out on their own, speaking themselves, getting applause. He was a lip-syncher, pretending he had a connection to the words.

Before long the Candidate was able to make out the faces of his wife and daughter and mother and friends, people who would love him even if he lost control of his bodily functions, but he wasn't going to, far from it, he was fine.

Lars and the photographer walked in the door, and Cormier nodded at them, colleagues from his former and future life. Now he could hear what he was saying and wanted to end with a flourish. "Let's face it, folks, these have been tough times for progressives, in Hartsburg, in Ohio, nationwide. It's hard not to feel overwhelmed sometimes, even powerless, right? You watch the news, and you know that things have *got* to change, but you don't know where to start. *This*, my friends, this campaign is a place to start. You listen to President Bush, and you get pissed off, and you want so badly to do *something*, but you don't know what. This, my friends, this campaign is what you can do. Do *this*. Instead of feeling overwhelmed, do *this*. Instead of complaining about how messed up things are, do *this*. Instead of letting Jon Wedgwood and his foot soldiers win again, instead of allowing them to force-feed their dark, devious, drastically wrongheaded views to our children, all of us can do *this*."

The Candidate was mobbed, people shaking his hand and literally patting him on the back. The Candidate, unlike the Intellectual or any of his predecessors, had it in him to make chitchat and laugh at nothing and bask in attention.

The photographer wanted a picture, and the Candidate posed with his wife and daughter, who both seemed excited by the excitement, which hadn't visited this house often enough in recent years. The reporter asked whether the Candidate really thought Wedgwood was dark and devious. No, he was talking about the political views of the man, not the man himself, he was sure that Wedgwood was a fine chap.

Cormier was so loose he gave Stu a good-bye hug. "Easy there," Stu said, and Cormier released him. "Good speech," Stu said. "Almost made me care."

"Yeah, right," Cormier said. "You care. You care more than anyone."

Stu grunted an unconvincing denial. Then he walked out.

Cormier's jubilation gave way to a delicious tiredness, and he was happy to collapse onto the couch with a beer in his hand and Robin's thigh resting on his.

"You did even better than I expected," Annie said. She was getting her neck rubbed by Star Mourning, and Cormier was glad for her, what with Star's strong hands.

"Who knew?" Robin said. Tepid praise, he felt, but while her words said one thing, the heat emanating from her crotch said another. The Candidate's eloquence had turned her on, and tonight the drought would end.

"Thank you, all of you," Cormier said through a yawn, which triggered yawns from others and then silence as the guests checked their watches, locating themselves in their lives, what they had to do tomorrow. This silence seemed to highlight his peace. Gone for the moment was the need to prove himself or impress anyone.

There was a thud on the porch, and the front door opened. It was Stu.

Cormier's first thought was that he wanted the beer he'd brought. He was chewing tobacco, his lip boxer-huge. He was also drinking a beer and smoking a cigarette. A parody of self-destruction, the viceroy of vice.

Robin was about to ask him to put the cigarette out; then she, like Cormier, saw it in his eyes. It was perfect somehow. Perfectly horrible.

"I just spoke to Jimmy," he said. "Jill's dead."

CHAPTER 13

BEVY CLOSED HER EYES. It seemed as if she'd been waiting three weeks, not three days, to hear the Reverend's voice, which she hoped would help her defeat her dark thoughts. Anger, worry, fear: each had taken turns at the mic in her mind. Guilt too, because she'd been struck by worry that Jimmy, a tragic, well-regarded figure, might endorse his old friend (who had to be sitting here somewhere). Talk about self-centered.

"God of all comfort," the Reverend said, "in the silence of this hour, we ask thee to sustain this family and these loved ones and to deliver them from loneliness, despair, and doubt. Fill their desolate hearts with thy peace."

Bevy opened her eyes to look at the Lynns. The boys, who could have been twins, went to the junior high with Loretta. Their daughter, Shannon, was, to Bevy's surprise, a woman. Jimmy had on a gray tweed jacket so small it was raised in points at his shoulders. Remembering the unwanted kiss that Jimmy had given Jill, Bevy took Peter's hand, and Loretta, on her left, took hers.

"May this, Blessed Father, be an occasion of rededication to thee. Help us live according to thy will and provide glory so that we will be prepared to meet thee. Let us remember that for all our pain this is a moment of hope. The Bible says, 'For me to live is Christ and to die is gain.' The believer, and only the believer, gains in death. The brutal fact of death has been conquered by the resurrection of Jesus Christ."

Bevy's tears cleansed her of confusion. Not of pain, though; her pain remained, but it felt pure, untainted by selfishness or fear or anger. She was simply sad. How could the Truth be so obvious and yet elusive? Did it speak poorly of her faith that she had to keep learning life's essential lesson? She needed to be grateful that she had learned it at all. Millions hadn't. Billions. How could they live? How could they die?

Peter's grip on her hand was gentle yet firm.

"For the person who has turned from sin and received Christ as Lord and Savior, death is not just an ending, but a beginning, a beginning of a glorious new life."

"You've got to be kidding," Robin said. "This is a fucking pep rally."

"Shhh," Cormier said. All he needed was an article in the paper about his heathen wife. Not that this was a time to be thinking about the campaign.

He couldn't believe the size of this place. Rows of seats slanted down on three sides toward the dais, which was an ovular platform fit for a political convention. The sound system was amazing; intolerance had never sounded so good, vileness in Dolby surround sound. Why didn't the prick just come out and say that nonbelievers were going to hell? The funeral, safe to say, would bring Cormier no peace. But then even normal funerals had never provided him with comfort or catharsis. The pressure to feel precluded any chance of feeling. His emotions had a way of sneaking up on him; like sleep or the police, they appeared only when he wasn't looking for them.

He'd sat numb through his father's memorial service as speaker after speaker testified to James's hatred of injustice and his love of his family, in that order. Grief didn't strike him until months later, when he was having lunch at Burger King before walking next door to Cinema Center. It was a post-bowling Saturday, and the grease seemed necessary. A fat black man in a cheap pin-striped suit sat down across from him, removed a wood-handled fork and knife from his vinyl briefcase, tucked a napkin in his collar, sighed, and proceeded to eat two Double Whoppers, a large onion rings, and a small fries. With his cheeks rounded to accommodate his bites, he poked his straw into the corner of his mouth and pulled milkshake into the mix. Cormier's eyes filled, and when he wiped them with his napkin, mayo stuck to his cheek. On the edge of his vision a shred of lettuce protruded from the glob, and it struck him as heartbreaking.

It wasn't until he was in the eighth row watching *Footloose* that he understood what was happening. When the conservative preacher played by John Lithgow announced from the pulpit that he would at long last allow the town's teenagers to hold a dance, Cormier started to bawl. The complicated emotions—anger, guilt, regret—would come later. This was a simple sense of loss. But it wasn't simple, in fact, because the pain contained a kind of joy, a cherishing of life expressed by the people dancing on-screen. No one in the world gave *Footloose* a more favorable review.

Wedgwood had a folksy charisma. There was sex in his appeal, but he was avuncular enough, and chunky enough, not to come across as threatening. The ideal American man, as defined by people between the West Village and the West Coast. Real men, after all, love Jesus. He seemed more suburban than country. You could picture him in a Hawaiian shirt and wraparound shades, playing blackjack in Vegas. Or as a college quarterback turned midmarket newscaster. Or, yes, as a preacher; this was a good role for him, and a role it was. There was no reason to doubt that most of the people here were sincere, but the only power that concerned Wedgwood, Cormier felt, was the earthly kind. The very notion of a cult-of-personality preacher didn't jibe with the ethos of this place.

Wedgwood said, "For the believer who has been to the cross, death is no frightful leap into the dark but an entrance into the beautiful kingdom of Heaven."

Robin groaned. "This is cheating, that's what this is, cheating."

"Please shut thy mouth," Cormier said.

"Every one of us should be thinking about death," Wedgwood said. "We're going to have to face Almighty God with the life that we have lived, the life that we are living right now. What matters is not how other people see you, but what the scorecard of Heaven says. Tell me, friends, what does your scorecard say?"

The thought of winning—of beating Wedgwood—filled Cormier with such yearning that he hugged himself and hunched over, as if in grief.

"I should go say hi to Wallace Cormier," Bevy said. "Come with me?"

She waited as Peter finished eating his mini-egg-salad sandwich. Half her life, it seemed, was spent waiting for him to swallow. While the Lynns attended the commital service, everyone else had gathered in the central room of the event center. It was a grand room, majestic, with a domed ceiling and a balcony, where Kay was standing with the twins. The room made Bevy think of olden times, kings and queens, heroism on the battlefield, honor and grace.

A toothpick decorated with a red frizzle had come with the little crustless sandwich. Peter put it in his mouth and actually started using it. "This is a funeral reception," he said. "Not a campaign event."

"You have egg salad on your lip."

Looking down at his lip, which he'd jutted out, he speared the food with the toothpick and sucked it. "You're in a mood," he said.

"And what kind of mood is that?"

"The kind of mood that comes, you know, *before*."

"Actually, I'm smack-dab in the middle of it, thank you for asking, and that's got nothing to do with you eating horribly."

"Okay."

"It'd be weird if I just ignored Cormier."

"But he's ignoring you."

"I want to go up to him before he comes up to me."

"I don't feel like talking to those people."

"You think I do? Look at how short his wife's dress is. That is not what you wear to a funeral. She's kind of funny-looking, don't you think?"

"Come on, Beverly. I'm not going to get into that kind of stuff."

"I'm going over there, and you're coming with me."

"You're just going to make me go with you?"

"No, you're going to do it as a favor to your beloved wife."

A crowd had formed around the Cormiers, but Bevy wasn't daunted; far from it, she felt energized. Prior to the campaign, she'd had no idea how much she'd missed this sensation. Riding horses used to give it to her, as did drag racing. And, yes, cocaine too, at first. It was a revving up but also a slowing down. The energy gave her calm, and the calm gave her energy, the feelings feeding each other.

As she strode across the grand room, it seemed as if all the people on the balcony were watching her and she couldn't swear they weren't.

She caught Cormier by surprise, as she'd hoped to. "Figured I'd come over here and wish you good luck." The man next to Cormier's wife, a fidgety, bug-eyed little fellow, was looking at Bevy's breasts. She didn't mind. "Also," she said, "I know you're friends with the Lynns, so I wanted to give you my condolences."

"Thanks, yes, you," he said, strangely. He looked better than he had when they'd met but was too girly to be good-looking. "Oh," he said, as if snapping out of a daze. "This is my wife, Robin, and my mother, and friends—we all went to high school together."

"This here is my husband, Peter," Bevy said.

His mother stepped forward and took hold of Peter's hand. "We've met once before," she said. She had a butch haircut and sounded English or something. Snobby, for sure. "I've done some work with your mother."

Kay appeared on cue, the twins in tow. "Good to see you, Annie," Kay said, and the two of them hugged. Cormier looked as shocked as Bevy was.

"How do you two know each other?" Cormier's wife asked.

"There was a dear woman who had medical bills that she couldn't pay." Annie made eye contact with different people as she spoke. Maybe she was classy, not snobby. "Kay's church and my nonprofit worked together to defray the costs."

"We were a good team," Kay said.

"Indeed," Annie said.

"In-dubitably!" the little man said, clawing at his neck. The other men were well dressed, but this one wore a plaid shirt and knit tie. He didn't seem like a liberal and maybe wasn't, this being Cormier's high school gang. The little man reminded her of men she'd known, hard men who worked with their hands and drank themselves to death. It was time now for him to stop looking at her breasts.

Pauline came by and squeezed Bevy's arm, but it was the little man she'd come to see. They kissed and he said something that made her laugh. So Cormier was friends with the Lynns, Cormier's mother was friends with Kay, and the little man was friends with Pauline. Maybe they ought to call off the Culture War. They could all go get a cup of coffee and talk about Jill.

"So . . ." Cormier said. He ran his fingers through his hair and looked past Bevy. "I guess I should thank you for telling me about the race."

"My pleasure," she said. "To tell you the truth, I wanted an opponent."

Cormier stuck out his lips and gave her some rapid-fire nods, as if to say, Sure you did. The perfect words came to Bevy. "Wasn't that the most beautiful service?"

"Oh, yeah," the little man said. He slapped his thigh. "Damn good."

Peter coughed.

"Yes," Cormier said. "It was beautiful and . . . good."

His wife put her hand over her mouth, then bent over and spit something into a napkin. A shiver went through her, freezing her neck. Pretty blue eyes: Bevy would give her that. "Excuse me," she said. "I'm sorry. I thought that was chicken salad."

The little man laughed. "The pink didn't clue you in?"

"Ham salad," Cormier said in a knowing voice, and the other men giggled. So these people were too high and mighty for ham salad.

"Holy cow, was that repulsive," Cormier's wife said, wiping her long tongue with a napkin. Talk about repulsive.

"Holy *pig*," said the little man, and Bevy laughed. It was funny, funny on a few levels, and they all laughed. Laughter was the best thing for releasing tension, and she felt herself relax, but she also became aware of how deep her tension ran. She was, she remembered, at a friend's funeral. She liked her laugh and didn't like people who didn't, but there were times when she wished it were easier for her to stop.

She stopped, finally, when a girl barged into the circle. She got real close to Cormier's wife, face-to-face, and put her hands on her shoulders. Their daughter. Bevy wouldn't have tolerated such rudeness, but Cormier's wife was just standing there gabbing and giggling like they were best friends.

"You more than said hello," Peter whispered, but Bevy wasn't ready to leave. What did she want from these people?

"This is my daughter, Carly," Cormier said.

Carly turned around, and Bevy introduced herself, remembering to be nice. "Why, you've got your mama's pretty blue eyes."

"Oh." Carly blushed. "Thanks."

Cormier stretched out his arms and made a show of yawning. "Carly must go to school with your children," he said.

"Yeah," Carly said. "Ronnie, right?"

"That's right," Bevy said. "That boy's around here somewhere. And Brent too. You must know him."

"I don't think so, but Ronnie, he's totally nice."

"Thank you. We think so."

Bevy managed to break away and as she and Peter walked across the room, the twins rejoined them. "Totally nice," Peter said. "Not sure how I feel about that, coming from her."

"She's at the top of the class. Ronnie could have worse friends."

"Next time you want to play smiley-face with libs, you're on your own."

Karl tugged on her dress and Kyle got under it. She knelt down and hugged them and thought about the debate. Monday afternoon she would meet with Arch Cook to prepare. A forum, it was called. Hogwash. It was going to be a brawl.

"What's up with that woman's arms?" asked Scott, the only one of their out-of-town friends to stick around; the others were headed back to the airport. "Or lack thereof."

"Birth defect," Stu said. They were walking across the church grounds to Stu's car, where Jimmy would join them. "That's Ricky Bumpers's wife."

"Who?" Scott said.

"He was a year behind us," Cormier said.

"And he worked next to me on the line," Stu said.

"How's he feel about her arms?" Scott said.

"Doesn't bother him," Stu said. "She's got all the essentials. I mean, there's no chance of the reach-around, but good relationships require compromise. Or so I'm told. Nicest people in the world. Really. They're religious but they actually practice what they preach. Do unto others, the Golden Rule, all that shit."

"I think 'do unto others' *is* the Golden Rule," Scott said.

"What happens to the Golden Rule if you're a masochist?" Cormier said, making what he thought was his best joke in a long time, but neither of them seemed to like it.

"Their son's in Iraq," Stu said. "Great kid. *Great* kid. If he gets killed, I'm going to kill someone, probably myself."

They pulled up at an intersection of walkways as a group of men, most of them black, passed by. Not even a funeral slowed the wheels of the Christian machine.

"This is quite an operation," Scott said.

"It's your shadow government," Stu said. "You better learn to like it."

"Very nineteenth century," Cormier said.

When they started moving again, Cormier turned around to see if Jimmy was on his way. He wasn't. Cormier had forgotten to put on an undershirt, and the sweat that had formed during his interaction with Bevy chilled him now as the wind blew. A cool drop of sweat fell from his armpit onto his love(less) handle.

"The things I would do *unto* Bevy Baer," Stu said.

"That laugh of hers?" Scott said. "That was like a primal mating call."

"Of the genus horny housewife," Stu said.

"I love Republicunts," Scott said. "DC's full of them."

Stu had parked in a faraway spot in anticipation of their little service. It was a clear day, October pure, and the view was as good as it could be. Cormier looked past Lincoln Ave. for the chimney of the factory, but it couldn't be seen.

The smell of beer against the burnt-leaf air brought back specific memories: they used to drink in the woods before going to watch Jimmy play football.

"Schlitz is just as gross as I remember," Scott said. He was sitting with Cormier on the back of the Buick. The cooler was in the backseat.

"I guess the counselor was hoping for a microbrew," Stu said. "Perhaps something in a nice amber?"

"I was hoping for Michelob," Scott said, "and expecting Bud."

"Wasn't in the budget," Stu said.

"You want some cash?" Scott said, reaching into the inside pocket of his suit jacket.

"Put your fucking wallet away," Stu said. Cormier's group of friends stretched across the social landscape; Scott and Stu had always stood at the poles.

"Are you still working at Wal-Mart?" Scott said.

"You better believe it. In fact I just got a new job. You're looking at the assistant manager of the produce department."

"Wal-Mart has produce?" Scott said.

"Not all of them," Stu said. "You see, Hartsburg is fortunate enough to have a Wal-Mart Supercenter."

"Very fancy," Scott said

"Yessir," Stu said. "This town is blessed. We've got a Jesus Supercenter down here and a Wal-Mart Supercenter up there."

"I cannot believe you work at Wal-Mart," Scott said. "You're one of the smartest people I know."

"That's because you live in DC," Stu said.

"You don't like the job, do you?" Scott said.

"Fuck no. Do you like yours?"

"No, but I get paid. Can't you find something else?"

"Not around here."

"So move."

"Nah. I'm going to die in this rat-hole. Maybe sooner than you think."

Stu grabbed the end of his tie and held up his arm, pretending to hang himself. It was quite a performance, complete with choking sounds and bulging eyes. His face got pink, he went up on tiptoes, his face got red. Scott and Cormier started to giggle. It was the intensity of his effort that was funny, and they needed to laugh after that funeral. When Stu fell to his knees, then forward onto his shoulder, they lost it.

They, too, ended up on the ground, Scott on all fours, Cormier on his back. They stayed on the ground long after the laughter had passed.

"So," Stu said. "I guess this must be Hell."

"Welcome," Scott said.

Stu smiled and Cormier felt love for his friends, and for himself for having these friends. Their relationships had gotten stronger over the years and were strong enough now to support grown-up pain, even if they still acted like teenagers.

When an SUV needed to get by, they staggered to their feet and waved at the girl in the backseat who was staring at the vagrants. Cormier got another round.

"Boys," Scott said, raising his can. "I'm glad to be here."

"As am I," Stu said. "And I can't for the life of me understand why the other guys didn't stick around."

"Two days' notice," Scott said. "People have lives."

"Fuck that," Stu said. "You get a babysitter, you tell your boss to piss off, you ask your wife for a favor. You show up."

"They did," Scott said.

"Barely," Stu said. "Did you see Bone with his cell phone? And they could have hung out for a few hours. Pull your head out of your ass so you can see what matters. That Jesus fest was for Jill. This is for Jimmy. They missed the main event."

"I agree," Cormier said. "They would want to be here. They're weren't thinking."

"Nope," Stu said. "Your buddy's wife only dies once."

There was no laughter at this. The three of them looked back toward the church, hoping to see Jimmy, and there he was, cutting across the lawn, looking at the ground. Without slowing, he took off his jacket and untucked his yellow shirt.

"What's up with that jacket?" Scott said.

"I think that's what he used to wear on game days," Stu said.

"No one to dress him," Cormier said.

"His daughter's all grown up," Scott said.

"*I'll* say," Stu said.

"Don't," Cormier said. "Please."

"Is this all right?" Scott asked once Jimmy got close. "Us drinking here?"

"I'm not sure," he said.

"Bad for your scorecard?" Stu said.

"Stu," Scott said.

"Let's get in the car," Jimmy said, and when they did, Stu started it.

"Let's go for a ride," Cormier said.

"Talk radio?" Scott said. "You're not a ditto-head, are you?"

"I'm *a*political," Stu said. "I hate them all, with extreme prejudice."

"Put on one-o-two-point-nine," Cormier said.

"Still?" Scott said.

"And they still play the same music," Jimmy said.

"Only now it's called classic rock," Stu said.

"With extreme prejudice," Cormier said, making only marginal sense.

"The Moody Blues?" Scott said. "This won't do."

"Leave it here," Cormier said. "They'll come through."

Cormier had gotten into jazz when he was in LA, and punk when he was in New York—he'd been there during its heyday. He'd even gone through a stage of pretending to like hip-hop. But he always returned to the music of his youth. After a time away, he longed for melody, guitar, and a big fat chorus. Rock, that is. He had a special fondness for practitioners of what he thought of as Midwestern, white-boy funk-rock, black music made undanceable enough for young white men, bands like Rare Earth, Grand Funk Railroad, and the James Gang. It was an unillustrious and possibly imaginary school of music, but it had provided the soundtrack for their teenage years.

Leaving Hilltop, they got caught in a mini-traffic jam. "Just think," Stu said, "all these people were here for Jill."

"It was a nice service," Jimmy said. "Wasn't it?"

"Definitely," Scott said.

"It was pretty religious," Jimmy said.

"You think?" Stu said.

"But that's what Jill wanted, right?" Cormier said. Stu gave him a look in the rearview, which said, Don't lie to him. "Usually you go to these things and the religion is a formality. Here it meant something."

"I think she would have liked it," Jimmy said. "Or maybe she did. I mean, maybe she was there. Fuck if I know."

"Fuck if anybody knows," Stu said.

"Look out," Scott said. Stu stomped on the brake and they pulled up just short of an old man in a wheelchair getting pushed by his wife. The woman, an apostrophe of a person, froze and squinted in an attempt to make out the source of her terror.

Stu gave her the finger. "Stu," Cormier said.

"Jesus," Jimmy said, sinking down.

"That was so incredibly wrong," Scott said.

"What?" Stu said as the woman started moving again. "The bitch is blind."

"And you're drunk," Scott said. It was true. After just two beers. Reverse tolerance, perhaps. Or he'd been drinking from a flask. Cormier sometimes talked to Stu about his drinking, usually when they were drinking.

"Want me to drive, Drunky McDrunkfuck?" Scott said.

"No," Stu said. "But I wouldn't mind if you shut your piehole."

"I used to think the piehole was your asshole," Jimmy said, and Cormier laughed.

"Why would your piehole be your asshole?" Scott said.

"Mary, Mother of God," Stu said, turning up "I'm Your Captain."

"Why is Grand Funk better than Steve Miller?" Scott said.

"Because you're a cunt," Stu said.

"Because it's high school," Jimmy said.

"That's a good thing?" Scott said.

"Sophomore year," Cormier said.

"Right," Jimmy said. "It's weird that it came on just now. It's . . ."

"Eerie?" Cormier said.

"Cool," Jimmy said.

The ride of the big Buick was smooth. They crossed Lincoln by the do-it-yourself car wash, then cruised past Water Tower Row, down to the bridge. The river moved quickly underneath them. Jimmy rolled down the window and closed his eyes.

They took a left after the bridge, looping around to The Drive, and houses gave way to businesses. Taco Bell. The Waffle House. The motor lodge where they used to rent a room for twenty bucks, fill the bathtub with beer, have a party. Cormier decided not to comment on Faith Evangelical's sign, which said, "If You're Ready to Die, You're Ready to Live."

Cormier had mixed feelings about memory-lane kind of occasions. Because of Robin, part of him viewed nostalgia as sentimentality, and sentimentality as weakness. But he had no illusions about his past: he knew he hadn't loved his life here as a teenager. He also knew that he hadn't loved his life anywhere else. This much was clear: he loved driving around and listening to music with guys he'd known forever. It was freedom, freedom mixed with security, which was Cormier's favorite kind.

What could be better? You were supposed to want more than this, much more, and Cormier did, but he wanted this as well. This, plus. It felt to him like an especially excellent thing to be doing right now, and he hoped Jimmy agreed.

It seemed like a long time ago, high school. At the same time, life was hurtling by. He was forty-four years old. Jill had been forty-two. Every Sunday of every football season for fourteen years, he'd gone to Jimmy's to watch Bengal games, yet not once had Cormier make a serious effort to talk to Jill. She would bring them food and he would say thanks. Not a tragedy that they hadn't been friends, maybe they wouldn't have taken to each other, but at the moment, pondering both his past and the oblivion that awaited him, Cormier felt that it was better to know someone than to not.

He could ask Jimmy about her, though, get to know her that way. Jimmy was still alive, and so was he.

They went past Wal-Mart and McDonald's and under the highway underpass. Jimmy was asleep. Cormier took the beer from his hand and started drinking it. Joe Walsh was singing "Turn to Stone," as was Scott, sounding surprisingly good. They came to a stop at an intersection known as Hunter's Pass, then went left, west, into the country.

PART TWO

CHAPTER 14

LIEUTENANT COLONEL LAMAR H. NORTHCUTT JR. had died a
Democrat. Thinking about her father now, Bevy wondered why he
hadn't changed parties like many Texas Dems had done, were still doing.
Maybe he'd felt an allegiance to the party of his parents—Lamar had been
big on loyalty—or had approved of government programs like social security.

His core values, in any case, were conservative and they became Bevy's
values, although prior to being saved, she didn't think much about them,
and to the extent that she did, they seemed like common sense. Of course
America was good and communism was bad, of course it was wrong to
kill unborn babies: did we really need to argue about this stuff? Guess so,
because debates were raging; but Bevy—busy being a good girl, then a
bad girl—wasn't even a spectator. In 1980 she was barely aware that an
election was going on and, to her shame, Reagan was elected without her
vote.

After converting in '82, Bevy got political. Lots of Christians were mo-
bilizing in those years as they realized they couldn't depend on politicians
of either party to govern morally (Reagan, for example, didn't deliver on
school prayer). Bevy looked to Scripture to clarify her own politics and it
confirmed what she already felt to be true.

The battle over abortion got most of the attention, but Bevy didn't
fixate—not then, not now—on any single issue. She was motivated, above
all else, by her belief that the family was sacred. It needed to be nurtured,
or at least left alone. Instead, it was undermined. Undermined by educa-
tors who thought they knew better than parents how to raise children.
And by judges who grabbed the godlike power to reshape families. And by
entertainment bigwigs who, like drug dealers, poisoned kids for profit.

The American family was in trouble. So, then, was the nation.

Bevy carried this sober reality in her heart, and a photo of her daddy in her bra, as she stood at the podium in the Hartsburg High School auditorium. The place was full, and Bevy could have run up a mountain. Oh, was she jacked.

From a table between the podiums, a representative from the League of Woman Voters asked the questions that audience members had submitted. The woman was a bundle of civic-mindedness under her flowered hat, and her voice was both high-pitched and monotone, like a foghorn. "This question is for Mr. Cormier. Do you believe that creationism should be taught alongside evolution?"

His response—blah, blah, blah—was exactly what Arch Cook had said he would say. Cormier was going for a laid-back, chitchatty style—Mr. Natural—but it was hard to pull off when you were pasty and pale and generally seemed to be turning into a hunk of mozzarella cheese. "A funny thing happened on the way to the forum," he'd said as an opening line, and the whole crowd had gone silent except for his mother, whose mechanical laugh was the only clue that a joke had been made.

He'd recovered somewhat from that awful (good for Bevy) beginning, but no one could call him strong, and Bevy hadn't even gone after him yet. She was waiting for the question that Arch Cook had planted via a Hilltop member.

Right now, though, it was time for her rebuttal. "Yes, that's right. We Christians hate science. I hereby declare that all Bunsen burners should be banned! I mean, this is just ridiculous. No one's opposed to science. Once again Mr. Cormier has tried to scare you. Here's what I believe: that evolution is a legitimate *theory*. It's possible that we used to be animals. It's possible, for example, that Mr. Cormier's great-great-great-great-great-great-great-great-great-great-great-granddaddy was a blue-butted baboon."

She paused so that the crowd could hear itself laugh. At least a third of the people here were Hilltop. The Reverend had spent a good part of Sunday night's service talking about the race; an army was finally rising.

"His butt wasn't blue," Cormier said, his glasses giving off a glare.

Was that another one of his "jokes"? He had a pimple on his nose. For a quick, uncomfortable moment Bevy felt bad for him. "Most parents believe it's possible that evolution is not correct, and numerous scientists agree, so why not give the competing theories roughly equal weight? It's a simple matter of balance."

"This question is for Ms. Baer. I was very concerned that a student had expressed a desire to blow up the school. What would you do to improve student safety?"

Bevy nodded several times like a TV news correspondent about to give a report. She was standing up straight—past straight; her back was arched, and she was wearing a peach suit with wide shoulders. She'd had her hair done and every strand was where it belonged. A perfect hairdo gave her confidence; it felt like part of her brain. "I'm a strong supporter of the zero-tolerance policy, which says that if you're found with a deadly weapon, you get expelled. But now a student has found a hole in the policy. He wrote a note saying he wanted to, quote, 'go bin Laden' on the school. He was suspended but not expelled, because he didn't have a literal weapon. Most parents, I think, would want the policy to be broadened so he and others like him can be expelled."

"Mr. Cormier?"

"This is an important issue, but it's perhaps more complex than sometimes people make it out to be, because these students—for example, this troubled kid is clearly troubled and he needs—well, I agree he needs to be punished. My daughter, as I've mentioned, is a junior at Hartsburg High, and I want her to be safe and sound, and I think we, as parents, have an obligation to *all* students, not just our own, which was my point originally regarding this bin Laden kid"—Cormier put his hand on his forehead, as if checking for a fever—"Should he be expelled? I don't know. But does *anybody*? I mean, suspension seems like a prudent pending further—"

"Time's up."

". . . evaluation of his psychological, yes."

"Just to be clear," Bevy said. "You think that the bin Laden boy should be allowed to come back and go to school with our children?"

"Here's what I think." Cormier had already taken off his jacket; now he rolled up his sleeves and turned toward Bevy. "We should suspend him and monitor his progress. Punish him? Yes. Give up on him? No."

There was applause, his loudest of the night. Arch Cook was sitting

145

with the Reverend in the second row, behind Bevy's family. Pretending to smile at Peter, she looked at Arch. A scratch of his nose meant that she was to go after Cormier without benefit of the planted question; there was a chance it wouldn't get asked at all. But Arch Cook nodded once as if to say, here it is. Maybe it was God, maybe it was serendipity, maybe it was the wisdom of Arch Cook, but the question came: "Why would you be better than the other person at representing the values of Hartsburg? In short, who *are* you?"

While Cormier gave his answer—some arrogant gobblygook about the "innate dignity of human beings"—Bevy said to herself the first three words of her response: Who am I? The rest, she knew, would come spilling out.

Preparing for the debate in a Hilltop classroom, she'd stood in front of the blackboard while Arch Cook asked questions. Toward the end of their four-hour session, he asked a question that she couldn't even begin to answer. It was so open-ended. "Don't worry," he said, squinting behind his glasses. Like drawing a bow, the weird guy pulled on the band of his accordionlike folder until it snapped; then he removed a piece of paper and folded it into a paper airplane, sucking his thumb every time he needed to seal a crease. "This'll win you the race," he said, and launched the plane, which did two loop-to-loops, the second larger than the first, and glided to a soft landing in Bevy's palm. To add to the magic of the moment, the Reverend stopped by. He wasn't wearing a tie and his dark chest hair rose in a reverse widow's peak to his Adam's apple. His chest hair unsettled her in a way that seemed useful as she delivered the monologue.

The words tapped into a reservoir that had been building in her at least since the early seventies, when she had seen the hurt inflicted upon her father and his friends by Jane Fonda and other antiwar traitors. Her reservoir had been fed when she visited her cousin Dicky Don at Tulane University and his roommate from Long Island, New York, got stoned and mimicked the way she talked. And when she went to Washington, DC, to watch Lamar accept an award and the girls at the gala afterward let it be known that something was wrong with her dress. And last year when she was handing out flyers at an antiques show and the event's organizer asked her to stop "harassing" people. After Bevy said she had a right to spread the Word, the woman peered out over her bifocals and told her that only "fearful, weak-minded people" believed in God. Bevy's certainty that this was a lie, a lie that came from the woman's own fear, didn't make it sting any less. But Bevy respected the woman's directness. She'd dared to say what all elites believed.

"Who am I? I'm Beverly Carmen Baer. I'm a proud wife and mother. I try to do the right thing and I pray to God that I am. I moved here from Texas because I fell in love with Peter Baer." She blew him a kiss, the smack loud in the mic. "I'd been through some dark days following my daddy's death, and it was Peter who brought me to the Lord, then brought me to Hartsburg. Y'all welcomed me with open arms. I'm running so that I can give something back to the town. Mr. Cormier, on the other hand, has a history of attacking both the town and the values it holds dear. When he was in high school, there was a war going on, as there is now, and to protest the war Mr. Cormier refused to stand for the Pledge of Allegiance—the very same Pledge, mind you, that people are trying to ban today because it contains the words 'Under God.' Now, we all make mistakes, but Mr. Cormier has never, to my knowledge, apologized. Then he went off to Greenwich Village in New York City, then to Hollywood, where he wrote movies that, safe to say, aren't what anyone would call family-friendly. Then he moved back to Hartsburg, so you'd think he liked it here, but he's used his platform in the *Informer* to bash the town. He's called the town 'close-minded' and, quote, 'blind to the pain in its midst.' Is this the town y'all know? The Hartsburg I know is *compassionate*. The Hartsburg I know has a *good heart*. I guess liberals think it shows intelligence to complain, to focus on the little bit of bad instead of the whole lot of good. At any rate, do you all want to be represented by someone like me, who loves this town, or by someone who keeps talking down the town? Hartsburg is based on American values, on faith and family and patriotism, and surely we want school board members who embody those values."

Aside from talking too quickly toward the end, she'd nailed it. Maybe not: the crowd was giving off a murmur at best. But the noise steadily grew, like the sound of an oncoming train, and probably two thirds of the crowd stood up. Then the cheer got even louder, a cheer within a cheer, as if everyone had just realized what she'd said. She'd landed a major blow, a fact not lost on Cormier, who was nervously rubbing the side of his nose with a straight finger, as if trying to poke his way into his forehead.

Her control of the moment was so total it was like her flying dreams where she could do whatever she wanted: take off her clothes, dive off a building, kiss a stranger. Only after she woke up did the guilt come, sometimes not even then.

"Mr. Cormier?"

"I don't know where—that protest was when I was in junior high, not high school. I was thirteen, or twelve, so I hardly grasped everything that—"

"What is it about the Pledge of Allegiance that you find offensive?" Bevy said.

"I was making a statement."

"You sure were—do you apologize for it?"

"No," came a voice from the crowd. "He most certainly does not."

Cormier did his best to smile. "Hi, Mom," he said with a little wave. There were giggles and Bevy couldn't tell if this was a good or bad moment for him.

"I can't believe we're talking about something I did in junior high," Cormier said. "In fact I'm not going to. As for all the things you said I said—"

"You *said* them," Bevy said. "I'd like to know: who exactly is close-minded and delusional? Why don't you name names?"

"You're taking my words out of context."

"All right. Let me read a complete quote: 'Newcomers to Hartsburg, especially those with black and brown skin, should know that we're like the son-in-law who greets you at the door with a smile, then complains the whole time you're here.'"

People booed, and Bevy shook her head as if in sadness. "Mr. Cormier, it sure sounds to me like you're calling each and every one of us racist."

"No, no, no—it was a clumsy metaphor—although it's not like we don't have a problem with race. Look—"

"Mr. Cormier," said the moderator, "we need to move on."

"Okay, but let me, let me just say one thing. This is my town. I remember going to movies on Main Street. And when the factories were going. And Kohl's Brewery. Who remembers Schenk's café? Great Reubens. And pickles! Jars on the tables and you could eat as many . . . The guys I grew up with, most of them, were back in town for—I care about this town, and when I criticize Hartsburg, it's because I want it to be *better*."

A decent point, but he'd just about killed himself trying to make it. He'd gone past pale to pale green and was sucking his bottle of Poland Spring as hungrily as a baby on a nipple. The poor guy was beaten enough, for now.

From here on out she would make nice, stand tall, look good.

CHAPTER 15

THEN CAME THE SAUSAGE.

It wasn't enough that he had bombed in the debate. Or that anticipation of the debate and its aftershocks had ruined his sleep for five days and counting. Or that the whitehead on his nose, which he'd popped the night before the debate, had come back to life. Or that as a candidate he'd had no choice but to come to the Octoberfest Festival, an übertacky event that he'd managed to avoid his entire life. Or that Robin had refused to come with him. ("Sounds great," she'd said. "I'll meet you at the swastika stand.") Or that Stu, who had agreed to join him, had left him in favor of the beer tent.

All that was prelude to the moment when Jenny Kohl, beloved foamer of his lattes, asked him to be a judge in the sausage contest. Her face was smiley and rosy atop her tight turtleneck sweater. He gathered from her tone that this was an honor, one he would be foolish and disrespectful to turn down. Zev would want him to say yes. What better way to seem like an ordinary guy than to hang with the townsfolk and eat their meat?

But even if not for his role as a politician, he'd have had trouble begging off. He couldn't tell her that aside from perhaps six turkey breast sandwiches and random bites of tuna, he hadn't eaten meat in a year. Or that his lack of sleep was, even as he stood there smiling back at her, juicing up his tum-tum. If there was a lie by which he could have both upheld his manhood and steered clear of sausage, it didn't come to him. Jenny was of German stock, strong, a car-fixing kind of broad who liked her men manly, and although she would never want to have sex with Cormier, although he wouldn't have had sex with her even if she had wanted to, he couldn't bear to render himself completely unworthy and would therefore eat too much sausage on a sour stomach to preserve the possibility of an impossible sexual encounter with a woman who couldn't possibly care whether or not he ate sausage. He was very tired.

"This way," she said, looping her arm in his.

These were the fairgrounds in the northeast section of town, between the athletic fields and the hospital. The single-day festival would draw maybe two thousand people, Ward Three voters among them. Upon arriving, he had talked to Dot Ferguson about sex education, shouting over the oompah band while she put away a midmorning piece of Bavarian cream pie. He'd realized that Dot looked like, of all people, Colin Powell. She was as white as a white person could be, and had a perm the color of a golden retriever, but she was practically the general's twin, right down to the shame in her eyes.

As he walked past the people gathered in front of the stands and stages and booths, his gloom lifted. No one, as far as he could tell, was pointing at him and giggling. Most of these people had not been at the debate, and the article about the debate had said that it had been "contentious and spirited." Thank God for overly balanced journalism. And maybe the debate hadn't been a disaster. Both Robin and Annie had assured him that he hadn't embarrassed himself—but what else could they say? The verdict would come in once Zev had watched the video that Cormier had sent him, but in any case, the Candidate wasn't a laughingstock. He was still in the race.

He should not have been touching Jenny, a fact made obvious by his half hard-on, which became whole as a result of his wishing it away. Trying reverse psychology, he pretended that he *wanted* to have an erection, that his life depended on his maintaining it. The ploy didn't work any better than it had the last time he'd tried it, when he was fifteen. Maybe would-be supporters could shake his penis. Pleasure to meet you.

Jenny's hair was up and he imagined kissing the soft skin behind her ear. As the cool breeze gave him Jenny's apple-soap smell, he knew he needed sex as much as he needed sleep. The sausage would decrease the likelihood of both.

Waiting in his chair for his judgeship to begin, Cormier spotted Bill-William and waved him over. Always glad to have a chance to use his body, Bill ran to him, weaving between festivalgoers like a running back.

"Nice moves, Icky," Cormier said, referring to an old Bengals back.

"Speaking of icky." He pointed at the coffin-sized grill where sausages were sizzling, sending smoke up and over the adjacent Little League field. Bill was a healthy eater, an eater of rice cakes. "You're a judge?"

"Afraid so. Whatever it takes."

"It'll take a colostomy bag."

Cormier's stomach made a noise that sounded like the groan of a chastened dog. "Having fun?" Cormier said, petting his stomach as if it were actually a dog.

"Nope. A day like this, I should be on a hike. This was Tina's idea."

"Where is she?"

"Buying stuff." Tina, a bank teller, was hot, shallow, and twenty-seven. Bill dated either young lovelies or more substantial older women whose sagginess and procreation plans always ended up scaring him away. He needed to live in a city, where there were more smart young women. And to stop expecting a woman to make him happy.

"The debate coverage was too kind to me," Cormier said.

"It struck me as objective."

"Ah, yes, blessed objectivity."

"You know what'd be nice? If just once when we saw each other, you could not bitch about the paper."

"You used to bitch too, before you were an editor."

"Now you go out of your way to bitch. My guess is, you're angry at yourself for writing fluff, and it's easier to give me shit than, say, write better pieces."

It eased the tension in his pre-sausage stomach to admit that there was truth in what Bill was saying. "So maybe I could write better, hard-hitting pieces and you could back me when Jeannette puts up a stink. That way I could stop being angry at both of us."

"If you give us hard-hitting pieces, I'll back you. As long as they're good. Now excuse me while I go try to stop my girlfriend from buying junk."

Jenny, it turned out, was the master of ceremonies. She walked with a microphone in front of their table, her good, big ass packed into Levis. "Welcome to the thirty-ninth annual sausage-making contest," she said with genuine cheer. "The winner will receive a hundred-dollar gift certificate to Bosch's Meats and the coveted Golden Sausage." She introduced

Cormier first, describing him as "a newspaper writer. And he's running for . . . school board? Anything you want to say about that, Wallace?"

"Please call me Wally." He decided that this was a moment to act like a politician; to that end, he stood up and told two lies and a bad joke: "This is a great event. I've been coming here all my life. But never in my wildest imagination did I dare dream that I would help pick the winner of the Golden Sausage."

There was laughter, quite loud, and one of his fellow judges, a frizzy-haired woman in a poncho, gave him a thumbs-up. Cormier knew her from somewhere. He knew most of these people from somewhere. They were good people, proud of their heritage, proud of their town. "If you live in Ward Three," he said. "I'd appreciate your support. If you don't, I love you anyway." He sat down, leaving them wanting more.

The other judges, he learned, were Barb Shellenberger, who worked at the reference desk at the public library, and Joe Upchurch, a bearded, lumberjack type who probably had sausage with every meal and Jenny Kohl for dessert. His forearm looked like a mass of cables. But Barb was small; if she could handle the sausage, then so could Cormier.

The judges were to give each entry a one-to-five rating in three categories: appearance, consistency, and flavor. They didn't have to eat entire sausages, only a bite of each. Twenty-six bites. Was that a lot?

Yes. Yes, it was. This became clear while he chewed on number two, which was gummy and studded with caraway seeds, one of which lodged between his front teeth.

"I could use a beer," Joe said, and blew out a burp that smelled like bacon, not sausage. Pitchers were brought over, cups poured. The ale cut the animalistic aftertaste and Cormier had three cups during the first ten entries. Not all the sausages were German. There were Italian sausages and Polish sausages and fancy sausages filled with fennel and duck. There were spicy sausages and sausages that had no flavor aside from an indistinct meatiness. Some sausages were dry, others horrifyingly gooey.

Cormier was grateful for number twelve, a classic sweet Italian. He gave it fives across the board and decided it couldn't be beat. Gastric juice moved in his stomach, creating a sound like the clucking of pigeons.

While they ate the pieces of sausage, Joe and Barb made faces that Jenny and the crowd tried to read, but Cormier, just trying to make it through, gave away nothing and earned the nickname Poker Face. By number fourteen Cormier was leaving the barely chewed sausage in the back of his throat to be washed down by ale.

During number seventeen, a dirt-dry bratwurst, Cormier became fixated on the seed still caught between his teeth and used his tongue to try to pry it free. "Uh oh," Jenny said, misreading the gesture. "Poker Face doesn't like it."

"Poker Face is drunk," said someone, an astute observer. Getting sloshed in public wasn't great politics, but ale had become essential to swallowing. Plus it was numbing his body to whatever physical effects he was incurring. It was possible that he already had diarrhea. Could you have a heart attack and be too drunk to notice?

He got a huge wedge of number nineteen, including excess casing that belonged to Joe's mostly naked bite. Nineteen was white and veined. The little paper plate was barely lighter than the sausage, and where the plate was wet with grease, it was darker. Cormier gave it a zero in appearance. Albino cock, he thought as he held his breath against the fishlike flavor, which was no less horrid than its raisins-and-rubber-bands consistency. Wrong. Nineteen was wrong the way violence was wrong. He stopped chewing and downed his beer, then let out an "Ahh" that turned into a moan.

He was drunk, and if you feel drunk when you're anxious, you're drunker than you think you are. The drunkenness and the flulike sensation inflicted by number nineteen made him feel as though he were behind glass. He couldn't hear what people were saying. Because they weren't saying anything, they were only chewing. He watched their mouths move. These people were fat and pale, their limbs too short for their portly bodies. Human heifers, human hogs. Cormier felt that he had just eaten a bite of them. Had they chopped up one of their own and turned him into number nineteen? Would they eat Cormier once they had fattened him up? What was going on here?

He looked past the grazing heifers and hogs to the sprawling orange-brick hospital, where he had been born, where his father had died. He wanted to feel something for his father. He searched his body for emotion but found only his body, his physical self, his meatiness. A beer was in his hand and he drank half in two swallows.

There was commotion. The attention of the heifers-hogs was drawn away. Heads turned, white necks bulged, entire bestial bodies rocked into motion.

When he saw Bevy Baer, he stood up halfway, knocking over his beer. "That's all right, Poker Face," Jenny said, "we'll get you another hunk of twenty."

Bevy waved at him and he managed not to give her a Nazi salute. Instead, he gave a military salute, or an impression of one, which seemed to amuse the herd. He doubted that the Octoberfest Festival would help his political fortunes. Octoberfest Festival was a redundant name, a stupid name for a stupid event for stupid people.

Number twenty had hair in it. Joe burped out bacon and poured Cormier a beer. Bevy and her entourage had moved on. Why was Cormier alone? Why was he eating sausage with a mustache in it? What kind of race was he running?

On the edge of his vision, he realized, was his pimple. Beyond his pimple, that snowcapped mountain, heifers and hogs were grazing in the valley, chomping and slurping. They wanted more, always more. Fullness they did not understand, these fat full beasts who were eyeing him and his sausage. They would not take kindly to someone who didn't eat their meat, meat that was part of them and now part of him.

He placed number twenty on his tongue and swallowed it like a pill.

CHAPTER 16

THIS HAD BEEN a good day, a perfect day, a day when the evil in the world had receded in fear of the good. The whole family went to the Octoberfest Festival, which Bevy found especially meaningful because her mother's great-grandparents had been born in Germany. It was an important event for Hartsburg, and the pride was palpable. For one day every year the silent majority of Hartsburgers took it back from the pessimists and whiners who, like Wallace Cormier, had access to the media. At the Octoberfest Festival you couldn't argue that the town didn't have lots to offer, not with all the spirit and talent on display. Who knew Hartsburg had so many skilled chefs, musicians, and artists? Peter, who had good taste for a man, spotted a beautiful ceramic vase, and Bevy, filled with goodwill, didn't mind at all when he said he was going to give it to Kay. Bevy ate a tasty veal cutlet sandwich and a piece of German chocolate cake that she allowed herself because she was doing so much walking. After lunch, Brent watched the twins while Bevy hooked up with a dozen volunteers from Hilltop. They handed out almost a thousand pamphlets, and not even Cormier's smug mug and mockery of the military could bring her down. The best thing was that Ronnie was in a good mood. On the drive home, he sang a song that went "Today was a good day." According to Brent, it was a rap song, but it seemed to have a message that was both hopeful and fitting. They all had eaten so much at the festival that Bevy didn't have to make dinner. It was the rare Saturday night that the whole family was home, and after the twins had gone to bed, they gathered in the family room to watch *The Rookie*, which had been recommended by Marybeth. Bevy lay on the floor and rested her head on JB's back. *The Rookie* was Bevy's kind of movie in that it was about following your dreams. It starred Dennis Quaid, who reminded Bevy of a man she'd once known.

Now, as she lay in bed skimming an article about "message discipline," she hoped that this special day would have a special end. It'd been three weeks since they'd last made love, and holy hogfish (as her old friend Colleen used to say) was Bevy ready.

She watched as Peter did what he did every night: set down his cup on the nightstand. On the side of the cup, which he'd had forever, was a faded picture of Johnny Bench. His pajamas, a Christmas gift from Kay, had a crisscross pattern, and if you looked closely, you saw that the lines were linked golf clubs. Peter opened and closed his mouth four times to get used to his earplugs, then folded back the covers.

But what he did after lying down surprised Bevy: he reached down to the side of the bed and grabbed what turned out to be the vase, wrapped in a red ribbon. "I should have told you this sooner," he said, handing the vase to Bevy. "I was real proud of you the other night. I loved seeing you up there. You were so smart, so poised."

Bevy was touched, touched in a way that intensified her desire. It was truly love that she would be making. "I thought you were going to give it to Kay."

"I only said that to throw you off."

"You devil."

Peter smiled and blushed. This was the moment to make her nonmove move, but when she kissed him, he kept his lips sealed. "Ahh," he said as if that had felt good, her tongue on his teeth. Peter picked up his book, put on his reading glasses, and looked at her. "I'm going to read for a bit," he said, his gray eyes looking huge through the glass.

"Mind if I take a sip?" She got up on her knees and reached across him, placing her breast on his chin. He tilted his head back and handed her the cup. Staying up on her knees, she let water dribble onto her nightgown and wiped it away with the tips of her fingers in such a way that her nipples said hello. Peter went on reading.

When she lay back down, she got close to him and put her hand on his thigh. "Today was a good day," she said.

"I really enjoyed that sausage sandwich."

"I'm glad, hon."

"Next year I'm going to try the sauerkraut balls."

This was ridiculous. There was no rule, biblical or otherwise, that said a woman couldn't ask for sex. "Peter," she said. "Please make love to me."

He looked up from his book like he'd heard a loud noise. "What did you say?" he said, staring out toward the street.

"You heard me. I want you to make love to me."

"Shush. You know I don't like it when you talk that way."

"I know no such thing."

"This isn't—"

She reached into his pants and he hardened immediately in her hand. "Hmm," he said, like he was puzzled.

"Hmm is right," she said. "We seem to have a situation."

"You're a bad woman, Bevy Baer."

"And you're a bad man."

She kept hold of him while he undressed, then, using it like a handle, pulled him onto her. He had a good body, small and trim, boylike. She stifled a squeal when he pulled off her underpants. After all this time, she still wasn't accustomed to quiet lovemaking. A cowboy named Clay once took her to a cabin in the mountains of Colorado, and a man from across the valley came by one night to make sure everything was all right.

After Peter had slipped inside, she took off her nightgown and put her legs in the air. She needed the angle to be right—with his penis, there wasn't margin for error—so she slid down and tilted back. She liked how his neck felt on her nose, rough. Then, wanting connection, she grabbed the back of his hair, pulled him down so that they were face-to-face, and looked into his eyes. Peter wasn't one to reveal himself, but during sex he couldn't help giving her a glimpse of everything: desire, fear, joy, sadness, love. Or maybe just desire. Whatever she saw, it made her feel closer to him.

"Do what I like best," he said, his eyes closed. "*Please.*"

"Just wait."

"Now, Bevy. Do it."

"Okay," she said, liking the authority in his voice. She put her middle finger in her mouth, then put the tip where he liked it.

"Woonch," he said.

The finger was only part of it. In addition, he liked her to talk in her Southern belle voice. A scandalized damsel was the idea. "My, oh, my," she said, wiggling the finger.

"What? What'd you say?"

She took out an earplug and spoke into his ear. "Mr. Baer, where oh where did you acquire such power? Does *that*"—knuckle-deep—"meet with your satisfaction?"

When he started to breathe heavily, she dialed up an image: Cowboy Clay, filling her up. "My goodness," she said. "I'm not entirely sure that I can handle your power, but I do intend to try." Now Dennis Quaid had her up against a locker, her knee at his chin, while Johnny Bench and the rest of the team watched. "Kind sir, your manliness is nothing short of extraordinary. I do declare that it is beyond compare."

The Reverend made an appearance. This was a first. She tried to come back to Peter, who was still pumping away, but the Reverend took her from behind. Arch Cook smiled and squinted. Her hands were on the blackboard. "Oh, goodness me. You, kind sir, are a large, powerful man of God. I fear that you might be too much man for this little girl from Texas." She commanded the Reverend to lie down on the floor and mounted him, clutching his chest hair with both hands. "Oh, my. I swear I've never in my life encountered such passion and power. I do hope you'll forgive me if I lose control. You are a man, do you hear me? All man, one hundred percent, grade-A, Christian-American man-meat. Good God, are you bad, bad, bad, bad . . .

When she arrived back in her bed via a tingly lemony cloud, she was trying to breathe. Peter had his hand over her mouth. She gasped when he took it away.

He rolled off her and almost off the bed. She reached out to catch him, but he held up his hand, not wanting to be touched. In one motion he put on his pajama pants and stood up. "If you can't be quiet . . . Where's my earplug?"

"I don't know." A lie. He wasn't the only one who enjoyed a certain sensation.

He marched around the bed and into the bathroom. Peter felt uncomfortable after they'd done the thing he liked best. The truth was, Bevy didn't know what to make of it: surely a husband and wife had some freedom to take pleasure in each other. On the other hand, that freedom had limits. And Bevy had gone well beyond them tonight. She'd forgiven herself her fantasies in the past—like Ronnie's music, they seemed passable if not quite right—but bringing Reverend Wedgwood into bed with them?

She waited until he turned off his light to get up. She peed, washed her hands and face, put on moisturizer. She looked every minute of her forty-four years and nine months. Her eye bags could have been made of brown paper for all the crinkles.

The phone rang and she raced into the bedroom as her mind dealt her the possibilities: her mother, Wilma, Ronnie, but he was in bed, wasn't he?

An unmistakable voice said, "I'm looking for B. C. Northcutt." Bevy looked at Peter, lying on his back like a corpse. But he had his eyes open. Like a corpse.

"Hello? Bevy?"

"God in Heaven," Bevy said, walking back into the bathroom. She sat down on the edge of the tub. "This sure sounds a lot like a girl I once knew."

Big laugh: vintage Colleen. "What's up, girlfriend?"

"How long's it been?"

"How long you been married?"

That was the last time Bevy had seen Colleen, at her wedding. Colleen and her date had put on a dirty-dancing display, which might not have been so inappropriate if there'd been dancing at the wedding. "Sorry I didn't call you back," Bevy said.

"Hey, that's all right."

"What'd you want to talk to me about?"

"I was thinking of driving cross-country and maybe passing through Ohio."

"Is that right?"

"Don't sound so happy about it."

"It's just that I'm real busy these days."

"Well, here's the thing. I was thinking about passing through Ohio and I did. I am."

"Where are you, Colleen?"

"Close to where you are."

"How close?"

"*Real* close."

Bevy heard a sputtering car pull up out front. She wasn't surprised exactly. It was almost like she'd been waiting for her. A visit from Colleen made a strange kind of sense—it did, anyway, until Bevy opened the front door. Backlit by the streetlight, Colleen came toward the house in silhouette, hair flowing from a hat, boots clicking on the walkway. This wasn't déjà vu. This was time losing meaning, ceasing to exist. This was the stack of experiences that Bevy called her life tumbling down, exploding.

She met her friend on the walkway and hugged her inside her white fur coat. To Bevy's relief, time came back when she pulled away and looked at Colleen. She was a fried kind of beautiful. Cracked forehead. Cheekbones setting off scooped-out cheeks, or maybe the other way around. Hair longer and blonder than it used to be. And cleavage. Middle-aged, yes, but still Colleen.

"This is too crazy," Bevy said. "One minute I'm in bed . . . I don't know what to say."

"First thing you can say is no."

"What do you mean?"

"Can I crash here?"

"Oh, Colleen, I don't know."

"That's fine."

"I wish you'd given me some warning."

"All right."

"I'm sorry if I'm not being welcoming."

"No, no, that's fine; I understand you've got your family to think about, but let me say this—and believe me, the last thing I want to do is guilt you—it's just that I kind of figured that even after all this time, I *was* family."

"Well, you are, Colleen. How long would you stay? What are you doing anyways?"

"I've got a job lined up in Rochester, New York."

"You're moving?"

"Yes, ma'am. The time finally came. Packed up all my things. You would not believe some of the stuff I came across."

"I don't want to know."

"I bet you don't. I hoped my car would make it, but something's gone wrong. Nothing serious, I don't think. Two or three days is all it should take."

"Stay here tonight, but as far as another night goes, we'll have to see."

Colleen smiled and put her hand on Bevy's cheek. "Thanks, darling."

Large and low-ceilinged, with wood paneling and a shag carpet, the guest bedroom was a shrine to the seventies. In some households it would have been a rec room, a place for teenagers to be bad. Kay always complained about all the junk; folding chairs and boxes and sports gear were creeping in on the bed in the corner. There was pleasure in seeing Colleen take off her pants and lie down in the bed that Kay considered her own.

In the light, she could see that Colleen's eyes were bloodshot. The black rose on her upper thigh was the only tattoo that was new to Bevy. Colleen had the wrinkles, freckles, and bumps you'd expect, but she still had her figure. No doubt she was still a hard-core exerciser; plus she'd had no babies to suck the life out of her breasts.

Bevy said, "I don't suppose I need to tell you that as long as you're here, you've got to, you know, keep it clean."

Colleen turned onto her side, curling up with her wrist between her scarred knees. "For all you know, I'm cleaner than you are."

"I'm serious, Col."

"You sure are."

"Not even alcohol, okay?"

"No problem. I didn't have a drink for entire states today."

"Let me ask you a question. If your car didn't act up, would you have come by?"

"I can't say for sure, since I tend to decide things last minute."

"That much I know. You all right, Colleen?"

"Just fine. This bed is like heaven."

"I mean—"

"I know what you mean." She scratched her calf, her nails making marks. "I'm scared, if you want to know the truth. I've been doing the same things for so long, seeing the same faces. Bored is what I was, sick to death of myself. If I had to have the same conversation one more time— I was stuck. I'm glad to be unstuck but I feel kind of . . . at sea, you know? I tried telling my friends I was nervous about leaving but they couldn't hear me 'cause everyone thinks I'm such a free spirit. The truth is, I've always kept close to home, and now that I've broken away, I feel like I might just drift off the edge of the earth. I knew I'd feel this way too. I'm ashamed to tell you that I stole money from the bar where I worked. So now I can't go back. I suppose that's why I did it."

Bevy walked to the other side of the room, or as far as she could go; an old air hockey table stopped her. She was taken aback, and moved, by this outpouring. Ask an Ohioan how she's doing and she's likely to say, Could be worse. But even for a Texan Colleen put it all out there, always had, and Bevy used to respond in kind.

"And you, Bev? How are you?"

"Me?" She turned around to find Colleen with her shirt off. Bevy looked away. The truth would sound like a boast, but what was she going to do, lie? "I'm good, real good. I feel blessed. I thank God for the life I've been given."

"You know, it's funny."

"What is?" On the edge of her vision Colleen had a straight leg lifted.

"Well, here you are with your flannel nightgown and your big house and your blessed life, but you still seem like Bevy."

She got close to Colleen so that she could look at her face but not her long dark nipples. "I'm *not* the girl I used to be," she said.

"All right."

"I've changed."

"But my God, Bevy, you're not an entirely different person, at least I hope you're not. You see, I loved that girl."

"We had some times, you and I," Bevy said, astonished that she was starting down memory road at one in the morning.

"Hell, yeah. Good times, bad times, and everything in between."

"Remember when I got out of the hospital?" Bevy said. "You were so sweet. I bet the massages you gave me sped up my recovery by a month."

"I liked taking care of you. And you more than returned the favor. Remember when that peckerhead tossed me around?"

"George. He broke your rib."

"You'd come home from work—where were you working?"

"Dentist's office. No . . . driving range."

"You took such good care of me, but then after a while, we decided you ought to go out, like we weren't going to let that prick-ass man lay us low. You'd have a night for both of us, then come home and tell me about it. That's what this right here reminds me of. It's like you just got home and were telling me about a bad lay or something."

"Come on, Colleen."

"What? Can't drink, can't smoke, can't say 'lay'?"

Bevy sat down on the end of the bed and stared down at her bumpy old feet. When she bit off a cuticle from her thumb, a strand of skin went with it, leaving a melonlike wound, pink and moist. What a night: Colleen in her basement, the Reverend in her bed.

"You all right?" Colleen asked, touching Bevy's back with her foot.

Bevy popped up and walked out the door before turning around. "I'm fine," she said. "It's been a long day."

"How many kids you got?"

"Five."

"Yikes." She rolled onto her back and let her hand slap down on her forehead.

"I got to get up and get everyone fed before church. Speaking of which, maybe you want to come?"

"That's real tempting, but I think I'll sleep in."

"Well, whenever you come upstairs, you'll be decent?"

"What a question." Like the dancer she once was, Colleen arched her back and sprung up onto her knees without using her hands. Her underpants were red and shiny. "What kind of woman do you think I am?"

"I think I might know."

"But you love me anyway." She puckered up and kissed the air.

CHAPTER 17

CORMIER'S ALL-TIME FAVORITE SUNDAY:
He wakes up in Robin's apartment. No hangover. With the help of the woman sleeping beside him, he's escaped his life downtown. From up here, he can see how sad it all was: the drunken debates about what was cool. Nerds in leather, wielding opinions, undersexed boys beating each other down, divvying up the unhappiness. He's left all that behind in spirit; a month from now, graduation day, he will leave it behind in fact.

Robin smiles at something in her dream. A gift is what this is. Love, perhaps. They met two months ago. Barnard girls, his roommate had said on the way to the party. Cormier escaped to the balcony, where Robin gave him a cigarette and said, "Let's talk about this party." She's more honest, more open, more in touch with her pain—her word—than any girl he's ever known; but then he never knew the others, not really. They were mysteries, even to themselves. Robin Birnbaum is knowable, reachable, real.

When he wakes up again, she wakes up too. No words. Slow is how they like it. Slow but hard. Sex with Robin is easy, was from the start. She can complicate a trip to the deli—she's all analysis and introspection—but sex for her is fun. Nothing he tries feels wrong. He puts his fingers in her mouth and she bites them. He says, "Oh, yeah" and she says, "You're really *fucking* me, aren't you?" She comes quickly. So does he.

There's a bench on Riverside that they call "our bench." That's where they eat bagels, drink coffee, and read the paper. Perfect silence.

The noontime sun gives way to something even better: rain, movie weather. They're compatible both in bed and in the theater. What more, really, does he need to know?

Back to her place for a joint. They'll see them all eventually but need the right one for right now. *My Dinner with Andre*? No way. *Raiders of the Lost Ark*? Absolutely.

Cormier is of the opinion that too much is the right amount when it comes to weed before movies and he has trouble with the advanced calculus problem known as the concession stand. He ends up fleeing, leaving his wallet on the counter, and Robin goes to retrieve it. When she comes back, he must rub and kiss her, and the teenagers next to them cheer. She takes his hand and leads him to his seat.

During the previews Cormier is so excited he has to stop himself from making noises. He wants to cluck like a hen, writhe like Iggy Pop.

The movie sucks him in and also delivers him back to himself, the way traveling lets you look at your life back home. He examines his insides with the passionate objectivity of a doctor. He takes an X-ray, does a scope, and discovers no shame. Fear, yes, but nothing terminal. He's up for the challenge sitting next to him.

With his friends a discussion of *Raiders of the Lost Ark* would be fraught with insecurity and gamesmanship. He couldn't admit to liking such a mainstream work unless he hinted that it contained value in the form of camp or irony, or unless he contrived to claim the counter-counter-conventional opinion, but with Robin he's free to give an honest reaction, which comes out as, "Jesus fucking Christ was that fucking good."

"A good matinee movie." Tepid praise, he thinks; indeed later he will learn that she liked it a lot less than he did, but it won't matter and its not mattering will matter.

As her apartment gets dark, they sit on the couch and drink beer. Robin has put on a Steely Dan record, and he likes them for the first time in his life. From now on, Steely Dan will feel to him like a rainy day in Manhattan. Monday is waiting, with his morning classes and his afternoon job, but there's life to be lived before then.

In bed she turns on the light. He's underneath her, inside her, and she's looking through his eyes into him. The courage he felt in the theater vanishes. Then they're hugging, trying to hold each other tightly enough.

The obvious thing to do afterward is to order in, but she wants to be sitting across from him in a restaurant. She wants to talk. "Don't worry," she says when he looks at her. "Nothing bad." He doesn't have to be talkative

with Robin, but he has to talk, has to tell her what he's feeling, which re-
quires him to know. He knows.

In the Chinese restaurant on Broadway they sit in the windowed area.
Her hair, wet from her shower, shines in the candlelight. That first night
on the balcony he didn't think she was beautiful, but he liked her face.
Now he loves it. "So," she says.

"So."

"What're you going to do?" she says. "What're you going to be?"

"I want to write movies." He's never told this to his friends at NYU or
to his parents. Only his friends from Hartsburg know.

"Yes. You *do*, don't you?" She giggles with excitement, officially becoming the greatest human. "You'll be good at it."

"Really?"

"Absolutely. It'll be hard, but so is everything."

"I'll probably move to LA."

"Would it be crazy if I moved there too?"

"No."

"I mean, I want to write and I can do that anywhere and—"

"Robin." He takes her hand in his, the way a man would. "I'm in love
with you."

She blows out, fluttering her lips. "Thank God," she says, and they
laugh.

"Say it too, please, so I can enjoy my pork bun."

"Oh." She puts down her chopsticks. "I love you."

"So I guess we're just getting started."

"Yup," she says. "We're going to California to write."

"And be happy."

"And be happy."

It seemed that his brain, that playful goblin, had given him a memory of
that Sunday to mock this Sunday. An anal-ice-pick sensation had awoken
him when it was still dark. *Good* morning! He'd raced downstairs to spare
Carly the final sounds of the 2003 Octoberfest Festival—the first of his
five sit-downs so far. The morning hadn't been a waste, however: he'd designed in his head a recliner that was also a toilet.

"I'm so not going to school tomorrow," Carly said into her cell phone upstairs, no less loud than Robin, who was in the kitchen having a long-distance whine-a-thon with her friend Julianne, also an embittered writer of fiction about embittered people. You Jewesses want to sell some stories? Try writing stuff that's fun to read!

He'd discovered that if he lay still and pressed his left temple against the leather and pulled the comforter up to his chin and cracked open his right eye, he could both watch football and not vomit. He was hot, unless he was cold.

"No, Jul," Robin said, "the work is not the only thing that matters. That is such trite, aphoristic garbage."

Yesterday the mail had brought Robin a depression in the form of five rejection letters. She could be despondent on any given day, but her depressions were discernible creatures, parasites that gobbled up her energy and hope, with life spans of up to a month. Meanwhile, Carly had it on good authority that Dave Chin had kissed her best friend and chief rival, Lisa Zimmerman. Somewhere in his ravaged body resided sympathy for his women, but he was hours if not days away from locating it. He would have bitten off the tip of his pinkie for quiet.

"But most people don't get it," Robin said. "Only other writers understand." She meant fiction writers. Fiction writers believed that their struggles were unique. They fancied themselves a kind of intellectual Marine corps, bonded in battles against the blank page, their hardships unknowable to the uninitiated.

Cormier farted without fear of leakage, a sign of recovery. But the less awful he felt physically, the more unable he was to ignore his emotional state. He'd dozed through most of *Meet the Press*, but had heard enough to know that Donald Rumsfeld had toyed with the host, Tim Russert. Rummy had kept lying and Russert had kept letting him lie and the war based on those lies raged on and Cormier couldn't do anything about it.

He could run for the school board, though. Yeah, he'd be great at that.

"Gross," Carly said, now nearby. "It smells like tuna fish in here."

"Squid sausage," Cormier said.

"Mom said you drank too much."

"Poison."

"Are those teal uniforms?" she said. "What is *wrong* with people?" Why couldn't he have one of those kids who hated spending time with her parents?

"How's the hangover?" Robin asked, blocking his view of the TV. The part of her stomach that was in her pants was puffy. Front bum, Stu called it.

"Remember when I had a hangover," Carly said.

"That was only two weeks ago," Robin said.

"My former life," Carly said. "Back when I didn't know I was disgusting."

There it was, sympathy. He wanted to hug Carly. And punch Dave Chin. Cormier could learn to deal with her having sex. He would have to. Move on in, boys. But if you treat her poorly, if you stoke her anxieties, I will make no attempt not to hate you.

"Dave doesn't deserve you," Cormier said.

"Dad, I don't know, but I'm pretty sure you're not supposed to judge sausage contests when you're a vegetarian."

"He was trying to appeal to the masses. This fucking town."

"We should move," Carly said. "Far away."

"We should," Robin said. "I mean, really. I'm serious."

Cormier needed to speak. "I thought we weren't going to have this conversation again until Carly graduated."

"Wouldn't that be good," Robin said, "a new start for us all?"

"If we moved to New York, I could go to, like, Trinity or Dalton, and it would totally help my chance of getting into the Ivy League."

Robin clapped: a firecracker. "Imagine living in a place where people read books."

"I'm going to go research other schools."

Carly walked out but Robin was still there, in front of the TV, front bum and all. "I'm so, so pissed off," she said. "Julianne thinks it's a sign of growth that I'm not taking the rejections as an authoritative judgment. But anger isn't healthy, and at some point, I need to question what I'm doing with my life if what I'm doing with my life makes me feel bad. I'm tired of feeling bad. Forget the psychobabble: I want to feel . . ."

Her stories were certainly better than many that were published, but he didn't love them. Did he like them? A few, yes, barely. Her work was bleak, humorless, and, at its worst, pretentious. But his opinion wasn't pure; it was colored by her view of his writing. He could forgive her for not liking his screenplays, but three years before, he'd written a memoir about his LA years that she'd called "romanticized to the point of dishonesty." She'd found things to praise, just as he found things to praise in her work, but their lack of love for each other's work was a problem. You could argue—and their therapist had—that it was their central problem. What they needed to do, Dr. Wolfsham had said, was to forgive each other and look elsewhere for professional validation. Simple as that.

When she stopped talking, he gave her what he hoped was a look of empathy and said, "I wish I were clearheaded enough to say the right thing."

"I wasn't asking you to say the right thing. Or anything. I just wanted you to listen, but I guess Mr. Stinky Fishface isn't even up to that."

"Squid," he mumbled as she walked away. "I had bad squid."

A twinge of tiredness behind his eyes suggested a nap but there was noise again. Carly, upstairs with her laptop, called out facts about schools they couldn't afford as Robin talked over her. "I'm so sick of this town," she said.

"You're sad, Mom, aren't you?"

"Sad? I'd love to feel sad. I'd love to feel *anything*. I'm numb."

Too much, Cormier felt, telling her that. Better for children to think their parents are invulnerable, or at least stable. Children will come to know the truth, but not, ideally, before they themselves are adults, and by then, if they're at all perceptive, they see that everyone is nothing more, or less, than a trembling glob of fear and want. Carly, though, had perhaps already intuited the truth about her mother, in which case being open with her was probably best, although there were different degrees of openness. His brain balked at doing any more work. So endeth the deep thought.

On TV a tight end hurdled a cornerback and fell into a first down. Coolness moved up from Cormier's legs, as though he were wading into a pond.

"We'll be back," Robin said from inside his dream, and the slam of the door woke him. He had been driving at night through the desert with his father. James was having an affair with a black blues singer who, when they got to the juke joint, turned out to be Robin. She needed a real man, James said.

Despite the dream, which was disturbing on at least three levels, his nap had restored him somewhat, and he decided to try to eat. He'd had nothing since number twenty-six, after which he'd jumped up and down with the husband-and-wife team that had won the Golden Sausage. Stu stole him away before he could do anything egregiously wrong, although now that he thought about it, telling Jenny that he wished her ass were number twenty-seven could not have been anything other than egregiously wrong.

In the kitchen he saw a box of yellow raisins, which brought back the sausage, the floor bouncing like an elevator, and déjà vu flickered until it became a memory: he's hustling to the bathroom after shotgunning a beer at Danny Pastorelli's, this house before it was his house. Back then he'd puked and felt better, but he was terrified of puking now. He put his chin on the toilet and begged his body not to feel nauseous.

If the nausea passed, he would be a better person. This was his vow. He would do his best not to complain or pity himself. He'd be grateful for what he had, for his family, his friends, his house, his health, his wealth. It was obscene that so often all this wasn't enough. It was a sin, a crime against people who had less. Now he wanted only one thing he didn't have: a body free of this horrible, horrible, horrible feeling.

His prayer was answered.

He stood up like someone not wanting to wake a baby and was indeed grateful. Grateful for his cushy Wigwam socks and for his recliner and for football on TV.

It was dark out, Sunday night feeling like Sunday night, and he longed to be with Robin and Carly. He feared that they weren't safe. An absurd thought, but he couldn't stop thinking it. He had the feeling, also irrational, that a winter storm was blowing in.

Football helped. The Packers were on and with Brett Farve playing football, with Brett Farvre throwing hard passes and getting hit and having fun, it was easier to believe that nothing out of the ordinary had happened.

But the game ended and he was alone again. He heard a sound—the cat door!—and ran into the kitchen, dropping to the floor so as not to scare Peeve off. The cute guy, munching away, didn't notice Cormier sliding on his belly, walking with his elbows like an army ranger. He let Cormier pet him and even stuck his behind in his face. "Hello, Peevey-poo," he said. "You're my sweet guy and I wuv you. Do you wuv me?"

Then he got serious, speaking man to man. "Listen, Peeve. I'm sorry I named you Peeve. I used you for a cheap joke. From now I'm going to call you—what? Pokey. That's the name of one of my favorite ballplayers." Cormier grabbed his head with both hands and pushed his ears down. "Do you like the name Pokey, Pokey?"

He squinted in affirmation and Cormier tried to hug him, but he slipped away and pushed through the door, into the night.

Cormier called Carly's cell, and when she didn't pick up, he called Jimmy. They'd spoken every day since the funeral but had barely touched on how Jimmy was doing, and now Cormier was calling not to comfort but to be comforted. He was going to talk to a friend who'd lost his wife about his irrational fear of losing his wife and daughter, although now that he thought about it, Jill's death and Cormier's fear were probably related, and even if they weren't, fuck it, he wanted to talk to Jimmy.

"I'm all right," Jimmy said. "You?"

"Not bad," Cormier said, not wanting to unload, after all.

"You watch the Bengals?"

"Some of it."

"They're going to be good." Jimmy was always optimistic on the subject of the Bengals, who had been bad for two decades and awful for most of that time. "Sorry to be short," he said, "but I've got to get dinner on the table."

"How's that going?" Cormier said. "The cooking?"

"I wouldn't know. Shannon cooks when she's here and when she's not, I just heat up one of the dishes people brought over. As a matter of fact, tonight we're going to eat something your girlfriend Bevy made. A casserole."

Bevy had made them dinner: what a strange world this was. "Talk to you tomorrow," Cormier said, and hung up feeling calmer but not calm.

Music, it dawned on him. Music was always the answer, whatever the question. He couldn't afford to take a chance. This was no time for cleverness or irony or even anger, no time for music of questionable strength or durability. He would climb into the tank that was *Born to Run*. The album had come out when he was a sophomore in high school, and it had spoken so directly to his restlessness and longing that upon hearing it for the first time he felt not so much joy as relief. *You're okay*, it had seemed to say, and that's what he heard now, as the harmonica wailed: *You're okay*. But he didn't believe it.

He was about to go search for them when he heard the Honda. He greeted them at the door, unable to conceal his wiggly-mouthed joy. "You're home," he said.

"You're gay," Carly said. "I know, I know, I'm not supposed to say that."

"Then don't," Robin said. "Uh oh. Bruce Springsteen. Could I have a Budweiser with tears in it, please?"

He took the grocery bag from Carly and kissed her cheek. "Maybe, like, a shower?" she said.

"It's great to see you," he said.

Carly had started up the stairs; now she turned. "You know I don't like it when you're weird," she said, and Cormier laughed. His daughter.

Robin put away the items that went in the fridge; he took care of the rest. Oatmeal on the top shelf, with the cereal. Almonds on the middle shelf, by the raisins, which he now dared to stare down. Healthy food on solid shelves in a bright kitchen.

When everything was put away, he said, "I know I'm a little gross right know, but do you think I could have a hug?"

She spread her arms. "Come here, icky boy."

As he hugged her, he knew that he would sleep well. He could hug her every day. She was soft and smooth and she would let him. He was almost disappointed when he got a hard-on. He humped her hipbone to the beat of "She's the One."

"Wall," she said. "That's not what this is."

"When's it going to be that?"

"Maybe the next time you're not hungover. Or smelly. Or drunk. Or anxious."

"I don't know if I can wait that long."

When he pulled away, he had to peel his cheek off hers. He looked at his wife, this person to whom he had woven his life. He wasn't sure if what he felt was closeness or distance, but it made excitement bounce from his gut to his chest to his mouth.

"I love you," he said.

"How's macaroni and cheese sound?"

"Perfect."

"It's that kind of night, isn't it?" She took down one of the heavy silver pots that hung above the stove. "Did you know it might snow? One of the earliest ever."

"Not *the* earliest?"

"I don't know and all of a sudden I couldn't care less. Listen, Carly and I talked about this moving idea. She's seriously interested."

"Of course she is. She had an awful week."

"It's deeper than that." Robin shifted to a whisper. "Does she seem good to you?"

"She's stressed out, but going to a cutthroat school isn't going to help."

"But think of the benefits: a smarter student body, better teachers."

"And my campaign?"

"That juggernaut."

"Wow. *Very* nasty."

"You have to admit."

"It's early. There's the debate next week, and Zev's coming."

"How about this? If you lose, we have a discussion about getting out."

"A discussion as in you say, 'Let's move,' and I say, 'Okay.'"

"That sounds about right."

"Can I say something?"

"On second thought, I don't want macaroni and cheese."

"When you were gone, I got really nauseous, but it passed, and I was so happy not to feel sick, and then I was just happy. I was happy about this house, and the two of you, the two of you above all, but everything else too, the oatmeal in the cabinet and macaroni and cheese on a Sunday night and those pots. I mean, *look* at those pots. They're like the crown fucking jewels. I know things could be better, but things are good."

"No," she said. "They're not."

CHAPTER 18

O**N SUNDAY BETWEEN SERVICES,** they drove to Kay's for a mid-afternoon meal, the twins and Colleen in Bevy's car, the older children in Peter's. This morning Bevy had hustled downstairs ahead of Peter and made a Mega-Egga, which was steaming in front of him when she asked if Colleen could stay. His face tight as he hunched over to tap out salt, he said she could stay for one more night; then they would see.

Bevy had told Colleen that Peter was taking a wait-and-see attitude, and when she hadn't made a comment or a face in response, Bevy had known she was short on cash. Likewise, if Colleen hadn't been so intent on staying with them, she would have passed on the meal, but not only was she sitting next to Bevy, she was wearing one of Bevy's dresses. Truth be told, Bevy didn't mind having a little leverage.

"But Mommy's from Texas," Kyle said.

"We both are," Colleen said. She spoke to the boys in a natural tone, as if they were grown-ups. It seemed like an odd way to be, but Karl and Kyle had taken to her. "Millions of people are from Texas," Colleen said.

"Millions?" Karl said. "Oh my gosh."

"They're precious, Bee," Colleen said, putting her feet on the dash. The red scorpion tattoo under her ankle had faded. "But I don't know how you do it. Five minutes with them, and I need—I'm done." Even if she'd stopped herself from saying "I need a drink" because she was shooting for room and board, Bevy was pleased that the girl was trying. Bevy wasn't naïve enough to think she could convert Colleen; if she'd had two years, not two days, then maybe. On the other hand, Bevy knew better than to underestimate the power of the Gospel. At Hilltop this morning, the sight of the Reverend had disturbed Bevy at first; it was like seeing the man she'd both cheated with and cheated on. But she was right where she needed to be, church. The message was about the sin of complacency in the face of sin, and Bevy took comfort in knowing that it was not among her flaws. God knew she was a fighter. She would never give in to sin, the world's or her own. Her mood was almost embarrassingly bright as the Reverend ended on a political note, tying together the war against terror and her very own school board race.

And it was her campaign that was on her mind as she pulled into the driveway of Peter's childhood home. Arch Cook had called this morning, and what he'd told her seemed explosive; for that reason, she'd kept it to herself.

But after she'd put her fruit salad sandwiches in the fridge, she found herself alone with Kay and couldn't resist. "How well do you know Annie Cormier?" she asked.

"Not very. We don't have much in common."

"You have no idea."

Kay was scrubbing a counter like she was sanding a board. The kitchen was open and bright, as was the sloping field it looked out on. Bevy liked the country feel of the place but was seldom at ease enough to enjoy it. "If you've got something to say," Kay said, "go ahead and say it. I don't care for coyness."

"It seems Annie Cormier has been carrying on with a history teacher at the high school. A black, *female* teacher."

Kay stopped scrubbing. "I don't believe it."

"It's true."

"I'm sorry to hear that."

Sensing Kay's sadness, Bevy felt bad she'd been breezy. This was no cause for celebration, whatever the political upside.

"I assume you know this has no place in your campaign," Kay said.

Bevy shouldn't have been surprised: Kay seemed to go out of her way to disagree with Bevy. In the early years, when they'd all attended the same church, Kay had been more supportive, a role model even. Sundays, in this very kitchen, Bevy would help with the meal and Kay would offer wisdom on everything from laying a table to saving the nation. In fact, it was Kay who'd first helped Bevy to understand the threat that homosexuality posed to marriage and therefore society.

"We're talking about the mother of my opponent," Bevy said.

"A child ought not pay for the sins of a parent."

"Do you figure it's a coincidence he wants schools to teach the gay agenda?"

"That's a separate issue."

"My goodness, Kay. Annie's lady friend could teach your grandchild someday."

"Another separate issue."

"No, it's not!"

Kay's raised eyebrows drew Bevy's attention to her own finger, which was pointed and shaking. She lowered her arm and, in a soft voice, said, "It's got to be relevant that Cormier's own mother is a practicing homosexual."

Kay opened the cabinet under the sink and dropped the sponge in the tiny trash can, the trash can of a woman with too much time on her hands. Her policy of using sponges exactly seven times was beyond irritating. "Love the sinner," Kay said. "I'm sure you Hilltoppers say that, but sometimes it doesn't seem to mean much to you. Well, it means something to me. If you want to try to save Annie, if you really care about her, I'll give you her address. But if you make a spectacle of her, I might—"

"What? What are you going to do?"

"Seventy-three years I've lived in this town. You don't want me as an enemy."

"I could swear you already are."

"Spare me your self-pity."

Bevy was about to say something sharp—self-pity!—but she saw Colleen through the window, taking a stroll around the house. She did a ballerina-like twirl—her shoes were off—and Bevy wondered if she'd snuck a line or a pill. She came in through the back door, and Kay looked down at her dirty, flaky feet.

"This is Colleen Stoddard," Bevy said, hoping Kay wouldn't remember her.

"Pleased to meet you," Colleen said.

"We've met," Kay said. "At the wedding."

If Colleen remembered the wedding, she wasn't about to apologize. Her motto, Bevy's too, used to be "No regrets." Mornings after, they would laugh and squirm and say, "No regrets." This, of course, was the kind of thing said by people with regrets.

"You know what I remember about that wedding?" Colleen said. She hugged Bevy from the side and kissed her ear. "How drop-dead gorgeous the bride was."

"Oh please," Bevy said.

Colleen rubbed Bevy's cheek. "Y'always were a blusher."

"Am not," Bevy said, although she could feel her heartbeat in her temples, and it didn't help that Kay was looking at her.

"This is some house you've got here," Colleen said. "It's like I stepped right into the pages of *Better Homes and Gardens*."

"Thank you," Kay said, handing Colleen a platter of chicken.

Peter's sister Laura arrived with her family, so there were fifteen people settling in. Colleen, already holding forth, was telling a story about a motorcycle trip to Mexico, and Ronnie was captivated. *There* was trouble. With Colleen visiting, Ronnie should have been the first person on her mind; but the first person on Bevy's mind these days was always Bevy herself. She had known the race would take from her family life; she had been sure it was worth it and now all of a sudden she wasn't. But Loretta was next to her; she could be a mother this second.

Loretta was checking her watch against the grandfather clock. She had her hair in pigtails, which brought out the smallness of her head. "Everything all right at school?"

"Was Colleen your best friend in Texas?"

"Yes, absolutely she was."

"But not anymore?"

"Well, I haven't seen her in so long. Your father is my best friend now."

"The other day Nikki said that we weren't going to be best friends anymore, because she and Taylor were getting really close."

"And what'd you say?"

"I told her it was fine with me, and that I have plenty of other friends who could be my best friend and it was silly, I said, ranking friends like that."

"That seems like a good thing to say."

"Yes."

"But?"

"Nikki was my best friend."

"Girls can be mean like that," Bevy said, wishing she could deliver Loretta straight to marriage. Nikki was Hilltop, and Bevy would try to resist the temptation to talk to her mother. "I know it's hard, but try not to take it personal. In high school you'll have a whole new group of people to meet. Maybe Brent will introduce you to his friends."

"Don't count on it," said Brent.

Brent gave Bevy a challenging look, and she knew not to react. Laura was in the kitchen tossing a salad. This, the dining room, was where Peter and his siblings, all homeschooled, had taken tests. What a schoolmarm Kay must have made.

"How about you, Brent?" Bevy said. "Anything going on at school?"

"Something pretty interesting happened on Friday. I was sitting in the lunchroom and I saw Ronnie talking to Carly Birnbaum-Cormier."

Ronnie pretended not to hear, keeping his eyes on Colleen.

"You want to tell me about this?" Bevy said.

Ronnie went all theatrical: closed his eyes, sighed, turned to look at Bevy like the effort took up his last bit of strength. "I can't talk to people?"

"She's not just people," Bevy said.

"To me she is," Ronnie said.

This shouldn't have bothered her, not unless she believed he would try to hurt her campaign. And she didn't; still, she felt exposed.

"Narc," Ronnie said, and flicked Brent's ear.

"Ow," Brent said, and put his hand on his ear. "That hurt!"

Colleen laughed, taking Ronnie's side. It was true that Brent came off as a bit of a weenie, but he was a good boy, and what did it matter what Colleen thought?

"May I have the honor of saying the prayer?" Colleen said.

Kay looked at Peter, who looked at Lou, Laura's husband. Lou bugged out his eyes and tugged on his collar. "I got the feeling everyone's looking at me," he said, imitating that comedian whose name Bevy never got straight. Lou was a ham even when there weren't pretty guests around. "Of course you may say the prayer," he said.

"Thank you, Lou," Colleen said, her accent on high. "I'd like to thank Almighty God for the tremendous meal we're about to eat. And for reuniting me with my dear old friend, and giving me a chance to meet her loved ones. Lord, I don't know why you brought us together after all this time, but I know it's a blessing, one I'm going to cherish, and you, Lord, are an awesome Lord, and you're . . . awesome."

"Awesome," Ronnie said, and then all the children said "awesome" instead of "amen." Even Kay didn't seem to mind. Colleen's presence wasn't causing any serious discomfort. As a matter of fact, this was about as loose as an event could be here.

"What are you looking for, Peter?" Kay said.

"Rice, or something?"

"Perhaps a tuber of some sort?" Loretta said. She was in one of her odd moods.

Something like horror rippled through Kay's face, and she darted into the kitchen. "Even Babe Ruth strikes out," Lou said, and Bevy laughed.

"My God," Colleen said. "How I've missed that laugh."

Steam streamed from the pie plate that Kay was gripping with oven mitts. "It's a little hot," she said, deadpan, and set the dish down by Peter. When he dug in, a burst of steam made him close his eyes, and once he'd scooped out a serving—au gratin potatoes—Bevy saw that the top layer was far past golden, almost burnt. Bevy might have taken pleasure in the screwup, but she sensed Kay's pain, and pain was not too strong a word. It surprised Bevy. She couldn't quite shake the idea that Kay never suffered. Which would have made her unique in the human race.

"Did you go to high school with Bevy?" Lou asked. He'd probably heard about the wild woman from their wedding but didn't seem to realize he was talking to her.

"No," Colleen said. "We grew up a couple towns apart. You know, it's funny but I can't remember how we met. Can you, Bev?"

"Through Betsy maybe?" In truth Bevy had a vivid memory of meeting her. Bevy walked outside at a party, and there she was, sitting on the hood of a car, wearing boots and short shorts, drinking with roughnecks, not caring what people thought. Bevy would come to learn that in truth Colleen cared too much what people thought, especially men.

"Bevy tells me you're moving to Rochester?" Peter said.

"That's right," Colleen said. "Should be quite a change."

"From West Texas?" Peter said. "I'll say. But Rochester is a good city, real down-to-earth. I used to go there on business. I bet you'll like it."

When Peter's eyes found Bevy's, she mouthed, "I love you." A lesser, weaker man wouldn't have given Colleen a chance, but Peter was treating her with respect.

"There's a great restaurant in Rochester called Nick Tahoe's," Peter said. "It's the home of the original garbage plate."

Kyle laughed. "Garbage plate?"

"That's right," Peter said. "You see, you get your choice of meat. I liked it with cheeseburgers." With his finger he drew two circles in the air; then, making like a fry cook, he scooped up the imaginary burgers and flipped them onto his plate. Peter was at his best when he was telling stories, showing oomph, talking with his hands. Too often he left his mind at work, but this afternoon all of him had shown up. "It comes with two sides," he said. "I usually went with baked beans and macaroni salad. They top it off with onions, mustard, and their special hot sauce, which has meat ground up in it. Then, if you know what you're doing, you mix it all up and scoop it up with buttered bread."

"Mercy," Kay said.

"Yuck," Laura said. " 'Garbage plate' is right."

"Quite literal," Loretta said.

"That's my kind of meal," Ronnie said, mixing up the food on his plate, and the twins followed suit, to Kay's obvious annoyance.

"You actually ate one of those garbage plates?" Laura said.

"Yup. Every time I was in Rochester," Peter said, and Bevy sensed nostalgia for his traveling days. He used to work for a rental car company; that was the job that had sent him to Dallas, where one morning he saw a woman on the floor of the airport. Like Bevy's, his life had changed for the better when they met, but he'd enjoyed his time as a single man. When not on the road, he'd spent a lot of time hunting and fishing and doing yard work with his father, who'd died of brain cancer on the same date as Bevy's father, one year later. During their very first talk, Bevy told Peter about Lamar. She didn't want to use his death as an excuse, but it was part of the reason she was where she was. She mentioned that he'd passed on March 5 and Peter's eyes went wide.

"I had a stronger stomach as a younger man," Peter said.

"Tell me about it," Lou said, patting his big belly.

"Your stomach gets weaker?" Brent said.

"Oh, the innocence of youth," Lou said.

"One time Walter Crane and me, he's who introduced me to Nick Tahoe's, we split three garbage plates. Not to boast, but . . ."

"Hon, I don't think that would qualify as a boast," Bevy said.

"Not to boast," Laura said, "but I had one and a half plates of slop."

"Not to boast," Lou said, "but I shortened my life by a week."

"Make fun all you want," Peter said. "It was quite an accomplishment for a small man. I was jogging every day back then. I was in great shape."

"You look like you're still in good shape," Colleen said.

"Nah," he said. In twenty minutes Colleen had made both Bevy and Peter blush. "I'm okay, but nothing like back then." He leaned toward Colleen, and now Bevy wondered if he was being too friendly. "Promise me you'll try a garbage plate."

"I think it'd be too much for me," Colleen said, pointing a finger from each hand at her trim figure. "But this food here is delicious."

Everyone agreed, but Kay, potatoes on her mind, had to work to smile.

"I like these potatoes," Brent said. "What do you call them again, au gratin?"

"Au gratin," Loretta said, using the French pronunciation. "It means, with grating."

"I'm sure everyone is real impressed," Brent said. "You're, like, the only person I know who takes French. I mean, what's the point?"

"She'll be able to understand the frogs when they talk down to her," Lou said.

"Frogs?" Karl said.

"Hey, Lo," Ronnie said. "Can you say 'cheese-eating surrender monkey' in French?"

"Right on," Colleen said. "*The Simpsons.*"

"You like *The Simpsons*?" Ronnie said, now truly smitten.

"I must have seen every one," Colleen said.

"I've only seen a few," Ronnie said. "It's banned in our house."

"And with good reason," Laura said.

"It's not as bad as you think," said Maureen, Lou and Laura's oldest child. "It's mostly about family values,"

"You cannot be serious," Laura said. "How about the depiction of the Christians who live next door? The Flanders."

"Sounds like you've seen the show a few times," Bevy said.

"I've been in the room when it's on," Laura said. "Lou lets the kids watch it because he wants to watch it himself."

Lou put on a sheepish smile and turned up his palms. "How else am I going to know if it's acceptable?"

"They speak French in several African countries," Loretta said. "It's a good language to know if you want to be a missionary."

This put a stop to the conversation. She didn't seem to realize her remark had come out of nowhere. "Do you want to be a missionary?" Bevy asked.

"Sometimes I think I do, but missionaries, I've noticed, are sometimes taken hostage or even killed, sometimes quite brutally."

There was another silence, and it was again up to Bevy to break it. "That's true, it's dangerous work. In fact, why don't we take a moment and pray for them."

Bevy joined hands with Loretta and Bobby, Lou and Laura's ten-year-old. Bevy said, "Let us pray for the safety of people doing God's work around the globe. Jesus Lord, may you watch over them and help them fulfill their mission."

Everyone amen-ed and got back to eating but a somber mood had set in. Talk of killing tended to put a crimp in the festivities.

"This is real nice," Colleen said. "Being with a family. I haven't had much family in my life lately, and this, well, it's good to be here."

"We're happy to have you," Kay said. Peter's decency didn't come from nowhere.

"It's rare, I think," Colleen said. "This kind of family feeling."

"We're practically like the Simpsons," Ronnie said.

"D'oh!" Lou said, and everyone laughed, Bevy the loudest, as always.

CHAPTER 19

SET OFF FROM DOWNTOWN by a Y-shaped intersection, the east end of Main Street was a pocket of poverty. Unlike the blocks between Main and the river, which had deteriorated in the last two decades, East Main had been shabby at least since the sixties, when James and Annie Cormier had gone looking for a space from which to launch their revolution. The Center hadn't changed the world, or even its block, but it had done a lot of good. Or prevented a lot of bad. Like thousands of other activists who had set out in the sixties to end poverty, Annie had spent decades trying to prevent it from getting much worse.

Only indefatigable people could work in social service, and Cormier was eminently fatigable, but Tuesday, waiting in the Center for Annie, he vowed to get involved. In the tutoring area, black and brown students hunched over books, and in the back room Elle Oliver, for the last decade Annie's replacement, taught stretching exercises to seniors. The sunlight pouring though the windows cast the scene in a heavy-handed, idyllic light, but there was no question that good was being done—a hands-on kind of good that was out of the reach of his campaign. Volunteering here plus serving on the school board plus writing columns plus reviewing movies would be a good life.

Since rising from the bathroom floor two days ago, he'd been having unmistakably positive thoughts. His mood was all the more mysterious because it ran counter to that of Robin, whose depressions he was usually at a loss to transcend.

The old women were now shaking their hips, and the jiggle of lumps made Cormier turn away. He was eager to get going—he and his mother were going to canvass for his campaign—but Annie, having hung up, was frowning at her computer. Her cluttered desk was in the corner: no offices here. "Are you good with computers?" she asked.

"Are you kidding?"

"This will have to wait for one of our high school volunteers. They essentially run the place. You should tell Carly to come down here."

"She's too busy as it is."

"Right. All those *clubs*."

"Mom."

"Star and her friends are going to canvass as well. And here they are."

Star was with a balding, blond-haired guy in red leather pants and a tall black guy who Cormier guessed was Star's boyfriend until he heard his effeminate voice. Cormier, ever hip, got the picture. "How's the campaign going?" Star asked.

"It's going," Cormier said. "I wish I'd done better in the debate."

"You did okay," Star said. The praise was meager enough for Cormier to trust it. Star seemed genuine, now and always. Hartsburg couldn't have been a comfy place for a black woman, but if Star had trouble being herself, it didn't show. "You've got to get meaner, though," she said. "These are not nice people you're dealing with. Christian, my ass. I know Christian. This ain't Christian, you hear what I'm saying?"

"Sing it, sister," said Terrence, the blond.

Annie gave Star's hand a quick squeeze. "Unfortunately, your friends in the black churches are joining forces with the white evangelicals."

"They're not my friends a-ny-more," Star said, poking Annie's sternum in time with the syllables. "But yeah, it's a problem. Scolds come in all colors, you know? As long as people are having sex, we're going to have trouble."

Annie said, "That's why the left needs to speak first to people's economic interests."

"Money first," Star said, "then the sex."

"Then the sex." Annie smiled, as did Star.

"So," Cormier said, venturing a fist-pump. "I really appreciate you doing this."

"No offense," Lester said, "but it's not for you; it's for us. If this town keeps heading in this direction, we'll have to up and move."

Star and her friends drove to the western part of the ward while Cormier and Annie walked across Main. "I need to talk to you about something," Annie said, slowing almost to a stop. A startled squirrel dropped an acorn and ran away. "I hear you drank quite a lot of beer at the festival."

"I concealed it pretty well."

"I'm not worried about the public perception. I'm worried that you drink too much."

He wanted to hip-check her into the pile of leaves on the Wendells' lawn, still wet from the Sunday-night snowfall. Annie, it seemed, was an optimist on all matters other than Cormier. While she was confident that murderers could be reformed, she seemed unsure if her son and his family could get their act together.

"I'm fine, Mom. I'm doing well."

They would visit houses belonging to people Annie knew, which were most houses; Cormier dreaded going for walks with her because they often required him to make chitchat. For someone who had lived in Hartsburg most of his life and who had a public profession, he had managed to maintain an impressive degree of anonymity. In the imagination of Hartsburgers, the town was a place where everyone knew everyone else, where people gathered round their neighbors in times of need. In fact, one of the things both he and Robin liked about the town was that it was possible to live and suffer in isolation—a quality that was threatened by the Christian soldiers. Indeed, the greatest counterweight to the Bevy Baers were not liberals per se but people like the Johns across the street who wanted to be left alone. For every busybody, there were several people who mercifully didn't care about you.

Annie stopped short across the street from Gladys Peters, who was sitting on the steps of her one-story home, smoking a cigarette under an American flag.

"Do I have to?" Cormier said. "She hates everyone."

"Perhaps she hates you less than she hates Bevy."

As he approached, Gladys moved only her eyes. "How's it going?" he said.

"Could be worse."

"I hear you," Cormier said, using a piece of banter he'd picked up from

Jenny Kohl. "So," he said, for lack of a better segue, "I'm running for school board."

"Are you that Bible thumper?"

"No, no, that's my opponent."

"I own a gas station out on The Drive, you see. Them Hilltop thumpers, for years now they give me a hard time about the signs I put up. Them signs is how I express my thoughts. And now there's a church nearby, and I got thumpers coming round, bothering me, bothering my customers. The way I see it, live and let live, you know?"

"I sure do. I'm your candidate."

"Let me see what we got." She looked at the flyer he'd handed her. The smoke from her cigarette didn't drift away; it swirled around her head like gas around a planet. "Are you for gays?" she said. "You see, I don't care for the gays either."

"Me neither," he heard himself say. "But live and let live, right? They should be able to do what they want."

"As long as they don't do it all over me."

"They won't," Cormier said.

"All right, then. Let me think on it."

He walked back to his mother feeling icky yet pleased, having done what needed to be done. He felt the way he might have if he'd bribed a maître d' or flattered his boss.

The houses on Middle Avenue, the formerly fancy part of town, perched a good eight feet above street level. As if out of frustration at the plummeting value of their homes, the people on Middle Ave., who presumably had the money to keep up appearances, chose not to. The whole block needed a paint job.

"Mildred Cox," Annie said as they walked up stone steps between rounded slopes of leaf-covered lawn. "Her husband, Fred, died years ago. Her daughter, Caroline, lives here in town, she's a hairdresser, and her son, Walt, is a gynecologist in Manhattan. If Mildred doesn't make mention of Walt's money, I'll give you a nickel."

"Care to make it interesting?"

"What do you suggest?"

"Five bucks."

"Goodness," Annie said. She wasn't tight with money, she said, she just preferred not to spend it. "You're on."

It took a moment for Mildred, peeking out from behind her door, to recognize Annie, but when she did, she smiled and shook both her hands at the same time.

"This is my son, Wallace," Annie said. "He's running for school board."

"My son lives in New York City," she said, shaking both of Cormier's hands.

"I went to school in New York City," Cormier said, glancing at Annie, who pushed her smile into a pout.

"Won't you come in for tea?" Mildred said.

"That's terribly sweet of you," Annie said, "but we have too much to do as it is."

"Oh poo," Mildred said.

"Election Day is only two weeks away," Annie said.

"I'll get biscuits!" Mildred said.

While Mildred went into the kitchen, they stood in a living room that was small and modern, as if a suburban town house had been stuffed inside the old Victorian.

Mildred, spry for a woman her age, zipped out of the kitchen. "Don't you just love peanut butter desserts." She held out a plate on which Nutter Butters had been arranged.

"I do," Annie said, taking a step back, "but I'm watching my sugar."

"Nonsense," Mildred said. "You silly goose!"

Cormier was glad to have no choice but to eat a Nutter Butter. If he were really lucky, some other old woman would force Devil Dogs on him. "Here's a flyer," he said. "It tells you who I am and why I'd be better than my opponent, Bevy Baer."

"She was here. Seemed like a nice Christian girl."

"Yeah, she's a fine person," Cormier said, "but her ideas would be bad for the schools and bad for our children."

"I'm a Christian myself, Methodist."

"But you wouldn't want to impose your beliefs on others, would you?" Annie said. "Because that's exactly what Bevy Baer would do."

"She had two biscuits."

"She's a Republican," Annie said, moving with Cormier toward the door.

Mildred followed, still holding out the plate. "Oh, I don't vote for Republicans."

"Then vote for my son." Cormier gave Mildred a military salute, a gesture that was threatening to become a habit, and took another Nutter Butter, to match Bevy's total. "And speaking of sons," Annie said as she stepped onto the porch. "How's Walt?"

"Oh, he's good, yes, very good. And rich!"

Once they were out of Mildred's eyeshot, he pulled a five-dollar bill from his wallet. Annie sniffed the length of it before putting it in the pocket of her denim dress.

"Never took you for a shark," he said.

"You didn't find my question organic?"

"About as organic as Nutter Butters."

"Poor woman."

"Something registered when you told her Bevy was a Republican. The problem is, I don't have a party affiliation."

"Oh, I know, but we might as well take advantage of the fact that there are still some blindly loyal Democrats out there."

"You really are a shark."

"I understand that politics is not patty-cake."

"Do you think Star's right? I need to get mean?"

"No, people don't like meanness. Star is a lot of things; politic is not one of them."

"She's pretty full of herself, isn't she?"

"Don't you like her?"

"She seems cool. I don't really know her."

"I need to tell you something."

She stopped in front of a driveway where a Cadillac was parked on the slant. Being irrational, he took a few backward steps and signaled for her to come toward him, removing her from the car's potential path. When she turned around, a yellow maple leaf, as big as a piece of paper, was draped over her shoulder.

"Star and I are involved," she said.

Cormier's first thought, fleeting and racist, was that Annie had lent Star money, that their involvement was financial.

"Involved romantically," she said just as he figured it out for himself.

She struck him as ridiculous, an old fool, and he almost laughed. It wasn't funny, though. "You couldn't wait till after Election Day?" he said.

"How heartless of me."

"I'm being selfish, I know that. I'm being selfish so I don't have to think about the fact that my mother just told me she's having a lesbian affair, which actually might not bother me if I weren't trying to win a school board race. I'm trying to win a school board race but my old columns make me look like a Hartsburg-hating traitor, and I'm married to a Jewish Manhattanite atheist depressive who didn't take my name and doesn't even hyphenate. As if that weren't enough, Liberace and his lover are out campaigning for me, and my mother is a Marxist who's dating a black lesbian who teaches at the high school. Meanwhile, I've given up lattes so as not to put off mainstream voters."

"Let me know when you're ready to think about someone other than yourself."

He realized that they were standing in front of the house that had once belonged to the Kettles. David Kettle had been his best friend in sixth grade, just before his family had moved away. Cormier had spent the night at his house several times. He remembered playing Risk, eating homemade french fries, and dry-humping David.

"Well?" Annie said.

"Still processing."

Annie had been in one relationship since James's death, with Henry, a doctor. Cormier had been happy for her because he had liked Henry. And he liked Star, so what was the problem? It wasn't the lesbianism per se; it was what? The trendiness, maybe. It was as if she were trying Tae Bo or Botox. He liked to think that Annie lived by convictions that couldn't be bent by the shifting winds of the culture.

"Hence the haircut?" Cormier asked.

"That had nothing to with it. They let you in the club even if you have long hair."

"I assume you don't, like, think of yourself as a lesbian?"

"I've never felt an allegiance to any particular label."

"Mom?"

"Oh, Wallace." She reached out to touch his upper arm, and the leaf peeled away from her shoulder. "I don't want to dump too much on you."

"Dump away. Dump, dump, dump."

"Fair enough. I've had two previous relationships with women, one before James and I were married and one after."

"After?"

"In Chicago, long before you and Marcie came along. I should mention that James also had a relationship with a woman after we were married. He knew about mine and I knew about his. We imagined that we were defying bourgeois convention."

"But Dad used to blast the whole free love thing."

"He knew of what he spoke. You see"—Dot Ferguson drove by, her Colin Powell face filling up the window, and Annie waved midsentence, with no sense of irony—"we learned that love comes in a beautiful multitude of forms, but that it is never, ever free."

"Does Marcie know?"

"She will soon. And I want you to tell Robin and Carly."

"About Star or everything?"

"That's your choice. I want all of you to know about this life I've lived."

He waited to speak. He had a tendency to tell people what they wanted to hear, only to jolt them with his feelings later on. Lesbianism wasn't Tae Bo, not for Annie and not for anyone. She still seemed like Annie, more so. But he wasn't thrilled.

"Are you in love with her?" he managed to ask.

"Quite, I'd say."

"You're happy."

"Extremely. Ridiculously. What is that phrase, 'happier than a pig in excrement'?"

"'Shit.' It only works if you say 'shit.'"

"I'd rather not. But that's what I am."

"I'm happy you're happy."

"Thank you, Wallace. You're such a good son."

He loved hearing these words, even as he disproved them by thinking again about the impact on his race.

"You're worried about your campaign," she said, reading him like no one else could.

"It plays right into their playbook."

"It makes me almost glad that Zev will be here. Speaking of sharks."

191

* * *

Maybe it was the new knowledge about his parents, maybe it was the effort to fight through the disinterest of strangers, maybe it was the lifeless face of his wife as she stared at the blank computer screen, but by the time he had installed himself on the couch in the study, his good spirits had left him. "I don't know why I just don't give up," Robin said, hitting the spacebar with her forehead. "Because I'm a masochist, that's why. I'm a big fat sadomasochist. But don't sadomasochists enjoy hurting themselves?"

"If you're really getting no enjoyment out of it—"

"No one *enjoys* writing."

"You used to."

"Did you enjoy being a writer?"

"I'm still a writer."

"You know what I mean."

"When I was writing screenplays? Yes, I enjoyed it, sometimes. There were days when it was just about my favorite thing."

"Oh please."

"It's true. It was right up there with seeing movies and having sex with you."

"None of that, okay?"

"Can't even talk about sex? Is this the Baer household? When I was writing well, I felt like I was getting away with something, like I was a kid skipping school."

"You're a fucking dork."

"That's nice."

She banged her forehead on the keyboard, again and again, then put her head in her hands. "I know I'm a bitch, a big ugly bitch. Do you think I like being like this?"

Cormier looked on as the man he wanted to be climbed out of his body like a ghost and comforted his wife. He held her and told her that he loved her, that he would love her even if she were the biggest bitch in the world. But the man he was, the boy, stayed on the couch, feeling hurt, wishing his wife weren't the biggest bitch in the world.

"I had my dream last night," Robin said. "The normal one, except I died. I used to think it was impossible to die in your dreams. Not so. I'm lying there in my coffin, crying, screaming, punching the sides. I know that I have three seconds of oxygen left, then two, then one, then I'm dead. Do you know what it was like, being dead? It was exactly like being depressed. It was like being alive and feeling nothing."

"I'm sorry," Cormier said.

"What are you sorry about?"

"I don't know," Cormier said. "That you're having such a hard time."

"A hard time. You make it sound almost pleasant. A hard time."

"Maybe you should take a break from writing. Get a job, maybe?"

"What would I do around here? Work at KFC? Yet more reason to move."

"You could volunteer at the Center."

"Yeah, that's what I want to do, get parenting advice all day long." She did an impression of Annie; the voice was the same as her Katharine Hepburn. "I have concerns that Carly's soul is not receiving proper nourishment."

Cormier knew that this was the depression talking, that she wasn't herself. Robin disagreed; she felt that her depression was an integral part of her, the source of her art, the swamp out of which her creativity grew. This was why she refused to take antidepressants. He had learned to accept her aversion to medication; what he couldn't accept was that she seemed to let herself get pulled down by the undertow. He saw little evidence of her trying to get back to the shore. When he had suggested this to her, she'd said that he didn't understand "the disease." He probably didn't, because he recoiled at her use of that word. But wasn't she wanting it both ways, calling it on the one hand a disease and considering it on the other her essential self?

"I want to tell you something," Cormier said. "Carly too. Would you call her cell?"

"Don't you hear that music? She's in her room."

"I don't want to yell and I'm too tired to get up."

"Ooh, vibrant." This had sexual undertones, a dig at his drive, yet it wasn't he who last night had removed his hand from her breast.

"Good evening, my dear," Robin said in her Annie voice, which had become vaguely British. "Your father requests your presence in the study."

CHAPTER 20

O N MONDAY, AS COLLEEN stood in the kitchen downing a glass of water—she'd taken her car in, then jogged back—Bevy was glad for the company. Peter had said she could stay until her car was fixed. Bevy, pushing her luck, had asked if he could give her a deal at his garage. He answered by mentioning the name of a cheaper garage.

Colleen was wearing black sweatpants as tight as spandex and a ribbed red thermal shirt, darkened by sweat at the collar. Bevy thought she detected alcohol in her smell. Cigarettes for sure, sweaty cigarette hair. "Can I fix you something?" Bevy said. She opened the refrigerator and stepped back to let Colleen see inside.

"I don't eat breakfast."

"It's almost noon."

"I'll take one of those Dr Peppers."

"That's diet. I've got the real stuff too."

Colleen paused to think with her fist on her mouth. Diet Pepper was good for a diet soda, but if you liked things sweet, and Colleen did, there was no contest. "Bevy Baer, are you trying to corrupt me?"

Bevy smiled as she handed her the can. Dr Pepper was what everyone drank in West Texas. "I'm headed out to Wal-Mart. I don't suppose you want to join me?"

"Why not? Just let me shower."

While Colleen got ready, Bevy checked her cell. For the second time in two days, someone had called from an unfamiliar cell phone and not left a message. Bevy worried that Wilma had called from someone else's phone, her boyfriend, Jerren's perhaps. Arch Cook had left a message displaying his usual charm: "Call me. Now."

When Arch answered, Bevy, feeling more and more comfortable with him, said, "Talk to me."

"I've got news."

"I figured."

"Star Mourning's been pushing the agenda in her classes."

"Mercy," Bevy said, placing a fork in the dishwasher.

"We want it fresh for the debate, so not a word about Star Mourning. But make sure you talk about homosexuality. We want to set it up."

"Thank you, Arch. I appreciate all your help."

"No problem. It's what I do."

"And you do it so well."

He giggled nervously, sounding like a fly buzzing around a light, and Bevy pictured him squinting. "Remember," he said. "Homos."

How nice it was to have a friend with her. The strangeness of being with Colleen hadn't worn off, but Bevy felt comfortable. It helped that Colleen was subdued, aiming to impress or unsettle no one. Her hair was in a sloppy bun, and she was wearing sunglasses and an old leather jacket over a sweatshirt. Mellow times like this used to be Bevy's favorite. Nights when they went out, Colleen had been a thrill but also a chore. Bevy had needed to keep up with her, to please her, to make her want more of her.

"Now I'm hungry," Colleen said.

"There's an Arby's up here."

"I don't eat that crap. How about that McDonald's? I can get a salad there."

The McDonald's was nice and clean inside, but Colleen, notoriously lazy for someone with so much energy, wanted to drive through. Ordering Colleen's salad, Bevy knew she should get the same thing—she hadn't made it to the gym in a month—but it just didn't appeal. "And a Big Mac," she said.

"Yikes," Colleen said.

"Nice up there on your high horse?"

"I got a nice view of your six hundred calories."

"I never knew you to be a killjoy."

"You're right. Sorry. I'm envious, is all. I'd love to chow down a burger."

"I'll tell you what. You take my Big Mac and I'll take your body."

"Your body's just fine," Colleen said, looking in the direction of Bevy's chest. Bevy gripped the steering wheel to shut off her view. "You're still hot, girl," Colleen said.

Bevy turned and smiled out the window, feeling like a fool.

"It's too bad you cover yourself up," Colleen said.

"What do you want me to wear, as a Christian mother of five. A bikini?"

This was a reference to Colleen's old getup of choice, a leopard-skin bikini top. Rape-wear, as dubbed by one of her charming boyfriends, who'd wanted to rein her in. Colleen wore them (she had two) when she was behind the bar. Bevy had been relieved when Colleen had started bartending—she'd figured the job would cut into their partying—but it turned out to be the beginning of Bevy's serious woes. She would sit at the bar, sipping free cocktails until Colleen got done, at which point the night really began. Meanwhile Bevy was trying to hold down a nine-to-five job.

"There's no need to show skin," Colleen said. "All I'm saying is, you could do better than that potato sack you're wearing."

"Give me five dollars," Bevy said. "And be quiet."

They ate in the car facing Wal-Mart. "I'm curious," Bevy said. "You won't eat a burger. A Pepper is a guilty pleasure. But you smoke cigarettes and drink and all that."

"Everyone picks their vices."

"What do your nights look like these days?"

"They don't look like anything right now. I'm moving, remember?"

"From one bar to another. It makes me sad to think of you still living that life."

"Pity, Bevy? Really? Deep down in your heart, beneath that potato sack of yours, do you really and truly believe I need pity?"

"Pity, no. Love, yes."

"After not seeing me for twenty years, love?"

"I feel badly we lost touch. But you're here now, and if you think I'm lying when I say I love you, then you really don't know me anymore."

Colleen stabbed her salad four or five times, stacking up a forkful. "Now, you know I like having good gut-spilling chats, but leave Dr. J. out of it, all right?"

"All right," Bevy said, but was at a loss for words. "How's your salad?"

"Fine. Your burger?"

"Good."

"Here's the thing that gets me," Colleen said. "It's like you view those years as some sort of dark chapter in your life. I can't say we were on top of the world—you were grieving and I was, well, I don't know, I was young—but I doubt there were two girls in all of Texas who laughed more than we did. We had fun."

"That wasn't fun."

"Oh no? Take me by my car and I'll show you pictures to prove it."

She understood why Colleen thought this. When you're twenty-one and dominating a dance floor and don't understand the concept of tiredness, you might not realize you're empty at your core. Probably five years into their six-year spree, Bevy was still getting excited for their nights out. Her favorite nights were when Colleen wasn't working. Before going out, they'd drink and do lines and dance around half-naked. Colleen's energy and anticipation would get inside Bevy, filling her with a sense of possibility, and she'd expect too much from the night. What exactly she wanted she couldn't name, but she always woke up feeling duped, the "fun" having vanished like smoke.

"I imagine our ideas of fun are pretty different by now," Bevy said. "At any rate, there are more important things than fun."

"Name two."

"Is it wrong for me to want you to be as happy as I am?"

"Who says I'm not?"

"You. You told me the other night you were sick of yourself. That's a direct quote. And you stole money, Col. A happy person doesn't do that."

"It's true I've had a bad run these past few years, mostly because I'd gotten lazy. I like my life when I'm working at it, you know? Changing, trying new things, which is what I'm doing right now with my move cross-country, so I'd say I'm actually doing pretty good. It's arrogant of you to tell me I'm not."

Bevy chewed on her last bite of Big Mac, which included a satisfying glob of special sauce. "It's arrogant to tell you how you seem to me?"

"I don't tell you how you seem to me."

"You could if you wanted."

"I don't want to."

"I *know* how I am."

"How are you?"

"Happy."

"What else?"

"You don't believe me?"

"There's got to be things in your life that are less than wonderful."

"Of course, Col. That's just common sense. But with how blessed I am, it's pretty pathetic to whine. I don't like to complain."

"I'm not asking you to."

"What do you want, then?"

"Nothing. I don't want you to tell me anything you don't want to tell me, but there's no way to have a real conversation without sharing your feelings."

This felt familiar. Years ago Colleen had wanted to hear about Bevy's troubles. If they weren't partying, they were analyzing themselves like their lives were movies and they were critics. Bevy would come to see that talking about problems helped create them. But Bevy had found it irresistible, the chance to show herself.

"I'm tired," Bevy said. "Run-down. Overloaded. Granted, I chose to run for school board, so I'm a lot busier than I had to be, but it's a good thing I'm doing and I think people—my friends, especially—could be more supportive."

"They know you're having a hard time?"

"They could guess it."

"You haven't told them?"

"I can't see myself admitting I bit off more than I can chew."

"Why not?"

"It'd make me sound like a bad mother."

"No, it wouldn't. If they think that, they're not good friends."

"I'm just not in the habit of telling them about my difficulties. Hilltop's like a big family, but I wish there was more . . ."

"Honesty?"

"No."

"Intimacy?"

"Maybe."

"You're lonely, Bev."

"No, I'm not. I'm not. But it's true I'd like a friend like, well, like you used to be."

"Tell me about it. It's hard to make friends like that as you get older."

"I want to tell you something," Bevy said. "But it's embarrassing."

"Embarrassing? This is me, Bevy."

Colleen, it was true, had seen Bevy at her worst. To this day Colleen was the only person besides Peter who knew that her accident wasn't an accident. Two weeks after her father's funeral Bevy drove a car into the side of a supermarket. She'd told herself that she wanted to join Lamar; the truth was, she'd swerved toward the brick wall not because she'd believed in heaven but because she'd feared she didn't. For the first week, Colleen slept in the chair next to Bevy's hospital bed. Most everyone else—fearful or judgmental of Bevy's wildness—stayed away. Colleen showed up.

"When I was making love with Peter," Bevy said, "I thought about my pastor."

Colleen looked away, probably to smile. "Is he some stud preacher man or what?"

"I shouldn't have told you."

"Sorry. Okay, let's see. My churchgoing days were limited, but I don't recall religion putting that kind of thing off-limits."

"I guess you didn't make it as far as the Ten Commandments."

"Oh. Well, let's look at it rational. I assume it gave you pleasure." Colleen looked at her and she gave no reaction. "Which means it made Peter feel good. So who's worse off? I mean, just think about all the damage done every day everywhere. The violence and betrayal and deceit, all the hurt, everybody ripping everybody to shreds. A thought in the privacy of your own mind—damn, Bev, cut yourself some slack."

"I don't deserve it."

"Yeah, you're a horrible woman."

"I am."

"A real wench."

"Maybe."

"Definitely."

They were both smiling now and Bevy couldn't deny that she felt better. What was it about confiding that made you feel hopeful?

"Where are you going?" Colleen asked as Bevy backed up. "Wal-Mart's right there."

"That's a curb."

"Why have a truck like this if you're going to worry about curbs?"

"I can't just drive up on there."

"Why not?"

"It's illegal."

"Look at the way they set this up. They want us to be rats in a cage. We're from Texas, baby. We can drive where we want."

"Don't mess with Texas," Bevy said.

"That's what I'm saying."

The SUV barely noticed the curb, dirt and wood chips flying up as Colleen let out a "Yee-haw" that Bevy could hear even over the sound of her own laughter.

The greeter in Wal-Mart, an old Hispanic guy, gave them an especially warm hello, and Bevy remembered what it was like to be part of a duo that turned heads. Sometimes she'd felt overshadowed, but she'd gotten more attention than she would have on her own. There was something about two women together that got men stirred up.

Bevy went to the food area while Colleen went to look at clothes. Thank God for Wal-Mart prices. She shopped off her own list and also picked up essentials for Pauline and her family. If Hilltoppers came forward and acknowledged a need, people helped you fill it. The Baers had never asked for help, but in the years when Peter was getting the dealership off the ground, Bevy had liked knowing there was a safety net.

By the time she'd made it to produce, her last stop, Bevy had been there for the better part of an hour, and she wondered what Colleen was up to. It was strange to trust and mistrust someone so much at the same time. Despite herself, she imagined Colleen living in Hartsburg. More miraculous things had happened. But if Bevy was going to fantasize about it, she had to start praying on it, so she bowed her head.

"Are you all right?"

The gruff voice was familiar and when she looked up, she saw Cormier's friend, the bug-eyed little fellow. She wanted to scold him, interrupting her prayer like that. But she realized that he was truly concerned about her. The poor worldly. It was like someone in a burning building fearing for someone down on the sidewalk.

"You're Wallace Cormier's comrade," she said.

"Comrade." He pointed at her with a fat finger, yellow and gnawed bloody around the nail. She had compassion for the man but wanted him to be far away. "That's pretty good." He picked up a grapefruit and pinned it with his chin against his chest, then let it fall into his hand. "Whoops. There goes my goiter."

"I need to get moving."

"Just wait, one second. Please. I've got a question for you." He picked up another grapefruit and put both of them under his shirt, making fake breasts the way a child would. "Do you think I'm going to Hell?"

Bevy pushed past him, leaning on her cart and surging with long strides toward the leafy greens. She finished in a hurry, not bothering to bag her veggies.

Colleen found Bevy at the register and pretended to sneak a package of tank top tees into her items. "Leave it," Bevy said. Peter barely ever checked receipts, and even if he did, he would think the shirts were for Ronnie.

The Bumpers' small house—yellow with dark green trim and shutters—was probably the best-kept on Deeb Street. It had been painted this century, curtains framed the windows, and there were fenced-in flowers and raked lawn on both sides of the walkway. The houses nearby, by contrast, looked looted.

Bevy asked Colleen to stay in the car, figuring that she should give her gift in private. As it turned out, Pauline showed no sign of discomfort or embarrassment. Bevy was relieved—she'd brought food to people who couldn't meet her eyes—yet she felt that Pauline could have been more grateful. "Stay for coffee?" Pauline said.

"I can't," Bevy said, wishing she'd allowed time for a visit. It was rude to rush off even when you'd brought a gift. Especially when. She watched Pauline dig into the groceries. Her nonchalance probably had to do with her disability; if she were prone to embarrassment, she could never leave the house. Maybe she was erring on the side of not seeming grateful, but when she pulled out the double chocolate Milanos and said, "Ooh. Pepperidge Farm," Bevy felt plenty thanked, and was glad she'd included a treat.

Pauline put food in the lower cabinets where most people would keep pots. The appliances had been spaced out to make room for stepladders that she could use to reach the higher shelves. It was a shelf above the kitchen table that caught Bevy's attention: a shrine to Zach, with photos old and new, everything from a grade school picture to a shot of him in his army uniform. With his round cheeky face, he looked like his mother, although his hair was a lighter brown. You couldn't help but notice his arms, wiry strong as he held a basketball above his head. He looked kind.

"I wanted him to be with us when we ate," Pauline said.

"It's lovely," Bevy said, wondering about Zach for Loretta. But the math probably didn't work: a six-year difference in age.

"There's something about your first child. I don't love him more than Lucy, but I love him different. Maybe I'm just having these thoughts because he's over there."

"I doubt it. Zach was there with you when your life changed."

Pauline, a loaf of bread pressed to her breast, looked at her, and Bevy felt seen-through, in a good way. She had two thoughts, each crushing: that she might give her son to the military, and that Pauline already had.

"Oh," Pauline said, realizing that she'd mashed the bread, and let it drop. She had to get on her knees to pick it up. "You bring me nice whole wheat and I go and ruin it."

Feeling guilty for having judged her, Bevy crouched next to her and, like an idiot, touched the bread instead of Pauline. "There are still some good slices."

"You're right." Pauline blew out, and her bangs lifted. "So," she said, standing up. "How's the campaign going?"

"Good. There's a debate next week."

"I'll be there." Pauline hugged her, her hands reaching only to Bevy's ribs, and said, "Thank you so much. I really appreciate it. Ricky will too, but I doubt he'll say anything about it. Too proud, you know?"

"What's the matter?" Colleen said as soon as Bevy got in the car.

"Nothing."

"Come on, Bev."

"Talk to me," Colleen said, squeezing the back of Bevy's neck.

"Oh. That feels good." She twisted at the waist to give Colleen a better angle, and when Colleen started using both hands, Bevy opened the door and swung her legs around. Colleen gripped her shoulders and applied sharp pressure with her thumbs. Physical strength was an accident of birth, but Bevy had trouble not seeing it as a moral virtue. Right away Bevy felt both sleepy and refreshed, like she was shaking off a nap. She was surprised by the sound that came out of her; she hadn't meant to moan.

"If nothing's wrong," Colleen said, "what's all this? It's like a tangled cord."

"That's normal."

"You've got a lot on your plate, Bevy Baer."

She moved her hands up to Bevy's head, which was her favorite thing, a head massage, and Colleen remembered just how Bevy liked it, a mix of rubbing and scratching, with a focus on the area above the ears.

"Pauline's son's in Iraq, and I got an inkling of what she was going through. We're considering the military for Ronnie, but seeing Pauline . . ."

"Yeah, don't."

Colleen knelt on Bevy's seat so that she could reach the front of her head. While Colleen massaged her temples, Bevy leaned back into her chest and breathed in her oatmeal lotion, which made Bevy thirsty. "Don't what?"

"Don't put Ronnie in the military."

"It's not like he's got a lot of options. And it might be good for him."

"It might end him too."

"That's a risk families have to take. Otherwise, well, we wouldn't *be* a country."

"I don't see politicians or CEOs sending their children off to Iraq."

Bevy's hairdresser had said the exact same thing. She wasn't sure if it was true, or what to make of it if it was. "Wow," she said as Colleen poked her cheeks.

"Yes, ma'am."

"My smiling muscles."

"Ronnie doesn't need the military," Colleen said. "He'll do fine. He's real smart—I don't care what his grades are—and he's handsome. The boy's beautiful."

"Thanks," Bevy said, referring to the massage, not to the mothering advice, which, coming from Colleen, Bevy couldn't take seriously.

"My pleasure. I love helping people feel better in their bodies." She gave Bevy a from-behind hug, and lifted her off the seat, then arched her back, arching Bevy's as well, and with her knee under Bevy's tailbone, bounced in such a way that Bevy's back cracked, her entire body falling into line.

The physical comfort brought joy, but it was the slippery kind of joy that was a sister to sadness. Driving along Riverfront, Bevy felt so good she wanted to cry. Maybe in heaven, joy never faded.

Colleen turned on the radio and found a rock-and-roll station. "Can't hear myself think," Bevy said, turning it down.

"That's the idea. You don't listen to music anymore?"

"Country, sometimes, not rock."

"Who can tell the difference these days?"

This was the Doors: "Break on Through." Bevy was amused that a song could come on and she could know it. Probably sing along if she'd cared to.

"This sure's not Texas," Colleen said, looking upriver from the bridge toward the old factory. "It was a good feeling, leaving."

Bevy knew the need to leave—she wouldn't have kept it together if she'd stayed in Midland—but Colleen was kidding herself. You brought yourself with you.

Colleen danced with her eyes closed to the Doors, then to Tom Petty. "The Waiting," Bevy had to admit, still sounded pretty good after all these years, and she let herself miss the days when she used to drive around and listen to Tom Petty. She wasn't happy back then, and she wasn't free, but she was young. And had days off. "I miss the times when you and I would just hang out," Bevy said. "Listen to music, go get a bite."

"Go to the drive-in."

They used to go to movies they knew would be bad and talk the whole way through. "Yeah," Bevy said. "That was fun."

When Hilltop came into view, she looked at Colleen for a reaction, but she still had her eyes closed, her long, thick lashes reaching almost to her cheeks.

"The twins have sure taken a shine to you," Bevy said as they pulled up in front of the school. "Why don't you go inside and get them?"

"All right, but if they start calling me Aunt Colleen, I'm going to stop being so nice."

Bevy grabbed her arm before she could get out. The leather of her coat was thin, like a glove's, and Bevy could feel the muscle of her biceps. "It'd mean a lot to me if you joined us here Wednesday night."

"Sure, why not? I'd like to get a look at this preacher."

CHAPTER 21

THE HARTSBURG INTERSTATE AIRPORT was on a barren road not far from Hilltop. Most visitors flew into Columbus and rented a car, but Zev Dreskin, a New Yorker through and through, didn't drive. Cormier, having spent the early afternoon canvassing, arrived late; Zev was standing in front of the little airport, which looked like a public bathroom. He wore a charcoal gray trench coat over his suit and held the smallest umbrella Cormier had ever seen. His hair was slicked back. He was smiling.

"It's the candidate!" Zev said, tossing his bag into the backseat. After a man-hug, made even more tentative because they were sitting, Zev stuffed the umbrella into a leather tube the size of a cigar. "This fucking car," Zev said as Cormier accelerated. "I was hoping there'd be a rental car place at the airport."

"Don't worry about my Saab. My mother is having a lesbian affair with a black teacher at the high school."

Zev looked at him, then let out a quick laugh like a sneeze, his mouth dropping into his hand. "How do you feel about that?"

It was amazing that Robin had left it to Zev to ask this question. Both she and Carly had been annoyingly unfazed. "I'm not sure. I'm having trouble separating it from the politics."

"Tell you the truth, bro, it's like a drop in the ocean."

"You watched the debate."

"You were just bad, not terrible, but *she*, she's a talent. It turns out she's getting coached by Arch Cook—he's a big outside-the-Beltway guy, with ties to the retarded right. Which makes my task all the more fun." He rubbed a clear spot in his window, peeked out. "I could use a stiffy."

"A penis?"

"What'd I tell you about jokes?"

"I like my jokes."

"A funny thing happened on the way to the forum?"

"We only have beer and wine at my house."

"A bar, then. A dive."

"I know just the place."

Tucked behind a warehouse on Lincoln Ave., Jed's Tavern couldn't be seen from the street. In a different town, one with tourists and college students, Jed's would have been ruined by tourists and college students. It was shaped like a spatula, with a bar in front and tables out back by the jukebox. Jed's had no dartboard, no pool table, and no windows—nothing, in other words, to distract the patrons from the task at hand.

Cormier had frequented Jed's in the weeks before Robin moved to town. The day before she arrived, six days before their wedding, Cormier had gone to Jed's with Stu and Jimmy for a bachelor party, staying from noon till midnight, leaving only to get meatball subs that they sucked down in the parking lot. Stu for some reason kept punching in "Shakin'" by Eddie Money, and on the fourth go-round, the bartender unplugged the juke. Stu went ballistic and the three of them got tossed. Cormier walked back to the house where his father lay dying. Before going up to his childhood bed, he sat on the porch and smoked a cigarette and thought, *My life is about to change.*

And it had changed—in short order, he had a house, a wife, a daughter—but in some ways his life had not changed, not then, not since. On the downside, he was still looking to make his mark on the world, express himself, be brave, whatever—whatever it was he'd always wanted he still wanted. On the upside, he was still doing things he'd always done, things he was increasingly willing to acknowledge he loved. Here he was, for instance, on a stool in Jed's, sipping a Bud and listening to the Allman Brothers.

"The one chick in here has no teeth," Zev said.

"I think her name's Desdemona, believe it or not."

"Actually, her mouth might make for nice nice-nice, you know?"

"I take it you and Denise broke up."

"More or less."

"Who're you calling?"

"Dreifort. Got to assemble the brain trust."

While Zev persuaded Dreifort to join them, Cormier felt a hand on his shoulder and smelled Stu: Old Spice and Wal-Mart, that stale popcorny odor. "Welcome home, Wally-wood," he said. "About time you got back where you belong."

"Stu, Zev. You two might have met before." Again Cormier was merging his different worlds, but he was confident that Stu and Zev would transcend barriers of class and culture to unite in their common cause: roguery.

"I'm not sure if we've met," Stu said, "but I saw you in that movie *Wall Street*."

"That's funny, because I saw you in that movie *Deliverance*."

Stu barked a laugh and clapped. "I love it."

"Want a shot, Billy Bob?" Zev said.

"Is pig pussy pink?" Stu said.

"Speaking of *Deliverance*," Zev said, "My friend's got a cabin in West Virginia. This weekend, Wally, you and I are going to the mountains to prepare for the debate."

"I've been itching to do some hunting," Stu said. "Can I join you?"

"Absolutely," Zev said. "That's perfect. We'll let the press believe Wally's going on a hunting trip. What kind of car do you drive?"

"Le Sabre," Stu said.

"Ooh," Zev said with a wince. "Is that French?"

"Yeah. It's like a Le Car." Stu looked at Wally and thumb-pointed at Zev as if to say, Where'd you get this guy? "It's a Buick, fucknut."

"Perfect." Zev froze just when he was about to take his shot of Jack, leaving his thick lower lip hanging as his eyes tracked the new arrival, a blond in a cowboy hat. Cormier couldn't see her face, but once she'd taken off her leather jacket and sat down at the end of the bar, he saw a toned arm and heavy breast.

"I just came in my panties," Stu said.

Zev shot his shot, slapped his cheek. "How do I look?"

"Perfect," Cormier said, and Zev made his way toward the blond.

"The guy's slicker than a rat's ass," Stu said, taking Zev's seat. "He's got stones, though, I'll give him that." It was remarkable that Zev had become someone who hit on foxy cowgirls. At NYU he'd been as nerdy as the rest of them, although he had been unique in his capacity for enjoyment. Unlike the other guys, for whom movies and music and even food had been burdens—things about which they needed to form correct opinions—Zev had been a hedonist, a consumer not a critic. In this regard, the man he'd become wasn't a surprise. He now had the confidence to indulge *all* his appetites.

"You seen Jimmy lately?" Cormier said.

"Not for a bit," Stu said. "We bowl next week. I'm hoping he comes out for that."

The bar became too bright, and an unmistakable body shape stood in the doorway. The day had turned sunny and Dreifort was letting in the light. "Shut the goddamn door," Desdemona said, and he obliged, but not before offering his Nixonian wave.

"I sense the presence of righteous riff-raffians," Dreifort said, inching along with his cane. "Sergeant Zev? Cormier?"

"Right here, Marlin," Cormier said, and between Dreifort's weak eyesight and the shift from light to dark, it took him a good twenty seconds to see Cormier.

"Can I get you drink?" Stu asked.

"Alas, with my unhearty heart, alcohol aside from the rubbing kind is verboten. But many thanks, whoever you be."

"I met you at Wally's. I also took your class back in . . . seventy-five, I guess. When I showed up for it, I thought it was pretty good."

"That's very kind of you." He put his face close to Stu's and opened his mouth to squint. "Are you the Gabe Kaplan fan?"

"Who?" Stu said.

"I had a student back in those days, a roughhewn fellow like yourself, who made it his mission to argue for the greatness of Gabe Kaplan. His passion persuaded me to set up a screening of *Welcome Back, Kotter*, and it was then that I did indeed discover greatness in the personage of John Travolta."

"What?" Cormier said, venturing an impression of Vinnie Barbarino, the clueless character played by Travolta, but his humor was, as usual, too subtle to register.

"As much as I'd love to drop to a stool and talk Travolta," Dreifort said, "I need to head back to the homestead posthaste. Where is Zev?"

"Right here, my man." Zev and Dreifort shook hands and Cormier smiled at this convergence of characters.

"Struck out, hunh?" Stu said.

"Au contraire, no hair," Zev said. "I put her digits in my BlackBerry."

"Well done!" Dreifort said. "Oh, how I yearn for the days of yore."

"I can't understand a word anybody's saying," Stu said.

"I used to imbibe bodaciously," Dreifort said. "Back then there was hardly a night that didn't end with a maiden's digits in my blackberry."

"I think I'm grossed out," Stu said.

"That's a first," Cormier said.

"Let's go to the back," Zev said. "Billy Bob, you're welcome to join."

"Politics? Fuck no. But count me in for this weekend."

"West Virginia," Zev said as they walked, single file, to the back.

"Mountain mama," Dreifort said. At the sound of Dreifort's voice, the cowgirl turned around and smiled at Cormier. She was older than her body led you to believe, with hard-life wrinkles and a not-small nose that suggested a touch of Mediterranean blood. Definitely foxy. Definitely not from Hartsburg.

There was a single booth in the bar. The table that belonged in the nook had been replaced with an army-green wicker coffee table, on which Zev rested his shiny, thick-heeled shoes. Sitting on the end of the booth, Dreifort clasped his hands underneath his thigh and carried it into alignment with his other one.

"Ah, Stephen Stills," Dreifort said, referring to the music. "If only the task before us were so pure or inspiring. Bevy has defined you into a corner."

"Yeah," Zev said. "No one seems to know what he stands for. Fuck, I don't even know what he stands for."

"That's not fair," Cormier said, kicking Zev's shoe. He wished he had the wherewithal to go word for word with these guys. It was his *life* they were planning. Robin seemed to be anticipating—looking forward to—his defeat and their subsequent move from Hartsburg. If Cormier lost, he might be eager to move, but it was a choice he didn't want to have to make. Now, on top of *really* wanting to beat Bevy Baer and Johnny Wedgwood, he *really* didn't want to lose.

Zev took his feet off the table and leaned forward, as if the people at the bar could hear him, or cared to, over the sound of the juke, now playing "Lord of the Thighs." Foxy cowgirl danced foxily on her stool while Stu, a fan of old Aerosmith, bounced his head with bulging lip. Zev said, "I'll help Wally become . . . decent. Meanwhile we've got to take Bevy Baer down a notch or two."

"Moralists, like giants, fall hard," Dreifort said.

"Come on, guys," Cormier said.

"Did I not warn you that the battle would get bloody?" Dreifort said.

"I'll play, you know, hardball. What I won't do is violate my principles."

"And I don't doubt that your principles are principled," Dreifort said, "but this race isn't about you. To be deathly frank with you, it won't be long before my maker makes what he will of me, and I'll pass more peacefully into the unknown knowing that my town is taken care of. Sure, Alex, I'll phrase it in the form of a question. Will the rest of us, Cormier, be able to afford your principles?"

"I can be tough. I'm just not willing to do anything immoral."

"Immoral?" Zev said, as though unfamiliar with the word. "I've got to say, Wally, I'm a little concerned: I'm giving you a week during a campaign cycle—an odd year, yes, but that doesn't make my time any less overpriced. My point is, do you want to win?"

Cormier nodded. "More than you know."

"Hallelujah." With two hands, Dreifort brought his cane to the floor as if planting a flag and stood up. "Some advice for Tuesday night, W.C.: Consider the importance of not being earnest. You made that fire-and-brimstone broad seem like Carol Burnett." He did his wave, supplementing it with a peace sign. "May a piece of ass be with you."

"Wow," Zev said, watching Dreifort give Desdemona his wave. "How'd he happen? Is that drugs?"

"I don't think so. I think he has some sort of autistic thing going."

"A savant maybe: he was on the money again. You were too heavy."

"I'll accept that, but the problem is, Bevy doesn't come across as fire-and-brimstone. That's what's maddening: they've figured out how to conceal how wacko they are."

* * *

When you went to Jed's at night, you courted oblivion; you fell down a hole and didn't climb out till the next morning at the earliest. But when you went, and left, during the day, as long as you didn't have more than three drinks, you emerged with heightened senses, saw things anew, especially when you were looking at the town through the eyes of a visitor. In the early clear-sky twilight, Lincoln Ave. was dim yet vivid, tinted blue. On the island that split the four lanes, a wailing toddler stood in a shopping cart pushed by a thin ratty man who wore no shirt under his jean jacket and jeans—a Texas tuxedo, Robin called it. Behind them ambled a woman, handicapped or maybe just obese, contorting her body like someone taking off a jacket while driving. Beer cans and cigarette packs adorned the low, prickly thicket that lined this stretch of roadside. Who knew there was plant life on Lincoln? In a box of brightness a man with a beard creeping up toward his eyes brought his hands to his mouth in rapid succession, munch munch. French fries, perhaps, or fried shrimp.

Stopped at the light, they could hear the fat woman shouting: "I can wipe my own ass, Sonny. I can. I swear to God, Sonny, I can wipe my own ass." Cormier's guess was that she was speaking metaphorically, but the image in his mind was all too literal.

"I can't believe you live here," Zev said.

It was a relief to get to the bridge, which offered a view that was also bleak but in a classic death-of-manufacturing kind of way. With the river low, mud was visible on both sides and you could smell it.

In the past, Cormier had been annoyed by Robin's fondness for Zev—his wife and his friend seemed to have nothing in common beyond their New Yorkness and Jewishness (which sometimes seemed like the same thing)—but he was glad for it now. Zev might be a welcome distraction for Robin, who perhaps had never been lower.

As it turned out, Robin had already provided for a distraction in the form of the Clymers, whom he hadn't seen since his campaign kickoff, and another couple, Lenny Finch and Belinda McNaughton. They were all sipping red wine in the living room when Zev and Cormier walked in.

"How's my sweetheart?" Zev said as he hugged Robin.

"I smell cigarettes," she said.

"That would be the essence of Jed's," Zev said.

"I can't believe Wally took you there," Paul Clymer said.

"When in Rome," Zev said, "drink your face off."

Lenny smiled until Belinda looked at him. A sculptor with a studio in an abandoned department store on Main, Belinda was the dominant one in the couple, at least when it came to matters of cultural taste. Lenny, a lawyer, sometimes sneaked away from their TV-less house to watch sports with Cormier. He liked Lenny. He liked Belinda too. What he didn't like was the smugness that prevailed when they all got together.

"Jed's is frightful," Paul said. "Even for Hartsburg."

"How would you know?" Zora said.

"Wally took me there once. It's a pit, an absolute pit."

"It's the best bar in town," Cormier said.

"A dubious distinction," Belinda said.

"Best fucking bar in the country," Cormier said, and Zev laughed.

"Looks like someone had a little too much bar," Robin said. "Wall, everyone's staying for dinner. I was thinking we'd order Thai food."

"It's edible," Belinda said to Zev.

"I like everything," Zev said.

"So you've come to right the ship of our little candidate?" Paul said.

"No easy task," Zev said, his hand wavering before landing on the mantel. He'd had two drinks to every one of Cormier's. "But by the time I get done with him, he's going be speaking in sound bites and lying without realizing it."

This provoked merriment all around: shared smiles, knowing nods.

"Well, I'd like to ask you about a different election," Belinda said. "That one taking place next year? What can you tell us?"

"That probably none of the Democrats can beat Bush, and no one can beat him less than Howard Dean. He's a disaster."

"Really?" Robin said. "He's the first politician I've liked in years."

"Of course you do," Zev said. "Pretty normal for a politician, right? But here's a helpful gauge. If the candidate is someone you can picture sitting here, drinking wine with all of you, he can't be president."

"He's right," Paul said, nodding at Belinda. "He's right."

"I, however," Zev said, "would love to drink wine with all of you."

"Oh, I'm sorry," Robin said. "Wall, get Zev a glass. And find the menu."

It dawned on Cormier that the presence of dinner guests was no coincidence. Robin had invited them over to show Zev that they had a nice little life here, chock-full of smart conversation, thirty-dollar pinot, and passable Thai. Cormier would probably end up having a decent time, assuming that the guests stopped apologizing for Hartsburg and kissing up to Zev. But he wanted to be back in Jed's.

CHAPTER 22

BEVY WAS BEING too careful. Taking pains not to say the wrong thing, she was coming across as stiff. The managing editor, a young woman with hair like hay, had said they wouldn't make an endorsement because of the conflict of interest. Still, Bevy didn't trust this trio. The interview would appear as a Q&A on the Sunday prior to Election Day, and she wanted to give answers that they'd have trouble distorting. So far, so good, but she wished she had her charm, which had won over even tougher audiences than this.

"You keep coming back to this theme of parents' rights," said the male editor, who had a sharp, clean face that Bevy might have liked were it not attached to him. "But it seems to me that you want to dictate to *other* parents what their children learn."

"Not at all, sir," Bevy said.

"You don't have to call him 'sir,'" said the managing editor, whose name was Jeanette Poole. "In fact, I wish you wouldn't." A joke perhaps, but she didn't smile.

"He's nobody's sir," said the third editor, a heavy woman with silver hair, dark at the roots, and dark eyebrows. The three editors could have been a family, and as in any liberal family, the child ran the show. Jeanette Poole was a teacher's-pet type. A virgin probably, but not by choice: an atheist virgin, a sorry species. Earlier in the interview, when Jeanette had talked about Christians' discomfort with sex, Bevy had wanted to point out the irony. Arrogant, insecure, and liberal: Meet the press.

" 'William' is fine," the male editor said.

" 'William' it is, then," Bevy said, trying not to think about the little tape recorder churning away on the table between them. "Take the issue of homosexuality. All we're asking is that schools not endorse it. Why discuss it at all? The test scores of Hartsburg students are not strong at all, yet the school board's time is spent debating sexual lifestyles? It's self-defeating. And strange, frankly."

Both Jeanette and Silver Hair started to speak, then stopped. Jeanette's nostrils got rhinoceros-huge. "Go ahead," Jeanette said.

"No, you go," Silver Hair said.

"Ask your question," Jeanette said.

"Some things *have* to be taught," said Silver Hair. "Like evolution. That's the only accepted scientific theory, yet you don't want it to be taught."

Bevy gave liberals too much credit. She assumed that they were only misguided, not stupid. "I think evolution *should* be taught. I also think that alternate theories should be taught."

"We've covered this already," Jeannette said.

"I'd like to add one more thing," Bevy said. "It's hard for y'all to see what's wrong with teaching evolution as fact or homosexuality as an acceptable lifestyle, because my guess is, you all believe in those views." They looked at her, giving away nothing. "But consider what it's like to have your fundamental beliefs undermined by teachers. Do any of you have children?"

"I do," Silver Hair said.

"A girl?" Bevy said. "A boy?"

"Both."

"What are their names?"

"We'll ask the questions," Jeanette said.

Bevy shifted in her chair to face Silver Hair. "Think about values you hold dear, values that are central to who you are. Values that *are* who you are. Like respect for other people, maybe? Or racial tolerance? Now imagine a teacher telling your child that those values are wrong. Imagine a teacher telling your child that *you* are wrong."

Silver Hair looked down at her pad and pretended to write something.

"One last question," Jeanette said. "We'll go off the record."

She nodded in the direction of the tape recorder, and William clicked it off. Her words were caught on tape, waiting to be diced and mixed up. She hated putting herself at the mercy of these people. Giving power to people she *trusted* was difficult enough.

"As you may have noticed," Jeanette said, "we're growing our coverage of religion-based issues. I'm wondering what you think of it."

Religion-based issues! These were the people who would edit her responses, put words in her mouth. Bevy had to work to breathe. The air wasn't good in here. It was thick and steamy with ignorance.

"A section is fine, I suppose," Bevy said. "But for most people, religion isn't a section of their lives. It's not something you do, like sports, and it's not like business; it's not a job. It's who you are. You can't separate it out. There should be religion in your sports section and in your business section and certainly in your news section. What you need, you see, are reporters and editors who believe in an Almighty God."

They stared at her, this liberal family. She'd expected them to tell her that someone on staff went to Hilltop, or to claim to believe in God themselves. Instead they were looking at her like she'd gone Pentecostal on them and spoken in tongues.

Checking her cell as she walked to her car, Bevy saw that someone had called from the mysterious number. Wilma, she feared. She called the number and a mechanical voice told her to leave a message, so she called information and got Wilma's home number, which, she learned, had been disconnected, so she called the head of Hilltop's drug counseling program, but she got his voice mail, so she left a message. Bevy had done all she could; now she wanted to get home. Last night the Reverend had sermonized on the Second Coming. With Colleen there, the message was pertinent but heavy—it was heavy even for the Saved—and it just about knocked Colleen out. She went straight to bed, declining an invitation to discuss the message. Her car would be ready on Saturday, which probably meant Monday, so Bevy had at most four days to make more headway.

Discovering a quiet house, Bevy feared that Colleen had run away; but the door to her room was closed and Bevy sensed her sleeping behind it. She cracked open the door and smelled cigarettes. Her eyes adjusted to the dark; seeing Colleen's hair splayed on the pillow, Bevy felt that old longing. Bevy had hated those times when Colleen hadn't been there for her. Days after sloppy nights, Bevy was in limbo until she'd spoken to Colleen. Or worse, she was still in the bar; images and sounds haunted her, a woman's dirty look, a man's hand on her stomach, Bevy's own voice, saying something ugly or unfunny. A conversation with Colleen released Bevy from the night.

One time Colleen left a bar with a man and disappeared. Bevy was worried—her choice of men was even worse than Bevy's—but mostly she felt stranded. When Colleen finally showed up days later, Bevy hugged her and punched her and said, "You *cannot* do that." Colleen made some crack about them being a married couple.

Bevy walked in and pushed apart the curtains on the little window, which gave her a view of brown grass and green hose. A fifth of Jack, almost empty, was on the bedside table, and so was a brown rubber thing that Bevy preferred not to think about. "Rise and shine, princess," Bevy said.

"Is this a joke?" Colleen said, her voice as gruff as a man's.

"Afraid not. That bottle's no joke, either. You drink all that last night?"

"Needed to."

"It was a lot to absorb, I know."

"Anyone home?"

At first Bevy thought she was making a crack about her intelligence. The interview had put her in a sensitive state. "Just us."

Colleen got out of bed—she was naked—and walked out. Bevy listened to her go up the stairs, and waited to hear the toilet flush. When the sound didn't come, she walked up and found her at the table, drinking a diet Pepper. She was naked on a chair, Ronnie's seat. As she brought the can to her mouth, the chain tattoo on her biceps expanded. But her face looked awful. Little blue veins by her nose swirled like paisley.

"Can we talk about last night?" Bevy said.

"Not right now. I need to sweat. There a gym I can go to?"

"You'd have to pay. Unless I went with you."

"Well?"

Bevy didn't want to let Colleen out of her sight, and she needed exercise. The housework, so much housework, would have to wait.

"I'll go put on my workout clothes," Bevy said. "I suggest you do the same."

"You mean I can't go like this?" Colleen put her heel in her hand and brought her leg up to her head, then over and behind it, leaving it there

218

while she took a sip. She tilted her head back to swallow, pushing on her ankle, and the muscles in her behind rippled.

American Fitness was on a road west of The Drive, near a florist and not much else. It was a scene after five, like a single's bar, but this time of day it was almost empty.

Bevy had begun to sweat inside her sweatshirt, which hung down almost to her knees; no one, not even Bevy herself, would get a look at her behind in stretch pants. On the Ellipse you gripped poles and moved your arms like you were cross-country skiing and lifted your legs like you were running. Bevy loved this machine.

With her headphones on, Colleen probably couldn't hear herself grunting on the bench press. Veins in her arms pushed against shiny skin. A muscle-head was looking at her, but she didn't notice, freed for a moment from her awareness of men. That's what exercise did, saved her from herself, temporarily. She filled herself with exercise and drugs and other people and thought she was full.

The Ellipse groaned as it shifted to a harder level. Bevy was pushing herself but not so much that she couldn't read *Mademoiselle*. Profiles of celebrities—this one was about the devil woman herself, the mother of all licentious libs—angered Bevy, but she couldn't resist them. An increasing number of stars, such as Tom Cruise and John Travolta, belonged to the "church" of Scientology, which was a cult that put actors on a pedestal. What a surprise they didn't pick real religion. Let's see, God or me?

Fame itself, the hunger for it, was a serious problem—reality shows were an abomination—but if there had to be celebrities, why not Bevy? If she became, say, a senator, women's magazines would write about her. Fired up by her fantasy and infuriated by the photo of Susan Sarandon—frog face!—Bevy picked up her pace.

Bevy's phone rang—she kept it on her in case Arch Cook called—but the number was Hilltop: Jerry Dawber, the head of drug counseling, who told Bevy that Wilma had stopped showing up. "Someone's got to track her down," he said.

"This someone's got a race to run."

"I'll take care of it," he said.

"Thanks," Bevy said, a little ashamed. "Keep me posted."

Colleen had joined the aerobics class. The other women in the class were lazily raising their arms, but Colleen was punching the air. Bevy pumped her arms sort of in synch with Colleen's, like they were dancing. Or fighting.

Driving down The Drive, Bevy wished they had showered at the gym. She wanted to talk and couldn't imagine a real conversation between people wearing sweaty underpants. Colleen's shorts—maroon with white trim and shorter on the sides—could have been part of a junior high gym uniform. "I'm a little drunk just smelling you," Bevy said.

"Yeah, I got it all out, I think." Colleen sniffed her armpit, then rubbed it and licked her fingers. "Ahh. There's nothing quite like Jack sweat. Reminds me of my stepfather, may God unrest his drunk-ass, pecker-head soul."

Bevy refused to get pulled into an argument that'd let Colleen make her out to be a scold. "I need a Gatorade," she said.

The Mobil Mart was busy for a weekday midday, with cars at every pump and so many people walking into the shop that Bevy decided to take a handful of pamphlets with her. "Get me an energy bar?" Colleen said. "Peanut butter."

It was an inviting shop, clean and spacious, with a wall of beverages prettier than a lot of paintings and a variety of food options: pizza, chili, hot dogs, burritos, gourmet coffee, baked goods. Americans took so much for granted. You could walk into a gas station and get a nice hot meal for four dollars.

The man behind her in line was reading the pamphlet over her shoulder, so she handed it to him. "School board," she said, too wiped out to go into detail.

He was really just a boy playing grown-up in his blazer. Fat had flooded his face, making his features small. There was a mole like a wood spot on his head, visible through gelled-up hair. The droplets of sweat on his forehead might as well have been tears.

"Do you know if you live in Ward Three?" Bevy asked.

"What? Oh. No." He looked down at his slices of pizza, their pointy tips drooping from the plate, pepperoni shining like medallions. He missed his mouth with his straw and poked himself in the nose. "I don't live in Hartsburg."

"Well, you might still like being part of the campaign. It's exciting. Usually we meet at Hilltop church. Have you heard of Hilltop?"

"Yes. I live out that way."

"You should stop by sometime and check it out."

He shrugged and looked down at his pizza and drink, as if she'd asked him to hold something. "I'm not—I don't know."

"Just think about it, please."

"That's three twenty-eight," said Gladys, the dried-up woman behind the counter, "and this ain't no place for preaching."

"Is this China? Did I just leave America and enter communist China?"

"Big fan of free speech, are you? You ought to talk to your friends across the way. They kept harassing my customers 'cause they didn't like a sign I had made. I called the police, but they didn't do nothing once they saw the sign. I had to take it down."

"What'd the sign say?"

"You want to know what it said? I'll tell you what it said. It said, 'Dear Dubya: No WMD? No War. Our boys ain't your toys.'"

"I can see why they had a problem."

"My son's in the army."

"In Iraq?"

"Not yet."

"Well, God bless him."

The woman slapped the drawer as she slid out coins. She hated Bevy, but Bevy didn't hate her, not even a little.

Bevy turned to the boy, squeezed his doughy arm, and smiled her good-bye. There was no horror in his life, she sensed, other than the horror of loneliness.

Colleen wasn't in the car.

Or near it. She was gone. Her car was ready early, she'd walked to get it, then zipped back to the house to gather up her things. Fear had sent her packing. She couldn't bear to see the truth, and now she was out of Bevy's life—

Colleen was on the edge of the lot, near the road, in her short shorts and little tank top, hugging herself with one arm and rocking from foot to foot. The relief Bevy felt was physical, almost painful, like she'd jumped out of the way of a car.

The lot was so huge that Bevy drove to her. "What are you doing all the way over here?" Bevy said, stepping out.

"People don't like it when you smoke near gas. Check this out. Seventy-five cents for air. Air ought to be free, don't you figure?"

"It's the pump you pay for."

"Even so, it's free in Texas."

Few things were sadder than a woman smoking and shivering. A woman in running shoes, no less. Cars cruised by. "Let's talk about last night," Bevy said.

"It was depressing."

"It doesn't have to be."

"Don't, Bevy. I did what you wanted, went to your church."

"Yes, you did, and it touched you. I saw what you were like afterward."

"I was creeped-out is what I was. I'm not one to tell a girl what's good for her, but that's some pretty whacked-out stuff you're inhaling."

Bevy jerked at the sound of a horn, a truck driver honking at Colleen. Bevy's heart was working too hard. "I believe that you're scared," Bevy said.

Colleen's hand was shaking so much that she held her wrist and guided the cigarette to her mouth. The cold had brought out her nipples.

"You're shaking, Col. You're shaking and I want to give you a hug."

"Please don't."

"It doesn't surprise me that you have doubts. It'd be weird if you didn't. The End Times, that's hard to get your head around. I sort of wish the message had been about something a little more, I don't know, down-to-earth. Because coming to Christ—"

"Fuck off, Bevy, all right?"

"Being born again isn't just about the next life; it's about this one. It's liberating and comforting and I want it for you so, so badly. Let me try to help you see it from my perspective. Remember when you discovered John Prine's music?"

"Of course I do. I wanted to marry the man."

"You came home, all excited, and told me to listen to "Hello in There," said it would change my life. You *needed* to share it. Now imagine if I'd refused to listen to it."

"Except I've already heard the song you're singing. I must have heard it a thousand times and it never gets any better."

"You're not open to it. It takes work, you see. I can help you. I've loved having you around, and I can't help but imagine what it'd be like having you around all the time."

"You want me to stay here?"

"It'd be the best decision you ever made."

"You're serious."

"Dead serious."

"Oh yeah, I can just picture it, you and me going to the Wal-Mart, grabbing a bite at Mickey-D's." She smiled, going from pathetic to arrogant in no time. "I mean, did you actually think this was going to be my *life*?"

Colleen laughed, and kept laughing. She tried to stop when she saw Bevy's face. Bevy wanted to stay strong, but her body wasn't obliging—her lips and legs were shaking—so she got back in the car and slammed the door. The effort to hold off tears gave her a headache, and the pain brought clarity. It was nothing short of a revelation, twenty-five years in the making. Back in Texas, Bevy had been too close to Colleen to see her clearly. Colleen was cruel. Sure, she was a great friend when Bevy was in the hospital or in grief, but she needed Bevy to be needy. Bevy's happiness threatened her, showed by contrast the darkness of her own life. Colleen's behavior was easy to read, as obvious as a child's.

Why, though, was Bevy so hurt? Why did it seem that nothing, not even the Lord, could make her feel better right now, unless by some miracle she became a child again and could crawl into her parents' bed and wedge her body between theirs? Why, when she was supposed to be saving her friend, was she hiding from her?

"Come on, sweet pie," Colleen said, standing at Bevy's window. Her lips got huge and white as she kissed the glass; when she took her lips away, there was a mark, an island of frost surrounded by a wet blur. "You know I love you."

CHAPTER 23

CORMIER ALWAYS WANTED other people to tell him what to do. Hence Zev. It seemed reasonable to put the campaign in his hands; Zev was a pro as well as a friend. There was a problem, however. Zev's top priority this week was not to help Cormier but to have fun, his version of it, which involved drugs and alcohol. This all became clear to Cormier as he lay on his back in front of a roaring fire in a cabin in West Virginia.

From the moment that Stu had picked them up to the moment that Cormier's only hit of marijuana had taken effect, he'd had fun, his version of it, which included the company of friends and escape from his depressed wife. It was great, hitting the road, hanging with his boys. The air cooled as they climbed; the forest was thick and protective. Having handed off control of the weekend, Cormier had assumed that it was serving its intended purpose, which was to prepare him for the debate.

This had still been his assumption as they settled in at the cabin. When Stu had announced that he was going to stay up all night before heading out to hunt, Cormier had been amused. The weekend was going to go well, so it was going well: this was the tautological case put up by his lazy brain.

But then he'd taken a hit of Zev's joint, and now Mr. Marijuana, District Attorney Marijuana, poked holes in the case. Marijuana wasn't being showy about it. He seemed almost rueful, as though pained to put away such a well-meaning defendant. Marijuana pointed to the rocking chair, which held Exhibit A: Stu Nedney. "Why is he here?" Marijuana asked. "There was the notion that Stu's fondness for killing animals would allow Zev to tell the press that defendant Cormier was headed to the mountains—in a Buick, no less—for the purpose of engaging in that most manly of ordinary-guy activities. But no one aside from his family knows where he is, and no one, in any case, would believe that Wally 'Can't Kill a Spider' Cormier was hunting. Don't get me wrong, members of the jury, Stu brings much to the weekend, but nothing, alas, that serves the trip's purpose."

The floor creaked as Marijuana walked over to the couch, then behind it, and looked down at Exhibit B. "Here we have another good guy, someone you can trust. Or can you? Please consider Zev's tendency to overlook the best interests of others in pursuit of his own indulgent interests. Members of the jury, direct your attention to the screen. It's a photo dated April 1980. It shows the defendant and Zev, sitting in Washington Square Park on a Tuesday morning, bag-drinking forty-ounce malt liquors. Zev had intercepted the defendant on his way to class and lured him to the park with his insistence that there was more to be learned from getting drunk than from sitting in class. Zev was right, or harmlessly wrong: the stakes were low back then. Not so now."

Marijuana took a breath—he was something of a showman, after all—and, in his coup de grace, pointed at the defendant. "I call Wallace Cormier to the stand."

Fuck.

"Mr. Cormier, are you stoned?"

I only had one hit.

"Please answer the question."

Yes.

"And is it not a fact that, although you love marijuana, although it has been throughout your life an important aide to self-discovery, it is a substance of which you should not partake when you're in a tenuous emotional state?"

Yes.

"And given the impending debate, your daughter's anxiety, your wife's depression, the secrets revealed by your mother, the not-all-that-distant death of your mother, the inevitability of your own death, the growth of American militarism, the heretofore unacknowledged financial problems incurred by your month without an income, the suspicion that not even victory in the election would give your life a sense of purpose and accomplishment, would it be accurate to describe your emotional state as tenuous?"

" . . . "

"Please answer the question."

"Mr. Cormier?"

"I will instruct the jury to take the defendant's silence as a yes."

"Ladies and gentlemen of the jury, clearly an unproductive weekend is not only possible; it is likely. You've seen evidence demonstrating beyond a reasonable doubt that Mr. Cormier is guilty of negligence, cowardice, and really bad decision making."

"Guilty as charged."

"Sentence: humiliation this Tuesday, defeat the following Tuesday. Would the defendant like to make a statement?"

I would, Your Honor. While the verdict is just, the sentence is not. It's only Friday—okay, Saturday. But still. I'll sleep, wake up, prepare. With every second that passes, I'm less stoned. I plead for mercy, Your Honor. I will atone!

Cormier, caught in the white rapids of his thoughts, grabbed hold of a rock in the form of his glass of bourbon. "Jesus," he said. "This weed."

"I told you," Zev said, and Cormier, his view blocked by the coffee table, sat up so that he could see him. There was something ridiculous about a guy with slicked-back hair wearing a flannel shirt. Also: sweatpants, white socks, loafers.

"I don't feel the weed," Stu said, rocking quickly. He looked about as mellow as Cormier felt, his dark eyes catching firelight.

"Bullshit," Zev said.

"I want to put that rifle in my mouth," Stu said, "but that's nothing new."

"Yeah," Zev said, "that's some Snoop Dog shit we smoked."

"Are you a Negrophile?" Stu asked.

"I dig African American culture, if that's what you mean. Especially the music. I mean, *listen* to this." Zev pointed at the stereo-box just as Sly Stone's "Love and Hate" began, and even Stu would have to admit that it was good, *true*.

"I don't like it," Stu said. He put his legs up like a kid on a swing and inadvertently kicked the coffee table. This cabin was cramped, with beds in the two corners that weren't part of the kitchen. "It sounds like someone tugging on a rubber band."

"Are you a racist?" Zev asked.

"Because I don't like this music?"

"Because you said 'Negrophile.'"

"Trust me," Stu said. "I've got more dark friends than you've got friends. The Mart's like Guadalajara. It loves exploiting browns."

"That's *Latinos*," Zev said, pronouncing it in Spanish, not joking.

"Brothers work there too. They dig me because I'm just as lazy as they are."

"Uh!" Zev said, pointing at him. "There it is."

"It is a problem, Stu," Cormier said.

"Fuck you, Wally. You laugh at my Negro humor when it's just the two of us."

"I used to, yeah, because I thought you were making fun of racist people. Now it seems like you're a racist person yourself."

"I'm making fun of all of us," Stu said, confusing Cormier. The bourbon had dulled the pot's knife, but he was still good old-fashioned sta-honed.

"It really bothers me," Zev said. "Not as a person, but as a political strategist. You see, Stu, you're a Wrench—"

"A mensch?" Cormier said.

"Wrench," Zev said.

"I know," Cormier said. "What's a Wrench?"

"It's shoptalk for white working-class men," Zev said.

"'Cause they're good with tools?" Cormier said, thinking about Something-ski.

"Also because the shift of white working-class voters to the Republican Party has been *wrenching* for Democrats."

"Ooh," Stu said. "Two meanings!"

"My guess, Stu," Zev said, "is that you vote Republican."

"Wrong," Stu said. "I don't vote."

"You sound proud," Zev said.

"I'm not," Stu said. "I assure you." His face reddened as he sucked on the end of a joint, a branched vein appearing in the middle of his forehead. "I don't vote because I don't like being part of anything. No group, no institution, no organization. No family. To tell you the truth, I don't even want to be part of myself."

"That doesn't make sense." Zev said, looking at Stu and smiling hugely, his hands clasped behind his head. He loved the entertainment that was Stu.

"Stu, you're part of me," Cormier said.

"Aw," Zev said. "That's sweet."

"And Jimmy," Cormier said.

"You think that brings me pleasure?" Stu said, now smoking a cigarette. "Actually, I don't mind being part of you guys. But the political system? Fuck me with a fork."

"Congrats," Zev said. "You don't get your hands dirty. You're pure. You're clean." Cormier laughed to himself, or maybe out loud, at the thought of Stu being clean. He looked like a strangler, revved up and sweaty after a kill.

Zev said, "But it's people who get their hands dirty—"

"Bloody," Stu said.

"No," Zev said, and licked a fresh joint. "I'm working to change the system."

"Bullshit," Stu said. "You're propping it up. You're—what's that word?"

"Validating it," Cormier said.

"No," Stu said. "But yes."

"I'm getting better people elected," Zev said, "people who will change the system."

"No, you're not," Stu said. "Change comes from outside the system. It bubbles up from the bottom like . . ."

"Bubbles," Cormier said.

"We need heat," Stu says. "But you're a fucking lid."

"A lid adds to the heat," Zev said. His hair fell over his eyes as he coughed, his head in a cloud of smoke. "I think we've stretched this metaphor as far as it will go."

"I'm not done with it," Stu said. "Zev, you keep the pot at a simmer."

"I thought you didn't care about the pot," Zev said.

"I didn't say that. Did I?"

"No, you didn't say that," Cormier said. "But you do say that."

"All right," Stu said. "I'm a liar. I still say the lid needs to blow off. If you don't trust me, then trust your brother here." He pointed at the ceiling, meaning the music: *The way they do my life.* "You don't think this cat wants to blow the lid sky-high?"

"Spare me," Zev said. "A call for revolution from a guy who doesn't even vote."

"Marvin Gaye?" Cormier said.

"By your logic," Zev said, "it doesn't matter whether Wally or Bevy wins."

"I forgot to tell you," Stu said, tossing his Skoal at Cormier, whose arms didn't follow the order of his brain, and the can plunked him in the forehead. Zev laughed. "I bumped into the holy hole," Stu said. "She was in the Mart."

"What'd you say to her?" Cormier said, scared to know. He wondered if he loomed as large in Bevy's consciousness as she did in his. Could she get beyond her prejudices to see him as a person, full of hopes and fears and gas? But could he see Bevy as a person? He tried to imagine Bevy farting. He could not. Bevy Baer did not fart.

"I fucked with her," Stu said. He smiled around his teetering cigarette and clapped once. "She was praying by the grapefruit and I went up to her, all concerned: are you all right? *Religion.* You want to talk about something that keeps the pot at a simmer."

"Ah," Zev said. "Marx has spoken."

"Groucho," Cormier said.

"Grimo," Zev said.

"Greaso," Cormier said.

"This must be college-iate humor," Stu said, slurring. "Here's a serious question. Should radicals accept religion and try to use it to blow off the lid—"

"Yes," Cormier said. "MLK."

"Or is it impossible to blow off the lid when religion is in the pot?"

"Yes," Cormier said.

"Democrats need to learn how to talk in religious terms," Zev said.

"Spoken like a guardian of the flame," Stu said.

"I thought he was the lid," Cormier said.

"I've got a clean conscience," Zev said.

"Bullshit," Stu said.

"*Fuck* you, all right?" Zev said, no longer amused.

"No, it's not all right." Stu stood up with a stumble. "I don't believe that you've got no guilt. I believe that if someone put a gun to your head, this gun, for example—"

"Put it down, Stu," Cormier said, standing up.

"It's not loaded," Stu said. "I don't think." He got behind Zev and pushed his head forward with the barrel of the gun. "Something about this music makes me want to play with guns." It was new rap, something heavy.

Zev, his chin on his chest and his hair over his eyes, seemed more angry than scared. "Is it loaded or not?" Zev asked.

"No," Stu said. "Or is it?"

"Fuck you," Zev said, and made a move to stand.

"Boom!" Stu yelled.

Zev froze, half-standing, then sat back down and smiled, as if realizing there was fun to be had, owned, a wacky story he could tell people. "All right," Zev said, leaning his head back against the gun. "Shoot. So to speak."

"Please stop," Cormier said. "This is how things you read about happen."

"But we're not famous," Zev said. "It's only cool if you're famous."

"I thought you were famous," Stu said.

"Not enough for shit like this," Zev said.

"Tell me about your guilt," Stu said.

"Here's your dip," Wally said, going behind the couch. "I'll give you your Skoal and you give me the gun."

"Sounds like a reasonable agreement," Stu said. Cormier placed the Skoal in his palm, but Stu kept the gun.

"You lied to me," Cormier said.

"He's a liar, remember?" Zev said.

Stu held the gun with his left hand while he packed the dip with his right, whipping it with his forefinger; then as he took a pinch, he propped up the gun with his stomach.

"This isn't funny," Cormier said. "It's not even interesting."

"I think it's a little interesting," Stu said.

"Me too," Zev said.

"Oh, Christ," Cormier said. "You guys are a perfect pair."

"You've had time to think," Stu said. "You're guilty about what?"

"Isn't it obvious?" Zev said.

"Not to me," Stu said. "But I'm just a Wrench."

"I treat women like shit. My girlfriends. I actually treat bimbos decently.

But my girlfriends, I break them. One after another. I get them to love me and I break them. I lie to them and cheat on them and break them. I steal years from their lives. I used to be a fat kid who could get no one, but now I can get women and I can't stop getting them. I get them and I break them. The worst thing is, I *want* to be that guy. A heartbreaker. I feel guilty because I don't feel guilty, but is that the same thing as feeling guilty? I don't think it is. I don't think it's the same thing. Oh, fuck. I'm fucked. Up."

Zev fell onto his side, and Stu, seeming disgusted with himself, walked outside, taking the gun with him. The springless screen door closed with a bang.

Cormier hauled his body to a bed as Sam Cooke sang. Bed was nice, although the blanket was rough beneath him. The fire brought warmth. The cabin smelled of other mountain cabins but also of places by lakes, wooden rooms in which Cormier had taken off wet bathing suits and put on comfy shorts before going to get ice cream, mocha chip for everyone except Marcie, who got butter pecan. Their family life had been good. They'd had problems, of course, problems of communication—especially between father and son and mother and daughter—as well as subtler forms of dysfunction that Cormier had identified and magnified in a psychologist's chair in West Hollywood, but his parents had created a nurturing home, a place of consistency and calm that had in no way been called into question by what his mother and father had done in Chicago.

From this bed in West Virginia, Cormier knew that he wasn't angry at his mother. This was typical: he didn't know what he felt until he was fucked-up and faraway.

What else could he feel? That he was going to lose the race. The good news was that it seemed unimportant compared to his own family life (which was related to the campaign, but he would choose—it was magnificent to have a choice—not to think about that). He would think about his daughter, whose home didn't have enough calm or consistency, and his wife, for whom he finally felt compassion. She was taking a break from writing—maybe a permanent one, she'd said—but seemed no lighter for it.

The door swung open, then banged shut, and when Stu turned off the light and fell into bed, Cormier realized that he was relieved; he'd feared Stu would do damage to himself when he went outside. Yet Cormier hadn't gotten up. He had taken laziness to a shameful level. Or was it a nod to powerlessness, to the impossibility of helping people?

But Cormier didn't believe it was impossible. He should have gotten up. He should always get up. "You lock the door?" Cormier said.

"What're you afraid of?" Zev said.

"Bears," Cormier said.

"Maybe Bronson Tavares is going to show up," Stu said. "Maybe the teenage terrorist is going to barge in here and blow us all away."

"I sense sarcasm," Cormier said.

"He's about as violent as you, Wallywood," Stu said.

"How do you know?" Cormier said.

"Remember when weed was just . . . fun?" Zev said. "Bong hits and *Barney Miller*."

"*Star Trek*," Cormier said.

"Meatball slice and chick Parm hero," Zev said.

"Cake," Cormier said.

"The gun wasn't loaded," Stu said.

"Hey, Stu," Cormier said. "Is it unfair to ask you to promise to never kill yourself?"

"Of course it's unfair. Unfortunately, it's also probably"—his voice got louder as he turned onto his back—"unnecessary. I'm full of shit."

"What do you mean?" Cormier asked.

"I mean I love all . . . *this*. Can't you see that? I thought you could see that."

CHAPTER 24

HILLTOPPERS COULD SPEND their lives going to gatherings and outings. There were prayer breakfasts for men, Bible studies for singles, square-dancing nights, Scripture-and-sushi lunches, biking clubs, parenting classes, and a bunch of support groups: for seniors, veterans, recovering alcoholics, recovering homosexuals, former Jews. On Monday, the day before the debate, Bevy longed for the company of friends—friends who weren't Colleen—so she went to the Women's Tea Club, which met at three o'clock in a closed-down clothing store on Main Street. Ladies picked up drinks at Kohl's beforehand.

As a reward to herself for making it through debate prep with Arch Cook, Bevy had gotten a triple-shot latte. She'd asked for half-decaffeinated, but Jenny had seemed annoyed by the request. Longing oddly for her approval, and always sensitive to any suggestion she was a priss, Bevy had told her to make the whole thing regular.

Packed into the three couches, they had their elbows on their ribs (as if they were all mocking Pauline, who was sitting across from Bevy). Lizette Bonderman was talking about her daughter, who, like Ronnie, was taking a zigzag path toward the Lord. Lizette was one of Bevy's better friends, but she tended to dominate. Words came to her in bunches, as if her mouth were her mind. While Lizette went on, Bevy gazed at the back of the old store, where men's clothes used to be displayed. She'd come here with Peter to buy a suit not long after she'd moved to town. The suit had been no bargain, but she'd liked the gruff kindness and expertise of the bald, big-nosed man with the tape measure draped around his neck.

". . . Andrea says she won't go to a Christian college," Lizette said.

"Are secular colleges out of the question?" asked Marla.

"They're out of our price range," Lizette said.

"Even the state schools?" Pauline said in the blunt manner that Bevy liked. Money, like sex, was usually discussed carefully at these gatherings. For a change Lizette had nothing to say. "Christian colleges can be sheltered places," Pauline said.

"And secular colleges can be cesspools," Carol said.

"Amen," Lizette said. "Dan suggested we split the difference and send her to a military academy. Which might be a good idea, except with the war in Iraq." Then, remembering Pauline, she said, "Of course, I'd be proud, but . . ."

"By the time she gets done with college," Carol said, "we'll be out of Iraq, right?"

"Definitely," Lizette said, but everyone else looked at Pauline.

"Zach said it was going to take a long time if we want to do it right. Years."

Then no one talked. The sound of sipping was loud and, Bevy thought, unpleasant.

"But he thinks it's the right thing to do, right?" Carol said.

"Oh yes. Yes. He's very proud."

"And we're proud of him," Bevy said, smiling at Pauline, thinking about that moment in her kitchen when she'd mashed the bread. Pauline would have crawled to Iraq to bring her son home. There was a war going on. Pretty crazy, if you thought about it.

"Would it be all right if I changed the subject?" Bevy said.

"That's the first time anyone's ever asked permission," Marla said.

"As some of you know, I have a friend visiting, and there's nothing that'd mean more to me than bringing her to the Lord, but she's only here a few more days. Meanwhile her worldly ways are starting to irritate Peter. She's leaving too soon and staying too long, and I don't really know what to do."

"Does she believe in God?" Sharon said this right into Bevy's ear, and her voice, powerful even from a normal distance, vibrated down through Bevy's spine, all the way to her fingers, giving her chills that convened in her chest. Too much caffeine.

"No," Bevy said. "She's pretty well lost."

"Has she shown any interest in Jesus?" Lizette asked.

"She went to church, but . . . no."

"Not everyone can be saved," Lizette said.

"That's God's own truth!" said Marybeth, who'd been blissfully quiet till now. Her son Patrick hadn't set foot in Bevy's house since the toy truck incident.

"I wouldn't give up," Pauline said. "I mean, I was born again only last year."

"But you were already a churchgoer," Lizette said, with a dismissive, backhanded wave. "And a family woman." She closed one eye to look through the hole in the lid of her cup. "If you can't win her for Christ, you'll have to lose her as a friend."

Afterward, as though they'd made a plan, Bevy and Pauline stayed seated while everyone else left. Someone hit the lights and they sat there in the dim gray light coming through the storefront. Bevy felt like she was inside a black-and-white photo.

"Lizette's a loudmouth," Pauline said.

"She's better one-on-one, when there's no real center of attention."

"Her outfit looked like a clown suit."

Bevy would have thought that Pauline, with her handicap, would be hesitant to make fun of people. It was probably a sign of health that she wasn't. Bevy herself wasn't above gossiping but didn't think she ought to right now. Lizette, after all, was her friend, and Pauline wasn't; they'd hardly spent any time together. On the other hand, their few conversations had gone a long way. Bevy felt close to her, and wanted to feel closer.

"I don't like her," Pauline said.

"You don't have to. Marybeth is the one who irks me."

"I can see why. A big church like this, there's going to be a few irkers."

"More than a few, I'm afraid."

"I think Lizette was wrong. I've got lots of friends who aren't saved."

"And what's that like?"

"Sad." She took a pull on her straw; for Pauline straws were a necessity. "But I believe they might make it to Heaven. The way I understand it, there's a chance."

"That's just not correct, Paul." Pauline didn't seem to mind her using a nickname, which had slipped out. "The Reverend is clear on this point, and I don't think you're doing your friends any favors by believing this."

"It's not like I don't want them to be saved any less. I mean, it's not something anyone can afford to leave to chance."

"Who's your friend who works at Wal-Mart?"

"That's Stu. He's a good example. He's messed up, but I love him to death. It's people like him who need our help the most."

Bevy wondered if she should try to get Colleen to stay past Wednesday, which was now when the car was supposed to be ready. Suspecting a lie, Peter wanted Bevy to call the garage, but she doubted Colleen wanted to stay longer than she had to. In any case, she'd already pushed Christian hospitality to its limits. At the same time, she had, in her way, made an effort. Most nights at dinner she'd been polite, and one night she'd made the meal, tough but tasty pork chops that everybody had seemed to like.

"Why'd you ask about Stu?" Pauline asked.

"To be honest, he sort of freaks me out and I find it strange that you're friends with him. You seem so different."

"*Everyone's* different than Stu. After the factory closed, he practically lived at our place. His wife had left him, and he didn't want to go home. A lot of afternoons Stu watched the kids. Zach really took to him."

If Stu could be part of Pauline's life, why couldn't Colleen be part of Bevy's? Because she was leaving. Colleen, as ever, had control.

Maybe it was the caffeine, maybe it was Colleen being in control, but Bevy wanted to run out the door and down Main Street. This was just the kind of quiet time that she needed in her life; she was angry she couldn't relax into it.

"Let's you and I hang out some time," Bevy said.

"Isn't that what we're doing?"

"This is too quick. Maybe we could go to a movie or something."

"Are you asking me for a date?"

"No, no, no." Pauline was smiling her devilish smile, and now Bevy was in on the joke. "I mean, yes, a friend date."

"Friend date: I like that. Busy as we all are, it makes sense. I'll tell you what: the Friday after you win your election, I'll make you lunch."

"Sounds good. I'll bring dessert. I make a mean jelly roll." The thought of jelly roll made Bevy's stomach growl. She hadn't eaten since breakfast. Which was probably why the caffeine was acting like a drug. Yet like an idiot she gulped down the last cold bit, wanting it because she didn't, like an addict. "I'm a little nervous for our date," Bevy said, and pretended to nibble her nails. "I mean, what on earth will I wear?"

"I don't know, but I wouldn't ask Lizette for advice."

She was pleased about her chat with Pauline, but as she drove away, Bevy was thinking only about Colleen. Why weren't there rules for what to do with a friend like her? Lizette's advice seemed cold, almost un-Christian. What if they'd been talking about Bevy's mother? Deidre was a believer but what if she wasn't? Would Lizette have sat there and sipped her drink and told Bevy to let her go?

But Colleen wasn't her mother. She was someone she hadn't seen in twenty years, someone whose steps toward the Lord were teensy at best, and Bevy had a race to win and five children to care for and the chills in her chest had become a fixture, ringing and trembling like one of those old alarm clocks with the bells on top.

You couldn't call the feeling pleasant but she liked showing up at Kay's energized. She thanked Kay for babysitting and decided, what the heck, to give her a hug, and when the twins ran to the SUV, Bevy raced them, actually wanting to win and then winning.

"You're fast, Mom!" Kyle said.

"We did art," Kyle said. "Landscapes!"

"Grandma said we did excellent work," Karl said.

"She said *mine* was excellent."

"They're both excellent," Bevy said, looking at the watercolors while she floored the gas pedal. She had an urge to sprint, punch, kick, sweat, and imagined fat melting on her muscles like snow on rocks. What she really wanted was sex. She'd expected Peter to be hands-off after the night she'd asked for it; instead he'd been frisky: fits of cuddling, from-behind hugs while she did the dishes. Yesterday morning he'd reached out of the shower when she was brushing her teeth and squeezed her behind.

Her sexual longing became a general longing—it was just *life*, maybe—and it kept growing until, moments later, tiredness overcame her. She shut down.

Kyle—who, she realized, had been trying to get her attention—let out a scream that made her feel like her ear was being used as an electric pencil sharpener. The beginnings of her headaches were usually hard to pinpoint. They built slowly, often while she slept, but this one, she knew, started at exactly four fifty-six.

"Quiet," she yelled, and drove the rest of the way with one eye closed.

When they got home, she went straight to the downstairs bathroom to get an Advil, but the bottle was empty, so she focused on the discomfort in her gut. It wasn't just pee that'd made her feel bloated; gas seeped from her, a hot puffer that smelled like some demon version of fried bananas.

When she walked into the kitchen, Brent looked at her funny, and she worried she'd brought bananas with her. The creamy brown smear on his cheek—he was his father's son—spoke of snacking but Bevy couldn't care.

"You're winking," he said. "Why are you winking?"

"I have a headache."

"Look it," he said, pointing at the fridge. "My chem test. A minus."

"That's good, hon." She wanted to get back to a life where nothing mattered much more than her children's tests, because nothing did. Right now, though, she wanted something else. She wanted to lie down while Colleen rubbed her head and listened to her whine about her headache and all the other burdens of being Bevy.

But Colleen, Bevy saw when she went downstairs, already had company. Ronnie, sitting shirtless on the floor, was gazing up at Colleen, who was lying there in her shiny red underpants, her head propped up in her hand. "Hey, Bevy," she said, all breezy.

"What's going on here?" Bevy said.

"Do you know where my white button-down is at?" Ronnie said.

"Go upstairs, Ronnie," she said.

"Are you all right?" Colleen said.

"I want to wear that shirt tonight," he said. "I'm going to that thing at Hilltop."

"I'll find it," Bevy said. "Go upstairs."

Ronnie sighed, then turned into an eighty-year-old man rising to his feet. When he was finally standing, the band of his briefs was visible above his brown jeans, his sharp hipbones curving down. Mr. Cool nodded at Colleen, then limped away.

"That make you feel good?" Bevy asked. "Displaying yourself for my son?"

"Come on, Bevy. He knocked on my door."

"And you made a real big effort to cover up."

"I didn't even think about it."

"I don't buy that for a second. You're well aware of what it does to a seventeen-year-old boy to see you like that."

"What?" She slapped her thigh. "These old legs?"

"Teenage boys aren't too particular."

"Ouch," Colleen said. She pulled her white UT sweatshirt down over her underpants and tucked it between her thighs. Then she looked up at Bevy, smiled. "That better?"

"You need to leave."

"What?"

"You heard me."

"Because of *this*?"

"Because you've been here ten days, because you've been smoking in here again, and, yes, because I don't need my son being treated to peep shows. I want you out in the morning."

"Just give me till Wednesday. Please. My car will be ready."

"Is that right? Because it was going to be Friday, then Monday."

"Oh. Wow. I get it." She swung her legs around to the side of the bed and slid down until her feet hit the floor. The bedspread, caught beneath her, came halfway off. "Is it just me that people don't trust or does nobody trust anybody?"

"I didn't mean that."

"So you said it just to be cruel?" She reached down between her legs and pulled her duffel out from underneath the bed.

"You don't need to pack this minute."

"Can't leave without packing."

"I said you could stay here tonight."

"And I'd feel mighty welcome."

"Stay here tonight."

"You can't kick me out and ask me to stay at the same time."

"I'm not going to let you make me feel guilty."

"You don't need my help for that. You've always been a natural."

"And you're just the opposite, aren't you? Shameless."

"Good Lord."

"I'm sorry."

"Leave me alone, all right? Go away. I need to get changed."

When Bevy got up to the kitchen, she had to stop herself from going back down and begging her to stay. A strange power Colleen had. Bevy wanted to punch her in the face.

Bevy needed to make dinner and with the throbbing in her head, it was all she could do just to put water in a pot. This would be the third night in a week they had pasta, but this being Monday, she'd call it the first time and Kay's meatballs would help the Ragu. With Colleen gone, Kay would get back to helping out and butting in. Things, for better or worse, would get back to normal.

Before the water had come to a boil, Colleen was ready to go, wearing the same things she'd arrived in: hat, boots, white fur coat. Stylish or cheap, it was hard to say.

"Where are you going, Colleen?" Kyle asked.

"Away, darling."

"When are you coming back?"

She wrapped her arms around his waist and picked him up. Karl came running, and she managed, strong as she was, to kneel down and pick him up as well. She shook them until they giggled. JB ran over and jumped up on her and barked.

After she'd set the twins down, Colleen sped out the door, forcing Bevy to chase after her. Every footstep was an explosion, like she was a giant in a cartoon, or Godzilla. "You going to leave without saying good-bye?" she shouted.

Colleen, stopping in the street, lifted her knee up to her neck and with the heel of her boot kicked the telephone pole. The streetlight flickered, then went back on.

Bevy walked into the street, and Colleen turned around. Bevy took a step toward her, and Colleen took a step back, so Bevy stopped. "Where are you going?"

"I don't know."

"Can I give you a ride?"

"No. You've done enough."

"Is this really what you want to be, an ingrate?"

"I'm serious when I say you've done enough. Ten days is a lot to ask, I know that. I don't mind you asking me to leave; what I mind is you not trusting me."

"I didn't mean that the way it sounded."

"There's only one way to mean it."

Bevy tried to think of another explanation but could barely think at all. The usable part of her brain was the size of a corn nut.

"You have a headache," Colleen said.

"Yes." Her eyes were squinted so much that the image of Colleen was flashing, as if the streetlight were still flickering. "I don't feel well at all."

"Sweetie, you can barely stand up."

"I had too much coffee. Forget about it. I'm fine. You've got your own problems."

"That's for sure. I don't suppose you have any money you could lend me."

"No." It seemed important to be honest about this. "Peter gives me an allowance, and I haven't gotten it yet this week."

"Check out these two middle-aged gals. I'm cash-poor and you're getting an allowance. I'm not sure we've come all that far."

"Speak for yourself, all right? I've come a ways, there's no doubt about that."

"No doubt, hunh?" Colleen smiled and Bevy squeezed shut her eyes. For the first time in years she fantasized about doing violence to herself, a drill to the temple, pain to relieve pain. Of course, way back when, she hadn't merely fantasized about it. In 1978 it was Colleen who she'd seen by her hospital bed when she'd opened her eyes. And now when she opened her eyes, she saw Colleen walking away.

CHAPTER 25

ONE FIFTY-FOUR, and he hadn't slept, would never sleep. He would face Bevy Baer on no sleep.

It started along his hairline, hot and prickly like a sunburn, and moved into his cheeks and chest and, like an actual burn, strained his organs, his heart, his lungs, and he sat up, stood up, walked out, paced. He longed for his little life of writing columns and seeing movies and failing in private. Private frustration was so much better than public humiliation. Why in God's name had he put himself in a position where he would reveal to the world how pathetic he was? Because he'd wanted to, that's why; this had been the plan all along, all his life, the scheme devised by his self-destructive, self-loathing subconscious, which had identified his worst nightmare—a public poop-in-pants breakdown in his hometown—then taken steps to ensure that it happened. Wow, was he fucked-up, a lost little boy who'd gone looking for validation, for love, but whose self-sabotaging brain would allow him only humiliation, scorn, pity. He would have to be escorted from the stage and taken to a mental hospital, embarrassing everyone in the auditorium (except for a jubilant Reverend Wedgwood), securing his fifteen minutes of infamy (a half hour on Fox), and ceding the school board once and for all to the religious right—the key event in the Christianizing of Hartsburg, which turned into a theocracy where Hilltop was City Hall and where people occasionally, out of compassion and condescension, prayed for the soul of Wally Cormier, the town's most notorious mental patient and its last liberal, who, having lost his mother to death and his wife to his former friend Zev Dreskin, and having been subjected to shock therapy and weekly visits from Bevy Baer, ultimately surrendered and accepted Jesus, a final act of fear and self-hatred that he was too mentally ill and medicated to recognize as such. He paced and tried to find a way out of this bad place. What were you supposed to do when you were *here*? Talk to someone. Your wife. Robin had comforted him in the past, she had rubbed his back and kissed his forehead, and it was a sign of the distance between them now that even as he was going crazy he couldn't bring himself to ask her for help, and he knew that his distance from her was a reason he was going crazy.

He managed to listen past the noise in his head and heard the TV, so he put on his robe and went down to the living room, where Zev was in the recliner with his silky black shirt unbuttoned, revealing a surprisingly hairless belly that was smaller than it used to be but not small. The sight of his friend was enough to make Cormier feel almost sane.

"Check this out," Zev said. "*The Big Lebowski.*"

"Mary, Mother of God," Cormier said, with some sincerity. "It's just starting."

Zev pointed at Cormier's midsection. "Hello, Mr. Lovebean," he said as Cormier covered up. "How are you tonight? Not too big, and you?"

"You're talking to my penis?"

"Yeah. Unfortunately, he's only capable of small talk." He raised his glass of bourbon, toasting the TV, where Sam Eliott was delivering the opening monologue. "America." Zev was referring, Cormier guessed, to the ability here in God's Country to watch *The Big Lebowski* in the middle of the night.

"Are you still a big movie guy?"

"Not really. I don't have the attention span. That's why I like *The Sopranos.*" He looked at Cormier and nodded to confirm that he'd revealed telling info. Prior to this visit, Cormier had believed that Zev enjoyed his life; if not quite healthy, he was closer to happy than most. But now Cormier couldn't deny that he seemed as sad as most.

"What'd you do tonight?" Cormier asked.

"You should be sleeping."

"I would if I could. Do you have any pills?"

"Do I have any pills? Is pig pussy pink?" Hearing him use one of Stu's sayings, Cormier was moved almost to tears, and he curled up on the couch. "You're going to do well," Zev said, heading for the stairs. "You're ready."

There was a chance that this was true. Cormier had woken up Saturday with a full-body ache. Zev had assured him that the hangover could work to his advantage; preparing for the debate in such a condition was, he'd said, like swinging a heavy bat in the on-deck circle. They'd proceeded to have a productive weekend, with Zev coaching him and doing a credible impersonation of Bevy Baer while Stu, who'd decided he was too tired to hunt, dozed and read and drank. Stu didn't say a word while they'd rehearsed; occasionally he looked up from his Carl Hiaasen novel and shook his head.

Zev had the largest toiletry kit Cormier had ever seen. "You're a Jap."

"It's a job requirement. You'd be surprised how many candidates partake. They should drug-test before debates. Here we go: Valium. Tomorrow we'll get more exotic." He poured three pills into his palm, put one in his mouth, and gave Cormier two.

"I need water," Cormier said. "I've got no saliva."

"You're getting to be kind of a diva with your demands." Zev fell forward onto his knees, crawled to his drink, and crawled back using one hand—a sight that made Cormier question all over again his decision to place his trust in his old friend. Zev, having retained his drink, crawled like a wounded dog back to the recliner.

"What if these pills don't work?"

"They will. Have faith."

On-screen the Dude sneaked a hit from a carton of half-and-half in a peaceful supermarket that, despite the Cohn brothers' weirdness, looked like normalcy, the sort of lovely American normalcy that Cormier would gratefully reenter in a week, win or lose. He would take his time. Appreciate. He would go to the supermarket and pick the slowest line and read *People* magazine. He would add an Almond Joy to his haul and be friendly to the woman at the register. Slide his credit card through and feel fortunate. Be patient as he tried to remember where he parked. Secure the bag containing the eggs. Stick his hand out the window at the four-way stop to wave his fellow driver through, receive a thank-you wave. Drive around the block three times while he listened to the song that seemed like a masterpiece only when he heard it on the radio. Go home.

He'd squeezed out five hours of sleep, and with the help of a midafternoon Klonopin and a last-minute Xanax, whose soporiferousness had been counteracted with half a NoDoz, he'd walked onto the stage and started debating without much self-consciousness—without much consciousness of any kind. His entry had been so smooth that he hadn't even noticed it, the tranquilizers doing what Schlitz had done on that day at the lake at the end of junior year when he'd found himself neck-deep in the frigid water talking to the lovely Ava Klam without any memory of getting in the water or starting the conversation. Thank God for drugs. Also important was Zev's suggestion that Cormier not wear his glasses, which in the last debate had apparently given off a glare. Tonight his inability to see people in the crowd seemed to decrease their ability to see him, and he was able to embrace the illogic of this because he knew that his gauge of the crowd's focus on him was more accurate than it had been during the last debate, when his self-consciousness had been so extreme he'd looked downward to conceal his nose hair.

Whereas the crowd was all but invisible, Bevy Baer was all too visible. Her face was a mime's but all the makeup couldn't conceal the pouches under her eyes. Did Bevy have a bad night? You'd think that someone guaranteed eternal life, debate or no, would get eight solid. Her brooch looked like a vegetable steamer, and even for born-again hair, hers was immense and rigid, as if she'd stuck her head in the freezer after showering. It was all a bit much. He was debating Ronald McDonald!

Bevy was answering a question that Cormier had already answered, concerning the bête noire, or bête brun, of the campaign: Bronson Tavares. Bevy loved this issue, which allowed her to imply that Cormier was too weak to either protect children or stand up to them: let him on the board and some sort of 9-11–Columbine–*Lord of the Flies* situation would ensue. But he'd said he was "open to the idea of expulsion," so unless she wanted to send him to Guantánamo, he had gone a ways toward neutralizing Tavares as an issue.

". . . but Mr. Cormier, on the other hand, is prepared to welcome him back in three months. Mr. Cormier: What part of 'go bin Laden on the school' don't you understand?"

"You're misrepresenting—"

"We need to move on," said Rita Beetle, who'd also moderated the previous debate. Like most moderators—Jim Lehrer, to name a famous example—Rita had been chosen for her lack of personality; boringness seemed to suggest impartiality.

"She addressed me directly," Cormier said.

Rita looked at him, her closed mouth bouncing, her chin fat bulging like a bullfrog's. "I'll give you thirty seconds," Rita said.

"No one cares about student safety more than I do," he said, letting a rasp vibrate a word here and there. (Years before, a woman at the other end of the speaker at a KFC drive-through—a black woman, no less— had told him that he had a sexy voice.) "But I'm willing to allow for the possibility that he can be reformed. I would think that Mrs. Baer believes in redemption." This last bit was an ad-lib, an actual spontaneous remark, and it elicited applause from his supporters, thrilled by his new poise.

"And I do," Bevy said. "But I also believe in raising kids right to begin with, which brings me back to evolution. Don't you think it's better for children to learn that they are godly creations, not random globs of pro-toplasm?"

This, it seemed, was not a rhetorical question but one that Bevy and Rita and everyone else expected him to answer. "I don't know how one can, in good conscience, suggest that creationism could have helped this student."

"I don't know what *one* can or can't do." Here she did a little curtsy meant to mock his language. Hear that guy's syntax? What a fag! "All I know is what *I* believe," Bevy said. "I believe that evolution is a dark, de-pressing theory. Liberals are big on self-esteem. Well, what does it do to students' self-esteem to learn that they're nothing more than glorified apes whose ancestors were a bunch of cells that stuck together and rose up from the ooze like creatures in some horror movie?"

Crackpot. If there'd been any doubt, there was no longer, yet he couldn't ridicule her, no no no, because her beliefs were religious, and re-ligious beliefs, especially the Christian kind, had to be *respected*. "That's not a fair depiction of evolution. In any case, evolution is perfectly com-patible with the idea that humans are special. Humans *are* special; that's a fact and facts are what schools should teach."

"*Your* facts," Bevy said.

"We covered this already," Rita said. "This next question is for Ms. Baer. Please explain the role that religious faith plays in your life."

Bevy pretended to consider the question, as though she herself hadn't written it. "It's everything to me. May 17, 1982. That's the most important day of my life; that's when my husband, Peter, bless his heart, brought me to the Lord. I know the power of the Lord, because I've felt the power of the Lord. Jesus changed my heart. And I believe in the power of prayer. I pray every day, and if you all do me the honor of electing me to the school board, I'll pray for guidance. There's been an effort in this country and in this town to take God out of government. Well, I'll tell you this much, if you want a school board rep who does *not* pray to the Lord, then I'm *not* the person for you. One final thing: some people have suggested that Christians are intolerant, but the opposite is true." She looked at Cormier. Staring out from her mask of makeup were eyes softened by sincerity; it appeared that Bevy Baer, however well coached, believed what she was saying. "As most of you know, putting your faith in God is a profoundly humbling experience . . ."

How could he compete with this? How could he, an agnostic or atheist, convince an auditorium full of Christians that he embodied their values? He probably couldn't, but he was on drugs and felt that he could.

"Mr. Cormier?"

"I'm not accustomed to talking about my spiritual beliefs in public, and I'm not convinced that they shouldn't remain a private matter. One's relationship with God, after all, is very personal"—Cormier thought about his prayer on the bathroom floor—"and I would no sooner fill you in on my intimate moments of prayer than I would tell you about my intimate moments with my wife. But I will tell you that whatever I do in my life, I pray I'm doing the right thing. I have deep respect for people's religious beliefs, but we need to remember that there's a diversity of beliefs in Hartsburg. There are Jews and Muslims and atheists and Christians of all stripes. If Ms. Beetle is a Christian and I'm a Christian and Ms. Baer is a Christian, that doesn't mean we all have the same beliefs. Ms. Baer wants all of us to accept her version of Christianity."

"No, I don't."

"I didn't interrupt you."

"I didn't distort your views."

"Can I have my time back?"

"You have thirty seconds."

Cormier had just asked for, and been granted, time he didn't want. He had finished his prepared response and was now faced with the prospect of trying to rephrase his series of not-quite lies. Instead he heard himself saying something he hoped as true, a prayer in its own right. "Most Harts-burgers don't want religion imposed on them and they don't want to be preached to by anyone except their preacher."

"Are you saying we shouldn't have the right to preach the Gospel?" Bevy said.

"No," Cormier said. "I'm saying that when you're having a nice quiet breakfast and people ring your doorbell and try to push their beliefs on you, it's annoying and—"

There were boos and cheers and Star Mourning shouted, "That's right, Wallace." Cormier couldn't see her face but he could see her hair, which tonight she was wearing in an Afro. "Come on, now," she shouted. "You don't hold back."

"And it's offensive," he said. "People want to be left alone."

"And he thinks *I'm* intolerant," Bevy said.

This got a predictable rise out of her supporters. He had just staked his campaign on his assumption that to-each-his-own, leave-me-alone types— his neighbor Mr. John and his like—still spoke for the soul of Hartsburg. But this had been the underlying assumption of his campaign all along. He felt good, in any case, about his new bite.

"This question is for Mr. Cormier. Many parents are concerned that the homosexual agenda is being pushed in the public schools. Do you share their concern?"

This would have been a difficult issue for Cormier even if his mother weren't a born-again lesbian. He and Zev had managed, however, to come up with an answer that Cormier could believe in, and Zev, for some rea-son, had revised it earlier in the day to make it even more not untruthful. "Let it rip," Zev had said.

"There's no such thing as the homosexual agenda; what there is—are." He paused, trying to get his grammar straight. Who cared about gram-mar? Not these people. He wondered if the drugs were wearing off. "What there are are homosexual men and women, trying to live their lives with dignity. I understand that some people have qualms with homosexu-ality, so where does that leave schools, which are charged with educating children as well as responding to the needs of families? The answer is that on this issue, as on evolution and every other issue, Hartsburg schools should teach truths, and there's simply no evidence that homosexuality is anything but a healthy . . ." He didn't want to say "lifestyle," a word that seemed to trivialize the matter. "Lifestyle," he said.

"Is it a fact that Abraham Lincoln was gay?" Bevy asked.

"I don't know," Cormier said, his mind misbehaving as it had in the first debate, "but I know he chopped down the cherry tree."

Bevy looked at him and actually scratched her head. "I bring this up because there's a teacher at the high school pushing the idea that Abe Lincoln, the father of the Republican Party and the man who ended slavery, is a homo-sexual—"

"Here I am," Star shouted.

There were cheers, and Cormier had the misfortune of hearing his mother yell, "You go, girl." Rita Beetle tapped her microphone.

"I said there's a *theory* he's gay," Star said.

"Oh, I see," Bevy said. "A *theory*. Well, y'all are pretty darn good at passing off theories as fact. Next thing you know, some teacher will be pushing the *theory* that Christ Himself was a homo-sexual. My opponent claims that Christians want to push their views onto other people. Well, that's just about the biggest case of the pot calling the kettle black I've ever seen. Liberals are using the public schools to demean mainstream values." She let out a sigh, her microphone making it sound like a gust of wind. "As if raising children wasn't hard enough, we've got teachers undermining what we teach them at home. School should *help* parents, but here we have a teacher promoting her own personal beliefs, beliefs that most of us find distasteful and despicable and disgusting!"

Bevy backed away from the microphone, breathless and red-faced, her voice having risen into a shriek. The crowd, even Star, had gone quiet. For the first time Bevy had seemed like the radical she was—her flurry at the end had been full of scorn and saliva—and this would have pleased Cormier if not for his realization that it might have been George Washington, not Lincoln, who'd cut down the cherry tree. If so, he had come across as not only unfunny but also unpatriotic. Even as he told himself that this fear was unfounded—the joke, if that's what it was, had passed quickly—his body filled up with anxiety; to let it trickle was to feel it gush. It paralyzed his brain. Feelings trembled through him—shame at the thought of letting down Dreifort, guilt for burdening Annie with the wreckage his life was about to become, anger at Robin for wanting to move—but his brain slowed, or sped, to a standstill. His brain was capable of Nothing.

He couldn't understand Bevy's closing statement. Rita Beetle said something and he knew it was time to talk. Still his brain gave him Nothing. He felt the crowd's discomfort and pitied them having to suffer through this. Nothing.

He imagined Wedgwood's smile and saw himself through Carly's eyes. He opened his mouth. He began to . . . talk. It was as if he were holding together the disintegrating pieces of his brain at the same time that he used the makeshift contraption. Yet he kept using it. He discovered strength that a less atheistic man would have attributed to God. But he knew it came from himself, and he liked knowing this.

"I care about the town," he was saying. "Don't take my word for it. Ask Stu Nedney, who I've known since the fourth grade. Or my mother, whose example I hope to follow in helping out the people of this town. My opponent wants you to believe that I don't represent the values of this town, but this is where I learned my values. This is where I learned about the importance of strong families and strong schools. Families need to be able to raise children the way they want to raise them. Meanwhile schools need to teach truths. My opponent has every right to believe whatever she wants to believe. The problem is when she uses the schools to promote her beliefs and to punish those who don't share them. That's really the crux of it, I think."

CHAPTER 26

PETER AND ALL THE CHILDREN SAID, "Great job," but they were probably just being nice and there was no reason, in either case, to tell the truth, which was that politics was a game of expectations, and that Cormier had slithered over his low bar and won a "moral" victory, which could, with the help of the *Informer*, make a race of the race. Instead, she smiled through her headache, now pounding away into its second full day.

On the way home she pushed her temple against the cold car window and regretted not getting a college education. Her brain lacked facts. Even when she knew something, she wasn't sure she knew it. After Cormier had made a crack about Abe Lincoln cutting down the cherry tree, she didn't have the confidence to point out that he should have said George Washington. She'd doubted herself for an instant—Lincoln's nickname was Honest Abe—and then it'd been too late to capitalize on his mistake, a mistake that was telling in light of his hostility toward the ideals of the Founding Fathers.

Hartsburg looked watery through the window. Ronnie was telling Loretta about some band and Brent was asking Peter about carburetors. She didn't want them to suffer with her, but it was sad that she could sit here, all torn up, and her family could carry on, oblivious. But she couldn't expect them to give her sympathy when she'd gone out of her way to act upbeat. People couldn't read your mind.

She missed Colleen: there was no use denying it. Even though Colleen had contributed to Bevy's headache and near-sleepless night. Even though Bevy might have wrapped up the campaign tonight if Colleen had never come on the scene. Now that Colleen was gone, who was going to listen to Bevy complain?

Only Loretta and Brent had eaten before the debate, and Bevy, brat that she was, was waiting for Peter or Ronnie to ask her to make something so that she could say, You have *got* to be kidding. An argument was what she wanted, an argument she could win.

She was saved, and deprived, by Kay, who'd made a pot roast, freeing up Bevy to take a tumbler of water to the living room, where she swallowed the last of the eight Advil she'd put in her pocket and lay down on the couch. The sounds of her family were distant and not unpleasant: the scrape of a knife on a plate as Ronnie ate too quickly, the suctiony sound of the freezer door opening as Loretta went for ice cream, the monotone murmur of Kay's voice asking if Loretta had eaten dinner.

Kay brought Bevy a big ziplock bag full of ice. Bevy didn't have high hopes for the remedy but appreciated the thought, and it felt good, the ice on her forehead, with the bottom of the bag on her cheeks, her smiling muscles.

"Thanks, Kay. That's sweet of you."

Now Peter was watching baseball and Kay was doing the dishes. It was Bevy's life that she was listening to, and she liked it. She'd recommit to it, reclaim it, as soon as she'd won.

The jingle of keys pulled her out of sleep: Peter was headed out. When she called to him, she got no response, so she went into the kitchen.

"Where are you going?" Bevy said.

Peter looked nervous, as if found out. Kay was sitting at the table, sipping her nightly cup of warm milk with honey. "To get gas," he said.

"At this time of night?"

"You know I can't rest easy when the gas light is on."

"I didn't, actually," Bevy said as Peter walked out.

"He likes things the way he likes them," Kay said with a little smile, maybe making fun of her son. If she was, it was a first.

"The ice helped." Kay nodded to say she'd known it would. Bevy was grateful for her help tonight but annoyed she hadn't asked about the debate. "I'm curious," Bevy said. "It seems to me that at one time you were interested in politics."

"If you want to tell me about the debate, go ahead."

"No, no, that's not it." To cover for her fib, she turned toward the sink. Refilling her tumbler, she saw herself in the window. The icepack had matted down her hair into what could have been a toupee, and with her smeared eye makeup, she looked beat-up. What a sight for Kay, who'd have found a way to put herself together if her house was burning down. "I remember having discussions with you about politics," Bevy said.

"I still could. I keep up on things, watch C-SPAN. I like that Brian Lamb."

"Correct me if I'm wrong, but didn't you tell me a few months ago that politics was no place for Christians?"

"That doesn't mean it's not important."

"So you care as much as ever about the condition of the country?"

"Of course. But I say: forget about winning votes, start winning hearts. What good are laws if people don't follow them? We need to pray and spread the Gospel. And set an example. I can't stand seeing so-called Christians like Bill Bennett and Tom DeLay preaching moral values. They hurt the Christian cause more than Ted Kennedy."

"That's a little glib, don't you think?" Kay stared at her over her mug, which she was cradling, and Bevy stared right back. What was the point of talking with Kay if Bevy didn't speak her mind? "What about the president? He's a good Christian."

"Forgive me if I have doubts. Christianity is about not compromising; politics is the opposite. You take money from whoever's got it. You work out *deals*. Tell me, would you vote for a bill that banned only the most gruesome form of murder?"

"You're talking about partial-birth abortion?"

"Yes, but more than that. Say you're a Christian politician. On the one hand, you fight for laws that are just symbolic, given the state of the culture. On the other hand, you end up supporting laws that violate your principles."

"I've stayed true to my principles."

"Glad to hear it. The reason I didn't ask about the debate is, I didn't want to find out that you made a political issue out of Annie Cormier."

"I didn't mention her," Bevy said, telling the truth. "I've got to say, Kay, I like talking to you. We used to do this more often."

"Same as I *used* to be interested in politics?"

"Your point being?"

"You seem to have a notion that things have changed."

"I believe they have." Standing limp-legged in the middle of the kitchen, Bevy didn't have the strength to hold back her words, and it felt liberating to let them go. "When I first married Peter, you and I were, maybe not close, but closer. I have this idea, maybe it's crazy, that you're still angry with me because Peter and I made the move to Hilltop."

"Mercy. You really have a knack for putting yourself at the center of the story. Have I changed? Am I less outgoing? More closed-up? If so, it has nothing to do with you, believe it or not. Have you considered what my life is like?"

"Of course I have."

"Do you think of me as a widow?"

It was hard to know how to answer; she went with the truth. "No."

"Well, that's what I am."

"Okay. But you didn't have a husband when I first met you."

"Let me tell you, there's a big difference between being alone and fifty-three and being alone and seventy-three."

"You're not alone. You have us."

"And I thank God for that, but there's no substitute for a husband."

"I suppose not. But you should lean on us. You never ask for a thing."

"You can't give me what I want, not unless you're willing to sleep next to me at night. And not unless you get to know me so well you can read my mind."

"I think I'll pass on the first," Bevy said, getting a laugh out of her, which was no everyday thing. "But I can give the second a shot. Talk to me, Kay."

"About what?"

"Jack. Tell me about him."

"Here's something you might not know. He used to get awful hay fever headaches, and I'd bring him ice packs, like the one I just brought you. Worked like a charm, until one night it didn't. It turns out ice doesn't help brain tumors."

She took a step toward Kay, thinking she might put her hand on her shoulder. "There's so much I don't know about your life. But I'd like to hear about it."

The garage door went up, and Kay said, "Some other time," before scooting downstairs, where she would sleep with no one next to her.

Bevy waited for Peter in the kitchen, and when he opened the door, he was holding a bouquet of flowers, all different kinds. "Special at the gas station?" she said.

"These are for you," he said, handing them to her. "I know you had a hard time tonight. But you did real well, and I'm proud as ever of you. I love you."

The flowers reminded Bevy of the years in the nineties when he had attended Promise Keepers rallies, which taught men to worship their wives. This kind of gesture didn't come naturally to Peter, and Bevy suspected that Kay had played a role. In any case, Bevy was thankful he'd be lying next to her tonight.

She hugged the bouquet and smelled the daisy in the middle. "Where on earth did you find these this time of night?"

"Wal-Mart. Where else?"

CHAPTER 27

A T THE PARTY—ZEV had invited people back to the house—the consensus was that he'd not just exceeded expectations but won outright. Star Mourning, the new bête noire of the campaign, was thrilled—"About time you muscled up"—as was Dreifort, who stayed at the party just long enough for him to announce: "Friends and Fools, we have a race on our hands!" Last night Cormier had been headed for a mental hospital; now he was celebrating a performance that at best had won him the race and at worst had put to rest his fears that he would make an ass of himself. A moment of triumph.

Yet he felt awful. He wished he could blame his mood on tiredness—a crash after an adrenaline-high was normal even when drugs weren't in the mix—but he knew it was a reaction to the reactions of his women. Annie had said, "Well done, Wallace," a constricted response for someone capable of enthusiasm, and Robin had remained silent until they'd gotten into her Honda, at which point she'd said, "I can't fucking believe you said you were a Christian." Cormier, sitting in the backseat while Carly rode shotgun, had lacked the energy to explain that he had skillfully managed *not* to say that. "What *are* we, anyway?" Carly had said, "What am *I*? Am I Jewish or nothing or what?" Robin's violent downshift was directed at him. "What do you want to be?" Robin asked. "I don't know," Carly said, "but I'd like to be something."

Now, alone on the couch, he wanted to escape into the crack between the cushions. No one would notice if he did. Carly had gone upstairs and Stu had gone to Jed's and Robin was talking to Zev and Annie was talking to Star and the Clymers were talking to each other and everyone was sort of talking to everyone else except for the man whose victory they were supposedly celebrating. He was drinking a bourbon and RC that he hoped would escort him to the party that was carrying on without him.

"People think New Yorkers are aggressive," Robin said to Zev. "But there's nothing more aggressive than the happy horseshit of Midwesterners."

"Why is it that horseshit is so often happy?" Zev said.

"It must be because horses have such nice"—Robin put her thighs together, bent her knees, slapped her ass—"behinds."

"If that's the way it works, your poop must be quite content."

"Not as content as it used to be."

"Your poop is very happy," Zev said. "Trust me."

Flirting was one thing (whatever it takes, babe). Flirting with the author of the lines she found so objectionable was another. It was hypocrisy.

So Cormier had given a response that was, God forbid, political. So he wasn't perfect; he was merely brave. I DID SOMETHING HARD, PEOPLE. I FACED MY FEARS AND ATE SQUID SAUSAGE AND STARED INTO THE ABYSS. I HAVE SUFFERED, AND NOW IT IS TIME FOR ALL OF YOU TO GIVE ME LOVE.

"Abe Lincoln?" Zev said to Star. "Anything else we should know."

"That was odious," Zora Clymer said. "I can't believe she went after you like that."

"I can," Star said. "I've been trying to tell ya'll that these people are not nice. We play nice; meanwhile they make us out to be perverts."

"Surely it doesn't hurt that the pervert in question has kinky hair," Annie said.

"The irony of the situation," Star said, "is that Bevy would actually like my class."

"Somehow I doubt that," Annie said, poking Star in the ribs. This was the first time Cormier had been around them since knowing they were lovers. He would have been comfortable had they not been so cutesy-poopsy with each other.

"I'm serious, A.C.," Star said. "I talk about Christianity more than any other teacher. You've got to when you're teaching American History."

"By the way," Paul Clymer said, "it was George Washington, not Abe Lincoln, who cut down the cherry tree. Or so legend has it."

"I must say, Wallace," Annie said, "I found your discussion of your religious beliefs borderline mendacious."

"There was nothing borderline about it," Robin said.

"I don't see that he's got a whole lot of choice," Star said. "This is a religious town, a religious town in a religious state in a religious country."

"He's got to appeal to the masses," Robin said.

"The asses," Zora Clymer said.

"The great unwashed," Paul Clymer said.

"He should say that it's a private matter and leave it at that," Annie said.

"I've got everything under control," Zev said.

"No doubt you do," Annie said. "I hope you don't plan on blunting his edges any further. May I remind you that your client was named after Henry Wallace."

"The segregationist?" Zev said, and Robin smiled.

"I hope you're joking," Annie said.

"Was Stalin Cormier already taken?" Zev said, and Robin smiled.

"You have anything to add, Wallace?" Annie said. "It's your candidacy, after all."

TO MENTION THAT I WAS NAMED AFTER HENRY WALLACE IS TO SAY THAT I HAVEN'T LIVED UP TO THE NAME IS TO IMPLY THAT I'VE DISAPPOINTED DAD IS TO STICK YOUR HAND DOWN MY THROAT, PULL OUT MY HEART, AND GRIND IT UP IN THE GARBAGE DISPOSAL.

"No," Cormier said. "I'm spent."

People took this as the hint that it was, and he felt like an ungrateful bore as the couples went home and Robin went upstairs without even looking at him. He and his wife now existed in separate universes, bubbles created by his campaign-related anxiety and her existence-related depression. Both prone to self-absorption, they had trouble enough when *one* of them was going through a hard time. Having done nothing to try to bust out of his bubble—his empathy in West Virginia had been short-lived— he had no right to blame her for not tending to his needs. But she could have said good night.

Although he'd come to suspect that tiredness was his chief problem— his most immediate one, anyway—he would stay up with Zev because this was his friend's last night in Hartsburg, and because, life being life, this was one of the last nights they would spend together. He estimated how many times he might see him again before one of them (Zev, more likely) died. Eight was his guess, every four years.

"Don't listen to the naysayers," Zev said, now crouched under the TV.

"Yeah, fuck them," Cormier said. He thought about Barb Shellenberger, the librarian with whom he'd judged the sausage contest. She'd hugged him after the debate tonight. "Thank you," she'd said. "Finally someone is saying what I've wanted to say for years." Barb probably represented a silent majority. Which now had a spokesperson.

"You know something?" Cormier said. "I'm pretty proud of myself."

"You should be." Still crouched, Zev spun around showing a smile of such delight and deviousness that Cormier felt preemptively guilty.

"What?" Cormier said. Zev stood up, walked toward the kitchen, and turned off the light. "What the hell is going on?" Cormier said.

Zev, still sporting that smile, dance-walked toward Cormier, who was afraid he was going to be made to dance. "Tell me what's happening," Cormier said.

"You, my friend, are about to see something very special." He reached into his pants pockets and pulled out remote controls like guns from a holster.

The video was homemade, a man mumbling as he tried to figure out how to work the camera: gray sky, the corner of a house, a deck with beer cans on the railing. And smoke, or steam. A hot tub, men with mustaches. The naked back of a blond-haired woman, who turned blurry as Zev, now next to Cormier, pushed Pause. "Are you ready for this?"

"I don't think so. Are we . . . Are we going to see Bevy?"

"Oh, yeah. Bevy at her best."

"Is this porn? Is this goddamned Bevy Baer porn?"

"No. It's better than porn. It's the *opposite* of porn."

"What does that mean? Where'd you get this?"

"Are you ready?"

"Play the tape."

The blond peeked over her shoulder. "Stand up," the cameraman said, and there were cheers. "Stand up, Colleen, and turn around." Colleen did just that, and the camera panned down to show skin, a dark nipple. She backed up, and the camera took her all in. An impossibly good body, the kind of body that didn't exist in real life, especially real life before the era of silicone. She froze, blurred: Zev again with the remote.

"You've got to be kidding," Cormier said.

"Did you see that?"

"Yeah, I caught a glimpse."

"I mean the dudes in the background doing blow."

"What's wrong with you? Where are your priorities?"

Colleen made like a model: all pouty looks and poses. She clutched her hair with both hands, pushing it into an even larger pile. "Get in there with her, Bevy," the cameraman said. "Yeah," Colleen said, and extended her arm. "Come here, sweet pie."

"Oh my God," Cormier said, woozy with a combination of arousal and nausea, as though he were getting laid on a rocking boat.

"Sometimes life is so beautiful I want to cry," Zev said.

There she was, unmistakably Bevy. But her shy smile made her seem like a different person. Her hair was as large as it was today but wilder; it swooped and sprouted the way certain hair did in the eighties. Her body, though not exquisite like Colleen's, was thin and shapely, with breasts hanging heavy in an orange bikini. Between her tits was a constellation of moles. "Take off your top," the cameraman said, and Bevy said something indecipherable as Colleen reached behind her and untied her top. Bevy let it fall into the water—her nipples were much smaller than Colleen's—and the two women put their arms around each other. The guys cleared out of the tub to get a better view. Colleen played to the camera. Bevy was more subdued, although she gave someone the finger and said, "Fuck off." Never had profanity seemed so profane.

"Look at that," Zev said. "Bevy loves her. She absolutely loves her."

He had a point. Bevy kept giving her friend longing glances, then rested her head on her shoulder. She was drunk, at least.

"Watch this," Zev said.

"Why don't you two kiss," the cameraman said.

"Why don't you kiss my ass," Colleen said.

"This," Zev said, pointing. "Right here."

Bevy gave her friend a kiss on her shoulder, a loving peck.

"Ha!" Zev said. "Now keep your eye on Colleen's tit."

Bevy reached out and cupped Colleen's breast from the bottom; still looking at the camera, she gave it a little lift, then snatched back her hand.

"Oh," Cormier said.

The two women put their cheeks together, and the camera zeroed in on their faces. Their smiles were heartfelt, their cheeks flushed. Bevy, a sloppy snorter, had blow on her upper lip. Despite their inebriation, the close-up was flattering because it de-emphasized their hair. They were drugged-up and happy. They were beautiful.

Colleen started to sniffle and wiped at her nose, and it was then that Cormier recognized her. The thickness of her nose gave her away.

"That's the woman from Jed's. That's how you got this tape."

The camera panned down to Bevy's black bikini bottom, then pulled back. Colleen turned toward Bevy, Bevy turned toward Colleen, and they hugged.

Colleen abruptly pulled away and walked out of the screen. They held hands briefly as they parted, Colleen tugging free of Bevy's grasp. Bevy's eyes followed Colleen; then she looked at the camera and smiled: the same shy smile she'd come in with. "Take off your pants," someone said, and the tape turned to snow.

"That's it?" Cormier said.

"That's *it*? Is that what you say at the end of *Casablanca*? Is your mind not blown?"

"My mind is pretty fucking blown, actually."

Zev laughed. "I've already whipped up two batches today."

Cormier had remained soft throughout. Was something wrong with him? "Did you have sex with Colleen the cowgirl?"

"What a film," Zev said. "Unfortunately, I don't think the public will grasp the story of unrequited love. They're only going to see tits, coke, and lesbian lovin'."

"Wait a minute," Cormier said. "I can't actually *use* this."

"What are you talking about? You can't not use this."

"How old is she in that?"

"Twenty-three. It's totally fair game."

"She's admitted she went through some dark times."

"Yeah, but here's the thing. This tape is dated October of eighty-two, months *after* she was supposedly born again."

"That's crap. As if people actually become different people when they—"

"Hey, *she's* the one using her alleged religious rebirth."

"True. But there's no actual sex."

"What do you want, a doubleheader dildo? And it's not just the sex; it's the whole scene, the drugs, the swearing. It's Bevy being—"

"Human?"

"It's Bevy being everything she rails against."

"I don't know, man. I did well tonight."

"Not *that* well. And don't you get it? By going after Star, Bevy went after your mother. This is personal now. Or it should be."

"I don't know, man. It seems extreme. This is just a school board race."

"*Just?*" Zev stood up and walked a circle around the living room, rubbing his face and the back of his neck. His lap completed, he retook his seat.

He said, "Remember when you assured me you wanted to win?"

"Remember when I said there are lines I won't cross?"

He sighed, leaned back. There was silence but for the hum of the tape.

"You're the boss," Zev said. "I don't suppose you've raised any money."

"No—oh, you had to pay for the tape. I'll pay you back."

"Could you? I mean, how are you, financially?"

"Honestly?"

"Forget it."

"No, I'll pay you back when I can. How much did it cost?"

"Forget it. Really. I've already gotten my money's worth." Zev closed his eyes and pinched the bridge of his nose. "You know not using this tape is killing me, right?"

"Yeah. But this way it belongs to us."

"We'll always have Texas."

CHAPTER 28

WEDNESDAY EVENING, walking down the aisle to a seat close to the pulpit, Bevy was shocked to realize it was only a week earlier that Colleen had joined them here. Colleen's stay in Hartsburg seemed distant and dreamlike, yet she was still with Bevy: her drawl, her smells, her sadness. The faraway-but-close feeling reminded Bevy of when she'd returned with Peter from their only real vacation ever; for their tenth anniversary Bevy's mother, using her new husband's money, sent them to the Bahamas. The sudden change of worlds disconcerted Bevy, and filled her with yearning: could she really have been in the Caribbean that morning? Yes, because she could smell the beach on her skin.

Bevy needed to put Colleen's visit, and the debate, behind her. Five more days. The Reverend would help her summon her strength.

Such was her confidence in the Reverend that not until she was back home did she realize that the service had brought no comfort. Her reaction seemed out of whack considering that the Reverend had used her campaign as a jumping-off point, and considering that even Ronnie, especially Ronnie, was inspired. "Now that was my kind of message," he said, using both hands to squirt chocolate syrup on ice cream. Peter was upstairs, putting the twins to bed. "That was a take-no-prisoners sermon, y'all."

Bevy liked that he'd taken to saying y'all, even though he'd picked it up not from her but from rappers. Or Colleen. On seeing Ronnie's reaction to Colleen's leaving—he'd pitched a fit and accused Bevy of kicking her out (which happened to be true)—Bevy had realized that the two of them had spent a lot of time together. Safe to assume it wasn't Colleen's intelligence or humor that had captivated Ronnie. Bevy had been slow to consider what sharing a house with Colleen would do to a seventeen-year-old boy. Slow, also, to realize the obvious fact that the fire burning within her son was, at least in part, lust. It was no easy thing for a teenage boy to stay pure (as she prayed and believed he still was). The good news was that, thanks to the Reverend, at the moment Ronnie was burning only for Christ. "That message was dope," he said. "Total punk rock."

"Can't be punk rock and Christian," Brent said.

"Shut up," Ronnie said.

"Be nice," Bevy said, serving herself some Chunky Monkey. Here they were, eating ice cream after church. It was possible—or should have been possible—to conclude that everything was back to normal. Better than normal, since Ronnie was in a good mood.

"How about you, Loretta?" Bevy said. "What was your feeling about church?"

"The Reverend was eloquent." She seemed to be counting the number of chocolate chips in her scoops. "But it was too loud for my tastes."

"That was *passion*," Ronnie said. "Rev was, like, stop caring about what people think. Stop apologizing. Christian pride, yo. Go out there and kick butt."

"That's not quite the way he put it," Bevy said, though Ronnie had captured the spirit of his words, which had been a direct response to Cormier's argument that Christians shouldn't be allowed to spread the Word. "The elites see you preaching the Gospel," the Reverend had said, "and they roll their eyes. They giggle at you. They despise you. They despise you because the Truth that you represent and embody is the only thing that stands between them and absolute power. So they want us to submit. Psychological warfare is what it is. They want us to want them to like us. But we don't need their approval. We can't be hurt by their judgment and mockery because we have the Lord's love. Make your presence felt, people. Be seen and be heard and be bold. Go out there and show Mr. Cormier and his kind that they can't insult us and get away with it."

Rising to her feet along with everyone else, Bevy had been excited, but her excitement had been mixed with unease, and now more unease than excitement remained. Cormier had turned the race into a referendum on the right to preach the Gospel, and the Reverend welcomed the argument.

As did Bevy: it was about religious freedom, the First Amendment, the stuff America was founded on. So what was the problem?

"Good gobble," Peter said, having stripped down to his V-neck T-shirt, which was still tucked in, his pants riding high, making his torso look cut off. "There's enough ice cream in here to choke a horse. Especially in your bowl, Ron."

"I've got a big appetite," Ronnie said. "Church got me hungry."

"Glad to hear it, son." Peter smiled, then got serious. "What the . . ." He picked up the container of chocolate chip cookie dough. "I thought we weren't going to get Ben & Jerry's except for Chunky Monkey."

"I know," Bevy said, "but I figured it didn't really matter since we were already giving them money."

"The less, the better," Peter said.

"How about not at all?" Bevy said, dumping her scoop of Chunky Monkey back into the container. "We can do without it, don't you think?"

"All right," Peter said. "No more B & J's." He snatched the container of Chunky Monkey. "After tonight."

She smiled at him and wanted him to smile at himself, but he still had that serious look on his face. "I love a man of principle," she said.

"No sense in wasting it." He tipped the container and removed Bevy's scoop, which was apparently unworthy of his bowl. "It's already paid for."

"Nikki's mother doesn't let her watch ABC," Loretta said. "Because Disney owns ABC, and there are gay days at Disney World."

"Not anymore, I don't think," Bevy said. "At any rate, it's near impossible not to give money to anti-Christian businesses."

"Christians should boycott NBC 'cause of *Will and Grace*," Brent said. "That'd be a good thing to do, don't you think, Dad?"

"General Electric owns NBC," Peter said.

"GE, we bring gay things to life," Bevy said. Loretta smiled and Brent laughed, sensing a joke in there somewhere. Bevy wanted to cry.

"Boycotts are lame," Ronnie said.

"No, they're not," Brent said.

Peter shook the can of whipped cream before spraying it, piling it so high that for a moment Bevy thought he was joking. "Enough cream, don't you think?" Bevy said.

"You used to love whipped cream yourself," he said.

The reference was clear. On the day that she had been born again, in the truck stop, she'd had chocolate chip pancakes with whipped cream. Saving someone was almost as fulfilling as being saved—Bevy knew this from experience—and Peter surely remembered all the details: the silver bolt of lightning on the waitress's necklace, the trucker who walked out in just a towel from the adjoining showers to refill his coffee cup, the flies buzzing around the jar of apple butter. When Peter placed his book-marked Bible on the table, Bevy had a moment of doubt, which God, working through Peter's kind eyes, wiped away. There was no real choice: to ask the question, to truly allow yourself to ask the question, is to an-swer it. Once God had entered her heart, she didn't cry, no, she laughed, she laughed and people turned to look. Now, as then, Bevy could not have been more grateful to Peter—he was right to be proud of what he'd done—but she resented him using her rebirth, their most cherished shared memory, to angle for advantage in an argument. My goodness, was nothing sacred? But it was possible he really was just talking about whipped cream.

"I still love whipped cream," Bevy said, "but I settle for five inches of the stuff."

"Well, aren't you virtuous," Peter said.

"I'll tell you one thing," Ronnie said brightly, choosing to ignore the bickering of his parents. "Rev wasn't talking about boycotts tonight. He was talking about getting out in the streets and making our voices heard."

"That was some message," Peter said. "A real humdinger."

Bevy wondered if it was too late to go back for her scoop, which was sitting, mostly melted, in the lid.

CHAPTER 29

O N THURSDAY MORNING, before he'd even opened his eyes, he knew things looked better. Yesterday things had looked bad indeed. He'd felt small and sour, like a crab apple. Zev had left, abandoning Cormier to family members who saw him as a reprobate. "Remember those gutters?" Robin said. "Or are you just going to *pray* it doesn't rain?" The article about the debate didn't help. The overly balanced style of journalism that had benefited him last time now benefited Bevy, who, the article said with gross understatement, "grew animated when discussing homosexuality." He called his mother and fished for approval; upon not getting it, he managed to be direct. "Are you disappointed in me?" She paused. "I wish you had an inspiring message, a vision of public education as a force for justice, the great equalizer. Instead, you presented yourself as a vaguely religious disciplinarian. I don't like thinking of you as the lesser evil." Ouch. "But I know it's not easy. Make no mistake, Wallace. I'm proud of you." Ahh. She'd picked up on his mood. "Things will look better in the morning."

And they did. Nine hours of Klonopin-aided sleep had revived him so much that he would have sprung out of bed and knocked on some doors were he not so comfy. Alone in the bed for the last hour, he'd moved to the middle. He had two pillows under his head, one on his face, and one under his knees. Robin maintained a magnificent bed, the sort that any-one with a penis was incapable of creating. He was suspended in a cloud. He'd ceased of late to appreciate the bed because it was the place where he wasn't sleeping or having sex. But now that he'd slept, could sex be far off? Yes, but the bed couldn't be blamed. With his shoulder, he nudged the pillows upward and regained his cloud.

The phone rang. He kept his eyes closed. There was no place he had to be until three, when he would meet with the editors of the *Informer*. He was glad the interview was taking place on the heels of his victory in the debate.

A thumping came from the study, where Robin was probably working on the copyediting job she'd just picked up. "Annie's on the phone," she yelled.

He grabbed the phone, eager to show his mother that he felt better. Her good, happy boy. "You were right," he said. "Things look better."

"Not from where I stand."

"What's going on?"

"I'm at Star's, and people are out on the sidewalk holding a protest. I suppose they would call it a prayer vigil."

"Oh, God."

"Indeed. They're holding signs and chanting slogans and a few moments ago a squat, mustachioed woman placed something on the porch— I don't know what, because I chose not to show myself. I'm staying hidden and I'm not sure why. I hope it's because I'm thinking of your campaign and not because I'm ashamed."

The image of the mustachioed woman mingled in his mind with the image of Annie and Star together, naked. "Those fuckers."

"There's no need for that language."

"Then there's never a need."

"Precisely."

He got out of bed on the hunch that he had his own protesters. "Star's at work?"

"Yes. She left before they'd assembled."

"So why are they still there?"

"Perhaps they don't know she left or perhaps they're waiting for her to return or perhaps they know I'm here. Or perhaps they've gone round the bend. I have no idea."

She was upset. Of course she was. "We've got thumpers of our own," he said, peeking out the front door. "About a dozen."

"Same here."

"Is the sidewalk public property?"

"I believe so. In any event, it wouldn't be wise to call the police."

A sign held by a slithery-looking guy said, "Hatred Is Annoying." As if he knew Cormier were watching, he turned the sign around with a flip of its wooden handle. This side said, "Religious Bigotry Is Offencive."

"This is exactly what I feared," Annie said. "This is why I didn't think you ought to turn the race into a piety contest."

He stopped the *fuck you* in his throat and put the phone against his chest. His anger was compounded by the image that had come into his mind: Star rubbing her head all over his mother's body, using her Afro like a loofah, scraping off dry skin. He counted down from seven but made it only to four. "They're doing this because I said proselytizers are annoying, which, as you can see, they are."

"But why are you talking about religion instead of education?"

"Because the Christian craziness is a problem that affects education. And it affects this town. Just look out your window."

"I suppose you're right." Not a phrase you heard every day from Annie. "It's just that I hate feeling trapped."

"Most people do." His mother's bravery was such a constant that he took it for granted. He'd not considered the boldness required to be with Star.

"I want to go outside, Wallace. It's a lovely autumn day, and I don't have all that many lovely autumn days left."

"Mom," he said, disturbed by the reference to her mortality. He would have to get better at talking to her about it. About her death.

"I want to leave here and go about my day."

"Please do. Please walk outside with your head held high."

"Okay. You try to do the same."

He was able to shake off her final jab; events this morning were proof he'd been right. He got dressed and walked outside, to the delight of the protesters. The noise they made was something like applause. Cormier got close to the slithery guy, an eel of a man whose dark hair was slicked back; behind his ears it reached the collar of his cheap leather jacket. He struck Cormier as a dry drunk, or maybe a wet one.

"Are we annoying you?" he asked.

"A little," Cormier said, and pointed at a cute redheaded girl whose heel was on his lawn. "Please get off my property." The girl looked at her mother, also a redhead, who told her with a nod to do as Cormier said. "Shouldn't she be in school?" he asked.

"I homeschool her." Her voice sounded like a creaking door, or Kermit the Frog. "Today's lesson is on free speech." This set off a chant: "Free Speech, Free Speech . . ."

It wouldn't be long before Robin made an appearance, and she wouldn't hesitate to call the police. "Who told you to come here?" Cormier asked, killing the chant.

"No one," the eel said. "We did this on our own."

"Sure you did," Cormier said.

"You see that?" the redheaded woman said, addressing her fellow protesters. "He thinks we're a mindless flock."

"No, I think you're a mind*ful* flock." His words were coming so easily that he was tempted to go over to Star's house to mix it up with the other dirty dozen.

The eel said something that Cormier didn't catch because he'd noticed Mr. John, squatting next to his snowblower. Mr. John waved him over with a screwdriver—the first time in sixteen years he'd initiated a conversation. A career military man, Mr. John had been retired for the entire time that Cormier had lived across from him. He seemed to spend his days taking things apart and putting them back together. He wore his white hair in a crew cut and still had a body that looked battle-ready. Cormier was a little scared of him, actually, and hoped that he wouldn't hold him responsible for the disturbance.

"What's that about?" Mr. John asked.

"I'm running for school board," he said, deciding that he would leave out the aspects of the story relating to gay rights.

"That much I know."

"They don't like the fact that I said proselytizing could be annoying."

"So they decided to be annoying."

"Right."

He scratched his chin, which was as wide as his forehead. Cormier imagined him using it as a hammer, driving home a nail. "A couple warning shots, they'd scatter. If you need a rifle, I've got one. Hell, if you need a rifle, I've got thirty-nine."

"No. Thanks. The best thing to do, I think, is just to ignore them."

He leaned back, looking past Cormier to the protesters. He shook his head in disgust. Cormier loved this man. "As long as they stay on that side of the street," he said.

Cormier nodded in full understanding. "Snowblower," he said inanely. "Are you fixing it?"

Mr. John looked at the machine and nodded wearily. "Damn thing."

Cormier thought he should say something about Brian. It seemed wrong not to talk about his son who was risking his life in a war that was talked about too little. Talking about it was the least they could do. Talking about it was all they could do. Cormier barely knew Brian; he got him mixed up with the Johns' older son. One of them had shoveled their walk one winter. "You hear from Brian?"

"He e-mails," Mr. John said. Cormier found it comforting to be living across from this man, with his silent strength and thirty-nine rifles.

The protesters got loud again—a tambourine was now part of their noise—and a girl who sounded like Carly yelled, "Get out of here before I call the cops."

Cormier realized that the girl walking up the steps of his home was indeed his daughter. She turned around and the crowd quieted. "You people are crazy."

Cormier stood there confounded as she went inside to a chant of "Crazy like Christ, crazy like Christ . . ."

"Thanks for putting up with this," Cormier said, snapping out of his daze.

"You bet," Mr. John said. "And remember: thirty-nine."

The crowd got louder as he walked by—"Crazy like Christ!"—and he stared at the redheaded woman, trying to communicate something, parent to parent. She stopped chanting, just for a moment.

With his house under siege, Cormier didn't have time to attend to whatever trauma had sent Carly home from school, but when he went inside, he heard her scream. It had always been like this: her weeping began with a scream. There was just one scream, always one, and it was a good thing, because the one had started Cormier shaking.

He went up to her bedroom, where she lay facedown while Robin rubbed her back. "I'm calling Champ Mullins," Robin said.

The principal of Hartsburg High. "What happened?"

"They harassed her," Robin said.

"Who?"

"A bunch of Christians," Carly said. She turned around, hugging a pillow, and sat up, her face a streaky mess. He hated her wearing makeup, never more than right now. It made her tears seem worse, like blood. Light from the lamp shone through the bras that hung there. "Ronnie Baer was, like, the ringleader. And I used to think he was nice."

There was no doubt, then, that Bevy was involved. "What'd they say?" he asked.

Carly made her eyes big and glazed. "Have you heard the news? Jesus loves you."

"Bastards," Robin said.

"Where'd they confront you?" he asked.

"Does it matter?" Robin asked.

"It might," he said.

A shiver shook tears from Carly's eyes. The older she got, the tougher it was to take. Her crying as a baby had barely pained him. She was a baby, after all, and he could pick her up, kiss her, make a funny face. What could he do now?

"I *hate* this town," Carly said with a slap of the bed. "I want to move." Robin put her arm around Carly and looked at Cormier, her raised eyebrows claiming vindication.

"I don't think you should call Champ Mullins," Cormier said.

"Why not?" Robin said.

"They're trying to provoke a reaction."

"I'm going to need a reason that has nothing to do with your campaign."

"I've got another way of dealing with it."

"What about the dipshits out front?"

"I've got that covered too."

"What, are you going to preach back at them?" Robin said. "Set up camp in front of Bevy's house, you and all the other fake believers?"

"I'm curious," Cormier said. "Do you think that being mean to me in front of Carly has no impact on her, or do you just not care?"

Chastened, Robin looked at the floor. It seemed that his debating experience had sharpened his verbal skills. "I'll tell you what," Cormier said. "If Carly gets harassed tomorrow, you can call Champ Mullins."

"What are you going to do?" Robin said.

Walking downstairs, he recalled his first meeting with Dreifort. Fundamentally naïve, Cormier hadn't grasped the old dog's wisdom. He'd failed to understand the nature of the battle in which he had pledged to fight.

It was with relief that he dialed Zev's number; Cormier had grown up, gotten over himself, just in time. "They're coming after us," he said. "They're in front of the house protesting, they harassed Carly, they had my mother trapped—"

"Who?"

"Who do you think? The funda-fucking-mentals. So, let's set the wheels in motion."

"All right," he said without enthusiasm.

"But?"

"If you were right that a lot of people don't like it when the crazies are crazy, maybe you're right where you want to be."

"Right where I want to be? Zev, my daughter's in *agony*. She's crying, and I can't stand it when she cries. Plus if I don't put a stop to this, Robin's going to raise hell—"

"We don't want that."

"No."

"There's another option. It's risky. We contact Bevy and tell her about the tape."

"And no one finds out about it?"

"And you win."

Upstairs either Carly or Robin was stomping around. "There's, like, thirty of them now," he heard Carly say. He did his best to think. There was value, he felt, in letting the world see the tape, which hinted at the world's complexity—a complexity that Bevy and the people out front were hell-bent on denying. The tape was worth a thousand speeches. The tape was the truth.

"Do it," Cormier said. "Put it out there."

"All right. Don't be afraid to be curious about the tape. A person who didn't know would want to know, you know? And practice acting surprised."

As it turned out, Cormier didn't have to feign surprise. He hadn't expected the wheels to turn in time for his meeting with the editors, nor had he quite understood what wheels he was setting in motion. Not only did the editors have a copy of the tape, but it was, according to Jeanette, also available on a Web site that specialized in sensational footage. He had known that he would be exposing Bevy's breasts to the world, but his anger had prevented him from knowing it enough.

"A tape?" he said. "What's on it?"

"So you don't know anything about it?" Jeanette said.

"Of course not. I'd love to, though. Seriously, what's on it?"

Jeanette looked at Bill-William, whose title was assistant managing editor. The executive and junior staff had greeted Cormier warmly, but these three editors—all of whom had from time to time confided in Cormier about their romantic travails—were treating him as if he were a stranger, apparently fearing that the great conservative media watchdog in the sky might perceive friendliness as liberal bias. "We can't tell you," Bill said. "Not until we've concluded that the tape is newsworthy."

"But you said it's on the Internet," Cormier said.

"So that makes it newsworthy?" asked Inez Bream, Cormier's direct boss.

"No, Inez, that makes it *public*."

Inez, a heavyweight in body only, looked to Jeanette for support. She was rumored to be a Wiccan. Dumb witch, Bill used to call her.

"Come on, guys," Cormier said, looking at Bill. "This is Wally here. Tell me what's going on. I mean, are we talking scandal?"

"That's not for us to determine," Bill said.

"Please step outside for a minute while we discuss this," Jeanette said.

Cormier's sigh was genuine. He walked out the door and down to the newsroom. His desk was as he'd left it, a monument to those innocent days before he'd become a candidate, before Jill had died. Under the *World Almanac*—which had told him what had happened in 1904, the year Margie Stone had been born—were the notes of his interview with her. He'd last sat here a day short of four weeks ago. He'd filed his column, then went to the bowling alley, spotting Faith Evangelical on the way.

It seemed that the desk belonged to a different man. Cormier studied the only photograph on this man's desk. And envied him. He was struck by the intelligent beauty of this man's wife.

A good day, that was, a Saturday maybe five years ago. Carly was spending the afternoon with Annie, and Robin, having just finished a story, suggested they go somewhere. "Show me something," she said. She was excited about her work. "I really think I'm onto something," she said as they arrived at the lake. This wasn't the lake they always went to but one farther away, the lake of his youth, and it was beautiful. There was a little sand beach and the water was muck-free. They changed into their suits and ran toward the water. Robin grabbed his arm to stop him. "Wow," she said, referring to the water, which looked like marble: no motorboats allowed. This was late September, so the beach was empty, as were the homes along the winding dirt road that led to it, and on their way out they laid a towel down on a lawn and had sex. After, at the general store he bought four bottles of dark beer and a can of cashews, then walked out to find Robin sitting at a picnic table, writing. He set down his bag and grabbed her camera. He wasn't much of a photographer, he'd never owned a camera, but her radiance that day, apparently, was such that even an amateur could capture it.

"Wall-ee! Hey, hey, what do you say?" Across the empty newsroom Bo Donnelly looked out above a divider. "We miss you, man."

"Oh yeah?"

"No, not really." He laughed raucously for two seconds, then clamped his mouth shut. "It's too bad about Jill Lynn." Bo, a sportswriter in his midthirties, had grown up in Hartsburg and still idolized Jimmy. "How's Jimmy doing?"

Cormier was ashamed not to have an answer. He would see Jimmy tomorrow. For the first time ever, bowling night felt like a burden; the campaign wasn't over, the videotape notwithstanding, and a rough night was not what he needed. "Okay," he said.

"Damn," Bo said. "Just goes to show, you know?"

"Yeah," Cormier said, though he had no idea what it showed. That even former high school stars could be struck by tragedy? Bo was a lunkhead.

Bill stepped into the hall. Cormier thought he saw a smile, but when he walked into the room, Bill looked no less constipated than the women. At the Octoberfest Festival Bill had said that he would help him get good pieces into the paper; Cormier had doubts.

"We've concluded that the tape is newsworthy," Jeanette said, "and at the end of the interview, we'll show it to you and ask for a comment—"

"Can you give me a hint?" Cormier said. "I'm dying to know."

Jeanette flared her nostrils. He imagined picking her up like a bowling ball and rolling her down the hall, knocking down Bo Donnelly. "There seems to be drug use."

"No shit?" Cormier said.

"That's not all," Inez said. "There's apparent homosexual nudity."

Cormier smiled like someone trying not to. He was having a good time, only slightly diminished by his emerging sense that he'd done something wrong. "Why only 'apparent'?" Cormier said. "I mean, what's in doubt, the nudity or the homosexuality?"

"We'll get to that," Jeanette said, not amused. "Meanwhile we'll cover other subjects." His once and future boss showed little enthusiasm for these other subjects, as she knew they would get overshadowed by the "apparent homosexual nudity."

CHAPTER 30

STANDING AT THE SINK she looked at her cell phone and got a rush because it said "restricted," which was what came up when Arch Cook called, but as soon as she heard his voice, she knew something was wrong. He sounded peppy. He sounded . . . nice.

When he said "videotape," it came back to her whole: she went from remembering nothing to remembering everything. "You should fight," Arch said. "Go all out."

She looked down at the swirls of grease in the soapy water and thought, *well, here it is.* She'd been running from it all these years even though she hadn't known she was running and now she could stop running and deal with it. Atone. Fight, as Arch Cook had said. But her mind might have been playing tricks on itself, yes it was, because the relief was already gone and she couldn't stand up much less fight.

"It's too late for a press conference today," Arch said, "so tomorrow."

"I can't." The strength of her voice surprised her; it was the voice of Bevy Baer, politician. That woman no longer existed. "It's over."

"People will understand. Maybe."

"I'm not worried about *people.*"

"Well, think about it."

She found herself standing in the backyard, looking at where the trees met the sky, wishing she'd appreciated the everyday beauty of her life when she'd had a chance.

The way she felt as she dropped to the grass wasn't unprecedented; no, it was *familiar.* The burn of shame was nothing other than the Devil's own torch. She'd built a new life in order never to feel this way again.

Arch Cook had seemed almost excited. Well, of course he was excited. A cringe made her curl up, and she bit her leg above her knee, her teeth breaking through slacks and skin. She got a whiff of JB's dung and deserved it. Fondling, Arch had said. She knew what he was getting at, but it wasn't that. It was wrong, wrong for a hundred reasons, but it wasn't *that*. Would her family be able to see what it wasn't? Could she make them see that it was just needy Bevy trying to please a needy friend?

The door slid open and out came JB. He circled Bevy, sniffing, and snuggled up to her from behind, draping his leg over her. Feeling his breath and the heat of his dense body, she thought about Colleen. Bevy could come up with "reasons"—she'd lived down to Bevy's mistrust, she'd wanted to make sure, as she had in Texas, that she could never come back—but none of that explained what she'd done. But Bevy already knew the explanation, had known since their pit stop at the Mobil Mart: Colleen was cruel.

While the shame was in her chest, the hurt was in her stomach and it called to her, she wanted to climb into the hurt like a sleeping bag to hide from the shame, which she couldn't blame on anyone else. But to focus on the hurt, to be a victim, was a luxury her soul couldn't afford. Self-pity was unacceptable, shame unbearable.

She forced herself to her feet, brushed off her clothes. What could she *do*? Be a mother. That's what she was. Her children would still love her, because they were her children and because she would become a better mother, the best mother in the world.

As her first act as the best mother in the world, she walked into the family room and checked on the twins, who were doing puzzles—good, educational toys that Bevy had given them. They were oblivious. She had two of five covered, and with love and the Lord's help, she would make things right with the other three. One of them, she realized, was in the house. From the sound of the steps in the kitchen she could tell it was either Brent or Ronnie. She leaned back against the side of the entertainment center.

Ronnie leapt into the room. "*There* you are," he said. "You should have seen what went down today. We witnessed to probably a hundred kids."

"That's great, hon." Finally it seemed that Ronnie was sufficiently submitting. Which made the hit his faith was about to take all the more heartbreaking.

"And guess who we witnessed to hardest of all. Carly Birnbaum-Cormier."

She gave him a smile, a real one: she was certain that Cormier was behind this. But she wouldn't linger on this fact. To fixate on Cormier—his dirty trick, his dirty mind, his hypocrisy, his ugly Jewish wife, his gay British mother—was to blame someone else.

"Are you all right?" Ronnie said. "You've got leaves in your hair."

"I need to lie down for a bit. Keep an eye on the boys, all right?"

As she walked past Ronnie, he brushed the leaves out of her hair, then followed her into the kitchen. "What's the matter?"

It was already a quarter to five. You'd think time would crawl when your world was crashing in, but she'd lost an hour, and now longed to be curled up in the backyard; she'd been chipper by comparison. She looked at her son and tried to find a way to tell him. "Something happened. Something from my past has come back to haunt me, us. It's going to be in the paper. Kids will be talking—"

"What is it?"

"An old videotape. Of me being a fool. Maybe you could try not paying attention to the whole thing. I should tell you now that there were drugs involved—"

"That's all right, Ma. You always said you were no angel."

"And here's proof." There was an opening; she could see past this. Good people would understand and she had good people in her life. "It looks worse than it was, but it was plenty bad. I made an awful mistake. I was only twenty-three, but I guess that seems old to you, doesn't it?" And just like that, the opening closed. "You see, what people are going to be focusing on and lying about is, well, there's nudity."

Ronnie glanced at her body, at her big boobs made bigger by her stupid push-up bra. Then he looked down, at the dirty linoleum. A strong woman would have cleaned the floor, then made dinner—putting food on the table would have said, I'm still your wife, still your mother—but Bevy wasn't a strong woman, not now, not ever.

She walked upstairs, dreading the sound of the garage door. She couldn't bear to see Peter's face. The day after the hot tub party she'd called him to say she'd relapsed, making sure not to mention the nudity. He'd told her that the Lord still loved her. It was then that she knew she

279

was falling for him. She'd fallen in love with him at the very moment she'd lied to him. Wow, she was *bad*.

The sight of her unmade bed reminded her of that morning, before she'd known. The lies we live, the fake security. The phone rang and she almost picked it up to stop the ringing, which was vibrating in her stomach, but there was no one she wanted to talk to except maybe her mama, although even that conversation would be a trial, with Deidre being as ignorant as everyone else about her daughter's past.

She found no comfort beneath the covers of her bed, none at all; she found an invisible hand strangling her, so she stood up and walked around and tried to slow down but was too terrified to slow down because she didn't think she felt His presence and there was the problem of her hair, it itched from leaves and dirt and sweat and she paced and scratched, longing to feel only as terrible as she'd felt in the kitchen. There was no floor to this feeling—what could she do with this feeling? She could cry, but tears weren't close, so she searched for the worst thought, which was—it was Kay, her finding out; no, it was the Reverend finding out. But that didn't bring tears, that sent her into the bathroom to look at the woman with glowing red eyes losing the battle to Satan—she would take care of her hair, which was infested with ants. She clawed at it, pulled it out, four clumps, five, six, three on each side, beautiful Bevy worrying about the way she looked even as she fell to pieces. The ants were all over her body now, so she locked the door and took off her clothes and *there* was the horrible thing, her body. She squeezed her breasts and pinched her nipples and put her nipple in her mouth and bit it, bit it until it broke, the pain bringing her closer to tears, not just the pain but her broken nipple and the blood on her lip and, more than anything else, this was the thought that did it: Loretta.

She turned on the shower and lay down in the tub.

Her sobs came in waves, and she moaned on release—she had no choice but to moan. The rate of the waves sped up, maybe two a minute, then three, the act seeming more physical than emotional, and the physicality provided relief, because she could focus on the clenching of her stomach, the shuddering of her body, the tightening of her neck as she moaned, head back, hot water falling on her chest and stomach.

She sensed that she could make herself stop but was afraid to be without the sob-spasms, which seemed to be a force outside herself, and as such, they were bearable—what came next might not be. So she lay there, head back, sobs working their way up from her stomach, ending with moans that echoed.

She focused on her burning stomach muscles, beautiful Bevy thinking this might be good for her body, like sit-ups, and her vanity triggered a sob, the pain in her stomach adding to her tears. Bevy kept her abs flexed, legs lifted, thinking only only only about the knives in her gut. She looked down half-expecting to see blood, and she did, blood from her nipple clouding the water as the tub filled up because Bevy, housekeeping fraud, had never gotten that drain unclogged. She stabbed herself with her stomach muscles and moaned, the water in the tub splashing as her body shook. She crossed her arms over her chest and felt her arms tremble and the next sob-spasm got lost in all the shaking.

All of a sudden she knew she was faking it, so she let go with a gasp, and gasped some more, the steamy air low in oxygen.

Her breathing slowed and then she was alone with her black heart. She tried to get up but the pain in her stomach stopped her. She'd done damage to herself. Masochism was the name for it and it was a sin, as sure as shit. *Shit. Fuck. Cunt.*

Her stomach hurt so much that she was in danger of vomiting, although—God help her—the idea appealed to her. With her stomach in this condition, she'd pass out and feel nothing and there was nothing that'd feel better right now than nothing.

"Mom," Ronnie yelled, knocking on the door. "Turn off the water."

Her finger was in her throat. "I'm sorry," she said, around the finger.

"It's coming in downstairs. Turn it off!"

She took out the finger and grabbed her shins and pulled her legs back, tucking them beneath her, and fell forward, but her arms couldn't support her, and she went under. She slid her knees up to her elbows and pushed herself up, then spit out the water she hadn't swallowed and sucked in air and hung on the knob with both hands and made it turn. "Is your father here?"

"He went to Grandma's."

"He knows?"

"It was on the news."

"And Loretta?"

"Dad took her with him. The twins too. He didn't know how to talk to Loretta about it, so he was going to have Grandma help him."

She pulled herself up to the side of the tub like she was getting out of a pool and pivoted on her behind, moving her feet to the floor, where there was a good half-inch of water, her hair floating in it. "And Brent?" she said.

"He knows, Mom. It was *on the news.*"

"What'd they say?"

"All I remember is, homosexual."

"It wasn't that, please believe me. It wasn't that." She looked through the steam to the door that separated her from her son. "Would it help if I told you that I was deeply sorry?" She waited for a response, worried that he'd left. "Ronnie?"

She was answered with silence, and when she didn't backslide, when she didn't bang her head against the toilet and stick her finger down her throat and vomit until she passed out, she knew the Lord was with her. But He'd been there all along, of course.

She stood up, bracing herself on the sink, and opened the door. The cool air brought her back farther into the land of the living. She wiped herself dry, then threw the towel on the floor along with two others to sop up the spill.

On shaky legs she walked into the bedroom, where Peter's suit jacket had been tossed on the bed. She imagined him coming in here, hearing her moan. He should have made sure she was all right. Maybe he hadn't heard her. Even if he had, she forgave him. She had no right to ask for forgiveness if she couldn't give it.

She opened the chest at the foot of the bed and dug out her only pair of pajamas, white flannel cozies. She'd given them to herself as a gift for getting an A minus in the class at the community college, English composition. She put on just the pants, then fetched her first-aid kit from the cabinet below the sink. Standing up was a chore, so she sat on the bed and rubbed cool, soothing disinfectant gel on her cut. She put a Band-Aid on the cut and got into her top. She longed to collapse but it seemed important to go about her routine. She peed. Wiped twice, always twice. Washed her face. Rubbed moisturizer on her face and neck. Brushed her teeth.

She slid her feet along the carpet to dry them, then slipped under the covers feeling almost safe. She really loved these pj's.

It was a surprise, then, when tears came. This crying was different, though—better. She was sad. She had a right to be sad, didn't she? Sad that her friend had betrayed her. Sad that her campaign was over. Sad that she was alone.

But she wasn't alone. She couldn't get through this if she was. She apologized to God for doubting him. He forgave her. Forgave her for everything.

PART THREE

CHAPTER 31

CORMIER WAS EAGER to see the newspaper but not so eager that he didn't stay suspended in his cloud. Zev had left him a stash of pills. Was there a reason not to medicate for the rest of his life? He raised his arms to stretch and breathed in the delicious clean of the pillow that sat on his face: Tide detergent. Perhaps he would find his way back to Robin through his love for the bed that she had created. He was tempted to turn onto his stomach and hump till climax the bed that she had created.

She was in the study. When she copyedited, she marked up the manuscript with a blue pencil. He heard nothing but knew she was there.

This was something like happiness, lying in bed after good sleep while your wife worked in the next room. It was something like happiness, rather than exactly happiness, because his wife was so far from happy. He was furious at her for being so far from happy. And there it was, the ugly truth. Not so ugly. Natural, in any case. Snap out of it, woman. Buck up. Go for a run. Think about Iraqis, the Sudanese, Jill.

He had to admit, however, that her husband hadn't done much to help. His selfishness was not just mean but also self-defeating because he and Robin remained connected. Their bubbles were illusions, finally. Codependent? Absolutely. Codependence was just another word for marriage. He needed to talk to her, and listen. The work he had to do on his relationship, though daunting, appealed to him more at the moment than campaign work; at least he wouldn't have to get dressed.

For all he knew, though, he was now running unopposed. With his sights set on the newspaper, he counted to three and burst out of his cloud.

He considered going into the study, then decided that French roast needed to precede any attempts at reconciliation. But in deference to Robin, who objected to his walking around naked, he grabbed his bathrobe from the hook on the bathroom door.

Downstairs, peeking through the front door, he saw that the sidewalk was empty. There was no commandment saying you couldn't mobilize when one of your flock got caught with coke on her lip and breast on her hand, but it tended to blunt your edge. He could be confident that Carly had made it to class unaccosted.

The newspaper waited for him on the kitchen table. An especially murderous day in Iraq had relegated Bevy to the bottom of the front page. The article, by Lars, ran next to an editorial explaining why the paper deemed the news news. "The *Informer*," Lars wrote, "has obtained a videotape revealing that Bevy Baer, candidate for the open school board seat in Hartsburg, engaged in illegal drug use when she was in her early twenties. The same tape also appears to show her engaged in homosexual activity, the opposition to which Ms. Baer has made a centerpiece of her campaign." The article explained that the paper had consulted with an expert at the DEA who "confirmed that, given the fact that people are seen using cocaine in the background, the substance on Ms. Baer's face is almost certainly cocaine." No experts in physiology were consulted to confirm that the body part in Bevy's palm was indeed a breast. That matter was taken up in the editorial: "We do not believe that such sexual activity disqualifies Ms. Baer from office. However, it raises issues of honesty and hypocrisy that need to be addressed."

Cormier didn't have time to feel pleased because Robin was on the stairs. He lunged for the coffeemaker and poured a cup, which was gone by the time he had to face her.

She struck him this morning as a parody of depression, the "before" image in a Zoloft commercial: schlumpy, grumpy, frumpy, and dumpy. In her baggy gray sweatpants and matching sweatshirt, she could have been a gym teacher dressed to make sure that even the most imaginative twelve-year-old boy couldn't bone up in her presence. Her athletic socks were also gray, a darker shade. Was there an outfit less sexy than this one? A McDonald's uniform? A body cast? A pantsuit made of garbage?

"Is that your doing?" She was pointing at the paper. "The video?"

A prospect he hadn't considered. "My sensors are picking up disapproval."

"Cute."

"Bevy opened herself up. So to speak."

"Oh, that's nice. A woman never would have done what you did."

"You don't think Bevy would put out a tape of me cupping a guy's sack?"

"A woman would have never put out *this* tape, of another woman."

"What are you talking about? Bevy had people protesting outside my mother's house. She had her trapped."

"I can't believe you have no compunction."

And to think that he was going to help her get closer to happy. And to think that he was going to hump till climax the bed that she had created.

"Did you even consider what this would do to her?" she asked.

"Of course," he said, trying to picture Bevy crying. "But you have to weigh one person's misery against all the misery she would cause."

"Fuck, Wall, you used to be a romantic. Now you're feeding me utilitarian crap?"

"Here's the most important point." He paused. He needed to get this right. "Bevy made a point of vilifying people based on their sexuality."

"She's a hypocrite."

"Yes!"

She peeled back the foil lid on a Yoplait, then licked it clean—not his favorite habit of hers even when they were at their best. "And now you are too."

"It's not that simple. It's not. Don't you think it's a little . . . self-indulgent to worry about being pure when the thumpers are taking over the town? I mean, Bevy's worldview, it's not just, you know, misguided, it's *dangerous*, and this videotape puts the lie to it."

"Does it really?" Robin said. "From the sounds of it, the tape makes homosexuality seem dirty and illicit, like drug abuse."

Another prospect he hadn't considered. "It wasn't an easy call. It was hard. The whole campaign was hard, and I wish I'd had a little more support from you."

"You feel like you've gotten no support?"

"Very little."

"Then you know how I feel."

"So we're having *this* conversation."

"When was the last time you even asked how I was?"

"How are you? Seriously."

"Shitty, thank you for asking only after I asked you to ask."

"What can I do to help?" he asked.

Robin turned to look at Carly, who had manifested in the dining room. "You're being loud," Carly said, blocking light from her eyes with both hands.

"Why aren't you in school?" Cormier said, stunned.

"Mom said I could stay home. Keep it down, all right?"

Once Carly had gone back upstairs, he looked at Robin, not needing to ask.

"She didn't want to deal with the harassment," she said.

"She wouldn't have to."

"I didn't know that."

"That's two days in a row."

"She'd be in school if not for your campaign."

"So it's all my fault."

"No. It's mostly this fucking town's fault."

"Oh, I get it. That's what this is all about, right? You're sorry I'm going to win because you want to move."

"I'm *not* sorry you're going to win. I'm depressed. I'm not despicable."

He set down his mug and went to her. Gingerly he put his hand on her back. It might have been the first time they'd touched. "But you want to move?"

She looked at him. Those eyes. "You asked how you could help? Well."

CHAPTER 32

LIFTING UP A SHADE, seeing sunshine and an empty street, Bevy pretended that everyone in town had taken the news in stride. No, they had been shocked and offended but had managed to forgive her. An act of communal forgiveness.

She believed in her fantasy until she walked into the bathroom, which smelled like an old sponge. Her breast stung only a little but her stomach was a problem. She had a normal stomachache on top of soreness from her unorthodox ab workout. *Now, ladies, first humiliate yourself.* The area from her pubic hair to her sternum felt like a bruise.

She dressed with the goal of making breakfast for Brent and Ronnie, but she got back in bed and listened to them leave. Then, seconds later, she heard the garage door. Had she been the woman she wanted to be, she would have met him at the door. Instead, she pulled the comforter up to her chin and waited.

There was a knock on the door, and it was just about the sweetest, saddest thing she'd ever heard, Peter knocking on the door to his own bedroom.

"Come in," she said.

"Are you going to sleep your life away?" Unless Bevy was delirious, it was none other than Kay Baer. They'd sent an arsonist to put out the fire. With her bruise, the butterflies in her stomach felt like wasps. Yet she didn't feel as bad as she might have, maybe because she was used to feeling judged by Kay.

This was one of the few times that Bevy had seen Kay in pants, light blue khakis that provided conclusive evidence that she had a rear end, though not much of one.

"There's a bad air in here," Kay said, walking to the window.

"It sticks," Bevy said.

Kay turned around and reached behind her with both hands, gripping the groove at the bottom of the window. To open it, she bent her knees, then stood up, and Bevy had the feeling that she'd worn pants for this very purpose.

"Get up," Kay said. "You've got a big day ahead of you."

"Did you take the twins to school?"

"I'm not going to tell you again: get up."

Bevy was embarrassed to show she had clothes on. A silly worry, considering. When she got up, Kay signaled for her to sit on the chest at the foot of the bed.

"I only have a few minutes," Kay said, stripping the bed. "Peter's going to drop me back at home on his way to work."

"How angry is he?"

"I'd say he's more hurt than angry."

Bevy, straining her stomach, twisted at the waist to look at her. She was sniffing a pillowcase, and Bevy felt flattered she hadn't just assumed it was dirty.

"And you?" Bevy said.

"I'm not surprised."

"You expected this from me?"

"Goodness gracious, Beverly. You always said you went through some dark days. I didn't think you were talking about stealing candy bars from the corner store."

"Right," she said, but what she was thinking was, Right! Bevy decided that standing would be easier on her stomach than sitting. Her thighs were sore but absorbed her weight, and she bounced on her legs like a baby seeing what her body could do.

"Here's what's going to happen," Kay said. "You're going to go get your hair done. It looks awful. Then at noon you're going to stand in your front yard and talk to the media about your sin and your redemption."

A press conference? Bevy tried to figure out how this was punishment. "You're serious," Bevy said.

"I'll be standing on one side of you. Peter will be standing on the other."

"He agreed to this?"

"I'll take care of Peter. You just get yourself ready. Everything's lined up."

She watched in amazement as her mother-in-law folded a blanket. "Why are you doing this?" Bevy said.

"Why wouldn't I?"

"About a million and one reasons. I swear, Kay. I don't understand you."

Kay glared at her with those Chinese eyes, and Bevy feared she'd jeopardized her chance at redemption. "What do I care about?" Kay said.

"Your family?"

She leaned over and squinted at something on the mattress pad. The old girl could annoy her even as she was saving her life. "With God as my witness, I've worked hard to love and support my family. That's what I've done with my life. I'm proud of it, and I've gotten back a lot more than I've given." She walked back to the window and looked out. "But this is larger than our family. I believe that you lead a good Christian life."

"I do. I try."

"People want to use that videotape to demean Christianity. They're saying it shows that it's all a crock. But exactly the opposite is true. That tape shows how far you've come. You see, the woman people will see out there today, she's a living, breathing testament to the redemptive, transforming power of the Lord Jesus Christ."

Bevy was brought almost to tears by the inspiring story of this woman who happened to be Bevy herself. But it was Kay's kindness, really, that had moved her. How could Bevy express how grateful she was? There would be time for that later. She had a more pressing concern: did Duane, her hairdresser, have an opening this morning?

Bevy, standing in the living room, saw four vans pull up, and she chided herself for not understanding the impact of her little movie. Her race had become a statewide story—nationwide since one of the vans said *CNN*. Arch Cook greeted the camera crews, as did Kay, who could have been mistaken for someone who didn't spurn politics.

Bevy had to give a press conference when she'd had trouble just walking into the salon. Duane, bless his heart, had put her at ease: "Girl, no one in here cares about that tape. Those big meanies are just throwing dirt on my diva." She had a worry that he'd forgiven her due to his own sexual problems—there were whispers—but Bevy had heard him talk about girlfriends, so probably he was just compassionate. Compensating for the hair she'd plucked, Duane had gone shorter than usual. He'd then teased her hair up into a decent shape, but she would have to face the nation without her best hair—she felt naked up there—and it made her nervous, so nervous she was having trouble breathing. Struggling to get oxygen past her throat, she was reminded of her father, whose lung had been damaged in Vietnam. He'd been unable to take a deep breath and it was hard to imagine Bevy taking a deep breath now, with the shame of her past and the knives in her gut. The scene outside went blurry and she turned away, thinking that if she could get one good breath, others would follow. Every Memorial Day, they'd walked to the cemetery where her father's father was buried, and one time she waited with her mother and brothers atop a hill while Lamar stopped halfway and put his hands on his knees. Seeing Bevy's tears, her mother said, "It helps him deal with his guilt for surviving. It's a blessing, really." Bevy's breaths were so shallow now they were barely breaths—she was going to die in her living room—but you couldn't hyperventilate to death, your body wouldn't let you, nor would God, and she prayed for just one good breath.

After establishing the site of the press conference, Bevy's advisers came inside. "How're you feeling?" Arch Cook asked, squinting.

"Okay," Bevy said, her breathing now almost normal. "But I wish I could eat."

"In here," Kay said, from the kitchen, and both Arch and Bevy followed.

"It's cold out," Arch said. "Maybe we should do it inside."

"It'll be fine," Kay said, playing mother to Arch, who did, in fact, seem nervous. Bevy was grateful that he was putting his name on the line for her, although a scandal probably appealed to a pro. The "Texas tape," he'd called it.

"Where's Peter?" Arch said.

"He'll be here," Kay said.

"And the Reverend?" Bevy asked.

"He said he'd do his best to make it," Arch said. "He has a busy day."

"I'm sure he does," Kay said, and Bevy chose not to come to the Reverend's defense. Kay, eyeing a container of vanilla yogurt, probably suspected that Stonybrook Farm was a save-the-whales-kill-the-babies kind of outfit. In the end, though, she dumped it into the blender with a banana, frozen strawberries, ice.

"Wait a second," Arch said. "Where are the children?"

"It's a school day," Bevy said.

"But we're trying to put across a family feeling," Arch said.

"It'd be too complicated," Kay said.

"All right," Arch said. "But Peter, we can't do this without him." On his way out, he checked the clock on his cell phone. "Fifteen minutes."

Bevy went down to the laundry room and was glad to find the dryer going. She was starting to enjoy the smoothie; she liked the taste, and more than that, the idea of nourishment, of replenishing the nutrients and fluids she'd lost sweating and crying. She sipped it and looked around. Her trusty old appliances. The string hanging down from the naked bulb. The plain wood walls that made the room feel like a cabin. The cheap wooden table decorated with wallpaper, orange and yellow flowers on a light blue background. Here was her laundry room.

Maybe Kay was right that this was a chance for Bevy to be an example; in a sense she would be witnessing to thousands. But she had trouble accepting that God would inflict such hurt on her family to achieve that end.

She leaned back against the gyrating dryer and finished her smoothie.

It came to her. It revealed itself in steps, one domino of logic knocking down the next. God had *wanted* her family to know about her past. It was wrong for a person to keep secrets from the people she loved. And having kept parts of her past secret, Bevy had been haunted by it. Trapped by it. She had run for office so that she could set herself free. Of course she had. Knowing deep down that she needed to face up to her shame, Bevy had invited her past into her house in the form of Colleen, then had all but begged her friend to betray her. She would use the press conference to speak to her family. Arch Cook had written her a statement, but she would ignore it and just talk.

Bevy jogged up to the kitchen and found someone who wasn't Kay poking around in her fridge. She was about to say something half-rude when she realized that the someone was Pauline. She smiled at Bevy over the door of the fridge.

"You came," Bevy said.

"I can't believe you're doing a press conference. I expected to find you in tears."

"There were plenty of those, believe me."

"But you're doing okay?"

"Yes, I am, I really think I am. This is what God wanted."

Pauline nodded like Bevy had stated the obvious. "I made you a couple of pies. Turkey and beef. The beef is Ricky's favorite. Zach loves the turkey."

Bevy thought about all the people she hadn't seen or heard from. Marybeth, Rhonda, the Reverend, everyone except Pauline. "You're a sweetheart, Pauline."

Pauline mouth-farted to say, big deal. "You paid for some of the ingredients."

"What comes around goes around," Bevy said. "I really don't know what to tell you about . . . you know."

"Well, you better think of something quick. The world is waiting."

"I think it's harder with people I know."

"Don't be embarrassed." With a flick of the wrist, she shut the fridge. Two readymade dinners were in there, and it seemed a hopeful sign that such a thing pleased Bevy. "I'm glad no one has a tape of me at twenty-three."

"You did some things?"

"That's one name for it, things. When you don't have what I don't have, you're eager—well, let's just say I couldn't keep men at arm's length."

Bevy felt free to laugh. "You're so positive."

Pauline winced. "Please, please don't think that. Am I supposed to thank God for the way He made me? Well, I don't. I'm just starting not to be angry about it. That's about all. I'm certainly not positive about it. Know that, all right?"

"All right." Bevy stood tall, let her arms fall to her sides. "How do I look?"

"Like a proud, beautiful, strong Christian woman."

"Funny, that's just what I was going for." Bevy tried out a smile but it bounced back on her tight face. "How many people are out there?"

"A lot. One of them stuck a mic in my face and asked who I was."

"What'd you say?"

"I told him I was your lover."

"That's not funny, Pauline."

"Sorry. Sorry. I make jokes when I'm nervous, and this TV stuff makes me nervous. I think I'll stay in here, if that's all right?"

"Of course it is. You just being here—thank you."

"Do me a favor?" Pauline approached her with her little arms raised. "Make yourself shorter." Bevy leaned over and Pauline put her hands on her cheeks. "They're going to try to make you feel bad about yourself out there. Don't let them. You're a good person."

God's plan having been revealed, Bevy knew Peter would be outside. And there he was, tight on Kay's hip. He couldn't look Bevy in the eye, but ever the good son, he pretended to, then kissed her cheek. "Hello. Dear," he said, sounding like a recording.

"I love you," she whispered.

Bevy and Peter followed Kay across the walkway to the center of the lawn. Microphones closed in on Bevy; a few were attached to spearlike poles. Twenty people looked at her, thirty, and beyond them a little crowd of neighbors in the street, dogs on leashes, Kelly Beale-Wallis holding her son and leaning over to say something mocking to Janice Haggarty. Bevy asked for a good breath and God gave it to her.

"Thank you all for coming," she said. "Welcome to the Baer household. My name's Beverly—people call me Bevy—and this here is my husband, Peter, and his mother, Kay. My own mama lives in Texas, so Kay's kind of become a mother to me too."

Bevy paused, worried that she was speaking too easily. "I made a mistake twenty-one years ago. I felt awful about it when I woke up the next day and I felt awful about it when I woke up today. But I take solace—pride, even—in knowing I'm no longer that girl you see in the hot tub. That poor girl is long gone."

There was movement: Reverend Wedgwood had arrived with an entourage, and Peter waved him over. The Reverend indicated with a shake of his head that he would stay where he was. She'd never known him to be camera-shy.

"With the support and love of my husband, I learned to live a moral life. It didn't happen overnight. I'm still a work in progress. But if you compare the poor girl in the hot tub to the woman you're looking at right now, you see what the Lord's love can do. God delivered me from the darkness into the light. I became a good wife and a good mother, and since y'all are here for the political angle, let me add that I'd be a good school board member." Bevy couldn't help but smile. "Questions?"

A burst of voices gave way to the loudest one, which belonged to a silver-bearded man in an expensive suit: "But the events in question happened after your alleged conversion, did they not?"

"They did," Bevy said, choosing not to challenge his use of the word "alleged." But his question made her realize that the time for honesty had already passed. Here it was smart to play dumb. "What's your question?"

"Well . . . It seems to call into question the sincerity of your religious convictions."

"Does it really? It might be hard to understand unless it's happened to you, but when you're born again, well, it's indescribable. But in some ways, it's the easy part. The hard part is learning how to live a godly life. I mean, it's not like flipping a switch."

"That's a great point," said an attractive woman with tightly bunned dark hair and freckles. The other reporters seemed taken aback by the woman's praise. The guy on her left was looking at her like she was insane. She had style: leather jacket, skirt, boots. "Don't you think there's been this uproar precisely because you're a Christian?"

Bevy smiled at her, the two of them sharing a moment.

"I do, actually," Bevy said. "The media loves it when Christians prove themselves to be human. That said, I don't think it's unreasonable that Christians are held to a high moral standard. We need to practice what we preach."

"Who's the other woman?" said a blond woman Bevy knew from the local news.

"Someone I used to know. I'm going to protect her privacy."

"Were there other times like this?" A follow-up from Blondie.

"What do you mean?" Bevy said.

"Other times involving drug use and, you know, naked hot tub activity?"

Having often been pegged as a ditz herself, Bevy didn't like to make assumptions, but some girls were as dumb as they looked. "I don't recall any other, as you put it, naked hot tub activity. As for drug use, yes, there were other times, but this was the last."

Bevy pointed at Lars Molofsen, who had been waiting patiently. "Did your family know about the behavior depicted in the tape?"

"They knew I went through some dark times, but they didn't know the details." She put her hand on Peter's back and looked at him. He kept staring straight ahead, all tight. But she felt Kay's hand squeeze her shoulder. "It dawned on me this morning that the tape was a blessing. It's given me an opportunity to come clean. It's not going to be easy, but my family and I will get through this. Our love and our faith are stronger than this."

"Do you believe that the Cormier campaign is behind this?"

"I do," said Reverend Wedgwood, striding toward the center of activity. Peter stepped back, making room for the Reverend. She was relieved to have the Reverend's support, but felt distant from him even as he put his hand on her back. "This is the politics of personal destruction," he said. "They couldn't beat her with their ideas, since they don't have any, so they're trying to impugn her character."

"Do you condemn Bevy's behavior in the videotape?"

"Of course I do," the Reverend said. "But I ask you, is she the only sinner on this lawn? There's only one perfect person and He walked the earth some two thousand years ago. It's my opinion that we'll see Him again soon, but that's a topic for another day."

"Ms. Baer!" yelled the bearded lib in Armani. "You've been crusading against homosexuality. What do you say to those people who say you're a hypocrite?"

"First of all," Bevy said, "I'd argue that what you see in that tape isn't homo-sexuality. It's just a lost girl pushing the envelope. But call it what you will. The important thing is that I accepted the Lord and that I stand foursquare against immoral behavior today. That's more than my opponent can say."

"Are you suggesting that you're more qualified to be on the school board because you were, in your words, born again?" The liberal beard again, dominating. No, Bevy was dominating; the Jew was just talking a lot.

"To be honest with you," Bevy said, "I don't know a thing about the religious beliefs of Mr. Cormier or Ms. Birnbaum. All I can tell you is that Jesus changed my heart."

CHAPTER 33

H E DOUBTED THAT ROBIN would ask him to move if he won. But he had sort of won already and she had already sort of asked him. She was expecting too much from moving; it wouldn't de-depress her. But then staying wouldn't do wonders either. He pictured Robin at the age of fifty, wearing a larger gray sweat suit and riding through Wal-Mart on one of those fat-person carts. Farts, Stu called them.

The image came to him Friday afternoon, at Jed's. On the stool to his right, Stu was holding forth on the decline of the American empire. Stu was in a jubilant mood not only because the American empire was in decline, but also because he'd found a slew of free songs on the juke, which he'd used to play the *Best of Kris Kristofferson.*

"What's the matter?" Stu said. "You're tighter than a teddy bear's asshole."

"Haven't heard that one in a while."

"So I watched the Bevy and Colleen show this morning," Stu said. "Or about half of it, if you know what I'm saying."

"I'm pretty sure I do."

"Were you shitting me when you said you didn't know about the tape?"

"Jimmy going to be there tonight?"

Stu smiled at Cormier's non sequitur, which was as good as a yes. "He said he'd show. Is Bevy dropping from the race?"

"I don't see how she can't."

"A nice dirty victory. How's it feel?"

The possibility that he'd ruined a woman's life to win a seat he would abandon didn't allow for a lot of joy. On the other hand, the thought of Wedgwood's face when he saw the paper this morning, that was pleasant. "Not bad," he said.

"Congratulations." Stu clanked the mouth of Cormier's bottle with the bottom of his, causing an eruption. An old teenage trick, not funny even back then. Cormier got most of the beer in his mouth. He was wary about drinking at the same time he was cultivating a Klonopin habit, but he was wary about *not* drinking at the same time that dark thoughts were amassing on the perimeter of his brain, waiting to charge.

"Whose tits do you like better?" Stu asked. "Bevy's or Colleen's?"

Before he could respond, his cell phone rang. The number was Zev's. Desdemona gave him a look, so he went outside. Behind the sub shop a wide-bodied black guy showing ass-crack checked a trash can for goodies.

"What are you doing?" Zev said.

Cormier was proud to tell him where he was.

"You don't even know about the press conference, do you?"

Robin held a press conference to say he was behind the tape's release?

"Bevy's hit it out of the park, I guess," Zev said. "I should have known: people eat that redemption shit up. I mean, politicians should make up bad stuff about their past."

Cormier waited for his brain to process this data, as if it were a seventies computer.

"Are you there?" Zev said.

"Yeah. Wow. Fuck."

"Don't worry. She's damaged. This is ours for the taking. Listen, a news crew will be at your house at five. We're going national, baby. It'll air Sunday night. Try to act normal. They want to hang for a few hours."

"But I'm bowling tonight."

"Bowling. That's perfect."

While Cormier waited for Jimmy and Stu to show up, the reporter, Suzy Rocker, delivered what she called "the bridge." Suzy was a glossy, anorexic blond with a huge head. She looked like a sunflower. Robin, still in her saltpeter sweat suit, had refused to come downstairs, so he'd left for the alley as soon as Suzy and the crew had arrived.

"Shit," Suzy said, distracted by a girl's scream a few lanes down. The cameraman, a black guy with little round glasses, wore a wry smile that seemed to say, I'm filming this bourgeois melodrama to fund my avant-garde movie, which will revolutionize American cinema. Cormier wanted them gone. All they needed were a few shots of him bowling and a word from Stu or Jimmy testifying to Cormier's hell-of-a-guyness.

One of the two producers—drinking a martini, of all things—sat down across from Cormier. "I was expecting the martini to be awful," he said. "And it is." Cormier probably preferred his arrogance to the presumption of the other producer, who seemed to think she knew everything there was to know about Hartsburg.

"Drinking on the job?" the female producer said. Between the wings of her leather jacket was an expanse of freckled skin. "At least get a beer," she said, fingering the stem of his glass. "You don't go to a bowling alley and get a martini."

"It's a virgin," he said, and they both smiled.

"The truth is," Suzy said to the camera, "it was *never* your average school board race. One candidate: a liberal who writes feisty columns for the local newspaper. The other: a conservative who attends the local megachurch. And both, remarkably, are advised by famous political operatives. But no one outside of Hartsburg paid any attention to this race until the videotape came to light. The conservative says she's a changed woman and that today her values are better than her opponent's. And that's what this story is all about, *values*: sex, drugs, religion. These issues are as explosive as issues can be, and this race is threatening to tear apart this close-knit community."

Cormier hated journalists as much as he hated politicians (and he was both!). The town wasn't coming apart, or if it was, hard-core Christianity, not the campaign, was to blame, and even hard-core Christianity was a symptom. Of what? Fear of terrorism. Fear of everything. The spiritual and material damage done by that amoral religion, the "free" market. Issues he hadn't mentioned during the campaign. But it wasn't his job to talk about that stuff; education was his issue. Had he mentioned education?

From his pants pocket he removed a ziplock bag, which contained pills of different colors. Red, white, and blue. He sneaked the white one into his mouth.

"I should have said *moral* values," Suzy said.

"No," the cameraman said. "That's redundant. All values are matters of morality."

"No, they're not," Suzy said. "If someone likes to, I don't know, spend time with their dog, that's not morality."

"Sure it is," the cameraman said.

"Well," Suzy said. "What if someone likes to . . . eat soup?"

"That's not a value," the cameraman said.

"It depends on what kind of soup," the guy producer said, thinking himself hilarious.

"Moral values is fine," said the woman producer.

"Thank you," Suzy said. "It's totally top-of-mind. When people hear 'moral values,' they know it means sex and God and all that, you know: the culture war."

Despite himself, Cormier felt a thrill at being a player in the melodrama. The feisty liberal columnist: that was one inaccuracy he didn't mind. And it would have been true once. Several years before, he'd been just a little bit feisty.

"Will someone get rid of them?" Suzy said, referring to the boys behind her who were mugging for the camera. One of them had turned around and was doing that thing where you hug yourself to make it look like you're making out with someone.

The woman producer waved at the boys, getting their immediate attention. While the camera stood out here, so did the two done-up women. "If you go and bowl," she told them, "you might actually get on TV."

"It's good to be in a town like this," she said once the boys had moved on.

"A town like what?" Cormier said, the Xanax maybe doing something.

"A town where people are real. Authentic."

It was hard to say which producer was more condescending. "Don't you think you're romanticizing Hartsburg?" Cormier said.

"Play it all night long," the guy producer said. Not wanting to want his approval, Cormier didn't mention that he understood the Warren Zevon reference.

"So then," the woman producer said, staring at Cormier, "Bevy Baer is correct when she says you don't think much of Hartsburg."

"No. I love this town but—but nothing. I love it."

When Jimmy walked in, Cormier met him at the counter, and they waited for his size thirteens. Having lost weight, he would have looked good if not for his eyes, which were red and pinched, like scars. "How are you?" Cormier said.

"Psyched to bowl."

As they walked toward the camera crew, Cormier knew he needed to prepare him. "The campaign's still going on," he said.

Suzy surged toward Jimmy and introduced herself. Blond beauts both, they could have been husband and wife, or brother and sister.

"It'd be great if you could talk to her for a minute," Cormier said.

Jimmy looked over his shoulder, maybe searching for Stu, whom Cormier should have warned. He should have warned both of them.

"We can practice without the camera," Suzy said.

"You don't have to do it at all," Cormier said.

"I'll give it a shot," Jimmy said, his clawed hand asking for beer.

Cormier went to the bar and got two Buds from Teresa, whose tenure stretched back to the beginning of their bowling nights. "Not much of a tip last time," she said.

"Really? I'm sorry."

He walked back toward the crowd that had formed around Jimmy. Teresa knew the bad tip had been unintentional. They'd always tipped well. He cared about service workers. Workers of all kinds. He was a good person. Compassionate. Even though he'd released the videotape. He'd tip Teresa, go home, sleep, campaign, not drink, be good to Robin, win the election, write feisty columns. The Xanax wasn't working.

"Good," Suzy said. "Just say that again." She giggled, smitten with the hunk of ruggedness in the ripped "Hartsburg Rec" T-shirt.

Jimmy's eyes got big at the same time that they wanted to squint in the light, creating twitching in his nose. A girl laughed.

"Tell me about Wally," Suzy said. "What's he like as a friend?"

"Good."

"Don't look at the light," Suzy said.

Jimmy took his beer and tilted back his head, spilling on his T-shirt. "Whoops," said the wiseass girl, whose eyebrow was traversed by what looked to be the prong of a fork. Cormier was glad Carly didn't wear eating utensils in her face.

"What was the question?" Jimmy said.

"You don't have to do this," Cormier said.

Jimmy let out a long wet burp, and Suzy laughed, easing the tension. "What kind of friend would you say Wally is?"

Jimmy burped again. "That's okay," Suzy said.

He stared at the camera, his forehead working up a shine, his mouth moving but saying nothing. "The guy's got total stage fright," said the wiseass.

"Sorry," Jimmy said, and turned to flee.

"What a puss," the wiseass said.

Chasing after him, Cormier pushed through the door and ran into Stu, who stumbled backward and fell. "The fuck?" Stu said. "Was that Jimmy?"

"Yeah. I brought the camera crew here and—"

"What are you, an idiot?"

"At best." He gripped Stu's hand, which felt like used tinfoil, and pulled him up.

"I have a contusion on my left buttock." He rubbed his ass with both hands and wiggled his hips.

"Do me a favor?" Cormier said. "Go in there and talk to the reporter. But please don't say *too* much, you know? And don't do your little dance for her either."

Cormier was driving out of the lot, on his way to Jimmy's, when he spotted his truck, still parked. He pulled up next to it, got out, and looked at Jimmy over the hood of his car. Jimmy rolled down his window, and they said "sorry" at the same time.

"You've got nothing to be sorry about," Cormier said. "I shouldn't have put you through that. Stay out here until they're gone."

"I'm going to take off. I'm not ready to be normal."

"You don't have to be normal. It's just me and Stu."

"I'm going to go home and try to sleep."

"You sure?"

He nodded, now looking straight ahead. He pounded the top of his steering wheel with his fist. "Listen, Wally. I've got to tell you something. Jill really liked Bevy. I feel like I should vote for her."

"I understand," Cormier said, although understanding wasn't the word for the prickly emotion filling him up. "I'm sorry if I screwed everything up tonight."

"That's the good thing about bowling night. There's always next month."

"I hope so," Cormier said to himself as Jimmy pulled away.

Walking toward the alley, he imagined Stu standing on a table, performing a strip tap dance while mocking the imperialistic designs of the United States.

But Stu was just meeting Suzy, who looked anxious to leave. A bowling alley, though great for color, was not where she wanted to spend her Friday night. It occurred to Cormier that despite Stu's verbal fluidity, and despite the barstool shift he'd worked at Jed's, he might be no more comfortable in front of the camera than Jimmy.

Wrong. "Wally's a great guy. Rock solid. Salt of the earth. I've known the guy since the fourth grade, and he's always been there for me. I'm sure you're thinking, well, he's got to say something nice, but I wouldn't say something nice if I didn't want to. He's a hell of a guy. The best. Not a very good bowler, though."

Stu had given them a perfect sound bite. Cormier was greedy enough to wish that it had been delivered by someone who didn't look as if he'd just fallen off a horse.

"So he really cares about his friends?" Suzy said.

"Oh, yeah. His friends are the most important thing in the world to him, except his family. He's got a great family. Me, on the other hand, I'm single"—he winked at Suzy—"so if you like Renaissance men: S-T-Nedney at AOL dot com. I'm an organic farmer. I also rebuild classic cars and write epic poems. I'm easy on the eyes, as you can see, and I like sunspots, NASCAR, and making salty love in the afternoon—"

"Ohh-kay," Suzy said, not angry, not amused. But the guy producer was cracking up. "Now if you two would just bowl a few . . . balls," Suzy said.

Cormier tried to forget about the camera as Stu punched their names into the computer. "You're up," Stu said. "Try not to look like yourself."

The thirteen-pounder felt like a cinder block so he went down to a ten-pounder, which was no bigger than a cantaloupe. The size of the ball wouldn't matter on TV; form was the thing. He held the ball at his side, letting it pull on his shoulder. Breathe, he told himself, follow through. He held the ball in front of his chest and bounced on his knees, conscious of his skinny ass. Breathe, follow through. Stepping toward the line, he pulled the ball back too far, and his balance was thrown off, but he went through with it. Breathe, follow through. The ball went directly into the gutter.

"Ha!" Stu yelled. "Nice shot, Holly."

Cormier had visions of twenty straight gutter balls, an anti-perfect game. "As much as I enjoyed that," Stu said, "don't do it again." He looked at Stu and his friend gave him a nod of encouragement, which reminded him that he had a choice to think positive thoughts. He still had partial control of his brain, and he could sure as death pick up a ball and knock down some pins. And that's what he did. All the pins went down. It would look like a strike on film, so he made himself do a dance, pumping his hips and moving his arms as if he were doing the backstroke, his body fighting itself.

"You'll edit that last part out, I hope?" Cormier said.

"Gladly," the guy producer said, and downed the last of his martini.

The cameraman and soundman packed up while Suzy and the producers took off, the woman producer lingering by the door to get a final whiff of authenticity. The guy producer put her in a jokey headlock and dragged her away.

"I don't feel like bowling," Stu said once all of them were gone.

Happy to leave, Cormier paid the bar bill, tipping twenty bucks. "That's more like it," Teresa said. "I'll see you dorks in a month."

He persuaded Stu to let him drive, and Stu told him to take a left out of the lot, away from town. "Where are we going?"

Stu held out his pack of cigarettes, and Cormier took one. He rolled down his window, and cool air filled up the car. "As far as I'm concerned," Stu said, "nothing is sacred. But bowling night comes pretty close."

"Point taken. I'm sorry."

"You should have asked. There's not much we wouldn't do if you ask."

They went past Wal-Mart and under the highway and when they came to Hunter's Pass, instead of going left as they had on the day of Jill's funeral, they went right, staying within the town limits. It was too dark to see the nice old farms, classic places with silos and red barns. Then the land closed up, forest lining the road on each side.

Stu's silence was making him edgy. He flicked the cigarette out the window and drove with both hands firm on the wheel. He had pills in his pocket.

He pumped the brake as they went down a steep hill. The land opened up, and Stu told him to turn left onto a dirt road that cut through a cornfield, then through the woods. They came to a village of trailer homes, and kept going.

"Veer left," Stu said as the lights illuminated a scrap metal roof. No nice old farms here. This was the rural poverty that Cormier often heard about but seldom saw.

They came to a clearing and Stu told him to slow down; there were more trailers here, but Stu told him to park on the dirt next to a small house. A cottage. A shack. "Where are we?" Cormier said, a little scared. "What are we doing?"

He followed Stu into the shack, which he'd entered after knocking once. Standing in the kitchen, or the part of the room that passed for it, was a Latina girl. She looked at them with one large eye, the eye that wasn't covered by her black hair.

"Hey there, beautiful," Stu said. "Your mother home?"

A door opened, and a short heavy woman in an apron ambled out. She had a necklace of little moles and walked as if her breasts were pulling her forward.

"Oh my God," she said. "Look what the dog drag."

"You should lock your door," Stu said. "This ain't the greatest neighborhood."

The woman gripped Stu's upper arms and kissed him on both cheeks.

"Wally," Stu said. "This is my friend and colleague Burrito."

She laughed, a squawk, and slapped Stu's chest. "Bonita."

"I believe you're familiar with her son, Bronson."

"Oh," Cormier said, relieved, sort of. "Yeah."

As Cormier sat down on the couch, Stu made for the fridge, and the girl scooted away to a back room. "Got any beer?" he said, already holding one.

"When are you going take me drinking?" Bonita said.

"When you start pulling your weight at work."

"Okay, right, sure. You the lazy one." Her little chair, completely concealed by her girth, creaked as she turned toward Cormier. "He better watch out. He come smelling like whiskey one more time, they going to fire him."

Cormier couldn't concern himself with the prospect of Stu getting fired. He wanted to figure out why he was sitting across from Bronson Tavares's mother. He could assume it wasn't because she loved what he had said about her son. In West Virginia, Stu had chastised Cormier for portraying Bronson as a threat.

"Where is he?" Stu said.

"Down the road," Bonita said, picking up the phone. "I call him."

Bonita spoke to her son in Spanish. She'd done her best to make the place homey, but carpeting and curtains couldn't make it feel solid. It was like a giant crate. On the wall above the kerosene heater was a large white cross.

"He's on his way," Bonita said.

"Nacho Bwainer," Stu said. Cormier was embarrassed by Stu's mock Spanish, but Bonita seemed not to mind. "Tell Wally what happened at his last school."

"Yes. Okay. The bullies, they pick on him. Very scared, very sad, he get in fight, and the counselor teach him the anger, um—"

"Management," Stu said.

"Right. Man-age-ment. They say, 'When you get angry, you get feel bad, you write down how bad that you feel.' Bronson, he's a very good writer. So he was doing better. Not so sad, not so scared. When he get angry, he write down his bad feeling. But they find his notebook, and the next thing to know, he can't go to school no more."

"And you told all this to the principal?" Cormier said.

She waved both of her doughy arms, as if throwing something heavy to the floor. "Mr. Champ, he say, 'Oh, bin Laden, very bad, very danger.'"

"And if you still don't think this is all a bad joke, I give you"—Stu raised his beer toward the front door—"the next Osama bin Laden."

It was true that Bronson didn't come across as threatening, but who was Cormier, who was anyone, to say what a dangerous kid looked like? Was it a rule that a sociopath couldn't have bright white sneakers, a tucked-in shirt, and hair so carefully groomed it looked like a helmet? In fact, it seemed a plausible look for a sociopath.

Bronson declined his mother's strange offer to sit on her lap and stayed standing.

"This man run for school board," she said. "He help you maybe get back to school."

"If I win," Cormier said.

"Talk about him tomorrow," Stu said. "Say you met him and changed your mind."

Now there was an idea. A bad one. He couldn't become the bête brun's champion, not if he wanted to win, and he did, more than ever. "Bronson," Cormier said, "do you understand why people were alarmed by what you wrote?"

He batted his eyes and fiddled with the cross that hung from his thin neck. "I was just doing what they told me to do at my old school . . ."

Cormier barely heard what he said because he was so taken aback by the way he said it. Did no one beside Cormier think it was relevant that Bronson Tavares was gay? Gayness probably wouldn't go over much better in this household than in Bevy's. Maybe Bronson wasn't gay, but some kids were, and they were the main reason schools needed to teach that homosexuality was okay. Cormier hadn't talked about gay students. Or students of any kind. He'd run a school board race without talking about students.

"I'll see what I can do," Cormier said. He found himself hugging Bonita good-bye. When he went to shake Bronson's hand, the kid turned away.

"Drink *after* work," Bonita said, pointing at Stu. "Not before."

"Mind your own business, Burrito," he said, and pretended to take a bite out of the top of her head, eliciting a final squawk.

Cormier leaned against the back of his car. Music thumped in the trailer next door: Green Day. He'd always been agnostic on the subject of Green Day, but now, standing in this shantytown, he felt the beginnings of belief.

"It'd be nice out here," Stu said, looking up at the stars, "if it wasn't so shitty."

"I've been doing some stupid stuff. Cowardly stuff."

"Not me. I'm perfect."

"You've got to stop drinking."

"Do you know why Bronson's a name below the border? Because of the *Death Wish* movies. That, Holly Hunter, is what's known as irony."

Maybe Cormier could give a speech in which he explained that he'd allowed himself to be goaded into getting tough—no, *seeming* tough—on violence by teenagers, that zero tolerance was a counterproductive, cynical policy, that he was sorry for demonizing a boy. This could be Cormier's own story of redemption. A born-again liberal. Nah, stupid.

A pickup truck cruised by menacingly, its tires undeterred by the ruts in the road, and Cormier made a move toward the driver's seat. "To answer your question," Cormier said when they were in the car. "Colleen's. I like Colleen's better."

CHAPTER 34

WHEN SHE REALIZED she was awake, she woke all the way, and her thoughts resumed their assault. Colleen, Peter, hot tub, the children, the Reverend, the race. The race. With tomorrow being Sunday, she really only had one day left. She was confident that her press conference had won back her supporters (aside from her family), but according to Arch Cook, lots of voters didn't focus on races until the final days, so their first look would show them Bevy in a hot tub. But also Bevy talking about her conversion. Even if she weren't opposed to betting, she wouldn't have bet on this race.

Peter was getting a cold, from stress probably. She felt responsible for the phlegm that was giving his breathing a rattle. "I'm sorry," she whispered. She wished she could snuggle up against up him, but he didn't like to be touched when he was sleeping. She'd long had hopes of changing their nighttime habits. Too much to hope for at this point.

"There she is," Ronnie had said yesterday afternoon. "The porn star." She preferred his hostility to Brent's shock and Loretta's fake indifference. After dinner Bevy had played them a tape of her press conference, which didn't seem to help. Ironically, it was easier to forgive people you didn't love. Voters could be inspired by her story; having never relied on Bevy, they didn't feel let down or lied to. Ronnie had argued that Bevy's misdeeds made his grounding null and void, and Peter had to yell to stop him from leaving the house. Doing his best to help her uphold their authority, the chain of command, Peter had been treating Bevy normally in front of the children, but when the two of them were alone, he retreated to a place she couldn't come close to reaching.

With sleep faraway, maybe a full day away, she walked downstairs and longed to see Colleen. She wanted to look into her pretty, nonjudgmental face and tell her about what she was going through; then she remembered that Colleen was responsible for what she was going through. Hurt filled her up. She felt bloated and nauseous, pregnant with hurt. She knew Colleen was cruel, yet some part of Bevy, some naïve or hopeful part, couldn't believe that her friend had betrayed her. Colleen had always used her power in subtler ways.

Hearing the TV, Bevy readied to do battle with Ronnie, but it was Loretta who was sitting in the glow. "Little late for you," Bevy said.

"I couldn't sleep."

Loretta had a busy mind that made insomnia a likely foe; Bevy's own sleep problems had begun when she was in high school. But it was possible that Loretta just wanted to stay up and watch this filth. Right away Bevy knew that the skit portrayed President Bush as a child. The more the elites turned their noses up at President Bush, the more popular he became with real people, but the skit was dangerous in that it ridiculed the Commander in Chief during a time of war. Bevy was all too familiar with *Saturday Night Live*. Once she'd watched the show, stoned on marijuana, in a roomful of her more redneck friends. She'd laughed along with everyone else until Eddie Murphy performed as Mr. Robinson, a poor, illiterate, alcoholic black man in the ghetto. It backed up the rednecks' darkest beliefs, and they howled with delight.

"If you're going to stay up," Bevy said, "you need to watch something else."

"I want to see the singer who's coming on." She tried to be matter-of-fact, confident, but couldn't pull it off. Sitting in the middle of the couch, she looked tiny. Her pullover pajama top revealed her little breasts. A girl, not a woman, not yet.

It was more important than ever that Bevy not bend. Loretta needed to know that the star of that horrid home movie was still in charge. "Where's the remote?" Bevy said.

Loretta held up the remote, then stuck it under her thigh.

"Give it to me," Bevy said.

"Why, do you want to watch a video? Like 'Christian Moms Gone Wild'?"

It was good that Loretta was expressing her anger. There were feelings you were better off fighting through—most feelings maybe—but Bevy knew that her family's anger over this wouldn't die a natural death. Pay now, or pay for the rest of her life.

"Loretta, please give me the remote."

She held up the remote, holding it over her head with both hands, and turned up the volume. Bevy tried to block the signal, then knelt down to shut off the TV but couldn't find the button, so she yanked the plug, putting them in the dark.

"I know you're angry," Bevy said. "But that doesn't mean you can defy me."

"Do you have any *idea* what you've done to me?"

"Why don't you tell me?"

"You've turned my life into a living hell."

"I'm sorry, sweetheart. So sorry. But trust me when I tell you it won't last."

"What's going to change? Is Kevin Sheets going to forget you were in a porno?"

"It wasn't a porno. I almost want you to see it, so you'd know what it wasn't."

"Fine. Let's go into Dad's study and watch it."

"No. I don't want you to see it, ever."

"Why not? It's supposed to be really good. Kevin Sheets beat off to it three times."

"Who is this Kevin Sheets?"

"He's only the most popular boy in the school."

"And he goes around bragging about masturbation?"

Loretta made a guttural sound, like she was about to cough up a clam. "You're clueless, Bevy. How can you be so clueless *and* so disgusting?"

Bevy's eyes adjusted to the dark just in time to see her daughter walk out. She was used to thinking of herself as disgusting so she was more stung by the charge that she was clueless. She'd always figured she'd be able to understand teenagers, but times change. In her school days, boys had ridiculed one another for masturbating. It was getting to the point where the word "shame" wouldn't be needed. It was just about extinct.

She looked at her family room—soft all around, edges smoothed out for safety—and curled her toes into the rust-colored rug that hid three years of stains. She wanted to wake everyone up, to set off the smoke alarm and tell them how much she loved them and couldn't they forgive her or at least hug her and tell her that they still loved her?

She got back in bed but wasn't hopeful about falling sleep with her mind spinning and Peter sniffling. He was sniffling so much that the bed was shaking. Peter, she realized, was crying. As far as she knew, it was the first time he'd cried as an adult. He sounded like himself: controlled, sweet. Except he was in tears.

She assumed he was asleep because he wouldn't have allowed her to hear him cry. By that logic, she wondered if she should wake him.

She decided it was good for him to cry, and good for her to hear him. She thought: *You can't understand why you need the Lord until you listen to your husband cry.*

CHAPTER 35

THE LESSER EVIL couldn't sleep. At the printing plant off Lincoln Ave., thousands of copies of the *Informer*, each containing the Lesser Evil's safe answers to easy questions, were getting piled on trucks. His bathrobe wasn't on the bathroom door, so he put on Robin's, which fit him disturbingly well around the shoulders. He was comfortable in it, because it was silk, but not entirely, because it was pink.

He sat in his recliner, phone in hand, trying to think of who might be awake. He focused on Los Angeles, where it was only one thirty, but he'd lost touch with his friends there. It occurred to him that his chief political adviser was perhaps out on the town.

"Jefferson Memorial, can I help you?" Zev said.

"You're at the Jefferson Memorial?"

"Long story. It involves a girl I thought was a guy who turned out to be a girl. She works at the White House."

"Naturally."

"Trouble in the heartland?"

"I'm feeling shitty about the race I've run. It was so timid and bland and I didn't talk about teenagers, except Bronson Tavares, who I demonized—"

"Ho, doggy, hold on, slow down. You've run a good, commonsense—"

"No, I haven't. It's had no heart, no theme, no passion, no philosophy, no nothing. I mean, what's it all been about?"

"Winning. You can't do anything if you don't win."

Right. He could redeem himself, and justify his campaign, by becoming a good school board member. "But am I going to win?"

"Hard to say," Zev said. "I liked where we were after the debate. I think you were smart to make it a referendum on the retarded right, but then you put out the tape . . ."

"It was your idea, fucknut. I never would have come up with such a slimy idea. And now you're telling me it backfired?"

"It gave her a chance to show people who she was."

"I should have shown people who I was."

"I don't know about that."

"Fuck you. I should have been myself."

"You still can be. Get some sleep, then get out there."

"The sleep part is the problem."

"Here's my new thing when I can't sleep: I pop an OxyContin and imagine that my head is tucked between Bevy and Colleen."

In the middle of the night a man at the Jefferson Memorial gives his friend in Ohio an image with which to pleasure himself. TJ probably could have never imagined such a scenario, but the dirty dog would have approved. "Talk to you soon," Cormier said.

He'd been saving his load for sex, but there was no stopping him now. Because he was a romantic, and because he could have gotten off by imagining a curvaceous gourd, he thought about Robin, that day at the lake. He put the bathrobe over his nose to smell her, and over his penis to feel her. On the lawn that day, they gripped each other's heads with both hands and put their unmoving lips together and came at the same time.

It could have been sad, a man masturbating to old images of his wife as her current asexual incarnation lay upstairs, but when he was done, he felt warmth for her, love.

He went upstairs and, wanting to wake her gently, crept to her side of the bed. He stopped breathing when he saw that her eyes were open.

"We should have had another child," she said.

"Oh, Robin."

They'd stopped using birth control without ever making a concerted effort to get pregnant. Did they want another child? Maybe. Let's talk about it. What's there to talk about? If we get pregnant, we'll have a child. If not, not. As was often the case, they didn't make a decision, so it was made for them.

He sat down on the bed with his back to her, keeping the gooey parts of the robe concealed. "We could adopt," he said.

"Spare me your passive aggression, okay?"

"I'm serious."

"No, you're not. And your pretense of seriousness amounts to hostility."

He couldn't even understand the charges against him. He leaned over and kissed her forehead, which was clammy and cool. "I love you," he said.

She pulled her head back to get a look at him. "Cross-dressing now? What *will* all your Christian supporters think?"

He thought about the woman he'd just had sex with on the lawn. "Robin, you need to write," he said. "I haven't been nearly as supportive as I should be. I don't know why. There's envy in there, and anger, since you haven't always been a fan of my writing, but we don't need to love each other's work; we just need to love each other."

She'd turned away but now lifted her head and looked at him over her shoulder. "I know what you're doing. You're giving me support so that I give you support."

"No. Or yes. I mean, that's the way it's supposed to work, right?"

He pulled on the comforter to roll her toward him, but she resisted and they had a tug-of-war that ended when he tried to dive over her and landed on her, flattening her with his stomach on her back. "Graceful," she said. "Get off."

"No."

"All right. It feels good, actually, your weight."

"Writing has always been your dream, and you need to keep it alive."

"Where'd all this come from, anyway?"

"I was thinking back to that day at the lake, on the lawn."

"Ah, yes, the glorious, idealized memories of yesteryear."

Someone was on the porch: the paperboy. When Cormier delivered the *Informer* one summer, he'd folded them and tossed them from the sidewalk. Tossing was the fun part, that and eating pancakes afterward. Now the paperboys were instructed to place the papers in mailboxes or between doors. What tedium. He would give the paperboy a huge Christmas bonus this year, assuming they still lived in Hartsburg.

Wanting to see the Q&A, and to protect their day at the lake from Robin's revisionism, he pushed himself up, making a point of putting a hand on her ass on the chance that it would remind her that she was a sexual being.

He was in the hallway when he heard her say, "Wait. Come back."

Daylight was coming in around the edges of the shade. "What?" he said.

"Huh?" she said, perhaps waking up.

"You told me to come back."

"Oh. Right. Thank you. I just wanted to say thanks."

"You're welcome, sweetie." After taking a quick look at the paper, he would come back here and sleep next to his wife.

The Q&A wasn't on the front page, but Wedgwood was, a picture of him between a man and a woman, parents of a soldier who'd been killed in Iraq, the town's first fatality. Brian John? No, these were not the Johns—the Johns wouldn't have let Wedgwood near them—but he recognized the woman, the man too. The Bumpers.

He went up to the bathroom and found an Ambien in his jar of pills. The one time he'd taken Ambien it'd given him an awful hangover—he'd felt as if his brain were covered in plastic wrap—but it was fast-acting. The world, with its dead young men and despicable reverends, would recede in twenty minutes.

He stopped the pill in his throat and coughed it into his mouth and tasted its bitter chemical flavor. With the war in Iraq on his mind, it was perverse—unpatriotic, even—to shut down his thoughts, so he spit the pill into the toilet. Then, before he could change his mind, he dumped in all the sleeping pills and painkillers and tranquilizers.

He made sure the flush carried all the drugs away.

He got in bed and let his thoughts have their way with him. During the lead-up to the war, he'd been surprised by his certainty. People he respected, both friends and public figures, were torn. They weighed the morality of invading versus the morality of leaving Saddam in power, but Cormier—possessing, it seemed, just enough knowledge and not too much—saw that no deep thinking was required. Did Bush want democracy for Iraq or empire for the United States? It didn't matter. Invading Iraq was a bad idea, as bad as an idea could be, an idea brilliant in its badness. It was like New Coke, or *Cop Rock*. It was like Mike Dukakis's riding in the tank. It was like remaking *Psycho*. Except people would die as a result. It was as if someone—Stu, to make it vaguely realistic—had proposed to raise money for veterans by driving home from Jed's blindfolded. Forget the illegality. Forget the immorality of endangering people (and of not helping veterans). The idea screamed "Mistake!" A noble purpose? Can a doomed act have a noble purpose?

The war would have to be a catastrophe not to be preferable to Saddam, but catastrophe was just the word to describe the occupation by the United States of a large, divided, oil-rich country at the heart of the Muslim world. This was slowly becoming obvious to everyone except right-wing ideologues, and Cormier couldn't deny that being right was a comfort, but a small one. The Bumpers had lost a son.

To try to calm himself, he imagined explosions in mosques and convoys and the presidential motorcade, Bush's bloody face, Condi's detached leg, Rummy's scream of anguish. Then he directed the violence at himself, his impotent self, lying in his cloud in the Midwest while bodies splattered like sauce in the Mideast. He imagined shrapnel ripping through his chest, his throat, and he woke up limbless in a V.A. hospital, which turned out to be a lab. Robin pushed his wheelchair down the hallway, the M.E. from *CSI* was waiting for them at a wall of yellow lockers, and Cormier realized that this was Dalton High School on the Upper East Side of Manhattan. The M.E. removed a knapsack from the locker, reached into it with both hands, and pulled out Carly's head, her eyes wide open, as if she had died startled. Robin kissed Carly's cold clammy forehead and said, "I love you."

CHAPTER 36

SHE WAS AT THE STOVE, cooking the scrambled half of his Mega-Egga, when Peter came back inside after fetching the paper and said, "Bevy, you need to see this." It was good to hear him say her name even though he was probably talking about the Q&A, which, she guessed, had made her out to be a fool.

"Just a sec, hon."

"Turn around, Beverly."

He was holding the paper in front of his chest. She saw the photo but couldn't focus enough to get the details. "Injured?" she said.

He shook his head. Behind his glasses, his eyes looked dry and cold.

"You were crying last night," she said.

"No I wasn't," he said, and she dropped to one knee.

She didn't stop crying completely until she was sitting in her car down the street from the Bumpers'. She'd put on a sweatshirt and jeans and her hair was in a rare bun. She wished she'd done more to get herself together. You'd think that the death of your friend's son would put to rest all your little worries, like your appearance. And your past. She'd be seeing Hilltop people for the first time since the video came out.

The sun was strong for a fall morning. Bevy let it soak into her cheeks and tried to remember the last time she'd really felt the sun; it'd become a thing you were supposed to avoid. But now, walking backward up the street, she questioned that belief.

The door opened, and Stu Nedney came out looking even more ragged than usual. He was far from her, on the other side of the little gate, but she picked up his smell.

"Bevy Baer," he said.

"Been here all night?"

"Yeah, and now I've got to go to work." He wiped his forehead with a stack of coffee-stained Dunkin' Donuts napkins. Bevy was tempted to go give him a hug but didn't, because she didn't know him, and because he smelled like pickled onions.

"A lot of people in there?" Bevy asked.

"I, I don't even know." To her surprise, he turned around and shuffled sideways through the thin space between the Bumpers' and the neighbor's house.

The kitchen was full of people, mostly Hilltop: Lizette and Don, Marybeth and Nate, Marla. There was almost no reaction—Marybeth didn't even look at her—but it was hard to know whether they were quiet in judgment of Bevy or in respect for the Bumpers, and she wasn't going to stick around to find out. She walked through the kitchen to the living room, where the crowd parted for her, and she saw Pauline on the couch.

And Pauline saw her. She waved her over, even made a space for her on the couch. Bevy nodded at the people she passed—she didn't know them—and squeezed into the spot between Pauline and a woman wearing a football jersey and drinking a beer. Pauline put her arm around Bevy as far as she could and said, "I like you without makeup."

Pauline, as she often did, surprised Bevy. She wasn't crying or grieving in any obvious way. And she knew it. "I haven't cried yet," she said to Bevy, but everyone was listening. "Once I start, I might never stop. I guess I'm in shock—course I am. Lots of drinking going on here, not exactly Hilltop behavior, but what can I say—we're Irish. Bevy, do you know all these people? Probably not, but you know Jimmy, right?"

Bevy smiled at Jimmy Lynn as Pauline introduced her around, giving a strange fact or two about each person. One guy—Carl or Chris—collected bandannas. Everyone looked concerned as words tumbled from Pauline.

"Shhh," Ricky said, trying to pull Pauline close.

"I'm just talking. My son is dead and I can sure as fudge talk if I want to. And I can sure as fudge say 'fuck.' Do you think I don't know I'm making people uncomfortable? Do you think I don't notice *everything*? All my life I've been trying to make people comfortable." She flapped her arms, and Bevy thought of a bird that couldn't fly. "My son's dead and I can sure as fucking fudge talk if that's what I feel like doing."

"Where's Lucy?" Bevy said, just to say something.

"Upstairs," Pauline said. "She doesn't want to see me. You see, she blames me for letting him go to Iraq. As far as she's concerned, it wasn't some terrorist who killed Ricky and it certainly wasn't President Bush; no, no, no, it was her mother . . ."

Ricky leaned back and Bevy did the same. They looked at each other behind Pauline's head. He was wearing a red hat that said, "Bengals." A football team on a baseball cap. But here was the strange thing: his orange scruff covered only half his face. The army people must have shown up when he was shaving.

Ricky's eyes asked Bevy to comfort her. But not knowing Pauline well—less well, probably, than everyone else here—she was reluctant to pipe up.

"I mean, really, Ricky," Pauline said. "Our boy's dead and you're worrying about how your wife's coming across? What if I start laughing, what would you think of that? Or start singing "Sweet Caroline"? What would you think of that?"

"That'd be okay," Bevy said. "We all love you, and you can do no wrong in this room. You can do whatever you want to do. Except that." Bevy put her arm across Pauline's chest to stop her from slapping herself in the face. "You can sing or swear or laugh or talk or scream, but we're not going to let you hit yourself."

Pauline looked at Bevy and swallowed. "I'm thirsty."

"Let me get you something," Bevy said. "What would you like?"

"Fresca and cranberry."

"It's her favorite," Ricky said.

Glad to have a concrete task, Bevy went into the kitchen, which had cleared out as people made their way to Hilltop. The Bumpers weren't going to church this morning, and Bevy would have to hurry to make it. She enjoyed prying the ice cubes free with her fingernail and almost started to cry when, searching for a straw, she found an industrial-sized box of them by the coffee machine. Five hundred, it said.

She went back into the living room, and Jimmy held a shushing finger to his mouth. Pauline had fallen asleep with her head on Ricky's lap and her feet on the lap of the woman in the football jersey. Everyone was silent.

Bevy tiptoed back into the kitchen and called home. She told Peter to go to church without her, implying that she would stay here, but after drinking the drink she'd made—refreshing, but too sour to her taste—she whispered her good-byes, kissed Pauline's forehead, and left. She stood in the street and felt the sun. If she went to church, she would focus not on the Bumpers but on people's reactions to her, and Bevy didn't want to think about herself right now. Or maybe she did.

After driving around for a few minutes, giving her family time to clear out, she went home. JB was asleep on the mat in front of the sink. A single dish, a cereal bowl—Loretta's probably—sat in the open dishwasher. All the others were scattered about.

She could hear JB's breaths. And the humming of the fridge. She was nervous and didn't know why until she was in Peter's study. She turned on the computer, sat down, opened up Google. It wasn't hard to figure out what to write. She typed, "Bevy hot tub." The third link down sent her to a site called Horndogs and Corndogs, which had the headline flashing at the top: "Hottie Tub: Christian Candidate's Texas Tit-Touch."

While it downloaded, Bevy looked at the wedding photo of Peter's parents on the wall above the desk. Eight years older than Kay, Jack had gray in his fifties flattop. He was bending down to kiss her cheek, and Kay—blond, radiant—had a white gloved hand on his arm and the kind of full-face smile that only love can make.

The video was ready. A young, blurry Colleen looked out from the screen. Bevy couldn't believe what she was about to do. It seemed that being with Pauline this morning had loosened her up, made her crazy or brave.

She didn't feel a need to see what was going on below their necks. She watched their faces. The pretty girl with the chestnut hair was Bevy but not.

As the tape went on, Bevy kept having two different reactions, contradictory reactions. On the one hand, the little movie seemed like a relic. She had so much distance on what had happened in the hot tub that she was angry and amused that people were using the tape to try to hurt her. On the other hand, she felt barely any distance at all. She knew these girls.

The blond and the girl who was Bevy but not were in the grip of drugs, any fool could see that, but a less-sympathetic, less-knowledgeable viewer wouldn't have noticed all the emotions coursing through them along with the tequila and the cocaine, emotions they couldn't name, much less handle.

Bevy braved a wider view, looked at their bodies. For a quick moment, she envied the girl who was Bevy but not: firm breasts, tight skin. Their behavior was disgusting, but Bevy wasn't disgusted. She tested herself, probed deeper, and still found no disgust. It was hard, she could tell, to feel compassion and disgust at the same time.

She wanted to yell, "Stop it! Get out of the tub, girls, and get your life together." Then she remembered that one of them had done just that.

CHAPTER 37

H E WALKED A CIRCLE around the greeter, then jogged between a pile o' woman cruising along in a Fart and a ponytailed dude in sleeveless denim testing whether an upside-down trash can could be a stool. Wal-Mart: an easy place to hate, especially if you had enough money to shop elsewhere. At a dinner party last year, annoyed by Zora Clymer's predictable anti–Wal-Mart diatribe, Cormier had done his best to defend it. But he hated it. He'd never made it out of there without feeling gross, complicit. Wal-Mart was a surrender, an acceptance of awfulness, a monument to moral relativism.

Plus it was like a fat farm in there.

He didn't find Stu in the logical places—the produce section, the bathroom—but he saw Bonita by the lettuce and asked if she knew where he was.

"You check his office?" she said.

"His office?"

She squawked and pointed to the back. "The loading dock." As he turned to leave, she grabbed his coat, hooking her finger in a buttonhole. "You no forget Bronson, okay?"

Her son had, in fact, faded from his mind in favor of Zach Bumpers. But the two young men, absurdly, were not unrelated, with Bevy pretending that Bronson was an ally of bin Laden and Bush doing the same with Saddam. The "War on Terror" was everywhere, everywhere and invisible. "I won't," he said.

Stu was standing and smoking, his back to the store. In front of him an empty eighteen-wheeler idled. Beyond the truck was forest, although less than there used to be. This part of Tripp's Trail, as Cormier had suspected, was gone.

Cormier said nothing and stood next to Stu, who didn't seem surprised to see him. It was weirdly warm today, and the truck was probably giving off heat, but the temperature didn't explain all the sweat on Stu's face. It pooled in the cracks on his forehead.

"I'm sorry," Cormier said. "I know you really liked him."

"What can you do?"

"Oh, come on. You're not going to pretend you don't care."

"I'm not. I care. I care and you're sorry but some other Zach Bumpers is getting killed while we stand here caring and feeling sorry, so like I said, what can you do?"

With its cab curled around, the truck looked like a scared animal checking its rear. "We could get out in the streets, protest."

"But here we are, standing in the asshole end of Wal-Mart." He threw his head back to inhale, spraying sweat like a punched boxer. "Smell that?"

"Fumes?"

"No, Wallywood. That's China!" He jumped down, landing with a grunt, and ran up the ramp to the truck, which gave his voice an echo. "It smells like China in here. This is the real deal, not like the Chinese we used to eat at Wok and Roll." He was walking back and forth along the edge of the truck, as if playing to a crowd below. "Okay, folks, so you've come here for advice. Here's the secret. Accept . . . Your . . . Powerlessness. Repeat after me: I cannot. I cannot. Do anything. Do anything. About anything."

"Are you all right?"

"Does it look like I'm all right? I'm giving a self-help seminar. I mean, isn't that crazy, *me* giving a self-help seminar. This crowd deserves better."

"Let's get out of here. I'll buy you coffee. And a doughnut."

"I'm at work, fucknut."

"They'll understand."

"Yes, that's what I've noticed about these people: they're very understanding."

"Tell them you knew Zach."

"I told my boss this morning. He said if I didn't come in, I was done." To put out his cigarette he pushed it into the back of his hand three times fast. Cormier had never seen him do this sober, if he was sober. "What am I doing here? Why am I wearing this fucking blue smock? A kid I loved got killed. In Iraq. I can't get my little brain around it."

"It's crazy."

"That's the word for it. No, it's not; there's no word for it. Except maybe . . . Allah-Achbar . . . Allah-Achbar-Bill-Clinton-Bush . . . blood-on-their-hands-hands-off-our-children-you . . . fucking-barbarians-in-caves. Corporatecaves! That's pretty fucking good actually. Did you like that, people? Now repeat after me: Allah-Achbar-Bill . . ."

Cormier wondered if he needed to be worried. It'd long seemed likely that at some point Stu's rage would overtake him. It was a relief when he stopped shouting and sat down. He lit another cigarette, his short legs dangling.

"Me and Ricky painted houses one summer," Stu said.

"I remember."

"The factory had shut down, and we were glad to be free of that place even if we knew we were fucked. It was like a second run at childhood; we got to be outside, make our own hours. Pauline had to take a job. Ricky's mother watched Lucy, and Zach came with us. He was seven. This was twelve years ago. Do the math, Holly Hunter. Zach was born in eighty-four. That's how young he was. Schenk's shut down in eighty-four. I was there the night it closed and I remember Philly Schenk watching the Olympics. When I said good-bye, he gave me a tub of brown mustard. It's still in my fridge."

"I would have thought you ate more mustard than that."

"It's a big tub."

"But you eat bologna for breakfast."

"Not the point."

"Sorry . . . He was a good kid?"

"*Great* kid. Nice, generous, upbeat without being annoying. Actually, he could be annoying . . ." Stu smiled. "Zach called me Uncle. Uncle Stu. They trusted me with him, and I didn't fuck him up. He's one of the few things in my life that hasn't turned to shit. Well, actually, he did. He's fertilizer now."

Cormier tried to think of something not-ridiculous to say. "I guess when a certain number of Zach Bumpers die, the war will come to an end."

"Wrong again. I'd explain all the flaws in your reasoning, but my break's over."

Driving out of the lot, he saw Robin's Honda go right into the adjacent mall. When he saw how fast it was moving, he knew it wasn't Robin. He followed.

The Honda jerked to a stop in a parking spot; driving past, he could see that Carly was with Lisa Zimmerman, who was apparently still her friend. He circled back and parked near the store, then got out and fiddled with his keys, waiting to be seen.

"Isn't that your father?" Lisa said.

He looked up and did an unfortunate sitcom double take. It was possible that Carly had been pretending not to see him; he suspected that she hid him from Lisa because he compared unfavorably—in a teenager's estimation—to Jack Zimmerman, a strapping, suit-wearing stockbroker who'd renovated their house himself. The good news for the Birnbaum-Cormier clan was that Lisa's mom was obese.

As he approached, he imagined the deep impression they would have made on boys, these two pretty girls armed with attitude, brains, and overstuffed book bags.

"Shouldn't you be out, like, campaigning?" Carly said.

"I just was," Cormier said.

"My parents are totally going to vote for you," Lisa said, looking away.

"Excellent," he said. "Please thank them for me."

"I definitely will." Carly often used this same tone: unenthusiastic politeness. It seemed that they'd figured out the words that appealed to grown-ups but were too lazy or honest to deliver them with conviction.

"Well . . ." Carly said. "I'll see you at home?"

"Can I talk to you for a second?" Cormier said.

"About what?"

He gave Carly a look to suggest it was serious.

"Order me my usual?" Carly said, and Lisa nodded.

They watched her walk away and Cormier was stupidly proud of himself for not looking at her ass. "What is it, Dad?"

The truth—that someone's child had died and that he wanted to hug his own child—was too hokey to go down well with Carly. A similar feeling had overcome him on 9-11; back then, though, there'd been no need to explain. He and Robin went to the high school. The hallways were full of parents looking for students and visa versa. Carly found them by the gym, and they hugged, the three of them.

"You heard about Zach Bumpers, right?"

"Of course. It's awful."

"It's got me thinking. About life. I don't really know what I'm trying to say."

"Can you maybe speed it up? I've got a history test tomorrow."

"If you want to go to an Ivy League school, I'll support you. But if you want to take a year off, that's fine too. Whatever you want to do, if you want to be a housewife or a drummer or an astronaut, you'll have my support. Probably you don't know what you want to do or be, and that's fine, that's *good*."

Avoiding her eyes for fear of losing his nerve—it wasn't easy in this ironic age to dispense how-to-live wisdom—he turned around and looked at Wal-Mart. "There's a balance to be found, a sublime paradoxical state where everything matters but—"

"What are you talking about, Dad?"

"I want you to walk in there and have a good time and enjoy your coffee because the Ivy League won't do you any good if you can't enjoy small things and you won't be able to enjoy small things, not really, if you're not living life the way you want to be living it."

She gave him a mystified shake of the head, more amused than annoyed. The speech was something she'd appreciate later in life, maybe. He'd give it to her again, soon, once he'd figured out exactly what he was trying to say. What he said, in any case, was less important than what he did. Did Carly know he'd put out the tape? Drug-free for the first time in a week, he started to sweat like Stu, and when Carly turned to walk away, he bit into the side of his mouth until he tasted blood.

He was still standing there when she sat down in the Starbucks in Barnes & Noble. He wiped sweat away from his eyes. Lisa pointed at something in a textbook. She tapped the book and Carly nodded. He watched them through the window.

CHAPTER 38

BEVY WALKED OUTSIDE as the sun rose on Election Day. She'd slept no more than usual, but it had been a good sleep. She'd left the world.

As she made her away across the hard lawn to the mailbox, her stiff body cracking and loosening with every step, she remembered her dream. She was riding through the sky in her father's green vinyl recliner. The lever on the side was the gas pedal. Not only was she flying around the country; she was flying around her *life*. She could do whatever she wanted. She zoomed to Texas, where she dipped down to cuddle with her father in the chair. Then to Ohio, where she rode around in the chair while making love with Peter. Then to DC, where Senator Baer gave a rousing speech from the chair.

She removed the plastic sleeve from the paper but wouldn't read it till she was sitting down with her oatmeal. Lars Molofsen had read her words back to her, but she was still nervous. Even a minor misquote could make her look bad.

Back inside, she heard someone get up and go to the bathroom—Karl, she guessed—and was relieved when he didn't come down. She wanted just twenty minutes with the paper and her oatmeal; then she would make breakfast for her family and face their anger. She had hope, maybe unrealistic, that it had peaked.

She took her oatmeal out of the microwave and added whole milk, raisins, bananas, brown sugar, and walnuts. She'd eaten oatmeal almost every morning from the age of five to twelve and ate it these days on special occasions. Yum.

When Lars Molofsen had called her yesterday, Bevy had been unsure if she wanted to talk about Zach Bumpers. But he asked her directly—"Do you think his death is relevant to your race?—and Bevy, still loose from being with Pauline, didn't hold back. "I want to stress that his death in and of itself is not a political issue. Everyone in town mourns for Zach and his family. But there's no question that issues related to his death are relevant. Do we want elected officials who wholeheartedly support the military and the War on Terror? Schools need to help parents pass their values on to their children, so we need school board members who share the values of parents."

Now, sucking on sweet oats, she saw that Lars had gotten it right.

Walking to the former grammar school where Ward Three voted, Cormier felt released from the race he'd run—the race that had run him over. It was as if he were the inconsistent, easily intimidated quarterback of a fractious football team. Somehow they'd made it to the big game, and all the failures and arguments during the season had become irrelevant: nothing to do now but win.

There were two obvious causes for the lift in his spirits: the story on national TV two nights ago and, more important, the woman walking next to him. Upon reading Bevy's comments in the paper, Robin had announced that she would accompany him to the polls. As for the piece on TV, it had been kind to Bevy in that it had depicted Hilltop as a benevolent outfit, but the bias could do nothing about the blurred-boob footage of Bevy in the hot tub, which contrasted beautifully with Stu's sound bite. *Now* which candidate had mainstream values? Not that Bevy was conceding anything.

"Truly shameless," Robin said, swinging her arms as she walked. "Exploiting Zach Bumpers's death like that. And what does that even mean, the War on Terror?"

"She's right: I'm opposed to it, whatever it is."

"Yeah, but she doesn't know that."

He realized that he was happy about Bevy's quote in the paper; it was a reprieve. Maybe it didn't justify what he'd done to Bevy, but it showed that in this race there was a candidate just as slimy as Cormier.

They moved into the street to pass a slow-moving pair of women, one of whom turned out to be Mildred Cox, who'd cost him five dollars two weeks ago.

"We're going to vote!" Mildred said, recognizing him.

"Can I count on your support?" he asked, slowing to Mildred's pace.

"Indefinitely!"

"She means yes," said the other woman. "Ma didn't care for that video-tape."

"I thought she was a Christian," Mildred said.

"The tape made me like Bevy more," her daughter said.

"Not enough to vote for her, I hope?" Cormier said.

"No way. I'm a hairdresser. Half my friends are gay."

They proceeded with half-steps toward the polls. This wasn't exactly MLK leading marchers to Montgomery, but he'd take it.

When they got there, Mildred and her daughter went inside while Cormier and Robin stopped to chat with Lars and Jiles, a photographer with a greasy bowl cut who asked if he could take their picture. Cormier looked at Robin and to his surprise she said, "Sure."

There was a loud noise. It turned out to be two noises: an army jeep and Bevy's bullhorn-amplified voice urging people to "Vote for Bevy! Because my values are your values!" In light blue paint someone had written "God, Country, Family" on the side of the jeep, which was driven by a man in camouflage fatigues.

"Where's a roadside bomb when you need one?" Robin said.

"That was off the record," Cormier said, and Lars nodded.

The other two passengers disembarked first. The guy had an absurd, pencil-thin mustache. The woman also had a mustache, which revealed her as the culprit who'd placed something on Star's porch. One of his mother's jailers.

A TV van had been following the jeep, and a camera was on them as Bevy climbed down and shook his hand. "Good luck," he said.

"Good luck to you." They stood there smiling and shaking hands, like heads of state who spoke different languages. Bevy had a pockmark near her ear. He pictured her at fifteen, pre–hot tub, pre-Jesus, trying to conceal the zit with makeup. He felt kinship—the kind of kinship he might have felt for someone with whom he'd been stuck on an elevator. They'd shared the same space, and the same worry, for a period of time.

"It's been a tough race," he said.

"Did you put out the videotape?" she said, and smiled.

He smiled. "Do you really think I hate this town?"

Thinking about the moles between her breasts, he told himself not to look down. She smelled like the candle display in a gift shop. They kept smiling and shaking. There was comfort in knowing that if he looked silly, then so did she. "Let's just stop," Bevy said.

"Okay."

Emilio Sanchez, on loan from the National Guard along with the jeep, had an aunt who was Hilltop, one of the few Hispanic members. Arch Cook had come up with the idea last week, before Zach's death, and it made even more sense now.

"Where to now?" Emilio said. His face, hidden by sunglasses, was a mystery.

"We've already been everywhere," Bevy said, getting a rush from giving orders to a man in uniform. "So just keep making the rounds."

Rhonda's head snapped back as Emilio hit the gas, and she cackled. Bevy loved the rumble of the engine, which she felt in her thighs.

Two policemen, standing between parked cruisers, nodded at Emilio. "Vote for Bevy," Ted yelled, and one of the officers gave him a thumbs-up. She'd once suspected Ted of spreading rumors about her past; either she'd been wrong or he was serious about atonement. She'd asked more than twenty Hilltoppers to join her; Lizette's excuse in particular had been far-fetched, and Bevy had hung up before she could start to cry.

Driving down Cormier's street, Bevy picked up the bullhorn. "Election Day, folks! Vote for Bevy, because this is no time for weakness. Bevy for the board!"

Deciding not to talk directly at Cormier's house, she looked in the other direction, and a striking, white-haired man stared her down.

"Did y'all see him?" Bevy said.

"Who?" Rhonda said.

"Military, I'd say," Emilio said to Bevy's relief: the man couldn't be her father's ghost if someone else had seen him. Plus Bevy didn't believe in ghosts.

"What'd you say to Cormier?" Ted said.

"I asked him if he put out the videotape."

"Of course he did," Rhonda said, gripping the seat with both hands. "He's w-wicked."

Bevy leaned forward and put her hand on the rounded muscle between Emilio's neck and shoulder. "Do you know what we're talking about?"

He nodded. "The video didn't bother me."

"I bet it didn't," Ted said, and turned around to make sure Bevy wasn't offended. She smiled. Maybe Ted was a good guy after all. They'd left Ward Three for a moment; they were on the lower part of The Drive, circling back toward Main.

"I mean, that was a long time ago," Emilio said. "You were a young woman."

"Not like now," Bevy said, "when I'm an old hag, right?"

"I didn't say that, ma'am."

"Oh my; now he's ma'aming the old hag," Bevy said, and they all laughed. Sometimes you found a family feeling in the strangest of places.

After voting, Cormier hung out in front of the school and discovered that some people didn't even know about the race. One of these cave dwellers, a man wearing rubber pants, asked why he should vote for him. "Because I believe in teenagers," he said. "My opponent fears them, and fears for them." It was rhetoric but it was true and having said it, he felt deserving of the victory that he increasingly sensed.

His optimism took a hit when Gladys, the Mobil Mart woman, entered the school without looking at him. But he couldn't picture her voting for Bevy. He wondered about other Hartsburgers: Something-ski, the Johns. An imaginary focus group of undecideds. He doubted that Something-ski would make it to the polls. The Johns, though, seemed like voters, especially the missus. Which way would they go?

Heading home for lunch, he had a chance to find out. Mr. John, scraping paint off the latticework grate on his porch, summoned Cormier with a tilt of the head and met him halfway, where his driveway spilled into the street. "I saw your opponent," he said.

"In the jeep?"

"An *army* jeep. That's wrong." He scratched his cheek with the scraper. Cormier imagined him shaving with the scraper, the scraper and spit.

The Johns' door opened and Mrs. John came out, her hair in curlers, which women apparently still used. "Lunch is ready," she said.

"Do you know the Bumpers?" Cormier asked.

"No," Mr. John said. "But I feel like I do."

"Lunch," Mrs. John said.

"I heard you the first time," Mr. John said, glaring at her.

Cormier had developed an idealized image of Mr. John, had practically designed his campaign to appeal to the Mr. John of his imagination, but he knew nothing about the man. Maybe he was a bad guy. Maybe he beat his wife.

"Can I count on your vote?" Cormier said.

"Sure can," he said, and Cormier wanted to drop to the pavement and break-dance, but Mr. John had more to say, "assuming I get the porch scraped."

"And your wife?"

"She went first thing."

He looked at Mr. John. His eyes were a deep ice blue. "And she voted for?"

"You."

Bevy made get-out-the-vote phone calls while she cleaned the kitchen. Dal Warren, her down-the-street neighbor, had promised his support a dozen times but still hadn't made it to the polls. His dog was sick and he didn't want to leave her alone. "Why don't you take her to the vet?" she said. "Then you can go vote."

"The vet? She's not that sick."

Bevy was going to lose a vote because Mimi the yellow Lab was sick but not sick enough. She didn't have much patience for nutty pet people. "Why don't you drop her off here. She can play with JB while you vote."

"Are you hearing me? She's not in the mood to play."

"How 'bout I give you both a ride to the school and sit with her while you go inside."

"You're going to be okay, Mimi. I know, dumpling. It's no fun being sick."

Bevy hung up and yelled, "It's only a dog." Then, feeling guilty, she went into the family room, where JB was lounging, and rubbed his belly.

The garage door went up, surprising her. Today, of all days, she had to make him lunch? On the other hand, maybe he was here to show support. He'd warmed up a little these past few days; he'd talked to her and even touched her, once.

But when he walked in, he kept his distance. He sat down at the table, a stack of paperwork in his hands, and said, "Whatever's easy. I know you're busy."

The only bread she had were ends, which she tried to improve by putting them in the toaster. "Dal's not going to vote because his dog's sick."

"So is her owner." Bevy laughed, and Peter said, "I'm not kidding. I've seen him out front having an in-depth discussion with his hedges."

"He'd be a good vote to get, then. You've got to figure that most mentally ill people are going to vote for Cormier."

"Most, but not all."

"No. My guess is I'll win about, oh, thirty percent of the fruitcake vote." She snuck a look at Peter and saw his smile. Here they were, just talking.

She put yesterday's tuna on toast and served it to him with Cool Ranch Doritos. "I guess after today," he said, "things will get back to normal."

"Does that mean you've forgiven me?"

"*Come* on." He slapped the table, and she stepped back, scared. "All I meant was, you wouldn't be out campaigning."

"So now I know. I can't read your mind, Peter. I mean, we don't talk about it."

"There's nothing to talk about."

"Of course there is. Tell me how you feel."

"How do you *think* I feel?"

"Awful."

"There; we talked about it."

"So awful you can't forgive me?"

Peter gave her a look like Bevy herself was a fruitcake. Eyes squinted, he pulled the paper towel from his collar, stood up, and put his hand on his heart. "Peter Baer—have we met? Do you not have a clue what I'm all about? Do you think this whole Christian thing is some kind of charade? Of *course* I can forgive you, Beverly, and I will. Believe me, I want to, but it takes time—you can't force it. I mean, being able to forgive, that's a gift from God. He'll give it to me when the time is right."

Cormier went to the Center and got a round of applause from the people making get-out-the-vote calls: Star, her gay friends, Barb Shellenberger, and a pale, dreadlocked couple who'd stunk up their corner with patchouli-sweetened BO. Here was his base: gays, blacks, teachers, librarians, and hippies. Absent only was his freshly energized Jewish constituency; she would arrive at six, with a platter of soy pigs in a blanket.

Star, on the phone, said, "What are you waiting for, book burnings? You need to smell charcoal-burnt Judy Blume before you get off your duff?"

Annie was in the big room out back, where the party would take place. "There's my boy," she said. "How do you feel?"

"Good," he said. "Great."

"Optimistic, are we?"

"We are, I think."

He recognized the old TV set, which he used to watch as a child. Back then, though, its antenna had been in better shape. Each rabbit ear was broken.

"Let's move, kids," Bevy yelled, itching to get to the event. Kay was doing dishes and Bevy was hanging near, hoping she'd say good luck or something.

Ronnie came downstairs wearing a tank top tee. "I hope you're joking," Bevy said.

"What?" he said, playing dumb.

"You need to put a shirt over that one."

"No."

Kay looked over, wanting to see if Bevy could handle it.

"You want to be left at home?" Bevy said.

"Can I?"

"For goodness sake, Ronnie," Kay said. "Put on a button-down."

"Okay," he said, and limped away.

"I guess he made his point," Bevy said, looking at Kay's back. She was taking a Brillo to the bottom of a casserole dish.

"I don't know if this needs to be said," Kay said, still scrubbing. "But I've noticed that you like things to be said, so I'll say it. I hope you win tonight."

"Thanks. That means a lot."

It seemed like Kay's words, along with Peter's this afternoon, should have put her mind at ease, but on the ride to Hilltop she found it hard to breathe in the silence. No one was thrilled about accompanying Chesty the Clown; Sunday night they'd all felt the stares, and even a win tonight wouldn't stop the judgment.

As they crossed the bridge, Bevy found herself missing Colleen. She wanted to scream, and complain. And hear someone tell her she was beautiful.

The TV's reception was fuzzy, so Stu bought a radio antenna at the pawnshop next door and pinned the cord high on the wall. "That's good," Cormier said.

With drunken agility Stu jumped down, went into a roll, and popped up. Using the moisture from the beer bottle that Cormier had handed him, he tried without success to slick down his hair. "That picture's almost perfect," Stu said with something like pride. The arms of the antenna were spread like Christ's.

"Good job, Wrench," Cormier said.

"I nigger-rigged it."

"Not tonight, please?"

Stu grabbed the bottle with two hands, as if it were a goblet, and took a drink, tilting his head back. Cormier saw the scar on his chin.

"Have you really been going to work drunk?" Cormier said.

"Oui, Madame Cooper." Their eighth grade French teacher.

"Jesus, Stu, you're going to—"

"What? Lose a job that makes me want to fuck myself with a fork?"

When she entered the event center, hundreds of heads turned, and it was useless to try to gauge the sentiments behind the stares. She would be the center of attention tonight, for better or worse. Rhonda started clapping, and so did everyone else. *Almost* everyone else: Marybeth had her hands at her sides. This wasn't a surprise; Marybeth had put together tonight's event, but the two of them had managed not to talk once.

Bevy had to admit that Marybeth had done a heck of a job. An American flag backdropped the podium, two huge TVs would give everyone a view of the announcement, and red, white, and blue streamers hung from the balcony.

The kids had left her. Ronnie was up on the balcony with his friend Dirk Freeman, who was Djing. But Peter was right here, holding her arm. Readying herself to make the rounds, she thought about the fearless woman who, a few weeks earlier in this same hall, had dared to go up to Cormier and his clan.

They started arriving around six-thirty, a steady procession that far exceeded his expectations. A woman with a buzz cut and hummus breath told him that he had inspired her to run for city council. A teenage boy with hair hanging over his eyes and pants touching the floor asked him to autograph a flyer. "I always liked your column," said a woman whose crystal green eyes stood out on her aged face like ponds in a desert. "But you've really outdone yourself with this campaign." He felt unworthy of the praise, but it persuaded him that his campaign had been better than bad.

A group of people stood around the TV, watching the national news. They shook their heads at the news from Iraq, booed at Bush, clapped for Dean. Cormier felt connected to the wider world. The Candidate was playing his part.

"Welcome, all," said Reverend Wedgwood from the podium.

Starting to loosen up, Bevy walked with Peter to the spot next to Marybeth, whose fake tanned skin was the color of bourbon.

"Tonight," the Reverend said, "will mark the beginning of the end of anti-Christian rule in Hartsburg. First, though, I'd like to talk about someone who's on all of our minds. Before Zach Bumpers shipped out to Iraq, he asked me if God approved of this war. I said, 'Absolutely.' I told him that there's no higher calling than defending and spreading freedom. So next time you're enjoying a nice meal or taking a hot shower, please think about the young man who sacrificed his life so that all of us might live in comfort and safety and freedom. Let us pray for the Bumpers."

Thinking of Pauline, the way she flapped her arms in grief, Bevy held Peter's hand. On the other side of her, Marybeth had her head bowed. When Bevy tried to take her hand, Marybeth jerked it away.

Annie urged Cormier to address the crowd, and it was a sign of his progress that he was only very nervous as the TV cameras targeted him. He plucked from the speech he'd written last night in the shower. "I'm really excited that so many people are here tonight. This campaign has been a learning experience for me. It was difficult to find ways to express progressive ideas to an electorate that's been so often lied to and talked down to. I didn't always succeed, far from it, but, well, I think I did okay."

"You did *better* than okay," Star said, and people clapped.

"Win or lose tonight," he said. "I hope to work with all of you to create a school system, and a town, where religion is an ally, not an enemy, of reason."

"You got something you want to say, Marybeth?"

"I've got something I want to hear."

"Go on."

"An apology."

"You think I ought to go around and apologize to everyone?"

"Why not? We've all had to explain your behavior to our children."

"I'm not going to apologize for something I did years before I met you."

"Why don't you apologize to me for running for school board knowing you had skeletons in your closet. There are plenty of clean people who could have run."

Dreifort walked in sporting a ragged tuxedo, a dented top hat, and a black, silver-tipped cane. "I've come straight from the polls," he said.

"There was a high turnout, which should benefit the more populist of the principals."

"Is that us?" Robin said. Cormier liked her saying "us," if not her question.

Dreifort hit Robin's leg with his cane, not softly. "I try to contain my expectations, as well as my expectorations, but I smell victory as sure as dogs smell death."

"Nice getup," Cormier said.

"Elegance is a lost art." Dreifort tipped his hat to Star and Stu as they entered the circle. "I grew up admiring Cary Grant."

"Yeah, that's who you remind me of," Stu said. "Him and the Cat in the Hat."

Star put her arm around Stu and lifted him up to his toes. "I caught this one smoking in the boys' room."

"I could explain why," Stu said, "but I don't think anyone wants me to."

"Ha!" Dreifort said, lunging forward like a fencer to poke Stu's belly. "Oh, where have you gone, Joe DiMaggio? A nation turns its vulgar eyes to you."

The circle opened up to make room for Annie, who looked Dreifort up and down and up. "Marlin, will you be performing magic this evening?"

"Yes. With a wave of my walking stick I will fashion a society in which men need not apologize for looking fashionable."

"Who's that boy with Carly?" Stu said.

"No one knows," Robin said.

"I guess the gang's all here," Annie said.

"Except Jimmy," Cormier said.

"Except Jimmy," Annie said, and smiled. There was someone else who wasn't here, and he knew from her smile that she was thinking about him.

Maybe it was adrenaline, or something deeper—Peter's love?—but Bevy was barely fazed by Marybeth or by all the other people who couldn't meet her eyes. A boy was headed back from the Middle East in a casket, and these people couldn't stop thinking about a mistake Bevy made twenty years ago. She could have laughed.

How many times had she told herself that it didn't matter what people thought? How many times had she managed to believe herself? Never before tonight.

She began to have fun. With Peter on her arm, she greeted everyone with an unapologetic smile. She was hesitant to judge people's faith—that's what people were doing to her—but she couldn't help thinking that the folks who smiled back at her were the better Christians. She'd try to have compassion for the rest.

The anchorman had a face that looked bed-marked and a soft pasty body that looked like an incubator of painful craps—a real newsman, hanging on to his job against long odds, holding off the models. "When we come back," he said, "we'll have the results of several races and ballot initiatives, including the results of a school board race in Hartsburg that has garnered national attention."

"I feel sick," Robin said.

"Lay off the soy pigs maybe?" Stu said, clearly nervous himself.

Cormier walked into the front room and out onto the sidewalk, where the air that he needed smelled of tar from a construction site, a few of the worst holes in the road having been filled in. The roads in Hartsburg were in terrible shape.

Cars passed by, bringing people home, and it occurred to him that most of them didn't care about the race. The race wasn't important in the scheme of things. But it was important in Cormier's scheme of things. If life mattered, and he had reasonably strong faith that it did, then what was about to happen mattered.

"The moment is upon us," said the Reverend, shaking Peter's hand. The Reverend used to send a spiritual charge through Bevy. Not anymore. She could even envision attending a different church in the near future, a smaller church that was more like a family, and less like a junior high.

The Reverend's wife, Millie, stared at her and Bevy stood there, comfortable in the silence. If there was tension, she couldn't feel it.

Peace had come over her, a feeling of safety, as if the world had no sharp edges, or the edges were there but couldn't hurt her. She felt cushioned.

Could you be born again again? Or maybe Bevy had reached the end of her walk, which she'd begun half her life ago with Peter by her side, as he was now. She'd finally moved on, by looking back. Standing in the crowd, naked before God, she saw herself through His eyes and felt only love. She wanted to win, but she didn't need to.

The commercial break ended. Bevy closed her eyes.

"We're ready to declare a winner in that Hartsburg School Board race that's gotten so much attention. The winner is . . .

Annie smiled and kissed his forehead.

". . . Bevy Baer. With eighty percent of the votes tallied, Ms. Baer has sixty-four percent of the vote, so it looks like a landslide . . ."

Bevy was standing at the podium before she noticed the applause, which was thunderous. It was snowing confetti. Everyone loved a winner.

Her family was standing behind her. She turned around and clapped for them and a cheer went up, an acknowledgment of all she'd put them through.

Be honest, she told herself, and be humble. "I want to thank my husband, Peter, my children, Ronnie, Brent, Loretta, Kyle, and Karl, and my mother-in-law, Kay. I love them all so much. And I want to give my humble thanks to our Lord and Savior. He's the best campaign adviser a girl could hope for. I believe that my victory, our victory, is part of nothing short of a revolution. We all are rising up to take back our country. As Hartsburg goes, so goes the nation. Yet we will not succeed unless we proceed with love and compassion. As we try to win people's hearts and minds, we need to remember that we're no better than they are. Luckier, that's all. There but for the grace of God we go."

She grabbed the microphone with both hands and let out a big ol' holler, which the crowd liked, or disliked. Didn't matter. "It's time to party, y'all!"

The music was slow and tromboney, like something you'd hear at a

Fourth of July parade. Craving something more upbeat, she asked Ronnie to talk to Dirk. A moment later Shania Twain's "Man! I Feel like a Woman" was pounding away. A few teenage girls had started dancing, and Bevy joined them. Did she still have it? Oh, yeah.

She wanted a partner but Peter, terrified, held up his hands and shook his head, so she tried to pull Ronnie onto the floor. "I'll dance, Ma," he said. "But not to this."

"Pick a song, then," she said. "Just keep it clean. Relatively."

The song Ronnie chose had a heavy beat. "This is Creed," he said, his head swimming side to side like Ray Charles's. "They're Christian. Trust me."

She put hands on his shoulders, her mouth by his ear. "I trust you," she said, but as she said it she smelled the oatmeal lotion that Colleen used. The undershirt must have belonged to her. Bevy wasn't about to ask. Whatever had happened between them, maybe because of it, he'd come out of it with a new commitment to God.

"What?" Ronnie said, because she'd stopped dancing.

"Nothing."

She felt the beat and began to understand what this band Creed was up to. She grabbed Ronnie's hands and they leaned back and spun around, holding each other up. He was smiling like a kid on a ride. She let her head fall back and laughed.

She guessed that people were staring at her, of course they were. They were wondering how a woman who was naked on the Internet could come out here and carry on like a tipsy schoolgirl. But God approved. He was a dancing fool, she knew He was. And she knew something else: that the people who were looking at her and shaking their heads, every last one of them, wished they were dancing too.

CHAPTER 39

AFTER DROPPING OFF the twins at school, she went home to an empty house. It was time to be a wife and mother. But Kay had cleaned the house top to bottom last night, leaving her little to do, so she took maybe her fortieth look at the front page of the paper, which showed her standing at the podium. She looked good. She looked *presidential*.

It occurred to her to call a plumber, and the man said he'd send someone in the afternoon. What now? Dinner, a nice dinner.

Caught up in the dancing, she'd missed Cormier's concession call, so he'd left a message, which she listened to again now as she flipped through a cookbook: "Hey, Bevy. I'm calling to say congratulations. Oh, and I . . . concede. This is Wally Cormier." He breathed. "I hope you have a good time tonight."

It was sweet, she thought, wishing her a good time. His voice all quivery, he'd barely been able to get those last words out. She took no pleasure in his pain; on the contrary, she was struck by sympathy, which made her feel duped, until she realized that this was just the kind of compassion she'd preached last night.

The plumber was a pierced, tattooed woman with bleached blond hair who'd voted for Bevy even though she was, she said, a "democratic social-ist," whatever that meant. The title canceled itself out. Was she also a freedom-loving fascist? "The power structure tries to deny political power to women who are overtly sexual," the plumber said. "I liked how you didn't let them force you out of the race."

"Thanks," Bevy said. "I guess."

She couldn't hear the twins, so before getting dinner started, she walked into the family room. There they were, building a Lego bridge to-gether. It seemed that Kyle was starting to go easier on his brother. Qui-etly, without talking, they worked. It moved her, and scared her, to think how close the two of them would be.

If she stayed in public life, and probably even if she didn't, the twins would learn about the video. It would be part of her portfolio, on the In-ternet forever. Still, she was glad that it had come out during this race as opposed to a race for, say, Congress.

Bevy sliced fat off the chicken breasts, trying not to be bothered by the sliminess. Her cell phone rang softly from somewhere; letting it ring be-cause her hands were sticky, she thought, for the first time in weeks, about Wilma. She put the chicken breasts between wax paper and pounded them with a rolling pin and wondered if those mysterious phone calls two weeks before had been from Wilma. Bevy would go to their session to-morrow; but Wilma, Bevy realized, probably wouldn't. She was too preg-nant by now, if she hadn't already had the baby. Bevy had faith that Wilma was okay, she had the Lord's love, and even if she wasn't, Bevy wasn't about to feel guilty. The race, as important and hard as it was, had used Bevy up. Strange thing was, she missed it.

"Oh, Jeez," Loretta said. "It's the dancing queen."

Bevy hadn't heard her come in over the sound of her chicken-pounding. She'd been moving her hips to music still beating in her head from last night.

"Easy on the snacks," Bevy said when Loretta opened the fridge.

Loretta opted for a slice of cheese and Bevy had trouble gauging whether this was defiance. She peeled off the plastic, making sure to keep the cheese intact, and folded it twice to create a little stack of squares, which she popped into her mouth. "Today was the worst day yet," Loretta said, taking a step back as Bevy went to get the eggs.

"Kevin Sheets?"

"Among others."

"I'm sorry, hon."

"I bet you thought winning would make everything okay."

"No, I didn't. I suspect things won't die down till next year."

"How do you know they won't be talking about this when I'm a senior?"

"Because that's not the way it works. You'll see. Something else will happen that kids are going to be talking about."

"You have something planned?"

Bevy cracked an egg, pulled it apart, and looked down at all the bits of shell trapped in the goo. She was reluctant to ask what she was about to ask. The question went against her parenting beliefs, which said you should never look to your children for validation. "Are you proud of me for winning last night, even a little?"

Loretta didn't give an immediate no. Wanting to know the answer herself, she closed her eyes. Bevy could sense that brain of hers buzzing away, and it almost made her cry, watching her daughter try to figure out how she felt.

Loretta opened her eyes and said, "A little." Her face twitched into a half smile. "But I still think you're disgusting."

"I don't believe that. Maybe you think what I *did* was disgusting."

"I don't even know what you did."

"Right. Well, sometime soon you and I should talk about that, about what I did, and about sex in general, okay?"

"If we must."

"We must."

Bevy heard the jangle of the plumber's tools as she came into the kitchen. "You're all set," she said. "Everything's flowing."

"Thank you kindly," Bevy said. "Did you use that snake thing?"

"No." She slapped her toolbox. "Got everything I need right here."

"I have to say," Bevy said, "you're the first female plumber I've ever seen."

"There are more of us than you think. But yeah, it was one of the final frontiers. And there are women pilots now too. All that's left now, I guess, is president." The plumber nodded at Loretta. "You're going to have to take care of that."

"I'd rather be a plumber," Loretta said.

"Me too," the plumber said.

"Not me," Bevy said.

"No kidding," Loretta said, and the three ladies laughed.

* * *

347

The ham smelled nasty but no biggie, she used bologna instead. She fried the potatoes too early but no biggie, she put them in the oven along with the cutlets while she sautéed the asparagus in margarine.

"Sixty-four percent," Peter said. He was at the table, reading the election coverage in the paper. "I can't imagine what percent you would have got if . . ."

"I think it helped."

"Are you serious?"

"People got to learn my story. It's uplifting."

"That's one word for it." Was that a joke? Whatever it was, it was a sign of progress. There was lightness in his tone.

"Ooh," he said as she set down the chicken. "It smells like a Bee-and-Chee."

"It's chicken cordon bleu," she said. "French food."

"Freedom food."

"Kids," she yelled. "Dinner."

The twins walked in together, as did Ronnie and Loretta. Then came Brent. She'd made headway with everyone but Brent, who'd been walking around in a stupor. She needed to help him talk about it, and she would, eventually. And her family would get over their anger. In the meantime she had this moment, this imperfect but pretty darn good moment, watching them eat the nice meal she'd made.

"Before we say grace," Peter said. "I'd like to toast the newest member of the Hartsburg School Board." Even the twins, even Brent, raised a glass. "I'm proud of you, honey," he said. "But boy am I glad the race is over. Thank God you're back."

CHAPTER 40

THE GUT-PUNCH in his dream was, in fact, a full bladder and he stumbled out of the recliner and, aiming for the bathroom, walked into the wall and fell backward onto his ass, pee squirting out. A bottle of Wild Turkey, not quite empty, rolled by. Liking the cool wood on his sack, he used it to mop up the pee. He breathed. It was past noon and he was Wallace Cornelius Cormier and he'd gotten 36 percent of the vote.

In the bathroom he realized that he'd finally fallen asleep to the sounds of Robin eating breakfast. There would be soothing, everyday sounds wherever they lived. People ate cereal in Brooklyn. As if they could afford Brooklyn. Yonkers was more like it.

He went upstairs to change his clothes, creeping by the closed door of the study. She'd been kind enough last night not to mention moving, but his luck wouldn't hold.

Latte! Free to be a latte-loving liberal, he went outside and sprinted down the middle of the street toward Kohl's. This wasn't the image he wanted to project: people looking out their windows had to suspect that the beaten Candidate was having a breakdown. But he wasn't. He just wanted a latte. He was suddenly bored and wondered if that's what a breakdown was, an attack of traumatic boredom. He found the thought fascinating, maybe revolutionary, and now wasn't bored at all, he was euphoric, then wasn't, he was bored again and couldn't imagine getting through the years till his latte.

Worn out after a block, he slowed to a fast walk. He was pasty inside his down jacket and his jeans pinched his waist. The jeans fit him when they were dirty and he was angry with Robin for washing them, although if he was going to be honest with himself, and today of all days he needed to be, then he had to acknowledge that he was angry with himself for growing a little gut and for not putting on his beloved L.L. Bean cords.

To save himself from boredom, he counted his steps. He guessed that three hundred and ten would get him there. He could have adjusted the size of his paces to make himself correct, but it seemed crucial not to. The total was three hundred and a half.

The sight of Jenny Kohl made him feel less bad. Her unassuming beauty started to stop his fear. "Sorry about last night," she said. "We still love you."

When she touched his forearm, he thought he might liquefy. He imagined her coming out from behind the counter to mop him up. "I love you too," he said, making it sound like a joke. It was a sign of something that he was excited for his coffee and glazed doughnut, a sign that he wasn't a depressed person. But his wife was.

Back on the sidewalk he ate his doughnut and thought its deliciousness, its sugary intensity, might save him, but then it was gone. He dialed Zev's number, and he picked up on the first ring. "Good," Zev said. "You're alive." They'd spoken last night after the results had come in, and Cormier sensed from his tone that they had spoken again.

"I want to pay you back for the videotape," Cormier said. "I insist on it."

"All right. I think I gave the dude five hundred bucks."

"Dude? You didn't get it from Colleen the cowgirl?"

"No, some dirtbag in Texas. Yeah, five hundred."

"Money well spent."

"Let's not have *this* discussion again."

"We talked about this last night?"

"You don't remember?"

"What'd we say?"

"You said that putting out the tape was the worst thing you'd ever done, and I said, 'You're not cut out for politics,' and you said fuck you and I said fuck you, and we went on like that for a while, until you said you had to puke."

"No more drinking for me."

"Then I have no desire to see you again."

"Fuck you. We're going to get together again soon. In a few months, not a few years, okay?"

"Definitely. We can meet in West Virginia. Bring your redneck friend."

People: that's what he needed. Jimmy lived nearby and he needed people too, so after saying good-bye to Zev, Cormier walked to the end of Main and rang his bell. No one came. He would have been sad if the coffee weren't triggering more immediate needs. He hadn't crapped his pants since college, and this seemed like an inopportune moment for the streak to end, although an opportune moment was hard to imagine.

He jogged to the gas station but the bathroom was out of order, so he decided to try to make it to Annie's, which, he realized, was where he wanted to be. Main to Elm to Looper to Weitz to Carroll to Bartlett: a route he'd walked, oh, a thousand times, but this was the first time he'd made the trip with a flexed sphincter. Avert your eyes, people: the Candidate was in a bad way. Yonkers was starting to look better.

At Annie's house he knocked on the door and, hearing nothing, walked in. The closetlike bathroom below the stairs was the same as it'd always been, right down to his father's bridge magazines, which were crisp from splashed water and maybe piss. The same magazines next to your toilet for twenty years. You needed change even when your life was pretty good. Especially when. Cormier had been lulled by the pretty-goodness of his life. If he was going to be honest with himself, and today of all days he needed to be, then he had to acknowledge that it might be unhealthy for his soul to stay in Hartsburg.

When he walked out he smelled garlic and knew Annie was in the house.

"Is that my boy?" she said from upstairs. Last night her good cheer had been preferable to people's pity, but he'd wanted to slap her nonetheless. No one could have reacted in a way he liked. Stu had come the closest. "Jed's" was the only thing he'd said until they were there. Then, while they waited for drinks, he'd turned to Cormier and said, "But whose *nipples* did you like better?"

Annie was in her office, which used to be his bedroom. His posters of Al Pacino and the band Heart had been replaced by a Diego Rivera print, and his mother now wrote letters to the editor in the spot where he'd dreamed peaceful childhood dreams and imagined sexual sandwiches with the two women in Heart.

"What are you working on?" he said.

"A letter to the *Informer* about its abominable coverage of the war in Iraq. But right now I want to check on my soup and talk to my boy."

He didn't speak until they were in the kitchen, he at the table, she at the stove. "I'm definitely down. And exhausted—"

"Is that what you call it, exhausted? You remind me of James. On days after he'd had two bottles of wine, he would say, 'I don't know why, but I'm very tired.'"

"Dad used to have two bottles of wine?"

"On occasion." She brought the wooden spoon to her lips and sipped. "Marlin looked peaked last night. I'm making him mushroom soup."

"That's nice, but isn't that kind of his wife's job?"

"His wife? What on earth are you talking about?"

"He doesn't have a wife?"

"Nettie Dreifort died in a motorcycle accident twenty years ago."

"But he's always talking about his beloved."

"That's just Marlin being Marlin. Either he's pretending she's still alive or he thinks she is. Or perhaps he's talking about one of his dogs."

"Jesus. *People*. People are fucking amazing." She looked at him, her face a web of lines in the sunlight. "We're moving, Mom."

She rubbed her thumb and middle finger together, sprinkling salt. "Is it definite?"

"Pretty much. It was part of the deal with me running for school board."

"I'm sorry. Of course I am. But not entirely surprised. You and Robin have never quite reconciled yourselves to this town."

"And what happened last night doesn't help."

"Hold on, Wallace. Stop right there." She walked over to him drying her hands, and Cormier had the sensation that she was going to whip him with the dish towel. "God knows there are reasons to move," she said. "Hartsburg is not exactly Barcelona. But what happened last night shouldn't affect the decision."

"Thirty-six percent?"

"You blame the town for that?"

"I didn't run a perfect campaign, but—"

"You were responsible for the release of the video, were you not?"

He looked down at the marks left on the table by drinks hot and cold.

"Whatever the dubious ethics of the move, safe to say it backfired. People seemed to rally around her in defense. If anything, I'd say that's a reason for hope."

"Oh, come on. This town is in trouble."

"Yes, it is. That's all the more reason to stay. I mean, to where would you move? Some enclave where everyone agrees with you?"

"Sounds pretty good."

"You could have won had you given people a chance to see what you believe in. I've always thought it's not essential that voters agree with *what* you believe in; they respond to belief itself. Bevy was a fountain of belief. You, on the other hand . . ."

"Maybe I don't believe in much."

"You believe in people."

"That's true. And I believe people are getting pissed on."

"There you go. I'd like to see that framed a little more positively."

"But I don't *feel* positive."

"Well, gloom and doom doesn't work."

"You don't think Bevy's campaign was all about gloom and doom?"

"No, I do. It was fear dressed up as hope."

Sleepiness struck him and he grabbed his dirty hair with both hands to keep himself upright. "Things are so screwed up."

"Things get screwed up, then they get better, and when they get better, they get better than they've ever been. MLK said, 'The arc of the moral universe is long but it bends toward justice.' That's the way it works. Right now there's too much power in too few hands. There will be a correction. I just hope I'm alive to see it."

An interesting notion: the country wasn't destroying itself. Cormier was often wrong; why wouldn't he be wrong about this? Maybe the Middle-Class Republic could be rebuilt stronger than ever. Maybe the nation wasn't beyond salvation.

"Dad would have hated my campaign."

"Oh, Wallace." She grabbed his head, kissed it. "It moves me to think of you wanting to live up to your father's ideals."

"But I didn't. I failed."

"Did you know that James always wanted to run for office? But he never summoned the courage. And there's something else worth thinking about."

"What's that?"

"An astonishing fact that I've come to partly accept: he's gone."

The walk home was something of a farewell tour, so he wanted to notice everything. The charcoal gray rocks clustered by the side of the road, rocks that were once part of the road. The slope of the grass as it rose to meet the trunk of a thick tree, the massive roots invisible yet palpable. The swishing sound as Mr. John primed his porch with long brushstrokes. The subtlety of Mr. John's nod hello. The pleasure of nodding back. The pool of oil below Robin's Honda, which needed to be serviced. The sound of his feet on the sturdy but hollow porch, telling his wife that he was here. The female voices coming from the kitchen. The sense that something wasn't right.

Walking into the kitchen, he recalled the awkward beginnings of high school parties—Danny Pastorelli's, maybe, in this house before it was his house—when the first people to arrive would huddle around the fridge. Cormier made it through those first bad minutes with the help of his friends, who were right there by his side.

But the only people at this party were his wife and his daughter, and this was his house, not Danny Pastorelli's. Still, he felt uneasy. Robin and Carly were sitting across from each other and smiling devilishly, like mean girls.

"Why aren't you at school?" he said.

"Because it's, like, three o'clock?" Carly said.

"Oh," he said, and their smiles widened. "I guess we need to talk about moving."

"We just were," Robin said.

"Without the head of the family?" Cormier said, half-serious.

"No, I was here," Carly said, half-serious.

"You can relax, Wal," Robin said. "Neither of us wants to move right now."

He didn't get the joke but knew it was nasty.

"Maybe we'll move someday," Robin said, "maybe we won't. All I know is that I don't want to move right now. Not like this."

She seemed serious. "Not like what?" he said.

Her beautiful puckered lips rose to touch her nose. "This doesn't feel right. This feels like we're getting run out of town. I can't say I love this place. I can't say I even like it, but it's my home. It's mine as much as it's anyone else's. I've lived here for seventeen years."

"Me too," Carly said.

"Like they say," Robin said, 'When I run away, I'm going to walk.'"

"I've never heard that," Cormier said.

"You've heard every saying?" Robin said.

"Oh no," Carly said. "He's crying."

He headed for the front porch but, remembering Mr. John, turned and walked into the backyard and put his elbows on his thighs and his head in his hands. This was the first time he'd cried since he'd grieved for his father while watching *Footloose*. And now, like then, he was crying for James. Also for Jill Lynn, finally. And Nettie Dreifort. And Zach Bumpers, the sweet young man who'd died for Dick Cheney's sins.

He was crying for everyone who'd died. For himself too, because he would die. He would leave what Stu had called *all this*.

Crying felt great, almost sexual. It was like getting wrung out, his head clearing as brain gunk, congealed pain, was washed away. He had the sense that his subconscious had been working toward this, breaking his body down so that he could cry.

He heard the door open, felt Robin's hand on his back, which made him cry some more, and he spoke through a slurp. "I'm not surprised that Carly wants this, but you. *You*." He stood up, pushing off his knees, and kissed her on the mouth.

"I stand by my man."

He laughed, then shivered. "We got so far away from each other."

She clutched the hair on top of his head. "Never again, okay?"

He nodded and wiped away tears with his palms, and when his eyes were clear, he saw the barren garden that next summer would give them tomatoes, which he would eat whole, with salt. Here was his life. A column, he realized, was due in two days; he knew his topic: the war in Iraq. With this column, with his next hundred columns, he would try to contribute a little something to Annie's correction. And in a few weeks he would bowl with his friends. There was one thing, though, one thing making him feel unworthy of the excitement dancing in his chest. "I shouldn't have put out that tape. What a despicable, stupid thing to do."

"You should talk to her, Wal. Tell her you did it, apologize."

"Ask her to forgive me?"

"No. Only you can do that."

He turned to look at her and could *see* her intelligence, its beauty: the light of her eyes was the light of her mind. "I'm ready to face the head of the household," he said.

Pokey, on the table, was luxuriating in the warmth of the sunlight and the feel of Carly's fingernails. At the sound of Cormier's sniffling, Pokey turned and looked at him. Unimpressed or embarrassed, he turned his head away.

"So tell me about this new boy," Cormier said.

"He's got a weird name," Carly said. "Nunna."

"Nunna?"

"Yeah. Nunna your business."

"Speaking of names," he said, "I forgot to tell you two something. I've given Peeve a new name. Hereforth Peeve will be known as Pokey."

"You can't do that," Carly said. "I mean, you couldn't just give *me* a new name, even though I'd like one."

"You don't like your name?" he asked.

"No, I'm just kidding. Carly Birnbaum-Cormier isn't beautiful, but it's who I am." He couldn't stop himself, he didn't want to stop himself: he walked over and hugged her from behind. "Gross, Dad," she said, "you're getting tears on me, and sweat and snot."

"That's all right," he said. "You can handle it."

"Any ideas about dinner?" Robin said.

"Let's go out and celebrate," Cormier said, ravenous. He wanted creamy pasta, tacos, German chocolate cake, french fries. "It's the first night of our new old lives."

The only sound was Pokey's purring as they tried to think of a place to eat. They always did this: thought long and hard about the options, as though they might suddenly realize that Chez Panisse had moved from Berkeley to Hartsburg. Maybe Alice Waters had set up shop in the vacant storefront next to Dolly's Doilies.

"Can't we just order Domino's?" Carly said.

"No, for the hundredth time," Robin said. "They're anti-gay."

"Anti-choice," Cormier said.

"Whatever," Robin said, and shook her head. "This fucking town."

CHAPTER 41

S HE DROPPED THE TWINS off at Kay's and, on her way to Wal-Mart, realized that she'd forgotten her shopping list. She tried with little success to rewrite it in her head, then thought about the work she had to do: clean the twins' room, the family room, and the downstairs bathroom; empty the dishwasher; make dinner. She wanted to do exactly none of it. What she wanted to do was school board stuff, but the next meeting wasn't for a month. Last night's meeting had disappointed her. She'd loved getting sworn in—she'd used her own Bible—but then after a half hour of bureaucratic nonsense, the liberal members used a procedural motion to put off debate about intelligent design. The other conservative members didn't object too much because, they said, no matter what, I.D. wouldn't be put into the curriculum until next year. *Next year.*

Maybe she enjoyed running for office more than she enjoyed governing. Waiting at the light where Kay's road met The Drive, she had a bad thought and knew immediately it was correct, like she'd remembered a name she'd forgotten: it'd be a while before she ran for office again. Years. Congresswoman Baer? Doubtful.

She found herself merging onto the highway. Going north. What was she doing? She turned on the radio. Country music was what she wanted, and she found that duet by Sheryl Crow and a singer Ronnie liked called Kid Rock. They were hardly country artists, but the song was more country than a lot of country these days. Whatever it was, she liked it. She was driving fast. Colleen was right: an SUV was a truck in disguise. Till now Bevy had been wasting a big engine.

In Cleveland she could pick up the highway going east toward Rochester, New York.

The land opened up, cornfields on both sides of the road. Around where

Bevy grew up, the land was dry so there wasn't much corn. The fields in West Texas were mostly wheat, cotton, and oil. Around Austin, though, there was corn. Colleen used to know a couple of girls who lived in Round Rock, just north of Austin, and they visited them one night. This was early, before Bevy's father's death, before her suicide attempt, before cocaine. They went to see music, but what stood out in Bevy's memory was what they did afterward. They were driving back to the house when the girl behind the wheel said, "It's time to go rolling," and Bevy said, "What's that?" and they took a sharp left, straight into a medium-high cornfield, and then both of them, the driver and the girl next to her, climbed out their windows, onto the top of the car. That was the idea of rolling, you let the car drive itself while you climbed all around. There was a chance you'd run into a rock or a ditch or a piece of machinery, but the danger was part of it, that was what made rolling seem like something you weren't supposed to be doing, the danger and the trespassing and the possible damage to someone's crop, but you didn't really think about all that because you were having fun and feeling free and you knew that this was exactly what you were supposed to be doing. A big Plymouth sedan, it was a good car to roll in, or on. They slid around on their butts, or walked around, hanging on to each other for balance. At some point—it could have been a mile in, it could have been five—they settled down into a silence. They'd been listening to Carlene Carter, Bevy's favorite, but the tape had ended and the only sounds now were the polite rumble of the engine and the swishing of the stalks as they gave way. Four young women, looking up at the stars, riding a car like a raft through a field in the heart of Texas. Youth, they say, is wasted on the youth, but the preciousness of the moment was clear to Bevy as she lay on the hood of the car next to her new friend Colleen Stoddard, their shoulders touching, both of them protected from the chill of the night by the warmth of the engine. And that's all it would be: a moment. You couldn't separate the joy from the pain of knowing that the field, and the night, would come to an end.

Bevy got off the highway at the exit in Ashton. This was as far from home as she'd been in months. And it was as far as she would go, for now. The song had ended, and there were things to buy, food to make, rooms to clean. As she went under the underpass, she thought about all the cars and trucks passing by above her, their speed and weight. She got back on the highway and headed home, to Hartsburg.

ACKNOWLEDGMENTS

I want to say thank you to my family, which has recently grown: Alison Mizner (my first and best reader), Miri (who validated my wild romantic fantasies about life and love), Milo (who was minus two years old when I started the book), the Marstons (with a special thanks to the world's greatest flower girls), and the Navaskys (who welcomed me, fed me, housed me, and helped to get this book published).

And to my friends who've given me edits, support, and shit through the years: Ted Webber, Neil Hare, Alex Sherwin, Kostya Kennedy, Julian Rubinstein, and Chris "Baloney" Stone.

And to Eric Simonoff, Gillian Blake, Benjamin Adams, and Elizabeth Peters, who forced me to part with some of my cynicism about the publishing industry.

And to the Simons, who let me use their lovely house, the best place to write I've known.

A NOTE ON THE AUTHOR

David Mizner has worked for political campaigns and political non-profits. He grew up in Maine and now lives in New York City. He contributes to InsidiousBeast.com, a blog that he created. He can be reached at davidmizner@yahoo.com.